Beth -

Thanks for [illegible]
friend and [illegible]
person could have. And thanks for
your support on the book as
well! All the best,

Lane

AXMAN

Lane T Loland

ISBN: 1540883337
ISBN 13: 9781540883339

PRESENT DAY

CHAPTER ONE

The rifle lay gently along his comfortably extended left arm with the barrel caressed lightly in his left palm. A modest, warm breeze, familiar and soothing in the southern California springtime, meandered from the north across the rifle and the left arm without any noticeable effect on either. The sniper glanced once again through the rifle scope to the front door of the house standing nearly three blocks away, although he knew that the appearance of the limousine would presage any human appearance at the door. The house remained as still as the rifle and the sniper resumed his focused, calm watch over the top of the scope.

Without breaking his visual concentration, the sniper found himself thinking about his hands and their lack of perspiration. He freed both hands from the rifle to rub his fingers lightly over the palms confirming their dryness. The palms probably should be damp, he thought, given that he was about to put an end to another man's life -- but then again, they'd never been damp before. A blessing or a curse, he wondered, before quickly ending the six-second lapse in concentration. A final slide of the fingers over the palms recorded no change, just as his eyes recorded no change at the front door of the house. His hands resumed their dry and relaxed, but lethal positions on the barrel and trigger guard of the rifle.

The focus of the sniper's watch would be described more properly as an estate rather than a house. It sprawled expansively both north and south of the front door, yet its extreme depth gave it an almost boxlike appearance from the sky. He had never seen the interior of the house, but it took no great strain when his mind's eye had previously pictured many ornate trappings of wealth throughout the far-flung walls. What he could actually see from the outside was an expensive, cobblestone circular drive that connected the quiet building with the equally quiet street out front, but only after passing through heavy, electronically controlled gates at both ends of the drive. A sturdy, uninviting iron fence connected the two gates and stood between the street and the dense bushes and trees that served to protect the privacy of the expensive home from the commonplace presence of the street. The sniper knew that through the northernmost gate and up the circular drive, would roll the limousine prior to the opening of the front door of the house. For now, the gate remained still, the drive remained empty, the door remained closed, and quiet dominated the landscape.

He briefly looked down from the makeshift hunter's blind he had erected in the tree where he lay silently and still. With a repetition demanded by an unwavering professionalism, he visually and mentally reviewed his exit strategy for what must have been the hundredth time. The blind provided the stability he needed for the anticipated shot, but could be removed quickly and easily once he descended in his well-practiced path. The fact that the tree stood in a watershed currently closed to all human traffic made his planned egress significantly less complicated than it could have been otherwise. Still, with his careful nature he wouldn't allow himself to make the mistake of any potentially costly assumptions. The planned steps down the tree jumped out to his eyes as though covered in fluorescent paint. The three exit paths through the woods were nearly as flawlessly marked in his mind. Nonetheless he reviewed each, in unchanging repetition, once again. The quiet stillness all around the watershed allowed the breeze to note its presence with the slightest rustle of leaves that were lifted slightly before returning to their natural resting place. No questions, no problems, no anxiety. The sniper returned his attention to the house.

He first glanced back at the street, the gates and the driveway and saw no change and no movement. Most of the circular drive was blocked from view by the foliage, as was much of the house. His perch, however, provided a clear line of sight, and therefore bullet path, to the front porch through a gap in the trees. He looked once again through the sight of his rifle over the estimated six hundred yards from his eye to the worn iron knocker on the door. He carefully noted the consistency of the slight northern breeze. The sight of his rifle brought forth remarkable detail from the front door of the house where most of the wood of the door stood out darkly against the crisp, white paint of the surrounding walls. Even so, the door contained numerous much lighter panels that were inlaid with geometrical precision in the darker wood, and those panels served to temper the contrast between the door and the house.

Without taking his eyes from the house, nor losing concentration for the task at hand, the sniper momentarily thought back to the door of the home in which he grew up as a child. The door had resembled many in the neighborhood of his youth -- painted wood, three small diamond-shaped panels of beveled glass at about eye level, and a black thumb-lever handle rather than a traditional knob. What stood out starkly in his memory, however, was an attention-grabbing gouge in the wood just inside the hinge near the lower left corner of the door. He had used a worn pocketknife to carve it out at the age of ten in some juvenile act of defiance that seemed both justified and exhilarating at the time. He remembered the shame and regret he felt when his father discovered his destructive act, and his even greater disbelief when he received no punishment for the vandalism. The gouge remained, however, and his embarrassment over the years proved to be more punishment than anything else his parents could have imposed upon him. In the eye of his memory he could still see the door clearly, with the gouge standing out larger than any other feature of the entire house. A replacement door was the only change he had made to the house before he sold it.

With his mind back to the present, he lifted his head from the scope and looked again at the entry to the circular drive without telescopic enhancement. He glanced to the east in the knowledge that the higher arc of the sun would make the shot more difficult, but he also knew that the appearance of the limousine was imminent. He rolled his shoulders and stretched his neck in relaxed preparation that reminded him of a sprinter about to step into the starting blocks. Just as he was about to look back toward the house, the dark hood of the limousine appeared through the trees. The massive car stopped, halfway turned off of the street and onto the drive, where a man stepped out of the front passenger door. He moved deliberately, but without hurry, around the front of the vehicle to the intercom box mounted to the left of the gate. Rather than speaking into the box, he punched a code into a numbered keypad and calmly returned to the waiting door of the limo. The gate slowly swung open inwardly toward the house and grounds. The limousine followed the swinging gate to move briefly outside the view of the sniper who noticed a momentary bump in his heart rate. The anticipated appearance of the limo meant that the time had arrived.

The sniper looked back toward the house -- first with his naked eyes, then with only his right eye through the scope of the rifle once again. He could see the carefully shined top of the limo where it had come to a stop directly in front of the dark, patterned door. Both the driver and the gate-opening passenger emerged from the over-sized car and walked up the steps to the front entry of the over-sized house. Without knocking on the door, the two men turned their backs to the house and faced the limo, one on either side of the porch. Both men showed off expansive shoulders and chests. Both had very closely cropped hair on top of serious, closely shaved faces. One stood at least 6' 4" however, while the other might have been 5'10". Mutt and Jeff thought the sniper as his view passed from one to the other. They stood rigidly erect but noticeably calm in their muted black shoes, dark creased pants, white open-collared shirts, and suit coats that matched their pants. With their feet spread slightly wider than shoulder width and their hands crossed in front of their crotches, they appeared to be mimicking the image of secret service agents as so frequently presented in movies and on television. In this case, however, they weren't protecting the president.

The sniper also knew that in this case, their seemingly menacing protection would prove to be utterly useless. Not that he felt sorry for them. From his concealed perch 600 yards across the darkening ravine, and before the two guards would even sense that anything was happening, a single bullet would take out the target. The guards would serve no greater purpose other than to remove the body from the front steps of the house.

The target, Samuel Jamison Benton, otherwise known as "The Supplier", had only minutes to live. Benton, 56, had accumulated a significant portion of his current significant wealth through the importation and wholesale distribution of heroin and cocaine. Those enterprises continued to provide a consistent stream of income, but more importantly had also provided seed money for what was now a far-flung, mostly legitimate business empire.

Benton's latest illegitimate endeavor, however, was proving to be far more lucrative than anything else he had undertaken. For a fee ranging from $500,000 to $1,000,000, Benton brought key, skilled workers into the country from various Balkan and Eastern European nations. The immigrant workers never actually worked for Benton, but would disappear shortly after their arrival in the U.S. Benton earned his fee merely by sponsoring their move into the country, and then carrying them on his books as employees. In exchange he pocketed the fees, which were always paid in cash. Benton asked no questions, but was fairly certain that the "workers" were tied to terrorist plans. No skin off his back, but he was prepared to raise his fee to $1,500,000 per worker, despite the fact that his net worth already measured into the hundreds of millions of dollars. Unfortunately for him, but also unbeknownst to him, whatever pleasure he derived from his wealth was about to come to an abrupt, but painless end.

Inside the house, Benton closed his briefcase and slipped into a tan camelhair sport coat. He patted his pockets to verify the presence of his telephone and his plane tickets. He would be gone for just two days on a trip that received much more publicity than was customary for him. Benton was on his way to San Francisco where a benefactor's award awaited him for his generous contributions to help with the refurbishing of the earthquake-damaged Graphite Art Gallery. He had resented the contributions at the time, but they seemed worthwhile in the building of his legitimate reputation. At least now he was getting the valuable recognition he had hoped that his money would buy. Or so he thought.

The sniper stayed relaxed but intent as he watched through the riflescope for the opening of the door. He continued to monitor the breeze, and noted that it remained light and consistent over his arms and the tan line where a wristwatch sometimes resided. He alternated his gaze between the guards on either side of the door, and the door itself. The moment was here. The view was clear. The shot would be easy.

The guards raised their chests and dropped their hands to their sides in unison as they heard the door open behind them. Their eyes looked forward above square chins that jutted out confidently. The sniper saw the door move into the house, but nobody immediately appeared in the newly created opening. Completely focused through his scope, the sniper knew he'd have at least four or five seconds in which to take the shot. His best options, however, would be when the target initially came out the door, or when he was about to enter the waiting limo. He prepared for the first shot, knowing he'd have the second opportunity if needed. He inhaled slowly, then fully released his breath. His heartbeat slowed to less than forty beats a minute. His entire body relaxed, except for his right eye, which stared through the scope, and his right index finger, which remained poised over the trigger of the rifle.

Benton stepped slightly sideways from the house on a quiet Friday morning and paused momentarily just outside the door while saying something to the taller of the two guards. The riflescope, adjusted for the slight northerly breeze, centered clearly on Benton's white-frocked head. The sniper squeezed lightly on the trigger.

CHAPTER TWO

His heart rate instantly jumped to over two beats per second before his finger jerked back from the trigger. He rolled away from the rifle and forced himself to concentrate while beads of sweat popped fully formed from his forehead. Had he heard the hammer fall? Had he fired the shot?

He quickly turned back to the scope, just in time to see Benton's white hair duck into the dark limousine. The sniper exhaled in visceral relief and prepared to extricate himself from the tree. First, he took one final look through the scope and saw the young boy smiling contentedly and waving by the side of the limo as it turned on the cobblestone circle to follow the drive out the southern gate to the street.

The boy had appeared in the sniper's vision in the last possible instant before he made the final hairbreadth of a squeeze on the trigger. He had aborted the shot. Benton would certainly die, but he wouldn't be killed in front of the young boy.

Barely more than an hour later, but in another world, the sniper looked up at the waitress in an overly bright yellow dress with a muted yellow and white plaid apron who stood looking down at him. She wore little makeup and her dark brown hair was pulled away from her angular face in a tight ponytail revealing multiple piercings in each ear. Despite her slightly haggard "seen it all" look he guessed that she couldn't have been more than 20 years old. From the look on the young-but-old face, he quickly perceived that she was expecting an answer from him.

"I'm sorry?" He realized she'd said something, but he hadn't heard it. He visibly shook his head as he brought his focus back to the diner.

"I said, do you want to hear about our specials today? It's breakfast time, but you can have anything, actually," she said without any effort to disguise her tired exasperation. He assumed she was nearing the end of a long shift and he imagined her legs were as worn out as her fact and voice.

"Oh, no thanks", he responded apologetically, but assumed she was just as happy to not repeat the offerings. "I'd just like a French Dip sandwich with cheddar cheese on it, and a Diet Coke." He ended the order with a half-smile and handed her his unopened menu. He noticed only two other customers, sitting far apart from each other at the counter.

"Fries?" She spoke while scribbling on her notepad. She looked down at him and took the menu with her writing hand.

"Uh, sure. Thanks." He knew that french fries could be a real crapshoot in a random diner, but he wasn't obligated to eat them if they turned out to be bad ones.

The waitress turned from the table as though she were grinding a cigarette into the floor and walked deliberately toward the kitchen while the sniper's mind turned back to his target. Benton's pending award in San Francisco had been reported in glowing fashion in the local papers providing enough information for the average killer. The formal event was set at the gallery for Saturday evening, following a private dinner on Friday, meaning that Benton certainly wouldn't return until sometime on Sunday. The sniper's secondary plan involved Benton's regular Saturday night rendezvous in Los Angeles. It bothered him that Benton wouldn't be there to keep his normal appointment this week Saturday; just as it bothered him that Benton was still alive to make the trip to San Francisco today. Spilled milk, he thought. Following Benton to San Francisco carried far too much uncertainty and risk. Now that he had missed his first opportunity, he had no choice but to wait until next week Saturday at the earliest. Regrettable as it was, he would have to be patient.

After finishing his sandwich and most of the fries, which turned out to be better than expected, he tipped the waitress heavily and got up to leave. He returned her smile, but without the same energy that he might normally put forth. The waitress had no clue that his response was muted by his thoughts of killing Benton in just over a week.

The sniper had driven to Los Angeles and had planned to drive out of town immediately after completing the job. The job wasn't complete, but he had no intention of staying in town for the entire ensuing week. He brushed his teeth in the men's room, then left the diner, settled into his car, and headed north on Interstate 5. He was late enough to miss the morning commute time, so the traffic was merely heavy, rather than unbearably immobile. By driving through the night he would reach Seattle by early afternoon on Saturday.

He drove with the radio playing, but with little thought to what he heard. Instead, he reviewed the details of the assignment that remained waving in front of him like a cape taunting a bull in the ring. He had received Benton's name nearly two months earlier through the established web site posting and as usual, the only information he received on the posting was the name and the city. Samuel Jamison Benton. Los Angeles. The rest was up to the sniper.

Through news reports, internet searches, a detective friend from Seattle, and a police department contact on the east coast, the sniper learned of Benton's legitimate and criminal activities. Benton currently owned significant warehouse space in the greater Los Angeles area, as well as a number of office buildings as his interests tilted toward real estate. Even so, he also owned a trucking company and a growing Pacific shipping line. Most of the seed money for his acquisitions came from his drug smuggling background, and little doubt existed about the intimidation techniques used to advance his current business enterprises. It was widely believed that Benton had ordered multiple murders, and arson seemed to be a favored business tactic as well. The sponsorship of illegal alien "workers" was less well established, but reasonably assumed. Despite all that was known and believed about his activities, Benton's official record remained spotlessly clean.

Following the web site posting, the sniper spent considerable time watching and following Benton and devising plans for his death. Such research and planning had always been the part of the "job" that he most enjoyed. Learning, piecing together parts of a puzzle, crafting solutions to the problems that arose. In this case, however, the process carried an added, underlying element of excitement as he knew that Benton's death would be his final assignment. The sniper was ready to retire.

The morning broke bright and crisp when he finally caught sight of the increasingly impressive Seattle skyline from his southerly approach to the city. His joints were stiff and his legs ached to be stretched after the extended drive, but he wasn't overly fatigued. A few hours of napping would be enough for now. In a week, he'd be back in Los Angeles.

CHAPTER THREE

The Patrons Auction at the 5th Avenue Theater stood near the pinnacle of prestige as an established and important annual social event in the city of Seattle. The wealthiest and most well known from local society gathered for an hour of cocktails, socializing and silent auction at 8:00 pm, followed by more cocktails, more socializing and a live auction. Each of them cheerily paid $500 per ticket simply to walk in the door and enjoy the opportunity of spending more money and thus confirm their status among the city's elite. The open bar certainly helped to open wallets. Throughout the evening, all the guests received pleasant invitations to make additional contributions beyond the ticket price and the cost of any auction items they might be lucky enough to win. The event typically raised in excess of $1 million for the theater, and the related publicity in the large city with a small town feel, provide nearly as much benefit as the direct fund-raising.

Thorne Stryker arrived shortly before 8:00 feeling slightly awkward in his tail-less tuxedo. He approached one of the two bars in the loud, ornately decorated theater lobby and gladly accepted a chilled bottle of water after finally gaining the attention of the somewhat frazzled bartender who looked as though he wouldn't survive the evening with an open bar and a large gathering intent on having a good time. Across the crowded lobby Stryker returned a wave from an elderly woman in a stunningly expensive looking black dress and began to move in her direction. As he made his way through the mingling socialites, Stryker smiled frequently and shook a few non-drink-holding hands, including that of the mayor.

Eventually, he made it across the room. "Margaret, you look younger every time I see you," he commented with a smile and a European style cheek brush / quasi-kiss / head bob as he reached the waving woman in the black dress under a triple layer of creamy white pearls.

"Thorne!" She might have been blushing, but the heavy rouge on her cheeks hid the evidence. "How wonderful to see you again!" Her smile revealed fabulously white and even teeth and her blue eyes sparkled unusually brightly for a woman in her sixties. Age showed around her eyes and in the skin on her neck, but she maintained a remarkably trim figure and Stryker admired the fact that she evidently hadn't given in to the obviously accessible temptations of plastic surgery or botox.

Margaret Chasen directed the board of the 5th Avenue Foundation and could be found in attendance at almost every major social event in Seattle and Bellevue. It was commonly whispered that her husband operated the largest construction company in the northwest, and that she ran everything else in the Seattle area. Stryker first met her nearly three years earlier and he knew that she had taken a strong liking to him. He enjoyed watching her well-practiced social charms at work.

"Mary, do you know Thorne Stryker?" Margaret grasped the arm of the tall woman next to her as she spoke. "Thorne, this is Mary Granderson – of the Watkins Gallery in Pioneer Square."

"Pleased to meet you Ms. Granderson," Stryker took the hand that she offered in a motion that seemed to exaggerate the forward curve of her shoulders. "I really like what you've done with your gallery lately. It's both unique and very compelling." The strength of her perfume startled him briefly, but he managed to smile as he held back a cough.

Granderson's pleasure showed clearly on her elongated face and her shoulders straightened noticeably. "Mary, please. And thank you! You've been to the gallery?" Her unnaturally light green eyes caused Stryker to wonder about the real color under her contacts.

He tried to ignore the combined disturbing effect of her eyes and her perfume and focused on the question. "Just last week, in fact," he responded with only a minor exaggeration. "A friend insisted that I go."

"Well, we could use more friends like that around," laughed Granderson with a light touch of her left hand on his shoulder. "Thorne did you say? That's an interesting name."

"Yes, well, my mother was a nature lover," explained Stryker with a concerted effort to avoid the reality of sounding as though he had told the same story many times before. "I'd have been 'Rose' if I were a girl."

Granderson offered a sincere chuckle. "Somehow I can't see you as a Rose." Stryker wondered if he noticed a hint of flirtation in her voice or if he were simply woozy from the cloud of perfume in which he found himself engulfed. He actually looked to see if the perfume might be visible in the air, so strong was its presence.

"Oh, he's just the sweetest thing around, aren't you Thorne?" offered Margaret Chasen with a mischievous smile and a pat on his arm.

Stryker merely smiled in return and sipped his water while trying to avoid breathing as much as possible. "Might I get you ladies something to drink?" he offered.

"Well, I see you have a monopoly on the hard stuff," smiled Margaret with a nod toward his water bottle. "I'd love another glass of wine myself." She handed Stryker her empty glass stained with maroon lipstick.

Thorne looked the question at Granderson with a nod and raised eyebrows.

"Sure, same for me," she replied. "White."

Thorne bowed slightly as he turned to revisit the bar while sucking in fresh air as if he'd just surfaced from an extended submersion in the ocean. He calmly shared smiles and nods with various dignitaries and CEOs as he wormed his way through the gathering. At the bar he requested the wine and waited patiently until he found himself next to Miles Elliot, current club president of the city's professional baseball team. Elliot had spent a lifetime in baseball front offices, but somehow managed to acquire the leathery, sun-tortured skin of a baseball man without ever actually playing the game himself. The lines deeply etched in his face reminded Stryker of a recently plowed, but not yet planted field.

"Mr. Elliot, Thorne Stryker," he swiveled to his right to offer his hand. "We met at the RBI Club luncheon in April."

"Of course, nice to see you again Mr. Stryker," responded Elliot with unexpected vigor. "And thank you for your contribution to our field development fund." The quizzical look on Elliot's face convinced Stryker that he carried the legacy of Granderson's perfume with him, but he decided avoidance was a better tactic than explanation.

"My pleasure, of course," nodded Stryker congenially. "Hey, nice start to the season this year. Kind of unexpected, huh?"

"Oh, I don't know," shrugged Elliot, also choosing to avoid the oddity of Stryker's aroma. "We're always expecting the best."

"So am I, in March," smiled Stryker with a touch of challenge in his voice. "It's often a different story by June, however." A cock of his head with an extended open hand made the statement into a question.

"Well, this year we'll stay with the original plan all the way through September!" promised Elliot with a healthy laugh. "Be sure to stop by my box the next time you're out to a game. It'd be nice to have time to chat when it's not as crowded and noisy as it is in here." He clapped Stryker on the shoulder with the practiced ease of a man accustomed to public encounters.

"Will do, thanks," promised Stryker with a nod as the still-harried bartender arrived with the wine glasses. "Enjoy the evening."

Stryker slipped his water bottle into his jacket pocket to free up both hands for the generously filled wine glasses. He maneuvered carefully through the crowd to the patiently waiting ladies who stood with two tuxedoed men and a third woman who matched them for both their style and their evident substance.

"Thorne Stryker, this is my husband Casey," offered Mary Granderson with a genuine smile. "And over here we have Bill and Sandra Wilkens. This is Thorne Stryker."

He handed off the wine glasses and gave hellos and handshakes all around. The newcomers already had drinks in hand, which evidently were not their first of the evening. They talked effortlessly for a few minutes about the theater and their love for charitable events before Stryker excused himself to peruse the tables of silent auction items.

By the end of the evening, Stryker had purchased a day in the owners box at Safeco Field for an upcoming baseball game, and a signed etching of Don Quixote by Salvador Dali. The bidding at the live auction began with a raucous flair and remained entertaining while eager patrons spent more than they should, but not more than they could afford. Stryker left the theater with his checking account nearly $7,000 lighter. Nonetheless, he felt good about both his contributions to the theater and the acquisitions his dollars had netted him. It was nearly 2:00 am by the time he arrived home, and his body loudly expressed the need for some sleep. He barely moved before getting up much later that morning.

CHAPTER FOUR

The week passed quietly and quickly for the sniper with the ultimate return trip to southern California marking the highlight of events. By 4:30 Saturday afternoon he had comfortably established himself at a table in a Starbucks shop across the street from the Belvedere Hotel in downtown Los Angeles. The coolness of the shop contrasted dramatically with the heat just on the other side of the glass doors. He slowly enjoyed a double chocolate chip frappuccino, which was his favorite offering on the menu despite the fact that he enjoyed many of the hot coffees as well. He slowly nibbled on an especially tasty and satisfying apple fritter. He pretended to read the newspaper at his small table by the large window, all the while keeping his eyes on the hotel entrance across the heavily trafficked street. It was highly unlikely that Benton would arrive before 8:00 that evening, but the sniper also knew that he couldn't stay at the Starbucks for more than an hour or so. He watched from his table until nearly 6:00, by which time his plastic glass was empty and his apple fritter nothing more than a distant memory. He left the shop with the mostly unread paper folded and tucked under his arm.

He spent the next thirty minutes in the increasingly comfortable evening temperatures strolling and window-shopping on both sides of the street while never fully taking his eyes off the entrance to the Belvedere. A glance at his watch told him that he was finally approaching the end of his prolonged vigil. If Benton were coming, as expected on a Saturday night, the arrival could be any time over the next two hours.

After a bit of random walking the sniper ordered a six-inch sandwich from the Subway store that stood two doors down from the Starbucks. Only a McDonald's was needed to complete a triangle of ubiquity. He kept one eye on the hotel while giving directions for turkey on wheat with lettuce, tomatoes and pickles. Lots of mustard. As in the coffee shop, he took a table by the window to eat and scan the newspaper. He planned about 40 minutes in the sandwich shop before he would head for the hotel bar, which was immediately to the right of the lobby as customers entered. He wasn't hungry in the least, but he ate the sandwich with a slow, methodical approach and enjoyed it more than expected. He washed it down with Diet Coke and continued to "read" the newspaper. It was nearly 7:15 when he cleared his table and left the shop with the worn but little read newspaper tucked under his arm once again.

As he waited to cross the street toward the hotel, he saw the long-awaited limousine approach and slow into the open drop-off/pick up area in front of the hotel entrance. He hurriedly crossed the street and entered the hotel lobby just as the two guards emerged from the limo. Mutt and Jeff. The sniper slowed his pace, but didn't look back. Benton and the two guards headed directly for the block of elevators with the sniper a few strides in front of them. He pushed the elevator call button and remained facing the block of doors, seemingly oblivious to the threesome behind him. The universally familiar ping indicated the arrival of the elevator car directly in front of the foursome. Nobody exited as the doors opened, so he stepped aboard, pushed the button for the top floor – number 14 – and slid to the back corner and looked down as Benton and the guards entered the elevator. All four men faced the doors and followed the ascending numbers as they ticked off behind the darkened glass covering. No one spoke or moved as the elevator rose to the 12th floor where Benton and the guards quickly exited without any acknowledgement of their fellow passenger. The sniper continued his ride to the 14th floor, then immediately descended to the basement of the building.

The two guards stood at attention outside the door of room 1217. One on either side of the door, their feet were spread and their hands crossed over their crotches as they had been in front of Benton's house eight days earlier. The stance must have been part of lesson number one at bodyguard school. Their heads swiveled slightly as they turned their attention to the right as the elevator stopped at the 12th floor. Both tensed and extended their chests as a room-service waiter in black pants and a white tunic stepped off the elevator and wheeled a cart in their direction. The waiter pushed the cart with his head down, but nodded at the two guards as he passed. Two sets of eyes followed as the waiter stopped in front of the last door at the end of the hallway and knocked. He entered the room after a moment's pause and the two guards relaxed as they resumed their stares at the wall across from room 1217.

The waiter stepped back into the hallway just over a minute later and pushed a now empty cart back toward the bank of elevators. Both guards looked his way, but not nearly as intently as they had moments earlier. The waiter kept his eyes focused on the front of the cart.

The waiter passed by room 1217 and the right rear wheel of the cart ran over the right foot of the taller, nearest guard.

"Hey!" exclaimed the guard gruffly as he looked down at his scuffed shoe.

In the instant that the guard looked down, the waiter's right hand flew from the cart handle toward the head of the shorter, second guard. The sap snapped hard just above the unprotected left ear. In one motion and just a fraction of a second later, the sap found the right temple of the first guard who looked up in reaction to the quick movement. Both men slumped quietly to the floor while the sniper immediately knocked lightly on the door of room 1217.

"Excuse me sir," he spoke into the door and then knocked lightly again. "Excuse me."

He could hear cursing inside the room that got louder as footsteps approached the door.

"What the hell . . ." Benton began as he abruptly opened the door. He stopped in shock when he saw the unfamiliar face over the two guards crumpled on the floor, but quickly regained his composure. "What do you want?"

The sniper pushed into the room, dragging the smaller of the two guards with his left hand while he pulled a silenced pistol from the back of his waistband with his right. Benton stared at the gun in panicked disbelief, but managed to say nothing. Standing by the bed was a beautiful young woman wearing nothing but an unbuttoned blouse, a short skirt, and heeled shoes. She held one hand to her mouth in shocked confusion, but didn't make a sound.

The sniper waved with the gun at Benton and the girl. "Pull the other guy in here," he directed them toward the door. The two conscious bodies seemed as frozen as the two unconscious ones.

"Now!" he demanded more forcefully.

Benton nodded at the girl and they both moved quickly to the door. After the second guard's body had cleared the threshold, the sniper pulled the service cart into the room and closed the door. Benton and the girl stood immobile and unspeaking.

"Into the bathroom," he directed the girl with a calm voice and a nod of his head. "Lock the door and stay there."

This time she moved without hesitation in response to his command and scurried across the room. As soon as the bathroom door closed, the sniper heard the lock engage. His attention remained focused on Benton the entire time.

Benton spoke first: "Who the hell are you, and what the hell do you think you're doing?" he demanded. Despite the barrel of the gun pointed in his direction he had regained sufficient composure to sound confident and in control. The sniper offered no immediate response.

"Comin' in here like this -- you're a dead man. You know that, right?" Benton sounded exactly like a man accustomed to giving orders rather than receiving them. He stared at his intruder without acknowledgement of the gun, and the sniper internally gave the man credit for maintaining his façade of control despite the weakness of his current position.

"One of us is a dead man," the sniper responded calmly and quietly with a nod at Benton's statement, "and I need to leave now."

"Who sent you?" Benton demanded, although with considerably less assurance than he'd just displayed. "What are you . . ." he tailed off as the sniper raised the pistol to point it directly at Benton's forehead.

"Wait! Wait!" Benton pleaded with an urgent display of desperation and recognition that the overly calm man in front of him wasn't there to threaten or negotiate. "I'll pay you double whatever you're being paid. Just name the price!"

A slight smile showed over the top of the cold and unwavering gun. "Let's see. Two times zero, I guess that's still zero, huh? You'd be getting off pretty cheap."

Benton's confusion showed clearly on his face as it competed with the now frantic fear rising in his chest. "Zero? You're not being paid? What? Why are you . . .?"

"Well, you know how it is," the sniper responded without real explanation. "Just trying to clean things up a bit."

Benton started to respond but his brain instantly lost the ability to send messages to his vocal cords as the pistol recoiled away from him. The sniper left the waiter's cart behind and quietly stepped out of the room with three bodies lying quietly on the floor. Only two of the three were breathing.

The sniper removed the waiter's tunic as he skipped quickly down the multiple turns of twelve flights of stairs and out the side door of the lobby. It was not yet 8:00 on a warm and beautiful California evening. Around the corner and two blocks from the hotel, he pulled a plastic bag from the pocket of his pants and into it he slipped his moustache, goatee, wig and glasses while he walked. Three blocks later he reached the lot where his car waited patiently.

CHAPTER FIVE

Three days after the death of Samuel Benton, the sniper awoke at home fully rested and relaxed. He enjoyed the luxurious feeling of waking up at his body's call even though he rarely slept past 7:30 am. His enjoyment expanded as the windows revealed the beginnings of another beautiful, clear, sunny day with the calendar shifting from spring to summer. Seattle certainly deserved its widely known reputation for gray skies and dreary rain, but few cities presented a more glorious picture when the clouds disappeared. Jumping eagerly out of bed, the sniper stopped and stared out the bedroom window where he could look across the Puget Sound to the Olympic Mountains on the western horizon. With the water in the foreground, the snowcapped mountains spiked into the crystal blue sky with a beauty unsurpassed in the natural world. He stared as if it were his first time experiencing the exquisite view. For some reason, the "been there, seen that," syndrome never applied to the view out of the sniper's own window. He marveled for a moment more before going to the front door to retrieve the morning newspaper.

The murder of Benton in southern California had not been reported in Seattle's major newspapers and the sniper didn't expect anything different on day three. Benton had no real ties to Seattle that would cause his death to be newsworthy in the Northwest. The sniper had previously checked the Los Angeles Times online, however, and had seen the news report the day following the murder. The article began with a brief description of the killing and possible robbery at the hotel, and then provided a more extensive factual summary of Benton's personal life and business career. The writer hinted at Benton's underworld connections and speculated that his death was more than just a random act, but also noted the absence of immediate suspects. The article made no mention of the two guards or the female companion. The piece closed by noting that Benton had just been recognized for his generous civic contributions in San Francisco. The sniper felt no inclination to shed a tear.

He read through the Seattle newspaper, spending most of his time on the articles reporting the victory of the Seattle Mariners the day before. A bagel while reading allowed him to complete breakfast along with the paper. He took an intentionally deep breath as closed the newspaper and rose to take a shower. Today was a big day and he wanted to get moving. It was time to retire.

He enjoyed a relaxed drive north of Seattle to the city of Everett where he exited the freeway and proceeded west to the downtown area and the main branch of the Snohomish County public library. The library provided multiple computers in private carrels not far from the main entrance and checkout desk. The backs of the carrels displayed colorful images from Native American art, but few visitors took notice. Patrons signed up at the desk to use the computers for half hour time slots. He needed less than two minutes. Only one computer sat unused when the sniper walked in, but he didn't approach the young man at the desk to ask for it. Instead, he took a personal finance magazine from the current periodicals shelf and positioned himself in a reading chair that faced the largest block of computers. The unused computer was soon claimed, while two other users vacated their keyboards. He remained ensconced in his chair, apparently engrossed in his magazine.

In a few more minutes, the computer user in the end carrel began to pack up the papers she had been writing on. The sniper appeared disinterested, but in fact watched closely. As soon as the computer patron walked away, the sniper casually, but without hesitation, approached the now empty chair.

He sat down and quickly used the keyboard to access a proxy server. Through the proxy he chose a search engine through which he logged on to the Axman website, which dealt with medieval executioners and their weapons. The sniper ignored the information on the screen and went directly to the button on the left side of the page to access the discussion blog. He didn't bother to read the limited postings in the discussion thread, but instead logged in as "Axman" and typed one word -- "RETIRED."

He had been on the computer for less than 90 seconds when he logged off the Internet and stepped away from the keyboard. He returned his magazine to the rack, left the library, and leisurely returned to his car where he sat for nearly two minutes in calm satisfaction before putting the key in the ignition. He rolled his neck, flexed his fingers, breathed deeply and even smiled slightly as he thought of the word -- retired. Finally, he started the car and headed directly for the freeway that would take him back home. He drove with the windows open and the radio playing loudly.

The clock has not yet struck noon when the sniper stepped into his condominium just under an hour later. The calmness remained as he opened a window and then sat in his favorite reading chair and stared at the wall. He thought about tilting at windmills as he studied his recently purchased etching of Don Quixote that was signed by Salvador Dali. Great art, in any form, was worthy of repeated admiration. He looked forward to admiring artistry on the baseball field as well, as he would take advantage of his other auction purchase to sit in the owners box at Safeco Field for the weekday afternoon game tomorrow. The first day of a new life.

10 YEARS AGO

CHAPTER SIX

Thorne Stryker awoke early on a calm and mostly clear Tuesday morning, without the benefit of an obnoxious alarm clock, and quickly resolved what previously had been the most vexing problem of his day. He chose light yellow shorts to go with a white, throwback Seattle Mariners t-shirt.

More than six months had passed since Stryker abruptly ended his fifteen years of service with the U.S. Army Rangers. The adjustment to civilian life had proved more seamless than he might have imagined – if he had actually thought about it before making the move. Which he hadn't. Even so, without any preparation or long-term planning, his separation from the military had proceeded remarkably smoothly and free of any genuine difficulties. Except for the clothes.

For fifteen years, Stryker never gave a second thought to what he'd wear when he got up in the morning. For most of those five thousand plus days, he wore his standard Army-issue fatigues. If a special occasion called for formal full dress, he knew about that well in advance and his uniform was chosen, pressed, clean and ready to go. When a particular assignment dictated non-standard military attire for some reason, it was chosen and laid out for him in perfect sizes. His job involved nothing more than putting it all on at the appropriate time.

Thus, when he left the Army, Stryker left behind fifteen years of keeping his uniforms crisp and clean, but other than that, never giving clothes any time, effort, or most importantly, thought. The entirety of his civilian wardrobe at the time of his sudden retirement consisted of one pair of unfaded blue jeans and a long-sleeved white shirt with a button-down collar. When he left the Rangers, he wore the jeans and the shirt for five consecutive and increasingly uncomfortable days before finally giving in to the civilian reality of a varied wardrobe.

Faced with the clothing dilemma of his new civilian life, he breathed deeply, took himself shopping, and dreaded every minute of it. Nonetheless, he ended up with a number of pants, shorts, t-shirts, dress shirts, and shoes. The now full (or at least less sparsely filled) closet and dresser, however, simply provided Stryker with an unanticipated daily dilemma. Would it be jeans today? Khaki pants? Shorts? What style shirt and what color? Did the shirt and pants fit together appropriately? The problem for the now ex-Ranger resided in the fact that he had always lived his life with the unspoken assumption that a significant and clearly identifiable reason lay behind the daily uniform. Without the certainty of uniforms and the reasons for them, Stryker struggled with the vagaries of civilian choices. For nearly two months, he dreaded getting out of bed in the morning knowing that the necessity of a daily clothing selection awaited. For a time he tried making the choice the night before, but merely felt equally stymied in the evening, and then second-guessed his choices the next morning anyway. After that failed experiment, he found himself spending more and more time standing in the shower to put off the pending decision. Then, for nearly a month he solved the problem by creating his own day-of-the-week uniform. Monday: shorts and t-shirt. Tuesday: slacks and dress shirt. Wednesday: jeans and sweatshirt. Etc.

Three times through the definitive weekly cycle he loved the exhilaration of knowing what clothes would come out of the closet each day without having to make the baseless decisions. He hopped out of bed early each morning and stepped confidently out of the shower after his customary three-minute cleansing. Civilian life was a breeze.

Then one day he accidentally put on shorts instead of jeans and came face to face with the absence of a reason behind the daily "uniform" other than for the sake of having an easy rotation. Why couldn't shorts and a t-shirt be on Wednesday? Stryker never considered returning to the regimentation of the military, but the showers got longer again.

Finally, Stryker awoke early one Tuesday morning and without any real thought or reason he wore blue shorts and a dark gray sweatshirt. The day passed without incident. The next day started off a bit cloudy and threatening, so he wore jeans with the same sweatshirt. Nobody noticed and nobody cared. On Thursday, the clouds remained but he slipped on shorts and a t-shirt simply because he felt like it.

And so, after six months of civilian life, the crisis of life without uniforms disappeared. And now, on another Tuesday morning it was light yellow shorts with a Mariners t-shirt and Stryker's only thoughts regarding the previously paralyzing decision were that the clothes were clean and he felt like wearing them.

Thorne Stryker jogged lightly to the bakery just blocks away from his wardrobe and shower. The air smelled clean and crisp on this bright September morning in Seattle, with the promise of warm temperatures coming in the afternoon. Stryker had heard the stereotypical stories of Seattle rain, but he also knew that while the summers might be short, they were typically beautiful in Seattle and his first direct experience supported that assertion with pleasant surprise. Thus far, September unveiled itself as brilliantly as July and August and Stryker enjoyed every idyllic day of it. His pleasure at the beauty of the outdoors easily transferred indoors as he stepped into Brotherton's Bakery and inhaled deeply with a raised chin and a half-smile on his face.

"Morning," offered the youngish clerk behind the counter, only slightly looking up from the meticulous job of slicing. He sported an unusually large amount of bright orange hair and the requisite freckles over pale skin to go with it. His lack of a sunburn indicated he didn't spend much time outside. He didn't have the large body type that Stryker normally associated with bakeries as his six-foot frame might have carried 140 pounds if all his pockets were stuffed with bagels.

"Morning to you," responded Stryker as he perused the goods behind the glass. He already knew what he would order, but he still felt the obligation of looking with an air of appreciation. A few of the doughnuts looked as tempting as the bread smelled, but Stryker remained undeterred. "Did you make the apple fritters yourself?"

"Uh, no," the clerk looked a bit puzzled at the question. He continued with the bread and his face seemed to redden slightly behind the freckles.

Stryker smiled and tapped the countertop as though troubling over his choice. "Oh, well. I'll take one anyway."

"Coffee?" questioned the clerk as he wiped his hands on his flour-encrusted apron and reached into the glass case with a flimsy paper to pick up the nearest fritter.

"No thanks, just the fritter. That'll be good." Stryker felt a touch of guilt at not ordering more at the bakery that seemed devoid of customers, but he felt certain that it didn't really matter to the skinny redhead. While not sharing the addiction of some, he enjoyed a good cup of coffee at times. This morning, however, he had already consumed a large glass of orange juice at home.

Stryker paid the clerk and took a large, satisfying bite of the fritter before he'd even left the store and almost turned around to buy another. He resisted the temptation, however, and once out on the street he decided to walk a bit while consuming his prize, rather than returning directly home. Another day with nothing much going on. He entertained occasional thoughts about taking on some sort of work since his departure from the Army, but since he didn't have any pressing financial need, he had been in no real hurry to change his relaxed lifestyle. More than half a year into his separation from Uncle Same and his inclinations had not changed. Most job options seemed insurmountably mundane in comparison to his fifteen years as a Ranger and he remained far removed from the point of taking a job simply for the sake of filling the days with something to do. There were books to be read, trips to be taken, exercises to be completed, movies to be watched, sights to be seen, and more. A steady job would merely get in the way he rationalized whenever the Puritanical thought reared its chiding head.

With a beautiful day unfolding, Stryker eventually made his way home with his mind set on an outside chair, the morning newspaper, and another glass of orange juice. Maybe the radio playing quietly in the background. The red message light blinking on his landline phone surprised him. He had made few civilian acquaintances since moving to Seattle and the rare occurrence of a ring on his phone generally meant a solicitation call, but not a message. He felt cheated that he had missed the ringing and instead encountered only the flashing red light. He pushed the message button with a curious expression on his face.

"Thorne Stryker, is that you?" Stryker knew that he recognized the deep and confident voice. "General MacAfee here, how are you son?" Stryker's expression instantly turned from curiosity to puzzlement. General MacAfee? "I know this must seem like a bolt out of the blue for you, but I'd greatly appreciate it if you'd give me a call back. As soon as you can, that is. I'm calling from this cell phone and, ah . . . . wait a second. Damn, I don't have a clue what the number is. Let me see." His frustration carried itself clearly without the need for supporting facial expressions. "Oh hell. Look, I'll call right back and leave the number once I figure out what it is. I never call myself, you know? Anyway, once you get the number, then give me a call, okay? Any time, day or night – just as soon as you get this message. Thanks, soldier."

Stryker found himself drumming his fingers on the desk as the message ended with a beep. Immediately, a second message began. It carried MacAfee's voice once again and contained a phone number and nothing else. He stared at the phone for a moment before he replayed both messages and wrote down the phone number the second time he heard it.

His mind raced. General MacAfee? It sounded urgent, but what could he possibly want? Stryker had not sought out contact with anyone in the Army since his resignation. After some initial pleas for reconsideration, the only contact coming from the Army had been to deal with the formalities of discharge paperwork, insurance, forwarding address, etc. And now a call from General MacAfee. Out of the blue indeed.

He pondered his options while he replayed the message from MacAfee in his head. His departure from the United States Army had been sudden and unexpected and from Stryker's viewpoint, it had not been what the normal person would call amicable. Even so, he had never shared his reasons for leaving with his superiors, but had simply claimed he was finished and it was time to move on to civilian life. Very few people knew the true cause of his resignation and he was fairly certain that General

MacAfee was not one of those people. Was MacAfee simply trying to lure him back into uniform, assuming that Stryker would have had enough time to become disenchanted with the civilian world? Sure it was possible, he thought, but certainly not within the normal realm of duties for a general. But then, Stryker had not been a normal soldier in a normal unit.

Stryker's initial inclination was simply to erase the messages, ignore the call, and go on about his unfettered civilian life. The newspaper and sunny reading chair still beckoned for his immediate future. His pursed lips and slight head nod confirmed the wisdom of that decision. His head then shook in immediate resignation however, as he thought of General MacAfee. If the call came from anyone else, it would already be erased and nearly forgotten. Stryker had tremendous respect for MacAfee, however -- probably more respect for him than for anyone else Stryker had ever met. He couldn't simply ignore the General's call. He wouldn't hesitate to decline any requests to return to the Army, but he had no choice except to return the phone call. General MacAfee deserved that much at least.

Stryker glanced at the Lone Ranger clock on the wall and saw that it was just past 9:00 am in Seattle, which would make it just past noon for the General on the east coast. Oh well, he had never been a big fan of procrastination and the chair and newspaper would still be waiting in the few minutes it would take to make the call. Feeling a bit of unexpected tightness in his stomach, he picked up the phone and carefully, with a bit of hesitation, punched in the number left by the General.

"MacAfee here," the voice boomed over the phone line as if the General's considerable presence shared the room with Stryker. Expecting or maybe hoping for an answering machine, and still hesitant about making the call, Stryker was momentarily silent. The General was not. "This is General MacAfee, hello?"

"Uh, good morning General," Stryker finally responded, feeling discomfort similar to his first day in training camp. "Thorne Stryker here returning your call from Seattle." Stryker was certain he had made the wrong choice by calling back, but now he was stuck.

"Oh, Stryker! Great! Thanks for calling back so quickly." The General's voice boomed even stronger than before and projected a sense of excitement that surprised Stryker. "How the hell are you, son?"

"Doing just great General. How about you?" Stryker felt completely awkward sharing small talk with the General, but he assumed it wouldn't last long. Even so, he felt a tingle of excitement at the mystery of the seemingly random call.

"Fine, just fine, thanks" the General replied pleasantly with a slight decrease in volume. "So, civilian life treating you okay so far?" Surely General MacAfee had never spoken so amiably to any man in the military for the past 25 years.

"No complaints sir, thank you," responded Stryker with an attempt to sound comfortable and nonchalant.

"Good, that's good." The decibel level coming out of Stryker's phone dropped once again. "Been keeping busy?" More small talk that seemingly grabbed Stryker's head and forced it to shake from side to side.

"Well, nothing too exciting, Sir. Just kind of figuring things out so far." Stryker wanted to say 'What the hell are you calling me about?' but he stayed patient and hoped that his voice didn't betray the confusion he felt.

"Yes, well, you're a smart young man. I'm sure everything's been very smooth for you." MacAfee seemed content to continue the meaningless patter.

"Can't complain sir." Stryker decided it was time to press the issue before they started talking about the weather or the upcoming football season. "I, uh, was a little bit surprised to hear your voice on my answering machine, however. I haven't heard from anyone in uniform for a while now, and I certainly didn't expect to get a call from you General. Um, what's up, if I may ask Sir?"

"Ah, yes," the sense of resignation carried clearly in the general's voice. "To be honest, I was calling to ask a favor."

Stryker couldn't have been more surprised if the general had said that the Army had rejected his resignation and was sending men out to pick him up for immediate reenlistment and deployment overseas. Despite his surprise, he waited quietly during the awkward pause that followed, but nothing more seemed to be forthcoming from the other end of the line. Clueless as to what sort of favor the General could possibly want from him, he finally spoke. "Well, of course, General. What can I do?"

"Thank you Stryker, but of course I won't take your answer as a commitment until you hear the details of what I have to ask." The general paused just long enough for Stryker to privately re-affirm his complete lack of understanding. "I have to tell you that this is not within the usual realm of favors, in or out of the Army, so I fully expect that you'll end up changing your mind. In any event, that's why I'm calling – I need to ask a favor." General MacAfee's voice was now more quiet and subdued than Stryker had ever heard, and in stark contrast to the cannon-like projections that rattled Stryker's phone just moments earlier.

"Okay," Stryker tried not to sound too hesitant despite the fact that he knew nothing. "So, what's the favor General?"

"Well, we can't talk about it on the phone," MacAfee asserted without clearing up any of Stryker's confusion. "We need to meet. My schedule's pretty flexible, but I definitely would like to talk sooner rather than later. What are you doing for lunch?"

Stryker's head now spun so that he felt compelled to shake it in an effort to regain his bearings. He had no interest in flying to the east coast and he sure as hell couldn't do it by lunchtime. "Um, Sir, I assume you know that I'm in Seattle now. That'll make meeting a little more difficult. Are you sure you can't explain over the phone?"

"Sorry son," the general began again. "I guess I didn't make myself clear earlier. I'm here in Seattle too. So, why don't you pick a nice restaurant where we can meet at, say, 12:30. Does that work for you?"

CHAPTER SEVEN

Stryker hung up the phone still shaking his head in disorientation. General MacAfee calling out of the blue and asking for a favor. A favor that the general wouldn't or couldn't talk about over the phone. A favor that the general believed Stryker was likely to turn down. And, on top of that, MacAfee here in Seattle, presumably because he wanted to meet with Stryker in person about this favor.

He tried to guess about the nature of the favor, but kept coming up blank. Something to do with the Army? Someone he had served with or under? Something personal for the general? Being completely in the dark left Stryker feeling a bit nervous, but also completely unable to think about anything else, which made the three hours until the scheduled lunchtime meeting pass as it would for a nine year old waiting in the lobby for his turn in the dentist's chair.

Stryker arrived at the J & M Café on 1st Avenue at 12:15. He had long maintained the habit of showing up early for meetings or appointments and it provided him with a level of comfort he wouldn't have felt otherwise. Lighting in the café was limited so that even at midday the atmosphere hinted at privacy and discretion, or maybe just dingy dreariness.

The J & M had operated at the corner of 1st and Washington for over 50 years. The stickiness of the tables raised the question of how often they'd been washed over those years and the overall décor hinted at significant dollars saved on aesthetic considerations. Still, the burgers were tasty and Stryker didn't know many places in town yet, so the J & M would have to do. He asked for a table in the corner, and sipped water for five minutes before he saw General MacAfee enter and he immediately wondered how many soldiers had ever seen MacAfee dressed in civilian clothes. He then wondered how long it had taken MacAfee to select the outfit of brown slacks with a pinstriped button-down shirt under a light jacket. Although still an imposing man, MacAfee's presence wasn't quite as intimidating as Stryker remembered it being when presented in uniform. The general's close-cut hair was a bit lighter and his shoulders slightly more stooped, but his eyes remained remarkably active and alert. MacAfee stood in the doorway looking around the dark restaurant until he spotted Stryker half-standing and waving from the corner. MacAfee confidently strode over and eagerly shook hands with Stryker who returned the handshake with a smile.

"General, nice to see you," offered Stryker as he withdrew his hand. "Have a seat. No trouble finding the place, I hope?"

"Good to see you soldier," replied the general. "Found it just fine – I'm actually staying at a hotel just a few blocks from here so it was easy as could be. Interesting place," he noted with a cocked eyebrow at the overall surroundings.

"Yeah, I don't know." Stryker joined him in the visual once-over of the restaurant. "They've got good food and I don't really know a lot of places in town yet. We can try somewhere else if you'd like," he offered sheepishly.

"No, no, this'll be great," MacAfee sat while still looking over the establishment. "Thanks for coming."

The younger man looked hard at the older one, searching for clues but finding none. "Of course. I was a bit surprised to hear from you, Sir. And even more surprised to hear that you were in town. What brings you to Seattle anyway?"

"You, Stryker," stated the general matter-of-factly. "I came to Seattle because I knew that you were here."

"I don't understand, Sir," responded Stryker honestly and a bit off-guard.

"I told you I wanted to ask a favor, right? And, I told you that I didn't want to talk about the favor on the phone." He glanced at his hand but decided to ignore the stickiness it had encountered. "It didn't seem fair to ask you to come to me, since I'm the one asking for the favor, so, I came to Seattle. Just got in last night. Never been here before, actually."

"Really? Well, it's a nice city, General, and I appreciate you coming all the way across the country. I'm a bit puzzled, obviously, about the favor, though. I'm not sure what I could possibly do for you, Sir."

MacAfee nodded and looked around, apparently contemplating his readiness to explain. At that moment the waiter approached the table and MacAfee remained quiet and held back whatever he was about to say. Both men ordered burger baskets, MacAfee with a local microbrew, and Stryker with a Diet Pepsi. The waiter took the orders without writing anything down, then left them alone. Stryker turned expectantly back to the general.

"How many years did you serve, son?" the general asked with a fatherly glint in his eyes.

Stryker was sure that MacAfee already knew the answer, but he responded anyway. "Almost exactly fifteen years, Sir."

"Yes, you were one of the youngest Rangers ever, weren't you?" MacAfee looked at Stryker but didn't wait for a response. "You did some great work for the country over those years. Lots of jobs, lots of places. Lots of good work. I was sorry to see you leave," he said with convincing sincerity.

Stryker wasn't sure if MacAfee expected a response, so he said nothing. He had often found silence to be his best option when confronted with uncomfortable situations. He merely looked at the general and drank more from his ice-filled water glass.

MacAfee looked slightly over Stryker's shoulder as he spoke again. "I don't suppose you're aware of it – no reason you should be – but I've announced my retirement as well. It'll be official at the end of the year." He nodded his head slightly and blew out air in a controlled version of a laugh. "Never really thought I'd see the day, but . . ." MacAfee lifted his water glass in an apparent toast to himself.

Stryker's shock showed clearly on his face. "Wow! Retiring, huh? Well, congratulations Sir, I guess." He offered a return tip of his glass toward the general. "Watch out for the clothes though, they can really get you."

MacAfee wrinkled his eyebrows in confusion, but chose not to ask. He looked across the room, apparently lost in thought for a moment. Stryker's mind quickly pondered the implications. Could the general's favor be related to his pending retirement? It didn't seem to shed any greater light on their meeting, and if anything, may have added to the level of mystery.

The waiter arrived with their drinks and seemed to sense the building tension between the two men as he set the drinks on the table and left quickly. MacAfee immediately reached for his beer and took a long, comforting drink.

Stryker watched him empty half the glass and decided he was ready to be led out of the dark more quickly than MacAfee seemed ready to lead, so he decided to force the issue. "So, about this favor, Sir. Is it related to your retirement?"

"Not directly, son," responded the general as he avoided eye contact and gazed over Stryker's shoulder once again as he set down the glass. "A bit, I guess, but not really." The darkness remained unaltered.

"Okay, well, congratulations anyway, Sir. I'm sure you'll enjoy civilian life after so many years in uniform. Still," Stryker continued pressing, "I'm confused about you need. You didn't want to talk about it on the phone, so here we are. What's up, Sir?"

MacAfee shifted his gaze so that he stared directly into the black eyes across the table. Stryker held the look, waiting for the general to speak. Finally, and very calmly, he did. "I want you to kill someone."

CHAPTER EIGHT

Stryker's eyes remained fixed on the general's eyes, lighter but just as intense. Neither man blinked nor spoke for nearly ten seconds. During that time Stryker hoped for, but could find no sign of jesting in MacAfee's statement. MacAfee wanted him to kill someone. Stryker finally broke eye contact as he looked down to reach for his glass and considered how to respond to the request heard none to often at a luncheon meeting. Killing someone wasn't high on his list of guesses regarding the general's possible favor, and the startling statement left him without any reasonable response other than an utterance of disbelief. It seemed like as good a place as any to start.

"Kill someone, Sir?" questioned Stryker in a near whisper. He looked furtively to both sides and across the restaurant as he spoke – suddenly feeling self-conscious, guilty and paranoid all at once. "I really don't understand," he implored, harboring the baseless hope that he had misheard or misunderstood the general.

"That's right, son," the general confirmed in a quiet but calm and still commanding voice. His eyes remained firmly focused on Stryker now. "I certainly feel bad about asking you, but I don't have a lot of options right now. And, truth be told, you were the best that I've ever known at your work in the Army. I know you're out of uniform now, but the job wouldn't be much different than what you've done before. And I'll make it worth your while." The general's sincerity overcame any evident discomfort he felt in making the request.

The possibility for an immediate response disappeared as the waiter arrived tentatively with their burgers and fries. He carefully set the baskets on the table and inquired about any further needs from the two uncomfortably intense patrons. His face showed obvious relief as both men simultaneously waved him off.

Stryker looked at what normally would pass as tempting food in front of him and quickly decided that his appetite was non-existent, despite eating nothing but the morning apple fritter. Seeing the general take an immediate energetic bite from his burger surprised him. "I don't get it, Sir," was the best response he could render.

MacAfee finished chewing and wiped the corners of his perfectly clean mouth before responding. "Look, I'll explain," he began, "but as I do, just keep an open mind for now. Can you do that for me?"

Stryker surprised himself by nodding.

"Good," said the general before taking another unbothered bite. "And thanks," he mumbled through a full mouth.

Stryker sipped from his soda, simply to have something to do, and waited for the general to begin again. He nibbled on a perfectly crisped fry without any real satisfaction, and contemplated tackling the burger. He figured he had to eat it simply to disguise his shock at the general's proclamation and thereby reestablish the demeanor that said he would never be caught off-guard or let his emotions show. Thus, he took a proud bite of the burger. It tasted much better than he expected and he chewed with expectant eyes on the general.

"So, here's the deal," began the general with surprising informality as he finished chewing and wiped his mouth once again. Stryker looked on silently as he took on two fries at once. "The target's name is Henri Touseau, although it's fairly certain he goes by any number of different names. He's originally from France, as you might guess from the name, but lately he's been living in Libya. We know that he's spent most of his adult life as an arms dealer, although we're fairly certain he has coordinated and probably participated in a number of direct attacks on U.S. bases and U.S. personnel. We believe that he enjoys the thrill of the violence as much as the money he makes." MacAfee could see the questions staring back at him. "And no, I can't say who 'we' are."

MacAfee took another bite of his burger and washed it down with a healthy drink of questionably healthy beer. Stryker continued eating slowly and silently while waiting for the general to continue. The time had not yet come for questions on his part. The restaurant seemed to have gotten warmer in the past few minutes, but Stryker felt relief at the fact that they still sat relatively alone in the corner. He sipped his Diet Pepsi and waited.

"There's no question about Touseau's anti-American sentiments," MacAfee began again after swallowing another bite. "And, I personally have no doubt about his direct involvement in a number of anti-American actions. I'm sure you remember the attack on the Embassy in Cairo about three years ago?" Stryker nodded after a moment's thought. "That was Touseau. There are others as well, but he's been completely untouchable, both legally and through any military action." MacAfee sighed in apparent frustration. "We now believe, however, that he's planning something even bigger. Something big, against us. And the rumors we're hearing is that it may be here within our own borders." MacAfee squinted slightly as he looked directly into Stryker's eyes and Stryker could feel the hate driven energy burning out of those eyes. MacAfee paused and gave his audience a moment of relief by looking down at the table.

Stryker stepped into the verbal void simply to keep the general going, still not seeing how he fit into the picture. "So, now you're ready to take him down?"

"I wish that were so," grunted the general as he rubbed his hands together. "Nothing's happening legally, and we can't get authorization to do anything militarily. That's why I'm here. I'm doing this entirely on my own. Unfortunately, I don't have the skills to actually kill him myself, or I wouldn't be here." He paused and pursed his lips. "I don't, but you do, so here I am." This time when MacAfee stopped talking he didn't resume eating, but instead kept looking directly at Stryker as if to convince him of the seriousness of his request.

Despite the assurance of seriousness, Stryker still didn't want to accept the words coming from MacAfee. "General, I know I don't need to remind you that I'm a civilian now. Sure, I killed for the Army and Double O," Stryker lowered his voice and again looked around to make sure that they weren't being overheard, "but I can't just go out now and kill someone on my own. Out of uniform. That's all part of my past. I know you understand the significance of the fact that I'm not in Omega anymore, Sir."

"I know, son, I know," responded the general quickly. "And believe me, I didn't come here with some half-assed idea that I haven't given plenty of thought and consideration to. I've decided yes and no on this at least a couple of dozen times over the past two months. Maybe a hundred. I realize that you're just hearing about this for the first time, but trust me – I've been over it and over it. I wouldn't be here in Seattle talking to you right now if I thought there were any other options. Any real options." The pleading tone of the general's voice surprised Stryker. The general was a man accustomed to giving orders, not asking favors, but he continued in the same tone. "I really need your help on this."

The questions tumbled over each other in Stryker's mind, each fighting against the others to be the first one spoken. "I'm sorry, but I still don't get it, Sir," he began. "Why now? If this guy's so important, surely you'll get him eventually, right? And why me? I assume you've never proposed something like this before, right? "I'm just . . ." Confusion overwhelmed his ability to articulate, so he stopped and merely stared at the general. Had MacAfee gone off the deep end? Was there something else going on here that he wasn't being told about? Should he simply get up and leave right now or was the person holding the hidden camera about to appear with a big smile on his face?

"Look Stryker," the general tried to explain. "You must know that I wouldn't be here asking this if I felt like I had any alternatives. Of course you're right, I've never proposed anything like this before. And why you? Because I trust you and I know that you can do the job. You've got to kill Henri Touseau." MacAfee paused and took a deep breath before continuing. Stryker thought that he saw a glisten of moisture in the general's eyes as the general focused on the table in front of him. "I suppose there's no reason for you to have known, but my son was killed in Somalia last month. His squadron was hit by three truck bombs simultaneously. You must have heard about the attack – seventeen Americans were killed. Jason was one of them." The general paused as his breath caught momentarily in his throat and he swallowed hard. "There's no question that Touseau was behind it."

With limited clarity now, Stryker still found himself puzzled in other respects. "I'm so sorry, Sir. Of course I heard about the attack, but I had no idea that your son was there. I can only imagine how devastated you must be." Stryker wasn't entirely sure how to continue. "Touseau needs to die, I get that. But I still don't understand why me. Why me, now?"

MacAfee stared at the table for a moment before responding with the next bombshell. "I told you that I'm retiring at the end of the year, right?"

"Yes Sir."

"Well, the truth is retirement is a great idea and I should be looking forward to it, but I'm not supposed to make it that long. The doctors give me four to six weeks, two months at the outside. Seems that I've got cancer eating me up all over the place and I never had a clue until a regular check up last month. They say it's going to get pretty ugly."

The shock waves continued to hit Stryker who found himself immediately looking for signs in the general that weren't evident. He said nothing while keeping his face calm.

"Anyway," the general continued, "I have absolutely no intention of leaving this good earth before that bastard Touseau. If I've got a month or two left, then Touseau's got to die before that. There's no way it's going to happen through any ordinary channels – legal or military. That's why I'm here." He looked Stryker squarely in the eye with an intensity Stryker had rarely seen from another human being. "You're the best option I could think of. The only option I could think of. You've got to kill Touseau for me. Consider it a dying man's last request. I can't die knowing that he's still out there. Please Thorne. I need you."

Stryker was sure that no officer, certainly not a general, had ever called him by his first name before. He was also sure that he couldn't say no to this man whom he respected and sympathized with as well. Stryker had never killed out of uniform before, but it looked as though that was about to change.

A faint, lingering smell was all that remained of the hamburgers and fries and they had finished off three drinks each – beer and Diet Pepsi – by the time they got up to leave. Once it was clear that Stryker would take up the general's favor, they spent most of their time discussing MacAfee's son, the military, and the problems of the world in general. They also discussed MacAfee's offer of payment for the killing, but Stryker was able to convince the general that he had no need for his money. They walked outside into the pleasant Seattle afternoon and proceeded to walk north along First Avenue without a particular destination in mind.

Once outside the restaurant, MacAfee returned once again to the issue at hand. "As you know, we try to keep an eye on characters like Touseau as best we can. He's proved to be incredibly hard to pin down, and he seems to have very few people close to him that we can use to track him either. However, we have reason to believe that he's coming to the U.S. sometime in the next few weeks. He'll maybe more vulnerable here than anywhere in Europe or Africa, so that's what I'm looking at. It also happens to fit my timeframe. We know that he'll travel under some other name, but I believe we'll be able to find that out."

"Okay," Stryker offered tentatively. "Will I have any time to plan and prepare?"

"There's really no way to tell," MacAfee admitted, "but I'll give you as much lead time as I can. I also want to minimize our contact, however. I don't want anyone tracking you down through me. So, here's what I propose." The general stopped talking while they stopped at an intersection with two other pedestrians who presumably were not discussing a pending murder.

With his calm, peaceful civilian life disappearing before his eyes, Stryker set his jaw and listened intently as they began to move again.

"First, I'll give you a password so that you can access Pentagon files. You'll be able to see whatever we've got on Touseau."

"Okay," was all Stryker could say as he took the proffered paper from MacAfee's hand. With the physical act of holding the small paper, Stryker felt the genuine commitment to the cause, from which he know there would be no turning back.

"Secondly, I fully intend for this to be the last direct contact between us. So, I've set up a website called 'Axman.' It's got information on executioners from the middle ages. Somewhat of a long-standing interest for me. Anyway, there's a discussion thread on there as well as the historical info, and that's where you'll need to go. Check it every morning. Once I have information for you, I'll let you know when to find it on the site. I'll have the information posted for a total of five minutes, and that's it."

"Whoa, whoa, whoa," Stryker interjected. "There's no way that's going to work. Five minutes? It'd be pure unbelievable luck, impossible luck, if I happened to see the posting unless I monitored the site twenty-four hours a day. You can't really intend for me to do that?"

"No, no, you misunderstand," said MacAfee as they continued to move along First Avenue past a Tobacco Shop next door to a Tattoo Parlor. Neither man had any inclination to stop. "Look, I've thought about this for a long time. What I'll post is the time for you to look for the information. I'll have the time posted at least twenty-four hours in advance. That way, if you check the site just once a day, in the morning, you'll know when the information's going to be posted, and you won't miss it. The information itself will only be up for five minutes, but the notification about when the information will be there will be posted longer. Does that make sense?"

"Yeah, I guess," responded Stryker tentatively as he thought about flaws in the proposal. "What about anyone else on the site? I assume we don't want others randomly checking in at the same time."

"Well, with a posting of only five minutes, I'm not sure there's much of a realistic chance of that happening," MacAfee rationalized, "but even so, I plan to post the time in code. Here, let me show you."

The two men stopped at a soon-to-be antiquated newspaper box that MacAfee used as a writing desk. Stryker looked around and felt certain that no one on the street seemed to be paying them any attention.

"I'll start with the month, coded as a letter of the alphabet – A for January, B for February, etc. Then, I'll list the date as a simple number. The time will follow. We'll use military time, of course," MacAfee smiled slightly, "but it will be with a 12 hour reversal. So, 1:00 am would be listed as 1300. 9:30 am would be listed as 2130. Make sense?"

"Sure, that sounds easy enough," Stryker offered.

"Well, that's the plan. So, what would this mean?" asked MacAfee as he scribbled H141745 on a napkin.

Stryker paused only momentarily. "August 14 at 17, so, 5:45 am."

"Perfect!" beamed the general. "And this one?" He wrote G22545.

"July 22 at 5:45 pm," answered Stryker.

"See, nothing to it," said an obviously energized MacAfee who turned to walk again. "So, just check the discussion blog on the site every day. I don't expect there'll be any other discussion going on, but it doesn't really matter. Just keep your eyes open for a code like these. Then, go back to the discussion blog at the indicated date and time. I'll post the name Touseau's traveling under, and the city where he's going to be. Remember, it'll be there for five minutes only, and then I'll delete the entry. Got it?"

With a somewhat heavy sigh, Stryker responded in the form of a promise. "Yes Sir."

MacAfee clapped him on the shoulder. "The rest will be up to you."

CHAPTER NINE

Stryker awoke the next morning after a fitful night of little sleep and urgently tried to convince himself that his encounter with General MacAfee had been nothing but a bad dream. He instantly knew better. Thus, he immediately visited the Axman website for the first time with stiff fingers on the keyboard. A drawing of an extremely muscular, hooded, towering executioner greeted him on the homepage along with pictures of a wide variety of axes, swords and smaller blades. Stryker glanced only briefly at the figure before looking around the page for a tab leading to a discussion blog. He found it on the left side of the pictures and clicked on it after just a moment's hesitation. The blog appeared instantly and Stryker could see an attempt at a discussion thread on the issue of whether or not medieval citizens might have considered executioners to be respected public employees. The discussion didn't seem to be going anywhere. There was no coded date and time, but Stryker hadn't really expected to see it so quickly.

He logged off the site, turned away from the computer, and found himself shaking his head at what he was doing. "I can't believe I agreed to this," he verbalized to himself. But in fact, he realized it would have been more unbelievable for him to turn down General MacAfee. MacAfee dying. MacAfee essentially contracting for a murder. Stryker accepting that contract – a contract without pay. A small smile accompanied a shake of his head as he noted the chasm between his current reality and what he'd envisioned for his relaxed civilian life.

Next, Stryker returned to the Internet and made a general online search for the name Henri Touseau. He found two news articles alleging connections between Touseau and acts of terrorism – basically confirming the picture presented to him by MacAfee – but nothing else. He then went to the DOD website and entered the user name and password given to him by the general. With that access, he was able to peruse research files, including the one he found on Touseau. Almost instantly, however, Stryker logged off the site and shut down his computer. Movies and thriller novels had taught him that computer users could be traced and tracked when they logged into systems like the Department of Defense. Was it a danger and did he really need to worry about it for a quick scan of Touseau's file? Stryker didn't have a clue, but for this instance, discretion seemed to be the operative byword. He really should learn more about computers, he thought. In the meantime, plenty of public libraries and Internet cafes stood open and waiting where he could use a computer in relative anonymity.

Just a few hours later, he sat in "Muffins and Macs" along with a stereotypical fifty year old hippie sipping tea while surfing the net, and a sixty-something woman nibbling a muffin and checking email. Stryker logged on to the DOD website and noted that Touseau's file drew connections to a variety of weapons deals dating back at least 15 years. In addition he found reports on specific attacks, some that Touseau had allegedly supported, and some that speculated more direct involvement, including the recent violent attack in Somalia that had taken the life of MacAfee's son. The supporting evidence included the interrogation results from two unidentified captured terrorists. The file also included extensive reports on Touseau's money and land holdings, but it all seemed speculative at best. In addition, Stryker found two photographs, but both were grainy shots taken from a distance, and more than five years old.

Stryker read through everything in the file, then logged off the site and sat back to think. Clearly, military intelligence supported MacAfee's allegations that Touseau prickled as a poisonous evil thorn in America's side for well over a decade. Or, more likely, MacAfee's allegations stemmed from that very intelligence. The file also indicated that despite the fact that the military considered Touseau to be a significant target for the preservation of national security, there was no evidence of any action, past or pending, attempting to take him down. Stryker understood MacAfee's anger and frustration, but he also felt more than a bit leery about the unreasonably tight timeframe established by the general's limited lifespan prognosis.

If the general proved to be right about a Touseau trip to the U.S., it might indeed prove to be the quick and reasonable opportunity for killing the terrorist. Stryker had plenty of experience killing targeted individuals, which had brought MacAfee to him in the first place. However, while Stryker's killing had always been on behalf of his country, it had never before been on American soil, and had always been in a direct military operation. Returning to the life he thought he had left behind gave Stryker a slightly nauseous feeling deep in his stomach. He looked down at his hands where his fingers stretched and clenched repeatedly, almost on their own volition. Suddenly, choosing clothes to wear for the day seemed like a pleasant distraction.

When he arrived back home later in the morning Stryker checked the Axman website again, as he had done at Muffins and Macs, but found no changes in the discussion blog. He chose not to bookmark the page, and immediately erased the history from his browser. Nothing to do now but go for a run.

As he ran, instinct began to return and he jumped significantly ahead of the current situation to consider his options regarding the killing of Touseau. MacAfee had promised immediate shipment of the weapons he'd requested – two different sniper rifles, three handguns, a Kevlar knife, a blackjack, and even blow darts with poison – all of which Stryker had used at various times over his fifteen years in the Army. He had no question about MacAfee's ability to deliver the cache quickly, secretively, and untraceably. Stryker's surprise came from the fact that rather than causing any sense of unease, the pending weapons delivery gave him a grounded feeling. These were tools that he knew well from years of use. These were tools that belonged with him. These were tools that made him feel both comfortable and in control. They enhanced his trust in himself. With his tools, he would fulfill his promise to the general. As he ran, he decided that the sniper rifle would be his first preference, if the circumstances would allow for that choice.

With a self-imposed calmness each time he sat down at the computer, Stryker checked the discussion blog every morning and again every evening for nearly a week, but the message he was now anxious to find failed to appear. The anxiety came from a concern about how much time he had before MacAfee died, and with it he despised the helplessness of sitting and waiting for a message that might never come. As he prepared to log on for yet another check of the site, the phone rang to distract him from the computer. He had received few phone calls during his limited time as a civilian, and even fewer during his years in the Army. The ringing tended to bring a sense of unease rather than anticipation, especially with the last phone calls having come from General MacAfee. Could the general be calling again with information despite his demand for no further direct contact? The phone rang again. Stryker wouldn't know until he answered.

"Hello?" he questioned more tentatively than he wanted.

"Stryker? Thorne Stryker?" the male voice projected a sense of excitement that surprised and puzzled Stryker, although he also breathed out with relief that the voice didn't belong to General MacAfee.

"Yeah, this is he," Stryker responded with only slightly more assertiveness as he tried fruitlessly to place the voice. "Who's calling?"

"Oh man, I can't believe it's really you!" the deep voice seemed discordant with the energy being expressed.

"Yeah, sometimes I have trouble believing it too. But, ah, who is this?" Stryker contemplated simply hanging up but the novelty of the phone call seemed somehow intriguing. At least it didn't sound like a sales call.

"Hey, it's Perkins, man! LJ Perkins! From Double O!" Stryker wondered if the telephone somehow amplified excitement.

"Well, LJ Perkins. Whadya know." Stryker relaxed at the familiarity, but he still puzzled over the call. "What's up, LJ?" Stryker and Perkins had crossed paths numerous times in the Army and ultimately worked closely together in the same unit for more than three years. Stryker remembered Perkins for the same enthusiasm he now heard on the phone. Perkins had left the Army after a twenty-year hitch, a full two years before

Stryker's departure. The two men hadn't been in contact since shortly after Perkins' retirement.

"Wow, I can't believe it's really you!" Perkins excitement didn't seem to be ebbing very quickly. "This is great!"

"Yeah, great," agreed Stryker with a touch of reluctance that he couldn't really place. "How ya been, LJ?"

"Never better, man. Never better. Civilian life is good, let me tell ya," He paused momentarily and Stryker almost spoke into the void when Perkins started again. "I couldn't believe it when I heard that you got out though. I figured you were a lifer if ever there was one. I just can't picture you as a civilian. What happened?"

"Long story, but nothing too exciting," said Stryker in avoidance. "I know you were in for twenty, but fifteen years was a long time for me. Just seemed like time to move on. You know how it is."

"I don't know," replied Perkins with evident skepticism. "I was talking to a couple of the guys not too long ago – Fernandez and Sugar – I keep in touch with 'em pretty regular. Anyway, they said that you had quit all of a sudden, just out of the blue, and didn't say nothin' to anyone. Surprised the hell out of both of 'em. Neither guy really seemed to know much about it – some kind of mystery to everyone it seems."

"Yeah, well, you know how everyone wants to make something out of nothing," Stryker continued his avoidance. "No big deal."

"Well, either way, now that you're out, you'll have to tell me all the details," persisted Perkins in a much calmer voice than at the beginning of the call. "Anyway, Fernandez said you were in Seattle. I can't believe you haven't looked me up, man." Perkins actually sounded a bit hurt which surprised Stryker.

"Looked you up?" suddenly it clicked. "That's right you're here in Seattle. I forgot all about that." Just as suddenly, Stryker's defensive antennae shot up. Two calls out of the blue in the past week. Both from his Army background. Both men here in Seattle. One wanting him to commit murder. What could Perkins want? "Well, I've only been here for a few months. Definitely a nice city, huh?"

"Man, we've got to get together," Perkins plowed forward with renewed excitement. "Been a long time. How about splitting a pizza tonight?"

Tonight? thought Stryker. What the hell happened to my calm, peaceful, do-what-I-want-when-I-want, civilian life? "Umm, I don't know about tonight, I . . ."

Perkins jumped in and cut him off. "Come on, man. You got anything goin'? A woman or something?"

"No, no woman," admitted Stryker while desperately seeking an excuse that would give him time to assuage his paranoia.

"Well then, why not? You gotta eat, right?" Perkins clearly had his heart set on this. "You know the Northlake Tavern? On Lake Union?"

"Yeah, I know it," admitted Stryker.

"Alright then. The Northlake at 7:00 tonight. Okay Stryk? For old times sake," Perkins almost pleaded into the phone.

Well, why not, thought Stryker, unable to come up with an excuse and unwilling to give in to conspiracy thoughts. He glanced at his watch and nodded to himself. "Okay, okay," he relented. "But let's make it 7:30."

"Sweet! See ya tonight, man," chirped Perkins before a dial tone took over the line.

Oh well, thought Stryker. Pizza with an old Army buddy might be good to take his mind off MacAfee and Touseau for a bit. The thought reminded him that he was about to check out the Axman site when the phone rang. He sat back at the computer and pulled up the page. The discussion tab sat there as it had each time before. This time when he clicked on it, however, he saw: 1271725. Two days away.

CHAPTER TEN

Stryker arrived at the Northlake Tavern at a few minutes before 7:30 pm after struggling to find a parking spot on the tight residential streets near the University District in north Seattle. He walked in looking for Perkins, but thinking about Touseau and the posting on Axman. Had he taken a phone number from Perkins he would have called back to cancel, but he couldn't just no-show on a friend from the Army. So, his eyes scanned the tavern even though his thoughts were miles away.

As per Army habit, Perkins had also arrived early and stood waving to Stryker from a table at the back corner of the rectangular shaped room. The fabulous smells took Stryker's mind off Touseau as he walked through the restaurant, and he was further distracted by the hugeness of the pizzas he saw on tables. He had already heard about the Northlake Tavern during his short stay in Seattle, but had never actually patronized the famed establishment. From what he saw and smelled, he knew immediately that he would not leave disappointed. And as an added benefit, the pizza completely brought his mind back to Perkins and the present. Stryker gave a return wave and made his way to Perkins' table.

"LJ, great to see you," he offered with an extended hand.

Perkins ignored the hand and pulled Stryker in for a massive bear hug in his thick arms. "Great to see you, man! Thanks for comin'." Stryker stood nearly two inches over six feet and weighed a solid 195 pounds. Even so, he felt dwarfed in Perkins embrace. Perkins was at least four inches taller than Stryker, and looked as though he may have added a few pounds to the 230 he carried in the Army. He remained as broad across the shoulders and back as Stryker remembered. His hug was strong and genuine and Stryker immediately felt good about being with his old friend again. "I already ordered you a Diet Coke. I assume you haven't discovered the joys of beer yet?" Perkins chuckled.

"Not yet, thanks," Stryker laughed along with the big man.

"Well, one of these days you'll grow up like the rest of us," Perkins needled as he tipped his glass toward Stryker.

Stryker had never seen a pizza as thick and piled high with toppings as the one he and Perkins worked on. After two hours of eating and catching up, Stryker realized that he hadn't been thinking about MacAfee or Touseau at all. Once it was back on his mind, however, his stomach clenched slightly and he brought it up to Perkins indirectly. "Hey," he began, "I heard through the grapevine that General MacAfee was retiring."

"No way, man! I figured he'd die in uniform," said Perkins expressing almost exactly the same thought as Stryker's. "But, like I said, I never figured you to pull out early either." Perkins paused momentarily, but then began again. "What gives, Thorne? What's the big mystery about your resignation? I know you don't need the money, but I still figured you to stay for at least the twenty year pension." Perkins voice seemed to carry more concern, rather than just idle curiosity. Even so, Stryker had no interest in revisiting that particular past at the moment.

"No mystery, Zip. Just had enough," Stryker fibbed. "You know how it gets sometimes. And like you say, I didn't need to stay in for the job or the pension. It just seemed like time before I burned out even more."

"Oh, man. Not with the Zip again," Perkins pleaded, ignoring the issue of Stryker leaving the Army.

Stryker smiled at his unintentional shifting of the focus of the conversation. The story was legend about Perkins during Boot Camp, nearly a decade before Stryker's entry into the Army. Apparently, there had been two consecutive days of morning inspection when Perkins, never much of a morning person, had arrived in formation with his pants unzipped. The first day, he was chewed out. The second day, the Drill Sergeant demanded to know if Perkins was trying to suggest something. The sergeant then spent a good ten seconds with his hand inside Perkins pants all the while yelling that Perkins didn't have anything worth offering to anybody. Thenceforth, Perkins had always been known as "Zip", although he had sincerely hoped that the name would have been left behind when he took off the uniform for the last time.

"Hey, you'll always be Zip, right?" laughed Stryker despite the look of disappointment on Perkins' face. "I'll work on the LJ, but it just doesn't seem to fit you as well."

"Yeah, well my Mom thinks it fits me just fine," whined Perkins. "Anyway, what about the idea of helping out sometimes?" Perkins had spent much of the evening describing the private investigation business he owned, and solely operated for the past four years. Mostly domestic issues, but insurance work had picked up recently and he shared with Stryker that he had considered expanding the business. He wasn't quite ready for a formal expansion yet, but he had jumped at the thought of Stryker taking on some occasional tasks. Perkins had no qualms about showing his exuberance. "Really, man. We'd be a great team. And it wouldn't be that much; it's just that sometimes the timing of cases hits badly. You could pick and choose what you wanted to do, but I could really use some help sometimes. I mean, it's not like you're exactly busy these days, right? So, whadya say?"

Stryker smiled slightly at the 'not busy' comment as he thought about his planned retirement and his now pending business with Touseau. He also assumed that Perkins would cool to the idea as soon as they were apart so he didn't feel compelled to turn down the offer at that moment. Besides, he didn't want to argue about it with his old friend. "Yeah, we'll see. You never know, I guess." Stryker took a long look at his watch while Perkins finished off what was left in his beer glass. The two men were not light eaters, but they still had pizza left on the table. Stryker shook his head while gesturing at the left-over food. "I think it's time to go now though, huh big fella?" Stryker reached for the bill.

Perkins reached out to grab the bill from Stryker but immediately thought better of it and laughed. "Yeah, I guess I'll let you get it," he agreed with a nod. He looked hard at the pizza for a moment, and then succumbed to the temptation and picked up a final slice for the road. "Thanks for coming though. And I'll call you in a day or two after you've had a chance to think about the business. I think you'd really like it, man."

Stryker merely smiled and nodded as he left money on the table to cover the tab and a healthy tip. The two men hugged as they got up from the table, and this time Perkins gave Stryker three phone numbers – home, office and cell. "Call me any time, man. Regardless of the business, we need to get together again, huh?"

"Of course," promised Stryker. "Soon." His immediate future, however, centered on MacAfee and Touseau. Perkins would never have believed it.

When Stryker arrived back home he went back to the computer to re-check the website. The discussion blog carried the same invitation: I271725. It would be a long two days

CHAPTER ELEVEN

Stryker got out of bed at 4:15 on the morning of September 27th. He had set his alarm for 5:00, but hadn't been able to sleep all night. As he lay fitfully in bed, the scenario of missing his five minute window kept playing over and over in his head, denying him any degree of rest or relaxation, so eventually he decided to hell with it and got up. With an hour to wait until the scheduled time on Axman, he turned on the early morning local news, completed some push-ups and sit-ups, and finally took a quick shower.

At 5:15 he sat at the desk where his computer resided. On the right side of the computer was a notepad and pen. On the left side an unused coaster and a small clock shaped like a baseball in a mitt. There were no pictures on the desk nor anywhere else in the room. The background screen on the computer remained the same generic blue that had been there when he first turned on the computer after purchasing it. The computer desktop was as clean and uncluttered as the physical desktop on which it sat.

Stryker quickly accessed the Axman website and logged onto the discussion blog with nervous anticipation. Nothing further had been posted since the coded date. Stryker closed the site and checked the latest news headlines, all the while keeping a careful eye on the clock. Finally, at exactly 5:25 am, he anxiously logged back on to the Axman page. The knots in his stomach were not from the sit-ups and his shallow breathing could not be attributed to the push-ups, so Stryker willed himself to relax. The site popped up and the picture of the muscular, hooded executioner stared out at him as before, but this time it carried a greater sense of foreboding for Stryker. Without stopping to contemplate however, he jumped straight to the discussion blog. He saw an entry posted under the user name "Halloween-27". It read: "Philippe de Grais. Houston." That was it. Nothing more. Despite his overall anxiety and continued disbelief about his involvement, he felt a tingle of excitement at the fact that the code had worked and the information stared out at him as promised. He scribbled down the name and the city, although he was sure he'd be able to remember Houston, and then logged off the site. At 5:31 he logged back on and the posting was gone, just as MacAfee had promised.

MacAfee had said that he believed that Touseau would be traveling to the U.S. Apparently, he would be traveling under the name of Philippe de Grais, and would be going to Houston, Texas, for at least part of his trip. Suddenly Stryker's momentary excitement turned to dread as he realized all that he didn't know. Touseau under the name de Grais. But where in Houston? And more importantly, when? Tomorrow? A month from now? How was he supposed to carry out his assignment without more information besides a name and a city? His frustration level elevated instantly and he chided himself for agreeing to MacAfee's plea in the first place. The plan obviously just wasn't going to work, and as Stryker saw it, he had two options. One, he could violate their initial agreement and contact MacAfee to seek out more meaningful information. Two, and the more preferable of the options, he could simply forget about the whole thing and go back to more important issues like exercise and old movies. He had promised MacAfee, he acknowledged, but the general would have to understand that in addition to being a questionable idea to start with, the job under its current parameters wasn't really feasible.

At virtually the same time as he thought about bagging the mission however, Stryker thought about his reputation for reliability. It was a reputation he had earned over time, and one that he had proudly put on the line, over and over again. He had always been a man to get the job done, regardless of the difficulty of the task or the roadblocks in the way. Being a civilian didn't change who he was as a man. While wearing a uniform he never would have said, "I can't do this" or "This is too hard." He'd have found a way to get the job done. With a sigh of resignation and semi-confident determination, he shook off his doubts and resolved to do the same thing now.

Two hours later, Stryker was back considering his first two options. He ate a bowl of cold cereal with banana slices while mentally flipping a coin – contact MacAfee or forget the whole thing. If Touseau / de Grais lived in Houston, the job would be relatively easy, Stryker thought. In his helpless frustration he had checked, even though he knew that Touseau lived in France or Libya and was simply traveling to Houston. As expected, he had found nothing. Because Touseau didn't live in Houston but was merely visiting, Stryker needed to know when and where. Without that information, the job was impossible.

In mid-bite of a spoonful of disappointing cereal without any banana, Stryker paused. He needed to know when and where. Of the two, the when was certainly the most important. If he knew the when, he could possibly figure out the where within Houston since he had the city to start with. He thought again about the discussion blog posting – "Philippe de Grais. Houston." Nothing more. And then it struck him. For his molasses-like approach to the problem, he struck himself on the side of the head. What an idiot, he thought. Of course MacAfee would give him what he needed. Because there was nothing more in the posting itself, it had to be in the name under which the posting had been made. "Halloween-27." A moniker of "Halloween" made marginal sense for a site on medieval executioners, but Stryker was now sure that there was more to it. "Halloween-27."

Excitement elevated with the possibility of an answer to the puzzle. He pushed aside the half eaten bowl of cereal and stood up to walk to the window. "Halloween-27." Would Touseau be in Houston on October 31st? That certainly seemed possible, but where did that leave the 27? Between the 27th and the 31st? Maybe, but in that case, why not have it written '27-Halloween?' Halloween minus 27? Twenty seven days before Halloween? That made more sense. October 4th. It had to be, he thought. Stryker glanced at the calendar and realized that October 4th was just a week away. It also made sense that whatever notice MacAfee could provide wouldn't be long into the future. October 4th seemed right.

If he were right, however, it gave him parameters for his search, but he still had to figure out where in Houston he could find Touseau. He smiled and nodded at what he hoped could be labeled as progress while he reached for the phone to make a plane reservation. He immediately set the phone down. Flying to Houston would leave a record of his coming to and leaving the city. Instead, he would drive. Besides, carrying weapons was much easier in his own car than on a commercial airline. He realized it would be three or four days from Seattle, so he prepared to move quickly.

Stryker planned to leave Seattle the next morning, which would be six days before the October 4th date he was now confident about, but before that departure, he intended to know where in Houston to find Touseau. To begin his quest, he went online and accessed a list of all of the five star hotels in the city. If Touseau were to stay in a private home, in a cheap hotel, or in some outlying city, Stryker would be out of luck. He might have a chance, however, if Touseau went the predictable route and opted for one of the nicest hotels available.

The immediate hotel list included more than twenty names in the downtown area. Not surprising for a large, big money city such as Houston, but not the best for Stryker in the current circumstances. Lacking any other means of discriminating among the names on the list, he began alphabetically – the Algonquin Hotel. Having mentally rehearsed his spiel, he took a deep breath and punched in the number on the phone.

"Good morning, Algonquin Hotel, this is Carmella. How may I help you?" greeted the cheerful but professional female voice on the other end of the line.

Stryker began with an exaggerated sigh. "Oh, please Carmella, I hope so," he pleaded into the phone. He tried to remove all confidence and forcefulness from his voice. "I'm gonna be in so much trouble. I don't even know, I mean," he gave an exasperated heavy breath and continued, "ummm, I need to talk to somebody about a reservation."

"I can help you sir," Carmella's voice replied with practiced reassurance, "what seems to be the problem?"

"Oh, thank you, thank you," Stryker began again with urgent gratitude. "Ummm, so, my boss is coming in to Houston next week. I was supposed to make his reservations for him, but I was out sick, so Jason did it," he ran the words together quickly with a slight effeminate affectation to his voice. "But now Jason's gone and nobody knows where he is and I need to confirm the reservations and plan transportation from the airport. Oh, boy," Stryker interrupted himself with another sigh. "Anyway, Jason made the reservations but there's no record here of where he made them and nobody can find him and my boss is already gone on the first part of his trip and I have to follow up and I'm sure my boss wanted to stay in a certain hotel – he's very particular – and if I don't get things figured out I'm gonna get fired and I really need this job and it's not really my fault but Jason's gone and now, I don't know . . ."

"That's okay, sir, I can help you. Just calm down," Carmella's soothing voice almost came physically out of the phone to massage his neck into relaxation. She was obviously very good at her job and Stryker marveled at her apparently well-practiced ability to deal calmly with his exasperation. "Now, do you know the day that your boss is arriving in Houston?"

"Yeah, yeah," Stryker offered hurriedly. "Well, it was supposed to be October 4th, but I guess it could have changed by a day or so since he's already started his trip. But it should be the 4th. That's what I was told, but then Jason made the reservation, so now I'm not even sure about that. But I don't know where the heck he is, and . . ."

Carmella interrupted politely. "That's okay, really. I can check our reservations both before and after the 4th, it won't take but a minute."

"Oh, thank you so much," Stryker put as much combined relief and gratitude into his voice as he could muster. He intentionally paused.

"So, I still need some help," Carmella prompted politely.

"Huh?" Stryker feigned confusion.

"Your boss?" she replied. "I need his name."

"Oh, jeez, what an idiot," Stryker continued the charade. "Maybe I should be fired. I'm sorry. It's de Grais," he spelled it for her. "Philippe de Grais. He's also traveling with his partner, so it could be listed under Touseau, but it should be under de Grais."

Stryker listened to Carmella at the keyboard. After a brief pause, she came back with her news. "I'm sorry sir, but we have no reservation under either of those names for anytime between now and the end of October."

Stryker exhaled into the phone. "Well, thanks anyway. Hmmm. So, Mr. de Grais only likes the best places, that's why I started with your hotel. If he's not booked there, do you know of any other likely spots?"

Carmella mentioned a few names that Stryker verified were on his list and placed small check marks next to them. He then effusively thanked Carmella again and hung up the phone to replay the entire performance with the next hotel.

The sixth hotel on Stryker's list was the Excelsior and Stryker found the reservations clerk there to be as friendly and helpful as all of the others. The wealthy must come to expect accommodating assistance everywhere they traveled. Stryker thought about the temperament required to work in any sort of service industry, and realized that he probably didn't have it.

After sharing the name de Grais, he waited on the phone with a bit less patience than he had at the beginning of the search. Eventually, the clerk, named Marco, came back on the line. "Well, you're in luck, sir. And you were right. We've got Mr. de Grais registered here from the 4th through the 7th of October."

"Oh, that's fabulous," Stryker gushed with genuine excitement. "The 4th through the 7th," he confirmed. "Thank you so much. You've saved my life."

"Not a problem, sir. I hope Mr. de Grais enjoys his stay at the Excelsior."

It'll be one of a kind, thought Stryker as he hung up the phone and continued his preparations to hit the road toward Texas.

CHAPTER TWELVE

Stryker paced his driving so that he entered the city limits of Houston on October 3rd, the day before Touseau was due to arrive. The calendar clearly indicated the arrival of fall, but the thermometer seemed to have missed the message as it registered 94 degrees at just past noon. Stryker had never previously visited Houston, but he had no trouble finding the Excelsior Hotel in the busy downtown area. He circled the block twice and then the surrounding blocks several times to get a sense of the territory, then parked in a nearby lot with covered, i.e. shaded, parking places. Stryker took in as much as possible on the street as he walked slowly toward the hotel but then passed by without entering. He could see that the building was one of the older ones on the block, and rose to at least fifteen stories. Unlike many modern hotels, which tended to separate themselves from other buildings, the Excelsior was surrounded by businesses and had no visible parking available. The awning over the front entrance reminded Stryker of east coast hotels of the 1920s, though he doubted that the Excelsior was that old. Taxicabs enjoyed reserved spots immediately in front of the building, and he noted two classic yellow, although hybrid, models waiting as he walked by. The entrance to the white stone hotel included large swinging doors, and two energy saving cage-like revolving doors, one on each side of the main entry. All of the doors were heavy glass encased in gold edging and shined immaculately from frequent cleaning. Stryker smiled in semi-surprise at the absence of a doorman who, in his estimation, should have been there in braided green uniform, black cap and shiny black shoes. Glancing at his watch, he imagined Touseau walking through those doors tomorrow and began pondering his options over the next four days.

One of the immediate problems was that with only the older, grainy photographs to go on, he didn't have a clue what Touseau really looked like. In addition, while he knew that Touseau had a reservation for tomorrow, he didn't know what time his quarry would be arriving. He only knew that tomorrow would mark the start of his very limited window of opportunity in Houston. He needed a plan and he knew that ultimately he'd also need some level of assistance. Immediately, that meant that he needed to think, for without clear thoughts, spending any further time at the hotel would prove useless. Thus, he wandered away from the Excelsior and stopped in at a nearby Deli and enjoyed a leisurely corned beef sandwich with split pea soup – certain that the combination would not be considered appropriate in the finer circles of society. As he ate and stared out at the street, an idea began to percolate.

Stryker didn't want to check into a hotel and thereby leave a record of his visit to the city, so instead, he spent the day driving, and mall visiting until nearly midnight. At that time, he stopped at a local Costco store with a huge parking lot holding a few random cars. He pulled in, parked, and slept fitfully in the reclined driver's seat of his Mercedes sedan until nearly 6:00 the next morning. October 4th.

After a breakfast of two apple fritters and a large orange juice, Stryker arrived at the Excelsior at shortly after 8:00 am. He was certain that nobody would be checking in before noon, at the earliest, but he wasn't going to take any chances. He entered the hotel and walked immediately to the elevators without a second look at the front desk, despite his curiosity about whether the helpful Marco might be working to solve the vexing problems of the pampered guests. He took the elevator to the top floor where he got out and began slowly walking the halls looking for the maids on duty as they began their daily room cleaning chores. He assumed that many of the cleaning staff would be Hispanic, which would be just fine, but he regardless of ethnicity, needed to find one who wasn't too old. A man would be great, but he knew that wasn't very likely. He decided to stay entirely on the upper three floors, and to use the stairs at the far ends of the hallways to move from one floor to another. For nearly an hour, he walked, climbed up and down stairs, and waited as inconspicuously as possible in the hallways assessing the workers on duty.

He finally settled on a slightly plump woman, probably Mexican, who looked to be in her mid to late thirties. She worked steadily but alone on the west wing of the 14th floor and gave the appearance of tired resignation in her chores. Stryker had seen her twice before deciding that she would be the one. He watched her enter a room with her cart in the hallway and he waited a few minutes before he approached. With nobody else visible in the hallway, he approached the entry to room 1417 and knocked lightly on the open door. He repeated his knock when the first attempt produced no response.

"Si?" came a tentative voice from inside.

Stryker stayed back in the threshold of the doorway while craning his neck and leaning his head into the room. He tried to fix a non-threatening half smile on his face. "Hello?" he called out softly and reassuringly.

The maid peered around a corner toward the entry of the room with a look of apprehension on her pretty, but tired looking face. "May I help you sir?" she asked in very clear, but slightly accented English.

Stryker knew he had to monitor his approach very carefully, but he trusted his instincts about the maid and about human nature in general. He noted her nametag, which identified her as Rosa. "I hope so," he spoke softly with as meek a look as he could muster on his face, "Rosa, is it? I need a really huge favor."

"Yes?" she asked suspiciously. "What is it you need?"

"Well," he began sheepishly as he pulled his head back from the room and dropped his shoulders slightly, "I need to find out somebody's room number."

"I'm sorry, sir," she deferred as he expected, "we cannot give out any information about our guests." Rosa began to smooth out the bed sheets in a return to her work, which she obviously hoped would lead to his exit.

"I know, I know," Stryker kept his voice meekly soft and timid. "That's why I didn't go to the front desk." He noted that as Rosa stood up and looked at him, her cautiousness remained clearly evident in her cross-armed stance. Her face showed no sign of sympathetic listening. This was it, thought Stryker. "Look, I'm not going to lie to you," he lied expertly with a continuation of his non-threatening demeanor. "I'm leaving town tonight – I'm moving to Milwaukee. You see, I was divorced just two weeks ago and I work in the same office as my ex-wife, so I quit my job and now I'm going to Wisconsin." Stryker was hopeful that he could see a softening in Rosa's eyes as he continued. "You see, my wife, we were married for 13 years, she started seeing another man who was a client of our firm. He's from France and she met him there on business, and well, that's what led to the divorce." Stryker's voice caught briefly and he blinked in rapid succession as though he were fighting back inevitable tears. He paused and placed his left hand briefly on his chest while he swallowed hard and looked at the floor in front of him. After a few seconds he looked up again at the silent but attentive Rosa. "Anyway, like I said, I'm flying out of here tonight, and I hope I never come back to Houston. But, I heard from a friend of Lisa's – Lisa is, or was, my wife – anyway I heard from a friend that her French guy is coming into town today. And I, well, I don't know, I guess I just wanted to see what he looked like." He looked for understanding in Rosa's face. "I'm, sure he hasn't checked in yet, but, I . . ." he paused and looked as forlorn as possible.

"I'm sorry, sir," Rosa began with the company line again, but Stryker interrupted.

"Oh, it's Ben," Stryker held out his hand in friendly introduction. "Ben Robinson." He pursed his lips in defeated resignation.

"I'm sorry, Mr. Robinson," Stryker smiled inwardly at her use of the name he had given, "but we really can't give out information on our guests. I could get in a lot of trouble." Rosa seemed genuinely sorry at turning him down, but didn't take his proffered hand.

"Look, I know," Stryker showed the palms of both hands in virtual surrender. "I'm not going to cause any kind of disturbance, and no one would ever know that you helped me out. I mean, chances are my plane will be leaving before he's here anyway. But, I don't know, I just would feel better somehow if I just had the chance to see what he looked like."

Rosa shrugged in helplessness.

"What time do you get off work?"

"I'm supposed to be off at 4:00," Rosa explained, "but sometimes I don't finish until an hour after that."

"Okay," Stryker nodded, "look, I've got to head to the airport by 5:30 or so, so it may not do me much good, but . . ." Stryker reached out, lightly grasped her forearm with his left hand, and pressed five one hundred dollar bills into her hand with his right. "I'll come back at about 4:00. If he's checked in, and you feel like you can give me the room number, I'd really appreciate it. If not, well, that's up to you. I'm leaving anyway, so you can keep the money. And I promise, no scenes, no confrontations, no problems."

"I don't know," Rosa hesitated, but didn't say no. "I really can't take your money."

"Hey really, keep it, " Stryker reassured with a sad smile and a shake of his head. "I probably won't get to see him anyway, so don't worry about it. Here's the name," he handed Rosa a slip of paper with 'de Grais' printed on it. "I'll swing by the lobby about 4:00. If you can help me, great, if not, I understand. No hard feelings. Thanks anyway for listening. Believe it or not, I feel better just talking to you for a few minutes."

Rosa smiled as Stryker stepped back into the hallway. "Well, I can't promise anything, but why don't you come here, instead of the lobby. 4:00."

"Okay," Stryker kept his voice soft and resigned. "Thank you again, Rosa. You've been very kind." His feet barely touched the carpet as he smiled all the way to the elevator without looking back.

By 6:00, and wearing an Excelsior uniform from the laundry room in the basement of the building, Stryker busied himself washing the walls of the 15th floor of the hotel. Two doors down from room 1539. The room number that Rosa had whispered to him two hours earlier. He assumed that dinner would draw the occupants out of the room sometime over the next few hours. It turned out to be less than thirty minutes. As soon as the door opened, Stryker quickly picked up his cleaning supplies and headed toward the elevator. He pushed the down button and glanced at the two men approaching from his left. Both men exuded casual professionalism, dressed smartly in slacks, sport coats, and open collared shirts. One was tall, very pale, and looked to be in his early thirties despite his heavily receding hairline. He looked straight ahead with his eyes focused on Stryker at the elevator doors. The other stood at 5' 9", at the most, and sported a deep tan that contrasted well with his sandy-blond hair. He appeared to be in his late forties or early fifties and he spoke quietly into a cell phone, eyes on the floor in front of him as he walked. Stryker knew immediately that the shorter, older man was Touseau, and with that knowledge he focused on the elevator doors in front of him.

As the elevator arrived, Stryker stepped on and held the door for the other two. He looked closely at Touseau who seemed to take no notice of him. The other man waved Stryker to go ahead so Stryker allowed the doors to close and pushed the button for the 2nd floor. As soon as the elevator reached the 2nd floor, Stryker jumped out and headed for the stairs. Just outside the stairwell he set down the cleaning bucket and while hurrying down the stairs he removed the Excelsior uniform and tucked it under his arm. When he reached the lobby he strode out and stopped at a table of tourist brochures occupying a space near the main doors to the hotel. Stryker appeared to examine a guide to local golf courses while keeping a careful eye on the elevators. The door of the elevator farthest to the right opened in a moment and Touseau and his companion stepped out and headed straight for the hotel exit. Stryker turned his back so that he fully faced the brochures until he saw the two men pass through his peripheral vision. Stryker walked toward the center of the lobby as Touseau's companion stepped out through the main doors onto the street. A black Lincoln Town Car stood double-parked outside of two taxis waiting in front of the hotel. Touseau waited in the entryway to the hotel while the other man opened the back door to the Lincoln. Touseau quickly stepped between the cabs and into the back seat where he disappeared behind darkly tinted windows. His companion moved around the back of the car and entered the back seat from the other side. Stryker hurried out of the hotel and watched the Town Car drive two blocks up the street before taking a right turn and disappearing from view. He looked at his watch and noted that it was 6:31 pm.

Stryker took up watch outside the hotel, splitting time between a drugstore across the street, the deli where he had eaten the day before, a jewelry shop with a large picture window, and simply walking the street. He walked slowly on the opposite side of the street and down the block at exactly 9:00 pm when the Lincoln reappeared in front of the Excelsior. Touseau's companion got out of the car first, and after opening the door for Touseau, the two men moved directly into the hotel. The Lincoln then backed illegally around the corner. Stryker expected to see the black car emerge from the side street and head in the opposite direction, but instead the car remained out of sight. He continued to walk past the hotel and up to the corner where he waited to cross the street. As he waited, he saw Lincoln sitting on the relatively quiet side street in a load-unload only zone. Stryker raised his eyebrows in interest and as he crossed the street and then turned to walk away from the parked Lincoln and the Excelsior. At the end of the block he turned around and noted the continued unmoving presence of the large black car. He then walked back to the Excelsior and took a seat in the lobby where he proceeded to read through a news magazine recently purchased from the drugstore. The cover story dealt with the "failure" of America's schools and Stryker had a genuine interest in what the article had to say. He had more of an interest, however, in the reappearance of Touseau, which he assumed was indicated by the nearby presence of the Lincoln. As he expected, about thirty minutes later Touseau and his shadow stepped off the elevator. Stryker glanced out the window to see the Town Car double-parked out front once again. He smiled to himself as he returned to the news article.

Stryker slept in his car once again and arose early the next morning. He felt a bit ratty and was sure that his smell would begin to bother the better folks of Houston, especially since the temperatures hadn't cooled off toward anything un-Texas like. He found a public bathroom, removed his shirt, and gave himself a thorough splash bath at the sink as best he could. Along with a clean shirt he felt somewhat human to start the day. Unfortunately, experience taught him that the "bath" in the restroom was likely to be the highlight of the day.

By 8:00 am Stryker had taken up residence on a bench outside of a barbershop situated across the street and about a half block down from the Excelsior. Armed with orange juice, water, two apple fritters, a bagel, an investment magazine, a news magazine and a novel, he settled in for what he assumed would be a long day. He planned to sit for fifty minutes and walk for ten during each hour. Remembering his years of practice from the monotony of the Army, Stryker prepared himself for a mentally challenging day. He had assumed that these sorts of chores would be left behind in civilian life, yet here he sat. The biggest challenge came from actually trying to read as Stryker's primary focus remained on the Excelsior at all times. Thus, two sentences of reading were followed by a glance up and across the street. He often found himself reading the same sentences over and over again and struggling to maintain any flow with the text. At various times he simply gave up and enjoyed people watching on the busy cosmopolitan street. He created games for himself and the people such as trying to pick out who was the richest person on the street at any given time. He also challenged himself to pick out the best looking woman he could see in a five second scan of the street. He'd lose if he locked onto a woman who proved to be less attractive than he thought, or who was surpassed by another woman he had missed.

Stryker finally reaped the reward for his vigil when a black Lincoln, maybe the same one as the night before, pulled up and double-parked outside the Excelsior at about 11:30 am. The driver remained in the car, and within two minutes Touseau's companion stepped out of the hotel, scanned the street, and opened the back door of the Town Car. A brief nod toward the hotel brought Touseau out and directly into the back of the Lincoln. As soon as the second man seated himself on the opposite side and closed the door, the car moved up the street and turned right at the second corner. Stryker looked at his watch and decided that he had a bit of time to relax, so he walked to the Deli for a sandwich and a Diet Coke.

The Lincoln didn't return until after 2:00 in the afternoon, by which time Stryker was hot and uncomfortable with a sweat-soaked back that ached from sitting. Even so, he maintained his patience. He saw the car stop in front of the hotel whereupon the companion jumped out and opened the door for Touseau who then walked directly into the lobby. The Lincoln immediately drove away and Stryker decided that the time to prepare had come.

Stryker cleaned up quickly again in the restroom of the Deli and then walked the two blocks to his car where he changed into black pants and a white shirt. He also filled a small duffle bag with two six-foot sections of nylon rope, a blackjack, a knife and two handguns, both of which were fully loaded. Stryker then returned to the street to a spot further down the block, refreshed and ready, both for waiting and for action.

CHAPTER THIRTEEN

The temperature hovered near 90 degrees again in the late afternoon, but shade from the surrounding buildings along with a soothing breeze provided some semblance of relief from the otherwise steady heat. Stryker immediately resumed his pattern of sitting and walking, with inefficient reading thrown in. He didn't expect to see the Lincoln again before 6:00, but the accuracy of his assumption failed to reduce the monotony of the wait. Once evening came and the temperature dropped, he began to watch the hotel more closely. He looked at his watch more and more frequently as 7:00 pm approached, and felt himself tensing with increased anxiety as he began to question Touseau's reappearance. He relaxed, however, as he finally saw the Lincoln approaching the hotel from the east at about 7:15. Rather than stopping in front of the Excelsior, the Lincoln stopped at the corner and backed around into the no-parking zone on the quieter side street once again. Stryker briefly considered moving immediately to put his plan into action, but thought better of it. Within two minutes the Lincoln reappeared and double-parked in front of the hotel whereupon Touseau, classily dressed in black with a white shirt and no tie, and his similarly attired companion, repeated the same routine of exiting the hotel and entering the back seat of the car. It was 7:21 pm, and the would-be assassin felt his heart rate quicken as he anticipated the return of Touseau and the Lincoln later that evening.

Darkness had taken over the city by the time the Lincoln showed up again at 9:55, but the street maintained a constant flow of traffic. Stryker held his breath as Touseau and his presumed bodyguard exited the car to go into the hotel. With pursed lips, he reached for his duffle bag and stood up, all the while wondering if the Lincoln would drive off straight down the street or back around the corner as he hoped. He exhaled deeply and clenched his right fist in victory as the car backed around the corner into its waiting spot. Stryker briskly walked down the street while slipping on his gloves and crossed to the corner where the Lincoln idled unobtrusively. He stood briefly on the corner and put on a show of looking at the street signs and at a paper in his right hand. The duffle bag hung loosely from the left. He shook his head and started to cross the street again, but then stopped in the middle of the crosswalk and moved back to the corner. Again, he looked up and down the street. Finally, he walked hesitantly to the driver's side door of the Lincoln and mouthed, "help?" with a practiced look of exasperation on his face. The window of the car moved down smoothly and the driver looked out with a bored expression.

"What are y. . ." the driver began until the nose of the pistol pressing against his left ear and pushing him into the car stopped him.

Stryker quickly dropped the duffle bag to the ground, opened the door and coaxed the driver over to the passenger seat with a wave of the pistol. Before the driver could settle into the seat and begin his verbal protest, a quick strike of the blackjack rendered him unconscious.

In the relative darkness of the side street, Stryker immediately removed the driver's jacket in what proved to be a rather clumsy activity despite the fact that the Lincoln's interior space provided more room than most cars. He quickly bound and gagged the driver and stuffed him into the foot cavity in front of the passenger's seat, then stepped out of the car briefly and slipped on the driver's jacket and tossed the duffle bag onto the passenger seat. In the right hand pocket of the jacket he found a cell phone. He breathed deeply and waited.

A long twenty minutes passed before the cell phone rang. Stryker hesitated briefly and took a deep breath before he opened the phone and grunted a greeting.

"We're coming down," was all he heard in accented English.

Stryker pulled his 9mm automatic out of the duffle bag and rested it on his lap with the blackjack while glancing at the unmoving driver who looked as though he would be quite uncomfortable if he were aware of his body position. He slipped on the driver's hat before driving the Lincoln around the corner where he double-parked in front of the Excelsior. He breathed normally despite the anticipation of imminent action.

Stryker left the car in gear as he stopped in front of the hotel, keeping his left foot on the brake while his right was poised at the ready over the accelerator. Within moments, the companion came out on the street, looked around, and then opened the back door of the Lincoln without so much as glance into the front of the car. Touseau stepped into the car and as soon as he cleared the door, Stryker stepped down hard on the accelerator and squealed away from the Excelsior knocking down Touseau's companion and slamming the door shut at the same time.

Three blocks up the street the Lincoln made a right turn and pulled into a parking garage, all the while ringing with shouts in

French from Touseau in the back seat. Stryker screeched to an abrupt halt in the relative emptiness of the back of the garage and immediately turned to train the gun on Touseau who froze in the middle of opening the door to escape. Stryker motioned him to close the door and sit back in his seat, which Touseau did with wide eyes giving away the swirl of thoughts in his head.

"Who are you, and what are you doing?" demanded Touseau in remarkably clear English, and with a calmness that belied his looking into the barrel of a gun in the hand of a stranger. He extended the image of confidence by carefully straightening his slim burgundy tie that now accompanied the white shirt, and patting out unperceived wrinkles in his expensive-looking charcoal jacket.

"Pleased to meet you, Monsieur Touseau," responded Stryker with feigned politeness complete with a half smile.

"Surely you are mistaken, sir," the Frenchman began. Stryker was impressed with the very real look of incredulous honesty on his face. "My name is Philippe de Grais. I am visiting your country from Paris. Who is this Touseau of whom you speak?" His left hand remained positioned on the door handle.

"Touseau?" Stryker played along with a glance at the door and the left hand and a forced smile on an otherwise stern visage. "He's a terrorist, a killer, an all-around bad guy and a true enemy of the United States." The gun remained trained steadily on Touseau's chest.

"But what has he to do with me?" demanded Touseau in a voice that revealed an increased sense of anxiety. "I do not even know this man, and you call me by his name."

"Sorry, but there's no time to argue. I've got to go now." Stryker noted the thin layer of perspiration on Touseau's firmly set upper lip.

"I am pleased to hear it," responded Touseau with clear indignation. "And you had better hope that I never see you again."

"Don't worry, you won't," promised Stryker. "One last thing before I go," he tilted the gun up and then down again.

"No, no, wait. Money! I have lots of money!" pleaded Touseau.

"I hope you've got a will too," responded Stryker who calmly proceeded to place two shots directly into Touseau's heart.

Stryker made sure that the driver remained unconscious, then with great effort he pulled him up off the floor of the car, removed the rope from his oversized wrists, and replaced the black jacket over his arms and back. He quickly re-bound the driver's hands around the steering wheel, placed the hat back on his head, and left the car with the doors locked. With his duffle bag in hand, Stryker calmly walked the four blocks to his car. He then drove through the warm night heading northwest back to Seattle.

News the following evening carried the story of the French tourist murdered in Houston. The car had been discovered relatively quickly with the assistance of the driver kicking loudly against the windows. The seemingly random nature of the attack against a visitor to the country caused the story to be of national significance, for at least a short period of time, despite the absence of any suspects or apparent motive.

After returning home, Stryker logged back onto the Axman website a number of times. He wasn't sure if he was expecting a "nice job" or some other sort of follow-up, but there was nothing, just as MacAfee had promised. Within a few days, Stryker thought less and less about the trip to Houston, and more about a resumption of what he planned to be a normal civilian life. The only difference now was that the life carried a very real skeleton in a closet.

Less than two weeks later Stryker received a phone call from LJ Perkins sharing the news that General MacAfee had died. He never had the chance to enjoy his retirement. Even so, Stryker was certain that the general died relatively happy.

It was December 7, Pearl Harbor Day, almost exactly two months after the killing of Touseau that Stryker went back to the Axman website. He had been looking to purchase a book online when his curiosity was aroused and he ventured back to the site simply on a lark. The site's main page hadn't changed at all, nor seemingly had the tabs on the left side of the page. Stryker clicked on the discussion blog to see if anyone had presented a real issue to talk about. He noted a new discussion chain had been started recently and his eyes opened widely and he sat frozen for a moment as he read the beginning of the chain: L121212. December 12th at just past midnight.

Confusion swirled in Stryker's mind. The message had been posted more than a month after MacAfee's death. No one else was supposed to know about their deal. Someone obviously did know. Did that mean that someone also knew that he was the one who killed Touseau? What the hell was this posting doing here?

Stryker read the next entry on the discussion blog, which proffered the question of whether medieval executioners would have been paid the equivalent of $200,000 today. Was this an offer of payment for another assassination job to be posted on the 12th? Stryker's stomach churned as he chided himself for revisiting the site in the first place. Curiosity killed the cat. At least, however, he was now aware of the fact that someone clearly knew about the site and his code with MacAfee. But did they also know about him and Touseau?

On December 11th, Stryker spent the evening at home reading and watching Clark Gable smirk his way through a 1930s love story. As midnight approached, his anticipation rose with the minute hand of his old-school, non-digital clock. At exactly twelve minutes past the witching hour he logged on to the Axman website and its discussion blog. Following the question about the pay for an executioner, to which no response had been written, Stryker read a posting of a name and a city. They had been posted under the user name "Justice". He wrote them down and logged off. He checked back on the site at 12:20 and the name was gone. In its place was a reply to the pay question. The responder, again "Justice", commented that $250,000 was more likely today's equivalent of pay for an Axman.

Research informed Stryker that the name posted on the site belonged to a relatively well-known American criminal who lived in the named city, and who had managed to avoid prosecution for all of his seemingly well-documented crimes. After long and tormented thought, Stryker came to the conclusion that the country would be better off without the named criminal. He wouldn't seek out the offered payment, but he would take and complete the job. And he did.

PRESENT DAY

CHAPTER FOURTEEN

The Seattle Tourism and Visitors Bureau could not have scripted a more perfect spring day to create an advertisement for the glorious natural beauty of the Emerald City. Nestled into the Puget Sound, the perfectly clear sky afforded views of the Olympic Mountains to the west, the Cascade Range to the east, and the stupendously isolated Mt. Rainier to the south. Stryker could also admire the downtown buildings of the city from his perch in the owner's box at Safeco Field. It was exactly the sort of day that was meant for baseball, and in all reality it would have mattered little if the contest were between two little league teams rather than between the Seattle Mariners and the Baltimore Orioles of the American League. The fact that the Mariners were playing well and the stadium was packed with excited fans only added to the perfection of the blissful afternoon. For Thorne Stryker, the reality that he had just announced his retirement on the Axman website simply provided the whipped cream on top of the perfectly crafted sundae of a day.

The Mariners scored three runs in the bottom of the first inning to further heighten the joy of the already ebullient crowd. Club President Miles Elliot seemed to watch little of the game, but instead spent his time alternating his talk between the telephone that never left his hand, and the guests in the owner's box where he clearly but graciously held court. At the end of the second inning he moved to the front of the box to sit next to Stryker who had just concluded a conversation with a local Internet CEO who claimed to be approaching "wealthier than God" status. Stryker worked hard not to express his jubilation at reaching the end of the strained encounter.

"Well, glad you could make it Mr. Stryker," offered Elliot as he sat heavily in the empty seat overlooking the 45,000 fans in the stadium. "Anything you need?" he waved his meaty right hand at the box behind them as if to indicate that anything could be had simply for the asking. The notion appealed to Stryker, but at the moment he couldn't have been more content.

"It's Thorne, please, Mr. Elliot. And no," Stryker offered up his half-eaten mustard and relish coated hot dog as evidence, "don't need a thing." Stryker couldn't help but smile at the present circumstances of his life. Elliot didn't even seem offended at his khaki shorts and light blue polo shirt, despite the fact that others in the box presented themselves much more formally – some might even say more adultly, if such a word existed.

"Well then Thorne, please call me Miles. Not even the batboy calls me Mr. Elliot," he laughed. "Stryker though, it's such a solid, masculine name," he gestured with his fist, "seems a shame not to use it don't you think?"

Stryker laughed along with him. "Well, I didn't choose the name so I can't take credit for it. But I've never been very comfortable with the 'Mister' part. If you get rid of that, you can call me Thorne or Stryker. Actually though, on a day like today you can call me most anything you'd like." Stryker smiled out toward the perfectly manicured deep green of the grass field as the Mariners pulled off a smooth double play in the top of the third inning.

"Yes, it's just about perfect isn't it?" beamed Elliot. "And some people honestly thought that Seattle would never be a real baseball town. Humph. But I tell ya, give 'em a nice ballpark and a halfway decent team, and these folks love baseball. Doesn't hurt to have weather like today either, of course. What about you, Mr. S. . ., er, Thorne? Always been a baseball man?"

"Oh yeah, as long as I can remember. I never really played myself, but I've been a fan since I was just a kid in the Midwest," Stryker sighed with a touch of nostalgia in his voice. "I'd love baseball wherever I happened to be, but I've been in Seattle for close to ten years so I'm a die-hard Mariner fan now."

"Well good, good. We certainly appreciate your support. Oh, look at that!" Elliot pointed at a great leaping grab by the Mariners' third baseman for the final out of the inning. "Great play, huh? I tell ya, this could be our year," he beamed.

"I'm hoping so," Stryker nodded in agreement as the teams trotted off and on the field. "Nothing I'd rather do than watch baseball in October. And I don't mean on TV," he chuckled. "So, you have any plans for a left-hander in the bullpen to help us get there?"

"Ah, another General Manager in the making, huh?" Elliot teased as he patted Stryker on the shoulder. "Actually, we've got a kid down at Double A that you're gonna like. Haver Mapp. Sixth round pick just two years ago – really been tearing it up in short relief. I wouldn't be surprised if we see him here by the All-Star break." He paused as he looked back out at the field and the full stands. "But, either way we're holding it together pretty well in the late innings. We might be in okay shape as we are."

"Don't get me wrong, you've got no complaints from me," agreed Stryker as he gazed out over the infield and wondered if high-level decision making took the joy out of the game for a man like Elliot. "Speaking of the break, do you go to the All-Star game?"

"Yeah, usually," nodded Elliot. "The game's always okay but it's really just a show for the fans. I watch, but mostly it's a good time for business with the trade deadline only two weeks after. Mick and I always go," he noted, referring to Mariners' General Manager Mick Tressling. "A few others too. I'm not overly thrilled with Atlanta in July, but, it's what comes with the territory," he chuckled once again.

"Yeah, tough life," Stryker consoled in mock sympathy before finishing the last bite of his hot dog and carefully wiping his mouth. He tossed his napkin into a nearby garbage can and sat back contentedly as he swallowed the last of his traditional ballpark lunch.

"You know, I probably shouldn't be saying this," offered Elliot in an exaggerated whisper accompanied by a conspiratorial look around the box as he leaned closer to Stryker, "but I can't believe you actually eat those hot dogs." The grimace on his face reminded Stryker of a six year old forcing down a forkful of spinach. "We've got lots of other food up here you know. Real food."

Stryker smiled and licked the corners of his mouth. "Sorry, but I just can't see Sushi or Club sandwiches at a baseball game. How can you *not* eat a hot dog? And peanuts?" he gestured toward the unopened bag in front of him.

"A true American fan," acknowledged Elliot with a shake of his head. "You almost make me feel like a traitor," he admitted as he nodded at his glass of wine. "I'm . . ." Elliot stopped as his cell phone rang and he looked at the number indicated on the screen. "Hmmm. Sorry, I've got to take this. Enjoy the game, alright?" Elliot slapped Stryker lightly on the back before stepping toward the back of the box leaving Stryker with his peanuts and the game.

Stryker was able to enjoy most of the game through various conversations in the box and left the park a happy fan with an 8-2 victory in the books. As he separated from the crowds and walked to his car in a nearby garage on First Avenue, Stryker couldn't help but smile to himself as he found continued joy in his newfound retirement. He had retired from the Army nearly a decade ago, but the circumstances at the time prevented that retirement from being the joyous occasion it might have been. Now, however, he was retiring entirely on his own terms and the prospect left him giddy. A true civilian life. Today was the first day.

Stryker kept the radio off and left the game behind both physically and mentally as he drove home and half-heartedly mulled over the past ten years of his life. His separation from the Army was supposed to bring him a quiet, peaceful, ordinary existence wherein he could pursue what he wanted, when he wanted. *If* he felt like pursuing. Instead, that extremely lofty and ambitious goal had been suddenly interrupted and dramatically altered by the completely unexpected visit and request by General MacAfee more than nine years ago. Thereafter, the secretive, strenuous and very abnormal missions to kill had frequently dislocated the calm and normal civilian life that he attempted to live on the surface. He was well aware, of course, that taking on the executioner's role had been entirely of his own volition. After the initial personal favor for MacAfee he continued to take jobs from the Axman website at the rate of one or two a year, and in none of the subsequent cases did he have a dying general making a personal plea in relation to those jobs. The postings appeared, he investigated the targets, and in most cases he made the decision to complete the job. The remainder of his life had developed in a seemingly normal fashion, but he was never far removed from the very different edge brought to his world through one or two killings a year.

Not that he regretted his choices, Stryker thought almost defensively to himself. In some ways the killing kept him connected to his Army life, wherein he had demonstrated great skill and success, and from which, his separation had been very abrupt and not entirely of his own choosing. In addition, the killings provided him with a sense of meaningful contribution to society through his personal elimination of fourteen clearly undesirable and rotten elements of that society. He had received no compensation for his contributions, nor any recognition of course, but he had no qualms about that. He had made the choices, he had taken the steps that made sense to him, and he had been successful. The moral questions found their resolution long ago.

Now, however, it was time to be finished. As he drove, Stryker momentarily wondered how he knew with such certainty that this was the right time to retire. Numerous jobs over the past years had left him contemplating retirement, but this time felt entirely different. He wondered if it might be his age, or simply the number of years that had passed. It certainly wasn't conscience or guilt since he felt nothing related to that. Fear? No, he knew that wasn't it either. He had always felt a bit strange about not knowing who was behind the postings following MacAfee's death, but he had gotten over his misgivings about that years ago as well. Whoever it was, the postings had continued to identify truly bad characters that somehow evaded the law. The few times that Stryker hadn't followed up on a posting, there had never been any mention of it on the Axman site. Instead, someone simply presented him with targets and he made the choice about whether to proceed or not. Who it was didn't really seem to matter in Stryker's mind. Now, however, he was finished and his retirement announcement had been posted. He directed his car into his driveway with a light heart and a smile on his face. A Mariner victory and a completely ordinary civilian life. What could be better?

CHAPTER FIFTEEN

Stryker awoke at just before 6:00 the following Monday morning ready to run and read the newspaper before his trip downtown. After washing his face and neck, he stretched, completed some varied crunches and push-ups, and drank a half glass of cold, filtered water. His body felt relatively loose and energetic this morning, which wasn't the case as frequently these days as it had been in his younger years. He glanced out the window to see clouds and a very light drizzle. Perfect for a morning run he thought, as he headed friskily out the door for an eight-mile loop.

When Stryker returned wet and tired from his run, the message light blinked at him from his phone indicating that he'd missed two calls in the hour he was out on the streets. Telephone messages didn't carry the same sense of foreboding as they did in his first year out of the Army, even calls early in the morning, but he still chose not to listen immediately. In this case, however, it was because he was getting cold and wanted to shower and change into dry clothes as quickly as possible. When he got to the messages fifteen minutes later, he heard the familiar voice of his broker on the recording.

"Hey Thorne," the message began in a typically upbeat voice. "I hope you get this message before you head downtown. I know we're planning to meet at 10:00, but I'm supposed to sit in for a partner with another client and I'm kinda stuck with that one. I'm really sorry, but could we move our meeting a little later? If you could make it at 12 or 12:30, I'll take you to lunch. Anyway, let me know right away. It's about 7:00 now and I know you're always up early. Call me on my cell or leave a message with my secretary Lisa. Thanks, and sorry."

After a beep, the second message began. "Hey Thorne, me again. Just trying to catch you and make sure you got my first message. It's just about 7:30. Let me know if a later meeting will work for you. Call me or Lisa, and like I said, I'm sorry about the late notice, but it's out of my hands. We can do a different day entirely if you need to. Let me know. Thanks."

Stryker immediately called Lisa and told her that he'd be at the brokerage office at 12:30, and would be ready for lunch. With his plans for the day now entirely organized, he sat down for a thorough and leisurely reading of the morning newspaper.

Stryker arrived at the downtown offices of Merrill Lynch in the Financial Center building on 4th and Seneca at 12:20 pm and rode the elevator to the 26th floor. He had thought about making things easier by suggesting that they simply meet at a restaurant, but he enjoyed visiting the Merrill Lynch office and the Metropolitan Grill where they would eat was only six blocks away.

The reception area for the brokerage office gleamed in immaculate cleanliness as it had been every time Stryker visited, which had been three or four times a year for the past nine years. He marveled at how they were able to maintain the image of newness, despite the fact that the office had been open at this location for nearly two decades. The shiny chrome and untouched oak on the walls combined with the brilliant black façade of the reception desk to leave Stryker momentarily self-conscious about his shorts, t-shirt and running shoes. The feeling was fleeting, however, as Stryker had grown quite comfortable with his normal state of informality. Even so, he approached the receptionist with a reverent sort of quiet.

"Hi," he greeted as she looked up from a message she'd been writing. A hands-free phone set curled off her right ear to the corner of her lip-glossed mouth. The mouth was already smiling in greeting and the smile revealed teeth that contrasted markedly from the black desk, but somehow were just as shiny. Her nameplate on the counter in front of her read Linda Simmons and she exhibited the confident air that Stryker found to be common among women of great beauty. He decided not to comment on the smile or the confidence or the beauty. Instead, he looked casually at his watch and politely announced himself. "Thorne Stryker here to see Sam Wykovicz. I'm a few minutes early."

"Of course, Mr. Stryker. I'll let Sam know that you're here." She managed to continue smiling as she talked and Stryker wondered if that had been one of the critical lessons in receptionist training. "Have a seat." She gestured to a couch and a pair of chairs across the center of the lobby from her desk. "Would you like coffee or something else?"

Stryker wondered how she would manage to get coffee while still manning the phones. What if he asked for coffee and a bagel with cream cheese? He decided not to find out despite his natural curiosity. "No thanks, I'm fine."

Stryker sat in one of the chairs and looked over the offering of business and local interest magazines on the coffee table in front of him while he heard the receptionist speak quietly into her mouthpiece to announce his arrival. He decided against any of the magazines and instead sat back to enjoy the lobby while ignoring the electronic ticker scrolling with stock symbols and prices on the wall behind the receptionist.

"It'll be just a minute," she assured him with her smile still in place. "Merrill Lynch, how may I direct your call?"

Stryker was almost ready to respond and was a bit unnerved by the fact that she had apparently answered the phone without any visible evidence and she kept looking at him while she spoke. He guessed her to be in her mid-twenties, seemingly very competent, and Stryker wondered if she had reached her goal in life with a receptionist position at Merrill Lynch. Perhaps she was taking brokerage classes at night and this was simply a foot in the door of the money business. Maybe it was a short-term job to provide extra income for her family while her husband started out at the bottom of the totem pole somewhere. Or, maybe she was on the hunt for a young broker who would become her husband and thus take her away from all of this. Stryker was tempted to ask as he watched her work, but Sam's appearance interrupted that possibility. Probably for the better, he thought.

"Thorne, nice to see you." Sam held out a hand in greeting. "I'm glad you got my message and thanks for being flexible."

"Hey no problem," Stryker smiled as he shook hands. "Multiple messages – I was out for a run. Anyway, you know that my schedule isn't usually very cluttered." He couldn't help but notice the stark difference between his shorts and t-shirt and the well tailored suit that fit Sam's frame perfectly. Maybe he wasn't quite as comfortable with his informality as he might lead himself to believe.

"Ah, we should all be so lucky," Sam laughed without any apparent notice of Stryker's clothes. "A morning run to start a leisurely day with an uncluttered schedule. I should be back by 2:00," she directed to Linda the receptionist as she and Stryker headed to the elevator. "I don't have any appointments until three."

Sam Wykovicz was a foot shorter than Stryker but she walked comfortably next to him with a relaxed, confident stride as they left her building and moved south and west to the Metropolitan Grill. Her dark brown hair fell loosely around her petite shoulders and bounced lightly as she walked. The morning rain had disappeared, but the day remained cloudy and cool. The sidewalks teemed with the business crowd taking a lunchtime respite from the offices and desks, but most of them couldn't separate themselves from their phones.

"So, what've you been doing," she asked with a hint of challenge in her voice. "Traveling the world? Seeing beautiful places? Sleeping for twelve hours a day?"

"What do you mean?" Stryker asked in feigned offense. "I was up at six this morning as you know very well by your call." He looked over at his broker and anticipated the next line. "I know, I know. You were in the office by 5:30, but that's your fault for working in Seattle where the market opens at 6:30 local time. I bet you aren't up that early on the weekends though, are you?"

She smiled and raised her eyebrows in silent response.

A few patrons glanced at his informal attire as they walked through the restaurant, but Stryker never thought twice about the incongruity. They were quickly seated in a quiet booth near the back of the restaurant, and they each ordered clam chowder and salad without looking at the menus. They talked effortlessly across the table while digging into the basket of three varieties of bread brought by the waiter. Stryker enjoyed watching the single dimple in Sam's right cheek as she talked and he wondered to himself if other brokers smiled as frequently as she did. He had always believed the brokerage business to be one of high stress and early burnout, but Sam never seemed negatively affected in any way. Suddenly, however, she turned serious.

"Thorne, I've got to ask you something I've never asked before," she began mysteriously after a moment's quiet. "I hope you don't mind."

"Go ahead," Stryker shrugged masking his curiosity mixed with mild anxiety. What could this be about he wondered to himself.

"Well, I've always wondered why me. I mean, why I'm your broker." She looked intently at Stryker across the table and showed no sign of the dimple.

"Is there a problem?" Stryker asked with a perplexed look on his face.

"No, no, of course not," she assured him with a return of the smile. "I'm just . . . I don't know. Curious I guess."

"Oh. Well, nothing mysterious," Stryker explained. "I started with a guy named Julius Zarmi. That was a long time ago. After that, you know that Bernie Lapchick was my broker for years and I moved here to Seattle about the same time he retired. Then, Stephen, your old boss took over, and I didn't really care much one way or the other, but I never really worked with him directly very much. I had talked with you a few times and then you got your license just before Stephen left, so, why not?" It all seemed pretty simple and innocuous to Stryker.

"Why not?" Sam asked incredulously. "You do know that you caused quite a stir don't you? I mean, there are a few guys in the office who still don't want to talk to me because of you."

Stryker was genuinely lost. "Won't talk to you? Why not?"

Sam laughed and shook her head without noticing Stryker staring at the slight gap between her two front teeth set next to her single dimple. "Look, you may not be aware of this, but you've got a fairly large account. Not huge, of course, but decent. And, you're the ideal client because you're very hands off and trusting of your broker. Anyone in the office would have loved to take your account. And the fact that it went to a complete novice like me didn't sit too well with a lot of the partners in the firm. It certainly helped me get started, thank you very much," she nodded graciously at him, "but it still ruffled a lot of feathers."

"Oh well," Stryker gave a palms-up gesture of unconcerned innocence and naïveté.

"Come on," she insisted. "You must have known something about this, right?"

"Well, I guess that maybe I did hear from a few people in your office," he admitted with a sly grin on his face.

"Really?" she leaned forward in excitement. "Tell me!"

"I don't remember," he evaded. "It was a long time ago. I'm sure they're gone by now, don't you think?

"Well, I could tell you if I knew who they were," she reasoned. "Come on. I'm just curious. It won't hurt to tell me." The gleam in her eye and overall excitement on her face made her even more attractive than usual, but Stryker didn't give in. Instead, he tried to redirect her energy.

"Nah, I don't know," he shook his head. "But, Stephen did call me a number of times to see if I wanted to move my account to wherever he went when he left your office."

"No way! Really?" she slapped his arm and seemed oblivious to other customers around them in the restaurant. "I'd bet anything his separation agreement prevented him from soliciting any of his Merrill clients. I can't believe him." She paused and looked directly at Stryker while the waiter set down the two bowls of steaming clam chowder. The inviting smell didn't distract Sam from her focus. "So, why didn't you go?"

"With Stephen?" Stryker was genuinely surprised at the question, although he'd never actually thought much about it. "I don't know. I never really had much of a connection with him and there wasn't anything about his new firm that would make me want to go there. It was just easier to stay with Merrill." He thought for a second. "Besides, I liked working with you."

"Now, there's a good answer," Sam laughed before picking up her spoon to sip at the hot chowder. "I always knew you had good taste."

Sam decided it was time to talk business once they finished with their meal. "So, your account is still doing well, as you should know if you look at your monthly statements." She looked for a response but continued when it didn't come. "You're sitting at about $15 million overall and we're keeping the fifty-fifty balance between your beloved dividend stocks and the growth stocks you allow me to play with. We just cashed in a significant gain on the French cell phone stock, and I'm about ready to sell the Canadian mineral company as well. Are you still okay with your current quarterly draw amount?"

"Yeah, works for me," Stryker responded agreeably.

"You know," Sam began again, although she already knew the outcome of the issue, "it would be both easier for me and probably better for you if you took your draw out of the dividend payments rather than out of transactions from the other $7 plus million. It wouldn't . . ."

Stryker held up his left hand to cut her off. "No, you know that I'm committed to continuing to reinvest dividends. We've talked about this once or twice before, I believe. You're doing great with the other half of the money – in fact you've been able to add to my dividend stocks. So, we'll keep the draw coming from there."

"But that's just it," she argued fruitlessly. "The non-dividend investments are doing great. And, through all your reinvestments and dividend raises over the years, you're getting paid a ton of dividends every quarter. Now, if you took your draw from the dividends instead, you'd be further ahead overall."

Stryker just smiled and offered her the basket of bread. "Thanks, but no thanks." He nodded and squinted his eyes a bit as he looked at her. "I know what you're doing," he kidded. "You're just trying to have more money to churn so you can increase your commissions. What's up? Got a new car in mind or something?"

"Thorne, that's not funny," she replied in a different tone of seriousness as she sat back heavily in her bench seat. "You can't be talking about churning and commissions, even if you're just joking. Now, take it back."

"Okay, okay," he laughed. "But if I see you in a new car . . ."

"You are bad!" she chided in good humor. "Now, do you want to talk about the reinvestments I'm planning?"

"Sam, Sam, Sam, you know better than that," Stryker took his turn patting her arm. "It's your job, you do it well, and I trust you completely. Just try to give me some warning if all the money is about to disappear or something. I'll need some lead time to get my résumé up to speed."

"Yeah, well, the dividend stocks will still be there won't they?" she smiled and then changed the subject. "So, is the handsome, millionaire bachelor seeing anyone these days?"

"Yep. I'm seeing you right now. That counts doesn't it?" Stryker returned the smile while tearing a piece of bread.

"Very funny, Mr. Wiseguy," Sam responded. "But I'm serious. I know it's not any of my business, but we've known each other for a long time so I figured it's okay to ask. So, what's the relationship picture look like?"

"Well," Stryker began quietly with a conspiratorial look at the booth across from them and then a very serious look at his broker across the table. Sam leaned forward in anticipation. "I'm seeing my buddy LJ Perkins tomorrow. And last week I sat near some very attractive women at the Mariners' game. In the owner's box at that. All in all, things are looking pretty damn bright on the relationship front."

"Alright, forget I asked," Sam sighed in exasperation as she rested her chin on her hands with her elbows on the table. "Someday though, you're going to figure out that being a complete and total loner is no way to go through life."

Stryker laughed briefly. "And this is coming from the ultimate career woman who's had how many relationships over the past ten years?"

"We were talking about you, not me," Sam responded defensively. "Besides, I'm *much* younger than you, so I've got lots more time for relationships."

"Alright, so from a complete and total loner to the ultimate career woman – whadya say we kill two birds with one stone, so to speak?" Stryker leaned back in the booth with his chin tilted up defiantly.

"What? How?" responded a puzzled Sam who also leaned back on her side of the booth.

"Saturday night. Dinner. You and me." Stryker offered with a touch of challenge in his voice. "Not a business lunch, but dinner. You got the guts, lady?"

"Guts?" Sam asked incredulously in response to the challenge. "Just name the time and the place, buddy."

Stryker walked Sam back to her office, then nearly skipped to the lot where he'd left his car for a mere $12 midday charge. The open lot offered entrances on both the west and north sides, while it nestled up against the brick walls of adjoining buildings on the south and east. It was carefully designed for nearly one hundred tightly packed spaces, marked by faded white lines and sequential numbers, in the middle of which stood a kiosk for the collection of payments and distribution of tickets to be displayed on the dashboards of parked cars. The lot sat as unmonitored as it had been when Stryker left his car two hours earlier, and he wondered how often the company bothered to inspect the parking spaces for the required tickets. With most customers paying on the honor system / fear of being towed system, it certainly made for an interesting cost - benefit decision on the part of ownership.

Almost all of the spaces were occupied on this weekday afternoon as Stryker worked his way to the rear of the lot. As he approached his car in space number 47, Stryker noticed movement of another customer in the deepest corner of the lot. He was about to open his car door when his instinct told him to look more closely at the movement in the southeast corner. Six cars down from Stryker's parking place, three men stood between the end car and the brick wall but the man nearest the car had his back toward the car door. Clearly, they weren't getting into the car. Stryker hesitated only a second before leaving his car to move toward the threesome at the end of the lot.

"Everything okay here?" Stryker asked nonchalantly as he approached the white Ford parked in the corner space.

The two men facing the car looked up in surprise while the third man, with his back to Stryker, didn't react to Stryker's voice. Stryker walked closer so that he cleared the end of the Ford before he stopped. Leaning against the car stood an elderly Hispanic man wearing a black fleece vest over a plaid shirt. He looked to be about 5' 5", and fairly slight overall except for a belly that protruded over his belted jeans. Facing him were two white men in their late teens or early twenties. Both were lean, close to six feet tall, and wore hooded sweatshirts over faded jeans. They looked markedly similar except for the fact that one had a shaved head while the other sported shoulder length, light brown hair.

"Everything okay?" Stryker repeated, relatively sure that everything was not okay.

"Yeah man, we're cool," responded the longhaired man.

"How about you, buddy," Stryker directed toward the elderly man as he took a step closer to the trio. "You okay?"

Without looking toward Stryker the man grunted slightly in a completely unresponsive response.

"I said we're good," said long hair in an aggressive tone as he turned toward Stryker. His partner remained focused on the elderly man. "You can go on with your business."

"Sure," agreed Stryker. "Just as soon as this gentleman here walks away."

"We're not finished talking," responded long hair. "But we're done talking to you, now get out of here before you end up regretting it."

Stryker smiled while he took another step forward. A couple of young punks who thought they were tough and clearly were used to getting their way by simple intimidation. Stryker wasn't one to be intimidated. "I'll go," he said, "but my friend here is going with me."

The two younger men looked at each other and then back at Stryker. Long hair sneered as he reached into the pocket of his sweatshirt to extract a knife. Both men moved away from their intended victim and toward Stryker. Stryker backed up as they moved forward, with the intent of clearing room for the elderly man to slip away from his trapped position between the car and the walls. The two hooded hoodlums kept moving toward Stryker, emboldened by his apparent retreat.

As they all moved away from the white Ford, Stryker called out to the man who watched the trio, but who hadn't moved yet. "Why don't you go call 911," Stryker directed in a calm voice. "I'm afraid we're going to need an ambulance here."

The man remained wide-eyed but immobile. "Now," yelled Stryker more forcefully. "Get out of here and call 911."

The man moved quickly while hugging the car to maximize his distance from his young tormentors. In a moment he was behind Stryker and fully removed from the situation. Stryker gave him no further thought as he focused on the two men in front of him.

Stryker stopped moving backward. "Better think twice here fellas," he advised. "I couldn't have you harassing that old man. Robbery was it? But that's over now, so no use getting yourselves hurt over it." He noticed the man with the shaved head looking at his partner for direction. Clearly long hair would make the calls here. Besides, he had the knife.

The two men stopped their advance as Stryker had stopped his retreat. Long hair sneered again as he moved the knife from one hand to another in classic 1950s teen rebellion movie fashion. "You talk big for a guy who's goin' down," long hair threatened with feigned confidence. "You think you're some kind of hero?"

Without responding, Stryker watched closely as the knife moved again from one hand to the other. At the instant both hands were together with the knife in front of long hair, they were met with the heel of Stryker's left foot, which broke one finger and sent the knife clattering to the pavement. Stryker followed the kick instantaneously with his right fist driving hard into the solar plexus, driving all the air from the lungs of long hair.

The young man crumpled to his knees, gasping for air and clutching his injured hand when Stryker knocked him out with a swift blow to the left temple. Stryker turned his attention to the shaved-headed follower, who had not moved yet, when he heard footsteps running quickly toward him from the north entrance of the lot. Out of the corner of his eye, Stryker saw that the footsteps belonged to another young man dressed much like the other two. Just as his third assailant jumped at him from behind, Stryker spun to his left and continued in full circle to drive his right arm into the back of the off-balance man who then fell hard to the pavement beside his unconscious companion. Stryker pounced upon him and squeezed the man's neck in the elbow of his right arm to cut off the blood flow to his brain, all the while keeping his eyes on the shaved-headed hood who was now backed up against the white Ford. In seconds, the man lost consciousness and Stryker released his grip before any permanent damage could be done.

Stryker quickly jumped up to face the third man who immediately dropped to his knees and sobbed. "Don't hurt me, man! I wasn't doing nothin'. I told Chaz this was a bad idea. I didn't even want to be here. Please, man!"

Stryker stopped his approach toward the man when he heard sirens approaching from a distance. Maybe the intended victim actually had called 911.

"I guess it's your lucky day," Stryker said to the man on his knees as he moved toward his car. "I'm going to make sure that you're still here when the police show up, however. Don't even think about running away."

With that, Stryker jumped in his car and pulled out into the traffic. Just one block up the street he saw two police cars and an aid car pull into the lot. Stryker headed home with his thoughts quickly focused on dinner with a stockbroker.

CHAPTER SIXTEEN

The office of Discreet Inquiries sat somewhat obscurely and discreetly in a small, quiet rectangular building shared by an insurance company and in serious need of exterior beautification. Stryker arrived at Discreet Inquiries shortly before 10:00 on Tuesday morning and found the door locked. Puzzled, he looked at his watch and mentally confirmed his discussion with LJ Perkins about the time and place of their meeting. A glance at the insurance company provided no more insight than he might have expected. Before he could knock on the office door, Perkins strode up beside him with a huge grin on his face.

"Couldn't show up without the apple fritters, could I?" Perkins laughed as he held up a paper bag in one hand and reached with his key to unlock the door with the other. "It's not quite 10:00 yet, so we're good man. Come on in."

The two men entered the small, subdued outer office and Perkins flipped on the light before leading Stryker into his inner personal office. The combined space of the two offices was less than 500 square feet, but Perkins was proud of every inch of it and kept both rooms neat and utterly professional at all times. The outer office had the requisite desk and phone for a receptionist, although Perkins had never employed one. Two client chairs sat against the wall opposite the desk and a framed Leroy Neiman golf print decorated the wall behind the desk. A tall, slightly dusty and completely fake potted plant stood in one corner and was offset with neat symmetry by a seldom-used oak coat rack that filled another.

Perkins' office sported a slightly larger desk than the one in the outer room, with matching client chairs that looked over the desk and out the window onto a greenbelt that occupied the space behind the building. Three perfectly squared steel file cabinets in classic battleship gray dominated one wall, and the Neiman print on another wall, similar in size to the one in the in the outer office, depicted boxing. Perkins sat on the desk rather than behind it, and handed Stryker the bag of apple fritters after first taking out the largest one for himself.

"Thanks for coming, Thorne," LJ mumbled through a mouthful of fritter. He chewed and swallowed and offered a bottle of orange juice, which Stryker readily accepted. "I need your help on a case if you've got a bit of time."

Stryker had already confirmed with Perkins that he had time to spare, but he did so again now that they were together. "Sure, if the pay's right," he smiled. "What's up?"

Perkins took an extended drink of orange juice and then a deep breath before he explained. "Well, I've got a couple cases going and one of 'em's turning out to be a ton of time. The other should be pretty easy, but I just haven't been able to get to it and I don't really want to just let it go. You know how it is, man. So, if you could at least get the other one started, then maybe the bigger one will break and I can get over the hump."

"Well, that's why I'm here," Stryker shrugged in acceptance. "Of course, if you really want results you'd turn the bigger case over to me. Otherwise you might never see that hump." Stryker smiled and tipped his fritter toward Perkins. "So, what are the cases?"

"Well, the one I'm working on is for a small industrial plant down in the south end of town called Puget Machine Works. The company's owner's convinced that someone, one of his employees, is stealing from him and maybe even undercutting his business to help a competitor. He's 'hired'," Perkins made quote marks in the air with his fingers, "me to work in the office, so I'm there like nine hours a day, but I'm also tailing guys at night. It's killin' me right now, and I just got no time for anything else."

"Well, you know what they say – 'better you than me'," offered Stryker with mocking sympathy.

"Yeah, thanks buddy."

"But," Stryker counted, "you wouldn't hand that one off to someone else regardless of the difficulty level, now would you?"

"Why not?" Perkins looked puzzled.

"Come on, Zip, I know you," Stryker shook his head. "The owner's being betrayed and that pisses you off even though you don't even know the guy. I've never known anyone in my life as passionate about loyalty as you are. A client hires you because an employee's being disloyal – you're gonna nail the guy's ass. It may not be easy and the hours might be killing you, but it's right in your wheelhouse."

Perkins shrugged without a verbal response.

"So anyway," Stryker proceeded with a knowing look at his friend, "you need help with the other case which presumably isn't too exciting or difficult. It's always nice to be needed," he smiled. "What's up with that one?"

"Hmmm," Perkins grunted through a bite of fritter before licking his lips and his fingertips. "Some lady up on Capitol Hill – got her name here somewhere," Perkins glanced around his desk before settling upon a manila folder and then continuing.

"Broke up with a fiancé, but says the guy's harassing her. You know – phone calls late at night, says someone's following her, that kind of stuff. She doesn't want to go the restraining order route, cause what're the police gonna do, right? So, meet with her, check out the guy, record her phone, whatever – just put her at ease. She's got money and she's willing to pay for a little peace of mind." Perkins paused and gazed into the bag of fritters with a look of serious contemplation. Giving in, he reached in to take one out and tilted the bag toward Stryker who willingly grabbed the last one. "I really think this industrial job'll be done in a day or so. Three at the most. I'm pretty sure I've nailed down the guy who's screwin' his boss. So, if you could just get this other one started, I'll be ready to take it over in no time." He looked up at Stryker with a smile. "You in?"

"I think I've heard you say 'a day or two' before," Stryker sighed, "but sure. I can do it. What've you got on this lady?"

Perkins handed him the slim manila folder as he lovingly bit into his third apple fritter.

Eight hours later Stryker knocked lightly on the door of a small but tidy duplex unit on Harvard Avenue on Capitol Hill just east of downtown Seattle. He had called ahead to arrange the visit so he knew the client would be home. The client was Karmody Fenn, 31 years old, single, and an associate – soon to be partner – in the Seattle law firm of Stanley, Jacobs and Utterhuis. The door opened leaving a screen door between Stryker and Karmody Fenn. Stryker's first impression focused on her height, as she had to be at least 5' 11", maybe even six feet tall. At the upper end of all those inches, her hair lay professionally short and closely cropped around a face that featured abnormally dark eyebrows, high cheekbones, a slightly upturned nose and large, dark, piercing eyes.

"Mr. Stryker?" she asked through the screen door.

"Yes, Ms. Fenn, but call me Thorne, please," he glanced over his shoulder at the street. "May I come in?"

"Of course, I'm sorry," Fenn apologized as she opened the screen door and stepped back from the entryway. "You're right on time," she smiled. "And it's Karmody."

Her smile revealed straight, stunningly white teeth and as he stepped into the duplex Stryker couldn't help but notice that her tall frame was also quite slender and well toned. He wondered how difficult her decision had been to go to law school rather than to pursue modeling, and then looked up quickly when he caught himself staring at her ankles.

"Karmody, great," Stryker said pleasantly. "That's an unusual name."

"A family hand-me-down, I'm afraid. But I never minded being a bit different. In fact, I always felt sorry in school for the kids who had three other kids in class with the same name," she laughed lightly and Stryker couldn't help but smile in return. "Now Thorne isn't exactly a name you hear everyday either is it?"

"No, I guess not," he responded. "And I never had three other kids in class with the same name." he paused. "So, we've got a problem to deal with, huh?"

"Yeah," Karmody sighed as she looked toward the door and gathered her thoughts with a deep breath. Stryker waited silently. "Well," she began with reluctant resignation, "I talked to someone else at your office, a Mr. Perkins," Stryker didn't bother to correct her about "his" office, "and told him that I was being harassed. The truth is, I'm a little bit afraid. You see, I was engaged for about two weeks until I realized it was a huge mistake and called it off. We had only been going out for about five months, and only seriously for about two months. And, oh I don't know, it was fun, and I kind of got caught up in things and I wasn't thinking very clearly I guess. Still, I knew it couldn't really be serious for me. Anyway, it caught me off guard when he proposed and I just couldn't say no, but then as soon as I said yes, I knew it was a mistake. Long story short, I finally got up the nerve to break it off and . . ., well, it hasn't been so good."

Stryker nodded reassuringly. "Not so good, in what way? What's been happening?"

"Well, that was last week Saturday. Allen, that's his name, he said I was just nervous and that I would change my mind, but I insisted that it was over. Then, mmmm, well, phone calls at all hours of the night. Flat tires on my car – three different times. I'm sure I'm being followed when I leave work." She stopped and rubbed both temples with her hands. "Nothing directly tied to him, of course, but I knew it was. Then, on Friday, just a couple of days ago, he came by late at night. I wouldn't let him in and he started getting really loud and threatening. He said no one breaks up with him and if he couldn't have me then nobody could have me. Stuff like that. Eventually he went away, but he clearly wasn't happy. He said he'd be here at 7:00 this Friday night to take me to dinner. I didn't know what to do, so I called your office."

It looked as though she might start to cry, which was the last thing that Stryker wanted. "Hey, it'll be fine," he consoled hopefully. "You did the right thing."

Karmody looked up and nodded at the encouragement. "My office works with investigators, and I know some people, but I was embarrassed about taking a personal matter to them," she explained. "That's why I called your office instead."

Once again Stryker decided to ignore the 'your' office reference. "Well, let's see what we can do," he decided that a professional, active approach would be best for keeping Karmody on track. "First, do you have pictures of Allen that I can see?"

"Sure," Karmody jumped up quickly and stepped into an adjoining room. When she took her distracting presence away with her Stryker took note of the room for the first time. It was extremely neat and probably would be considered 'modern' though Stryker had no real decorating sense to be able to make such a judgment. The furniture appeared to be all new and the prints on the walls seemed designed to coordinate with the furniture. Despite the attractiveness of it all, Stryker wouldn't describe the room as homey or even comfortable. It felt more like a display room for an interior design company. Stryker suddenly became self-conscious about his shoes and he hoped they were clean. He was about to look at the soles just to be sure when Karmody re-entered the room.

"Here you are Mr. Str, er, Thorne," she seemed to have regained whatever composure she might have momentarily lost. "Although I'm sure you've seen pictures of him before," she commented as she handed Stryker two photographs.

Stryker's puzzlement over her comment instantly disappeared as he looked at a photograph of Allen Nixon, small forward for the Seattle professional basketball team. She was right, he'd seen plenty of pictures of Nixon before, but now he was a bit taken aback. She was being harassed by one of the most recognizable sports figures in the city? This certainly wasn't what he had in mind when he agreed to help out Perkins, and for a moment he simply stared at the pictures while he thought about how this changed her situation.

Karmody sensed his hesitation. "Is something wrong?" she asked.

"No," reacted Stryker quickly while still gathering his thoughts. "Just surprised I guess. I wasn't expecting your ex-fiancé to be somebody that I know. Well, I don't know him, but I know who he is at least. It doesn't make a difference though, for what's going on with you," he lied. Of course it made a difference. This held the possibility of complicating things dramatically compared to what he'd expected, which was John Doe from the corner office. Dealing with famous and popular people always brought complications to any situation.

"Okay," Karmody responded, taking him at his word. "So what do we do now?"

Darn good question, thought Stryker. "Well, do you have anything written from him? Anything threatening?" She shook her head no. "Anything recorded from the phone calls?" Another silent negative response. "Anything at all beyond him coming by here last week?"

"No," she answered meekly without offering anything else.

"Okay, then we start from now," Stryker sounded much more assured than he actually felt. "First, I want you to hook up this recorder to your phone so you can record any phone calls you get." Stryker stood up to begin connecting the recorder. "We'll get one for your office phone as well. Your cell phone will be more of a problem, so I suggest that you not answer any calls from Nixon that come on your cell."

"Isn't it illegal to tape a phone conversation without the consent of both parties?" Karmody questioned, although she knew the answer.

"Well, it may not be admissible in court," said Stryker, "but it can still be important for us. Who knows, there may not be anything on the phone anyway."

"I suppose, but either way, I don't really expect any problems right now," Karmody went on, "since he's planning to take me out on Friday. I'm not going though, so that's going to be a big problem. He just won't take 'no' for an answer," she sighed at her predicament. "I'm sure he's never been turned down by any woman and the fact that he was ready to get married means that he's more invested in me than in any other women of his past. I know it's just an ego thing for him, but I'm really scared."

"Yeah, I know," Stryker nodded, "but being a basketball player doesn't change the rules for what he can and can't do." He saw the instant skepticism on her face. "I know, it seems like athletes can get away with anything, and I'm sure he thinks that he's exempt from the rules, but that's why I'm here, right?" Stryker smiled confidently.

Karmody returned the smile with a glow that lifted Stryker's spirits. "So, what do we do about Friday night?" she asked.

Perkins continued toiling away at the machine shop while Stryker followed Karmody Fenn to her home when she left her office shortly after 4:30 on Friday afternoon. Since he knew where they were going, Stryker didn't follow too closely and focused most of his attention on whether anyone else might be following his "client". Nothing was evident. Karmody pulled into the narrow driveway in the front of her home while Stryker parked by the curb nearly a full block up the street. He felt lucky to find a space that close. He walked back after locking his car and met Karmody where she was waiting for him at the front door.

"Thanks for coming," she greeted him with a tired smile. Apparently long weeks could be wearing on even the most beautiful people. "I'll be right out. Help yourself to something in the refrigerator if you want," she offered over her shoulder as she left him alone.

"I'm fine, thanks," said Stryker as he sat on the pristine reading chair positioned at exactly 90 degrees off the corner of the equally immaculate couch. "Busy day at the office grind?" he called the question into the bedroom where she had disappeared.

"Every day is busy," she called out. "But I left a bunch of stuff for next week so I could get out earlier than usual. I was kind of nervous about tonight," she admitted, "but I feel a lot better with you here."

Stryker chose not to respond, but instead picked up a U.S. News magazine from the coffee table in front of him. He glanced through without really reading anything while waiting for Karmody to re-emerge from the bedroom. Stryker hadn't thought of it as nervousness, but he realized that he'd been a bit on edge about the evening as well.

When Karmody stepped out of the bedroom, Stryker noted that she'd replaced her work clothes with nicely fitting, slightly worn jeans and a loose, violet colored blouse that most certainly looked better on her than it had in the store before she bought it. "So," she exhaled in an effort to relax, "you don't think we're going to have any trouble tonight, do you?"

"Don't know," Stryker smiled, "you're the one who knows Nixon. But, he hasn't done anything this week, right?" She nodded in agreement. "Okay, well, let's hope that a little more time has given him some perspective so we won't have any trouble tonight. Hey, you never know – he may not even show."

"Wouldn't that be nice," Karmody smiled and nodded. "Of course, I'd feel a little silly having you here if he didn't even show up. But . . ." she hesitated momentarily and looked at Stryker's waist. "Do you have a gun?"

"A gun? Uh, no," Stryker replied. "I mean, I do have a gun, but I don't have one with me right now. I'm sure there's not going to be any need for that."

"I hope you're right," uncertainness clouded Karmody's voice. "As you said, you don't know Allen. He can get a little crazy sometimes."

"Nah, we'll be good," he assured her.

"Well, he's not going to be here for two hours, and I'm starving," Karmody moved toward the next room. "Would you eat an omelet if I made you one? Cheese, sour cream and mushrooms?"

"Sounds great to me," Thorne agreed. "I should get hired by you more often. Anything I can do to help?" he asked as he followed her into a sparkling like-new kitchen.

"Sure. You can grate some cheese," Karmody pointed to the refrigerator and then handed him a cheese grater. "You can handle that, right?"

"I grate a mean cheese," Stryker boasted with his chest puffed out. "It's sure to be the best cheese on any omelet you've ever eaten."

Two hours later they had eaten and cleaned up and were sitting in relative quiet in Karmody's living room. Both checked their watches frequently as 7:00 approached. As the minutes ticked past 7, Stryker could see a glint of optimism from his client that maybe the big bad wolf wouldn't show up after all. The optimism instantly disappeared in favor of an anxious look from Karmody to Stryker when a pounding on the front door startled them both at 7:10. Stryker nodded at her to stay seated while he walked over to open the door.

"Who the hell are you?" came the question from the door pounder as soon as Stryker appeared in the open doorway. Stryker could see that it wasn't Allen Nixon and he looked over the man's shoulder at the Hummer H2 parked immediately in front of the house. He couldn't see anything through the tinted windows. "I said, who the hell are you?" came the demand again after Stryker's failure to respond.

"A friend of Ms. Fenn's," Stryker stated as if that explained everything. "She's staying home this evening." He looked hard at the man on the other side of the screen door. He was probably about six feet tall and Stryker would have guessed his weight at close to 240 pounds with a definite roundness in the middle. He was dressed nicely in a dark suit and white shirt buttoned to the collar but with no tie. His dark sunglasses helped to hide any expression on his face.

The expression was quite clear in his voice, however. "What the hell do you mean, 'stayin' home'? I'm pickin' her up and we're supposed to be goin' now." He roughly opened the screen door as if to come in the house, but Stryker remained unmoved.

"Not tonight, I'm afraid," Stryker said calmly while positioning his left foot slightly in front of his right with his knees bent just a touch. "Ms. Fenn has explained to Mr. Nixon that she has no interest in seeing him any more. Thus, she's not going out tonight. You can give that message to Mr. Nixon for her."

"What the hell you talkin' about man?" he blustered behind the sunglasses, but stopped his advance through the door. "Tell her Three Piece is here."

Nice name, Stryker thought sarcastically but didn't verbalize. "No, Mr. Three Piece," Stryker's voice was as calm and relaxed as his words were polite. "As I said, she's not going and you'll need to give that message to Mr. Nixon."

Three Piece took a half step forward, which brought Stryker's weight to the balls of his feet. Three Piece then thought better of it and stepped back from the door. "You all don't know what yer doin', man," he warned with a threatening scowl. "Al ain't gonna be happy 'bout this." With that, Three Piece walked back to the Hummer and slid into the driver's side door while Stryker remained in the entryway looking out. The Hummer didn't move and although Stryker couldn't see it, he was certain that Three Piece held a phone to his ear behind the tinted glass. Nothing changed for a full two minutes until finally the Hummer engine started up and roared off down the street with an angry growl.

"Well, that's that," said Stryker as he closed the door and turned back toward Karmody. Her face was ashen and her eyes were open as widely as they could be. "Hopefully he'll get the message this time and that'll be the last of it." He certainly wasn't confident in his own words and he could see that Karmody wasn't either.

"Will you stay for awhile, in case he comes back?" Karmody pleaded quickly.

"Sure," Stryker agreed quickly. "But, it might make sense for you to stay somewhere else for a few days – just till we see that things have calmed down. Do you have somewhere you could go for a week or so?"

"Yeah," Karmody sighed. "I think I'd feel better somewhere else. I'm not sure I'd sleep at all tonight if I stayed here." She reached for the telephone on the coffee table.

Less than an hour later Karmody had packed and Stryker was following her car as she drove to a friend's house across Lake Washington in Redmond. Stryker drove back west toward Seattle certain that they hadn't heard the last from Allen Nixon or from Three Piece.

CHAPTER SEVENTEEN

Stryker's recently announced retirement was still fresh and exciting enough to jump frequently to the forefront of his mind and he reveled in the thought each time he focused on it. It wasn't as though his "work" through the Axman website had been constant or time intensive, but it certainly provided a consistent measure of pressure and anxiety from which Stryker was thrilled to be freed. He could continue to help out Perkins when needed, as with the current situation involving Karmody Fenn and Allen Nixon, but he otherwise was fully prepared to live his life as he'd initially imagined it at the time of his departure from the military. And now, to top off his retirement, he had a date tonight with Sam Wykovicz, financial advisor and broker extraordinaire. Even General MacAfee would find little to criticize in his current state of affairs.

The time and place was 7:30 pm at Daniel's Broiler on Lake Washington Boulevard in the Leschi neighborhood of Seattle. Sam said her preference was to meet at the restaurant rather than have Stryker pick her up, so he was waiting on the street next to his car by 7:20. The evening was slightly cool, but dry and calm so Stryker waited outside and didn't mind the fact that Sam showed up at nearly 7:45. He hadn't seen her park, but he saw her approaching on the sidewalk from the north just after he glanced at his watch once again. She wore a burgundy jacket buttoned once on top of a white silk shirt and dark jeans with very short heels. Stryker admired her confident walk and the relaxed formality of her carriage. He was sure she would fit in equally well walking into a Saturday evening symphony or a Friday night tavern.

"Sorry," she apologized with a smile and raised eyebrows. "I was a little late getting out the door. You haven't been waiting too long have you?" she gave him an innocuous peck on the check as he stepped away from the wall he'd been leaning on. The muted aroma of her perfume lingered as she pulled away and Stryker breathed it in with the realization that he'd never noticed perfume on her before.

"Not a problem," he assured her as he held open the door to the restaurant. "I got here a few minutes later than I intended as well."

They talked easily through dinner on topics ranging from the stock market to high school to nursing homes to the military. They enjoyed the view of Lake Washington from their table while they feasted on perfectly grilled steaks and delicate garlic potatoes. Sam talked freely and laughed often, making her an easy and highly enjoyable dinner companion. Eventually, as she finished the last of her steamed zucchini, Sam focused on Stryker's current retired status.

"So," she began as the waiter cleared away their final dinner dishes and left a dessert menu that they both ignored. "You're retired awfully young, you know. You've obviously got plenty of money so you don't need to work, but – and I hope you don't mind me asking, but I've always been curious, so – what do you do with your time? I mean, I think I'd be bored silly if I didn't have some kind of work to do, at least part-time." She looked expectantly at Stryker as if his answer would hold the secret of life itself.

"Well, put yourself in my shoes," Stryker responded with his hands clasped in front of him. "What would *you* do if you were retired right now?"

"That's just it," she expressed in mild frustration. "I can't even imagine being retired right now. I guess maybe, if I had a family – you know, kids – but that's just another version of a full-time job, right?"

"I'm sure that's true," he agreed, "but I have absolutely no experience in that field. Seriously though, what would you do now if you didn't go into work every day?"

Sam looked up at the ceiling as if the answer might be written there. Her hands lifted off the table and apart, then came together in front of her mouth as if in prayer as she let out a sigh. Stryker admired the way she thought seriously about things, but still seemed to be in good humor all the time. He especially enjoyed the wrinkle in her forehead as she dove headlong into the issue at hand. "Well," she hesitated as she looked at Stryker across the table, "I'm sure I'd still follow the market. Partly out of interest and partly out of necessity since I'd have to have money if I were to be retired. But, I'd still need something to do. I guess I'd find some volunteer work or something like that. Or maybe a part-time job just for fun, rather than for the paycheck. There'd have to be something though, or I'd go stir crazy."

"Okay," Stryker responded with an open-palm gesture, "so you've answered your own question."

"Huh?" Sam was puzzled.

"You've just described much of my life. I enjoy exercise and reading and movies, but I also follow the stock market, and I do some odd jobs and some volunteer work – just to keep myself semi-occupied. There's really not much to it, and you'd be amazed at how time flies regardless. In fact, I remember an older friend telling me after he'd retired that he was trying to figure out how he ever had enough time to work a full-time job," he smiled and looked directly at her. "You know that I spent a long time in the Army – well, retired is the only way I've ever really known civilian life. I've never had a regular job of any kind, so it's not like retirement is a huge adjustment for me. That make sense?"

"Sure, I guess," she agreed without conviction before going on. "I didn't know you did part-time work or volunteer work. What do you do?" she asked in genuine interest.

"Well, I've done a variety of things," Stryker said vaguely while keeping Sam's eyes engaged, "but most of my recent work has been with an old Army buddy who's got his own investigation business here in town."

"Oooo, that sounds exciting!" Sam commented enthusiastically with a slight bounce in her seat. "What kind of stuff?"

Stryker proceeded to give a few examples without mentioning his current work for Karmody Fenn. He hoped to come off as something other than a complete slacker. From Sam's reaction he was apparently successful.

They both decided against dessert and Stryker paid the bill with a generous tip. He then walked Sam out to her car with the realization that by meeting at the restaurant, they were destined to leave separately. She beeped her doors unlocked as they approached and Stryker opened the driver's side for her.

"Thanks for dinner, it was fun," she said as she stepped toward her car and turned to face Stryker who was holding the door open.

"The pleasure was all mine," he stated honestly. "So, we're scheduled for my quarterly meeting in three months, but you never know, I may need an update sooner than that."

Sam smiled at him through the street light illumination and answered enigmatically. "You know what they say in the brokerage business – past results are no guarantee of future returns."

Stryker smiled and nodded, and this time he gave her a light peck on the cheek before stepping back so that she could sit in her car. He noticed her very light perfume once again. He carefully closed the door with a wave and walked happily back down the street toward the restaurant and his car. Sam sat for a moment watching Stryker's receding figure in her side mirror before starting her engine and driving away – not entirely sure what had just transpired.

Karmody Fenn called Stryker at home at noon on Monday. She hadn't been to her house since leaving on Friday night so she'd had no contact with Allen Nixon over the weekend. She was now back at her office however, and had a message from Nixon waiting for her when she arrived, plus two more calls that morning. She said the calls were increasingly abrupt and belligerent with the same bottom line – no one but Allen Nixon decides when Allen Nixon's relationships are finished. She had optimistically, but unrealistically, hoped that it would be over after Friday night's refusal to go out, but now she was feeling enough tension that it was hard to concentrate on her work. Stryker tried to be reassuring.

"Well, I guess we, as in me, will have to take a more direct approach with Mr. Nixon," he offered. "What can you tell me about how to contact him?"

She shared an address and phone numbers, which Stryker wrote down, but he had no interest in a phone call and wasn't particularly interested in initiating an engagement on Nixon's home turf. "Any regular appointments or hang outs that you know of?" he probed.

"Ummm, yeah, as a matter of fact," she responded. "The last month we were together it seemed like he was going three or four times a week to a club in Belltown. It's called 'Night Moves'. I don't know the address, but I think it's on Third," she paused for a moment. "I don't get it though. You don't want to see him there, do you?"

"Who knows," said Stryker who did know. "Just looking at all possible options since you never know what's going to work out. Anything else you can think of for me?"

Karmody thought for a moment. "No, but he never goes anywhere without at least few guys with him. Three Piece is always there, and usually a guy named Jackson. Sometimes others."

"Okay," Stryker thought about the complications of Nixon having a constant entourage. "Well, for now, don't take any of his calls and don't go to your house. You can stay at your friend's place for a few more days at least I assume?"

"Yeah, that's not a problem."

"Great. So, go back to work and let me worry about Nixon for now, okay? Don't want you getting sued for malpractice now do we?" he tried to lighten her mood. "Still, you can call me anytime and I'll let you know if anything develops on my end. Are we good?"

"We're good," she gave a relaxed sigh. "And thanks Thorne."

"Haven't done anything yet, but you're welcome anyway."

At 9:30 that same evening Stryker picked up Perkins for a visit to the Night Moves club. "You sure you're up for this, Zip? You're a working man you know." Perkins was still working full shifts at his industrial site job.

"Actually, this is perfect," the big man responded as he settled into the passenger seat. "Tomorrow's gonna be my last day at DeMar's. I got the guy nailed and the boss is gonna be in in the morning for me to turn everything over to him. I know it took longer than I thought man, but what can ya do?" he smiled.

"Surprise, surprise," Stryker smiled back.

"So, Allen Nixon, huh?" Perkins commented without really asking. "I guess our client lady came to Discreet Inquiries cause this wasn't just your run-of-the-mill investigation. Movin' toward the big time, man!"

"Yeah," Stryker responded with a laugh. "Either that or she randomly picked an agency that she didn't know anything about, but that looked cheap." He looked sideways at Perkins to see if disappointment had taken over his face. It hadn't. "I'm sure it was more greatness than cheap randomness though."

"Well, either way, we're on our way to greatness," Perkins smiled. "I just hope she wasn't too disappointed that I couldn't handle her case personally. You know how upset people can get when their expectations are crushed and they get stuck with the second string."

Stryker merely shook his head as he drove onward to the club.

The two men were approved by the bouncer and walked into Night Moves at nearly 10:30 pm. The dim lighting was constantly interrupted by strobe lights that reflected off of mirrors and glass tables. Music thumped indiscernibly and loudly so that Stryker could feel it vibrate off his chest. He wondered how long he could stand it.

Inside the club, Stryker went right and Perkins went left to survey the two sides of the establishment, agreeing to meet at the far right corner of the stage. Stryker moved slowly through the tables and groups of standing customers trying to eye everyone carefully without calling attention to himself. He had the advantage of looking for either Nixon or Three Piece, while Perkins knew Nixon, but only had Stryker's description of Three Piece to work from. He was surprised at the number of people in the club on a Monday night. He had expected a sparse turnout, but admittedly that expectation wasn't based on experience. Everyone seemed to be dressed in dark clothing, which made the task of looking for someone harder, even though he was looking at faces. Many danced, some sat, and everyone drank. Stryker made it through his half without incident and stood at the end of the stage waiting for Perkins. He continued to scan the crowd in case he'd missed his quarry, but occasionally glanced at the two dancers on the stage. They somehow managed to find a way to move to the obnoxious music, although the limited and inconsistent lighting may have helped the image they projected. Stryker was ready to hope they'd come up empty so they could leave when Perkins strode quickly toward him.

"Over there, man," Perkins pointed behind him with a rush of excitement. "Nixon and three other guys. By the stage."

Stryker looked over Perkins shoulder and saw four men seated by the stage near the center of the floor, but he couldn't recognize anyone. "You sure?" he asked.

"No question it's Nixon, man. Don't know the other guys, but one of 'em looks like the Three Piece guy you described."

"All right," Stryker began to move. "Show's on." He led Perkins as they picked their way through the other patrons to the edge of the stage very near Nixon's table. "This'll do," he said leaning against the stage and staring at Nixon's table.

The four men were seated around two-thirds of the table so they could each see the stage, with Three Piece facing most directly toward Stryker and Perkins. Stryker leaned over as if to whisper to Perkins, but in fact he said nothing. He kept his eyes glued on Three Piece.

It didn't take long for Three Piece to notice the two men staring at him, and it apparently took even less time for him to recognize Stryker as he quickly leaned across the table and spoke to Nixon, whose seat provided Stryker and Perkins with only a partial profile view. Nixon and his other two companions turned as if choreographed and looked hard at Stryker. Nixon's face turned to a sneer as he mouthed something that Stryker wasn't able to discern. He then turned his back and said something to the other three. In less than a minute, Three Piece and one of the other men got up from the table.

Three Piece leaned over to say something to Nixon and then led the other man over to Stryker and Perkins. The second man was both taller and wider than Three Piece but stayed a step behind with eyes that never wavered from Stryker's face. His tightly cut hair couldn't hide the fact that his hairline ran nearly down to his eyebrows leaving the smallest forehead Stryker had ever seen. More like a twohead.

Three Piece gave Perkins an assessing visual once-over and then addressed Stryker. "What the hell you doin' here starin' at people, man?"

"Me?" Stryker asked innocently. "Just enjoying the music. I can't believe I haven't been here before, it's so . . . intellectually stimulating." He smiled at Three Piece and at the big man over Three Piece's shoulder.

Three Piece shook his head in apparent disgust. "Just get the hell out of here and don't be botherin' nobody."

"Or?"

"Huh?"

"Or what? Get the hell out of here, or what?" Stryker said calmly. "Your order sounded like an ultimatum. I was just wondering what the alternative was. Thus, or what?"

Three Piece snorted and shook his head. "Smart ass, huh? Okay," he raised his palms and cocked his head, "don't say I didn't warn ya."

Stryker looked over the big man's shoulder again at the larger man whose glare hadn't wavered during the brief exchange. "You must be Four Piece," he offered with a smile, deciding to keep the forehead comment to himself.

Three Piece scowled and returned to the table. His larger partner stared a moment longer with an intense look that made his forehead shrink even more. He said nothing but cocked his finger at Perkins before returning to the table as well.

"Okay, that was productive," nodded Perkins while watching the four men at the table. "What now, partner?"

"Three Piece is a nice enough guy to hang out with," reasoned Stryker, "but I really came here to have a word with Nixon. Seems like now's the time. You ready?"

"Always, man. Always."

Stryker walked calmly over to Nixon's table with Perkins on his right shoulder. Perkins kept his eyes on the others while Stryker leaned over to Nixon, keeping his hands fully visible the whole time. The other three men all stiffened noticeably as he did so and chairs shuffled on the floor, but nobody moved from the table.

"I wasn't sure you got the message," Stryker said loudly enough to be heard over the music. "Ms. Fenn says it's over between the two of you." Nixon's eyes remained focused on the stage. "That means no more phone calls, no more visits. Time to find yourself another girl. Any questions, Mr. Nixon?"

"And just who the hell are you?" asked Nixon without looking up or around.

"Well, I'm flattered that you're interested," responded Stryker while looking across the table at Three Piece. "The name's Stryker. Pleased to meet you."

"Whatever, Stryker," sneered Nixon. "If you know what's good for ya, you'll keep your face out of my business. Time to find yourself another job. Any questions, *Mr.* Stryker?"

"Oh, I've got lots of questions," Stryker smiled, "but I can't think of anything that you and the boys here could possibly help me with," he paused. "Just so we're clear – I've got no interest in any of your business. But, Ms. Fenn is no longer your business."

Stryker stood up and smiled at Perkins. "Let's get out of here before this music kills me."

The two men walked through the tables and dancers partway to the door before Perkins stopped and spoke loudly over the music. "I'm gonna hit the head before we go out. I'll meet ya outside, man."

"Okay," agreed Stryker. "I'm definitely not waiting in here."

Perkins split off to find the bathroom while Stryker walked outside and took a deep breath in relief at being freed from the pounding music and the strobe lights. He walked a half block to the corner to get away from the entrance and pondered the possibility of Nixon leaving Karmody alone. Not likely, yet, he decided. He paused at the corner to wait for Perkins and thought about options for the next step in resolving the issue. When he turned to look for Perkins, he instead saw Three Piece and his larger, quiet shadow walking toward him not ten yards away. Stryker noticed a young couple walking on the other side of the street, but saw no one else on the block. The sidewalk behind the approaching men was empty as well, as the doorman had apparently taken a break inside the doors of the club, and Perkins was nowhere in sight.

Stryker relaxed his arms at this sides as the two men stopped about three feet from his position. "Well, Three and Four Piece. Out for a little fresh air are we?" he offered in greeting.

Three Piece smiled menacingly while his partner's face remained calm and unchanged. "Mr. Nixon don't like people bothering him, asshole. He suggested we get a little exercise. Guess how we're gonna get it?"

"If you're smart, you'll get your exercise by walking around the block before going back to your club," Stryker looked for the appearance of Perkins behind the two men, but saw only empty sidewalk. "If you're not so smart, you'll mix me into your plans. I suppose I can guess about how smart you guys are, but I'll ask anyway – what's it gonna be?"

"Ain't gonna be nothin' but bad news for you," Three Piece smiled again as he separated himself about three feet to the left of his partner. "Make sure you listen next time when Nixon tells you to stay out of his business."

The two men were both swaying slightly and the larger man contributed to the dialogue by cracking his knuckles. Stryker assumed it was supposed to be intimidating, but he focused on assessing the situation. Both men were larger than him, but neither looked incredibly fast. He also knew that they'd been drinking. In addition he assumed that they were confident, possibly overly confident from the fact that there were two of them, acting on their initiative, facing one smaller man. Whether they had any training or experience, however, wouldn't be clear for another minute or two. Stryker had both.

The bigger man, standing slightly to Stryker's left, moved first with his left foot stepping forward to lead a telegraphed right cross. Stryker reacted instantly by stepping toward the two men, which put him inside the arc of the big man's right hand. As he stepped forward, Stryker swiveled slightly with his left elbow coming up and his right hand moving back. He kept his eyes on Three Piece while he threw his left elbow into the side of the neck of the larger man who found himself off-balance as his punch wasn't hitting its target. In one fluid motion, Stryker's left elbow connected hard with flesh and bone while his right hand shot out toward the face of Three Piece who thought he was about to see Stryker go down. Instead, his vision disappeared completely as the base of Stryker's palm shattered his nose.

Three Piece screamed and bent over with his hands to his face filling instantly with blood. His screams stopped abruptly as Stryker followed up with his right elbow to the neck of Three Piece to send him face first to the sidewalk in a motionless lump. Stryker quickly spun around to see the larger man regain his balance and shake his head to clear his eyes. Menacingly, he stepped toward Stryker with his hands up in classic boxer fashion. He growled slightly while rolling his head on his shoulders and continuing his advance. Stryker waited.

The big man threw a left jab that Stryker dodged while moving to his right to avoid getting tangled with Three Piece on the ground. Another left jab barely clipped Stryker's shoulder and he knew that a combination would come next. The big man threw one more jab expecting Stryker to move into the right hook that was to follow. Instead, Stryker darted quickly toward his attacker on the outside of the jab and well away from the big right hand. As the big man naturally shifted his weight to his left foot, Stryker delivered a sharp side kick to the outside of his opponent's left knee. He heard the knee pop as it caved inward, the way knees aren't supposed to move. Four Piece collapsed on the ground with a howl, grasping his knee before Stryker eliminated his immediate pain with a swift kick that rocked back the head of his attacker. The two large men lay together on the sidewalk.

Stryker walked back toward the club without looking at the devastation over his shoulder. He was halfway up the block when Perkins stepped out the door looking up the street. Perkins saw the two men on the ground and gave Stryker a quizzical look.

"They were just delivering a message," Stryker explained calmly. "Unfortunately, sometimes I don't hear too well."

"You ever hear the line that says something about 'don't blame the messenger'?" Perkins asked.

"Well, sometimes you just don't have any choice," Stryker smiled as he looked back over his shoulder. "Where were you, by the way?"

"Me?" Perkins cast an innocent gaze while pointing a finger at his own chest. "I was gettin' Nixon's autograph, man. What'd you expect?"

Stryker couldn't help but laugh.

CHAPTER EIGHTEEN

Stryker woke up still reveling in his retirement and ready for the Nixon job to be finished as well. He began the day with a relaxed seven mile run for his body while his mind replayed the street corner encounter with Three Piece and his partner. Stryker felt badly about their injuries, but even in retrospect he didn't see that he had any other options. Their approach was clearly aggressive and if they hadn't ended up on the sidewalk, then that's exactly where Perkins would have found him. He decided that he was merely the instrument of the fate the two men had chosen for themselves. He certainly didn't enjoy it, but he didn't necessarily regret it.

He returned from his run with a lot of nothing planned for his day. He considered calling Sam but decided against it. He wasn't really sure how he wanted to follow up on their dinner, so the best immediate course of action seemed to be no action at all. Of course, he hadn't heard from her either. He leisurely breakfasted on cereal and the morning newspaper before the ringing of the phone interrupted with an agitated Karmody Fenn. She wanted to see him and they agreed to meet for lunch near her downtown office. Although she didn't share any details, it didn't sound as though the job was as much over as he wanted it to be.

Stryker arrived ten minutes early for their 11:30 appointment and was surprised to see Karmody stride into the reception area of her office immediately after his announced arrival. She evidently had the decks cleared and was simply watching the clock in anticipation of their meeting. Stryker sensed her tension, but they engaged in nothing more than meaningless small talk as they walked to the nearby Bakeman's restaurant for their lunch.

Bakeman's sits slightly below street level on Cherry Street between First and Second Avenues in the downtown business district. Most pedestrians passed by without even recognizing the restaurant's existence, yet it was full every weekday from 11:00 am until nearly 2:00 pm. They entered before noon, which put them on the early side of the lunch hour, but a line of fifteen customers already stood in place. The restaurant served in a cafeteria-style assembly line with no table service. Neither Stryker nor Karmody spoke as they approached the head of the line, instead focusing their attention on their orders as Bakeman's was famous for its quick service and the greatest faux pas for any customer was to hold up the line. They both ordered Turkey sandwiches and Stryker supplemented his with a pickle slice and a bowl of cream of broccoli soup. Stryker paid for both lunches after surviving the tense lunch line gauntlet, and they took a table in the back corner.

Before Stryker could introduce himself to his soup or sandwich, Karmody began with the business at hand. "Allen called me three times at the office this morning," she began stressfully with quick but quiet words. "I ignored the first two, but then I realized he was just going to keep calling so I answered the third call," she paused and looked at Stryker who waited with a half sandwich in one hand. "He was asking me about you and said you beat up some of his guys," she looked an unasked question into his eyes.

"A friend and I saw Nixon last night," Stryker explained calmly. "I had a bit of a discussion with two of his cronies."

"A discussion?" Karmody asked incredulously.

"It got a little physical," he admitted matter-of-factly.

"A little, huh? Allen said they were both in the hospital," she said with an accusatorial tone. "What happened? I never thought you'd be out beating people up. I mean, you're working for me, right? I can't have you just . . ." she shook her head. "I don't know."

"Well, if it'll ease your mind at all, Three Piece and his friend came after me, not the other way around," Stryker explained. "So I guess you could call it self-defense. Anyway, I simply gave Nixon the message that he needed to leave you alone. He sent his goons after me and in the end they got hurt. Now, it seems that he still hasn't gotten the message if he's calling you at work," he sighed. "So, what did he have to say?"

"Well, like I said mostly just asking about you, but still kind of threatening," she looked away and almost took the first bite of her sandwich before stopping. "I still don't think he'd actually do anything to me, he just wants control, you know? It's just his ego still telling him that I can't walk away from the relationship. I don't know, he's mad I guess."

"Control, huh? I guess I don't know about that, but you hired me to make him go away." Stryker looked carefully into her eyes. "He hasn't agreed to do that yet. Now I know you didn't plan for or expect anything physical to happen and I wasn't looking for it, but that's where we are. His choice, not mine. Are you saying you're changing your mind and you don't want me to make him go away?"

Karmody looked down at the table and let out a long, loud sigh. Her face remained placid, but her eyes were troubled.

Stryker assumed she had reached the inevitable point of blaming herself for the situation. If only she'd never gone out with Nixon. If only she hadn't let it get serious. If only she'd broken it off earlier when there was less at stake. If only she'd anticipated better. Blaming herself for creating the situation naturally led to blame for current events as well. Stryker didn't interrupt her silent lament.

Finally, she spoke. "No, I mean yes. I want this to end. I want him to go away. I just don't want anyone else to get hurt. Can you promise me that?"

Stryker smiled and tilted his head down toward the table to catch her eyes before responding honestly. "I'm afraid I can't promise that. Whether anyone gets hurt, that'll be up to Nixon. I can promise you that it's not my goal to hurt anyone – just like I didn't want to last night. But, if that's the way they play it . . ."

Karmody nodded in saddened resignation. Looking back down at the safety of the table she said, "Okay, I'll trust you." She finally took a tiny bite of her sandwich and chewed very carefully. Stryker stared in amazement at the gracefulness of it and took his next bite with extreme self-consciousness. She swallowed and dabbed the perfectly clean corners of her mouth with her napkin.

"I would like to move back to my house," Karmody said hopefully. "The commute from the east side's a pain, plus I don't have half the stuff I need. How soon, do you think?"

"Let's give it a couple of days," Stryker said. "I'll follow up with Nixon about the phone calls this morning, then we'll see where we are. Okay?"

"Yeah, okay," said Karmody after finishing off another three-calorie bite. "But remember, you promised."

"And I'm a man of my word," smiled Stryker. "Now, let's finish our lunch and then I'll walk you back to your office so we can both get back to work."

By 3:00 in the afternoon, Perkins still hadn't come up with an address for Allen Nixon. He had learned, however, that the team was working out at their practice facility until 5:00 or 5:30 that afternoon. With that knowledge in hand, but without a real plan, Stryker headed to the team's practice gym, which was located on the east side of Lake Washington in downtown Bellevue.

Stryker arrived at the gym at 4:15 pm and identified what he assumed to be the players' parking lot based upon the abnormally high percentage of Cadillac Escalades and Hummers, mixed in with two Mercedes SUVs and a couple of Lexus sedans. He parked outside the gated lot where he had a clear view of the entire parking area and of the two doors leading to the lot from the building. He cracked the window slightly, glanced at his watch, and began to read the magazine he had brought along to pass the time.

The first player didn't appear from the building until 5:55 pm. He fired up a Lexus and gave a two finger wave to the security guard at the gate on his way out of the lot. Stryker set aside his magazine and turned his full attention to the building and the remaining cars. Players came out individually and in small groups, and none of them wasted any time leaving the facility. Each drove separately from the others. Nixon was not among them.

Stryker began to wonder if Nixon had missed practice or if he had parked in another lot and had exited from another part of the building. Each time a door opened he moved his hand toward the ignition key in anticipation, but each time he sat back in disappointment. By 6:10, only three cars remained in the lot and Stryker was fairly certain he had seen all the players leave. All except Nixon. He chided himself for not bringing Perkins along to cover the other side of the building and was about to leave when the door opened once again. This time Allen Nixon exited the building by himself and quickly climbed into a silver Mercedes. Stryker exhaled in relief and started his own Mercedes 540 and pulled away from the curb. He made an immediate right turn onto a side street whereupon he executed a u-turn so that he sat waiting at the intersection and could easily follow in either direction once Nixon pulled out of the parking lot across the street. Nixon exited the lot and turned to his right, away from Stryker, and Stryker immediately moved his car onto the street behind him.

Stryker followed with the luxury of not caring if Nixon discovered that he was being followed. Stryker's only goal was to talk to Nixon one more time. If he followed Nixon home and talked to him there, so be it. If Nixon saw Stryker following and stopped somewhere else along the way, that would be just fine as well. Finding out where Nixon lived might prove to be advantageous in the long run, so Stryker didn't go out of his way to get Nixon's attention, but he also didn't work especially hard at being discreet. As it turned out, Nixon was evidently oblivious as he drove undeterred to a new-generation gated community in the Sammamish Highlands with a sign identifying the neighborhood as Eagles' Roost. Unlike the names of some communities – Antelope Creek, or Bear Falls – Eagles' Roost stood in an area where Bald Eagles actually lived and probably roosted. Stryker appreciated truth in advertising. Nixon pulled into the entrance drive to the community where he reached out his window to open a "keep the riff-raff out" gate by sliding a card into an electronic sensor. Stryker pulled up right behind Nixon, ignored the "No Piggybacking" sign, and followed him through the gate before it swung closed again.

At that point, Stryker had no question that Nixon was aware of his presence, but Nixon drove ahead three quick blocks and pulled his Mercedes into a driveway leading up to a four-car garage attached to a very large home. The home looked new, immaculately maintained, and gave off an aura of quiet respectability.

Nixon parked outside the garage and aggressively jumped out of his car when Stryker pulled up into the driveway as well.

Nixon moved toward Stryker's car as Stryker opened his door. "What the hell are you d . . ." Nixon began loudly before stopping in his tracks and his syllables as he saw Stryker step out onto the driveway.

"Allen," Stryker stepped forward with a big smile. "Well, isn't this something running into you, right here in your own driveway." Nixon remained motionless but Stryker moved forward until the two men stood just three feet apart.

Nixon stood 6' 7" and weighted 225 pounds. As the two men faced each other, Nixon curled his goatee-encrusted mouth into a sneer and attempted to employ the same physical intimidation that had worked well for him since he was in junior high school. In this case, however, both men knew what Stryker had done to Nixon's companions the night before and Nixon quickly dropped the menacing glower.

"You're trespassing Strider. What the hell you doin' following me to my house?" Nixon sounded confident even though Stryker had already seen him back off physically.

"The name's Stryker, Allen. Not Strider," Stryker maintained his amiable smile while exuding nothing but seriousness from his eyes. "And you don't need to ask why I'm here, cause you already know the answer to that, don't you Allen."

Nixon glanced over his shoulder at the house and Stryker wondered if he had friends waiting for him inside. For the moment, however, the house remained quiet and Nixon focused on Stryker once again. "I don't care why you're here. You're trespassing, so leave now or I'll call the police."

"Can't do that quite yet, Allen my friend," said Stryker. "You see, we seem to have had some miscommunication last night and I want to clear things up so that it doesn't happen again. You're okay with good, clear communication aren't you Allen?"

"Enough of the smart talk," Nixon said with a return of the sneer. "I told you to get off my property, and I'm not gonna ask again."

"No, I wouldn't bother asking again if I were you," responded Stryker in a measured voice. "I'm not leaving till we've had our talk. But go ahead though, and call the police if you want. I can wait."

Nixon made no move to his house or a cell phone, but still attempted to exert control over the confrontation. "Go ahead and talk all you want, man. All you can talk in two minutes at least – that's as much time as I'm giving you."

"Thanks Allen," Stryker maintained the ever-friendly smile. "First tell me about your pal Three Piece. How's he doing today?"

"You broke his nose and gave him a concussion, that's how he's doing. We should have gone to the police about that, man. Assault and battery."

"I'll say it again," replied Stryker, "go ahead and call the police. I can wait." Once again Nixon made no move to follow up on his threat so Stryker continued. "Three Piece'll be okay. It's actually the other guy I'm more worried about. I don't think he's gonna be too mobile for a while."

"Melvin's messed up man. His knee's tore up bad." The menace returned to Nixon's face as his jaw jutted toward Stryker. "That was wrong what you did to him."

"Well, I've got two things to say to that, Allen," Stryker said as he rubbed his hands together slowly. "First, tell your buddy Melvin to pick his battles a little more carefully in the future. Or rather, you pick them for him a little more carefully."

"Second, and much more important, what *you're* doing is wrong, Allen. You've got no right to harass Karmody Fenn and I've made it completely clear to you that it's going to stop. Now you need to tell me that you've received the message perfectly clearly." Stryker squinted slightly as he looked directly into

Nixon's eyes. "It's too bad about Melvin's knee, Allen, but at least he's not a professional athlete. I'd really hate to see something like that happen to you. It could mean the end of your career. Tough thing to take on over a little bit of ego, wouldn't you say?"

"You threatening me, Stryker?" Nixon instinctively tried to use his physical presence again as he rose up taller and puffed his chest out like a cobra facing an imminent threat. He then recoiled slightly but maintained his aggressive tone. "No way are you gonna threaten me over some stupid chick."

"Well, Allen," Stryker's calmness remained unwavering and unnerving for Nixon, "that's sort of up to you. Now you're smart enough to know you can't force her to be in a relationship and you're both going to end up miserable if you try. Plus, a guy like you – you've got to have plenty of women to choose from, huh?" The corner of Nixon's mouth turned up involuntarily as he snorted a breath and shrugged slightly. "So, the question is, do you really want to keep on making trouble for yourself and your friends over Karmody?"

"Hey, man, I don't give a shit about that chick," Nixon asserted as if saying it would make it so. "Bottom line, though, it's none of your business and you keep trying to make it your business. So you gotta walk away, man, and let me deal with Karmody."

"Sorry Allen, but that's just not gonna happen at this point," said Stryker as he mentally noted that he'd gone beyond his allotted two minutes. "I'll tell you what we can do though, if you're willing to listen to a suggestion." Nixon shrugged slightly but said nothing. "Why don't you pick some place tomorrow night – some place you like to hang out. I'll bring Karmody by and you can publicly dump her. Tell her to get lost. Tell her you never want to see her again. Whatever." Stryker looked for a reaction from Nixon but nothing was evident on his face. "The real bottom line is that it's over between the two of you, but if you want to do it this way, I'm sure Karmody will agree." Stryker paused and finished a bit more slowly. "Either way, I'm going to make sure that you don't bother her anymore. If you really want to take that on, I'm more than ready."

Nixon said nothing for a moment as he evaluated the man standing in front of him in his driveway. Finally, he said, "You think she'd do that?"

"Yeah. I'll make sure she does. You just name the place."

Nixon smiled and picked the place and the time.

Karmody willingly accepted the compromise and stood calmly for her public dumping by Nixon in front a large group of his friends. She even made a show of crying before rushing out of the restaurant where she gave Stryker a huge hug and kiss of thanks. Stryker drove her to her own home and reported the successful conclusion of the case to Perkins, although he made sure that Karmody was ready to contact him if Nixon were to renege in any way.

Stryker enjoyed a relaxing drive home and arrived back at his own condo ready to take on the challenges of retirement.

CHAPTER NINETEEN

The next morning dawned with a light haze that quickly burned away with the aggressive appearance of bright sunshine. The sun crested the Cascade Range early and bathed the Puget Sound region in a sparkling natural invitation to jump out of bed and revel in the optimism of the day. Most residents weren't thrilled with pre-6:00 am invitations, but most would enjoy the beauty of the day once they were forced to face it. Stryker didn't need an invitation and awoke early, refreshed and feeling good about life. He thought about a favorite line from a song – there's no place to go and you've got all day to get there. Not a bad way to start a new day in a new life. He assumed that the Nixon issue would go away for Karmody Fenn, which meant that he had no current jobs to assist with for Perkins. He was always willing to help out, but Perkins generally respected his time and didn't ask too frequently. Thus, unless Nixon decided to do something stupid, Stryker was completely obligation free for the time being.

Gazing out the window to follow the progress of an early morning jogger, Stryker thought that maybe it was time to call Sam again. He had fully enjoyed their dinner together and he sensed that she'd had a good time as well. He wasn't sure how, or if, he wanted things to progress, but he certainly felt interested in another date if she were open to it. He reached for the phone to call but then changed his mind. Instead, he decided to catch her off guard and simply show up at her office and see if she wanted to go to lunch. Worst case scenario – she wouldn't be there or wouldn't be able to get away, but for Stryker that would simply mean a trip downtown where he could stop in and check on Karmody and then have lunch on his own. All day to get there.

Stryker spent the morning doing little things that amounted to a lot of nothing while he passed the time before preparing to leave for downtown. He sat at his computer checking and reading through the Yahoo headlines when curiosity suddenly grabbed his focus like the all-in poker player dying to see the final card turned over to seal his fate one way or the other. In Stryker's case, however, it wasn't poker cards but the Axman website that he was suddenly dying to see. It had been eight days since he had posted his retirement notice. Would there be any kind of reaction or acknowledgement? Maybe the entire site had been disbanded now that he had taken himself out of the picture. After not thinking about it for most of the past week, Stryker suddenly faced an irrepressible itch to visit the site just to see what might be there.

Stryker decided to look despite convincing himself that in all likelihood there would be nothing to see. Because he was only going to be reading without posting any messages, he felt perfectly comfortable accessing the site from his own computer, although he did take the precaution of using a proxy server.

Stryker logged on as he had many times over the past decade and felt a twinge of nostalgia when he saw the familiar home page pop up on his screen. He glanced at it briefly – just enough to see that it didn't look any different than the last time he'd seen it – and then, as usual, he went directly to the discussion blog where he had recently announced his retirement. He was a bit surprised to feel his heart rate pick up in nervous anticipation. He didn't have any real expectations, but he thought that there was an outside chance of finding something posted in reaction to his retirement notice.

What he saw was something he had not anticipated. The discussion blog remained unused as a forum of conversation, which was not at all uncommon over the past ten years. In fact, Stryker was always shocked on the rare occasions when he came upon what looked like real discussions about the medieval executioners. For now, the rule of nothing remained in place, rather than the exception of actual postings. Even so, Stryker found one posting that had been added since his announced retirement. Posted just hours earlier. It read: F260420.

Stryker's eyebrows knitted in confusion as he stared at the screen and the hum of the computer droned louder in his head. He looked at the prior entry that he had posted: "Retired." Then an entry added earlier this morning: "F260420." A date and time in the Axman code as established by General MacAfee ten years ago. An invitation to check back on the discussion blog during a five-minute window to find the name of another target. The date was just over a week away. Another job to be posted despite his retirement announcement.

Stryker shook his head in disbelief. He had always ignored a lingering uneasiness stemming from the fact that he didn't know who was responsible for the postings following MacAfee's death, but it bothered him even more that whoever it was, now seemed to be arrogantly ignoring his announcement of retirement. He felt the temptation to log onto the discussion blog right then to reiterate the retirement statement, but he sided with discretion and wouldn't break his practice of only observing the website from his personal computer. He wouldn't allow anything to be traced directly back to him.

He sat back and thought about his options. First, it was possible that the poster was being careful, even about an acknowledgement of his retirement. Maybe that acknowledgement would come in the traditional five-minute window only – at the date and time indicated in the posting. It seemed like a reasonable possibility. Second, however, what if the posting was an indication of a refusal to accept his retirement? What did it matter? He was retired simply by saying so. He never had to check the site again, and he certainly never had to take another job. Whoever was doing the posting could post as many dates, times, and names as he or she wanted and it wouldn't mandate a comeback from retirement. Stryker was retired. The postings couldn't change that. Stryker felt satisfied with his reasoning as he moved away from the initial shock of seeing the coded posting. He resolved to check in a week to see what showed up at the designated time, but just for the sake of curiosity. For now, he had two women to see.

At 12:40 in the afternoon, Stryker stepped off the elevator and into the familiar, spotless lobby of the Merrill Lynch office. He walked up to the reception desk and was greeted with a smile and a finger indicating that he should wait while Linda the receptionist talked into her mouthpiece.

Without anything visibly evident to Stryker, she suddenly finished on the phone and spoke to him while brushing a loose cusp of hair from her right eye. "Good afternoon, shall I tell Ms. Wykovicz that you're here?"

"Yes, if you would please, but I don't have an appointment," Stryker said apologetically. "I just dropped in to see if by chance she might be available. If not, it's no big deal."

"Well, we can find out, sir," she replied in a light and airy voice. "Just one moment." She answered another call and then reached Sam in her office. "She said she'll be out in three or four minutes if you want to have a seat."

After nearly ten minutes, Sam walked into the lobby in a flatteringly tailored dark pantsuit and a puzzled look on her face. "Hey there Thorne. I wasn't expecting you – is anything wrong?"

"Not a thing in the world," he responded enthusiastically. "But, the market closes in a few minutes and knowing you, I'm sure you haven't eaten anything all day. So, I thought maybe I could talk you into an unplanned lunch." Stryker glanced over at a gawking Linda who immediately interrupted her intense gaze at the two of them to shuffle some papers on her desk.

Sam looked at her watch and seemed to consider a mental calendar in her head. "Well, I suppose we could, but I'm afraid I couldn't go until 1:30 or maybe even 1:45. That'd be kind of long for you to wait, huh?" she asked with a hint of hope in her voice.

"Actually, that would be just perfect," Stryker nodded with an agreeable smile. "I've got a client I need to stop by and see for a few minutes," he glanced at his watch, "so I can do that and be back here by 1:45. Should we plan on that?"

"Client? What do you mean, client?" Sam questioned with piercing eyes that danced with curiosity.

"Oh, nothing much. I was helping LJ with a case that I think we've resolved," Stryker explained. "The client is a lawyer who works downtown here. So, like I said, I can do that and I should be able to be back here in time to deal with your obviously famished state. Now, go sell some stocks before the close and make your clients happy. I'll see you in an hour."

Stryker smiled, waved and moved directly to the elevator. Sam watched him walk away as she shook her head and raised her eyebrows before turning to head back to her office. She ignored the impish look on Linda's face.

Stryker met with Karmody Fenn to provide what he hoped would be final closure of her situation with Allen Nixon and to make sure that, thus far at least, Nixon had followed through with their agreement. Lunch with Sam stayed low-key and enjoyable and Sam didn't seem put-off by his unannounced visit. When she asked about his immediate plans now that he'd resolved his case, Stryker couldn't help but focus again on the Axman posting. Luckily for him, however, this came as they were winding up lunch so he managed to hide any distraction.

"We should do this again sometime soon," Sam invited as he walked her back to her office. "Of course, it *would* be okay to let me know first, but I guess it's not entirely necessary – if you're willing to risk being shut out."

"You wouldn't do that to me, would you?" Stryker teased. "And here I thought I was your favorite client." He pouted slightly while she held back a smile.

"A good broker doesn't have favorite clients," she said sternly, "you should know that. If I did, though, I'm really not sure where you'd be on that list." Stryker continued his hurt look. "So, like I said, it's up to you if you want to take the chance."

"Gee, maybe I should take my account somewhere that appreciates me for the delicate human being that I am," he intoned with a mischievous smile. "Or maybe not. After all, you've got the best receptionist around," he smiled at Linda.

Linda was pretending not to listen but she couldn't help but look up and blush at Stryker's comment. She quickly returned to her work, however, as Sam glanced over at her. Stryker then bade them both goodbye and left the building once again.

Before leaving downtown, Stryker visited the Seattle Public Library in its relatively new and unquestionably grandiose location on Fourth Avenue to complete one final task for the day. The street outside streamed with both cars and pedestrians, but the library seemed unusually quiet, even for a weekday afternoon. The computer carrels were the one busy place in the library as was generally the case. It bothered Stryker that libraries, the traditional home for books, had become much more popular for seemingly everything else other than books. First it was newspapers and magazines, then it was movies and music to check out, now it was computers. It was difficult for Stryker to get too self-righteous, however, as his visit led him to the computers rather than the stacks.

He found an open computer, slipped into the chair and immediately logged onto the Internet and then onto a proxy server. In less than thirty seconds he saw the Axman site in front of him and he clicked on the discussion blog. He saw the same entry from earlier, F260420, and he logged on to add to the blog. He typed as he had once before: RETIRED, then logged off the site. He was out of the library just two minutes after walking in the door.

Stryker left downtown to head for home while pondering the possibility of an early evening run followed by an old movie at home. No place to go and all day to get there.

CHAPTER TWENTY

For three days Stryker focused on the leisurely life of the somewhat young, relatively comfortable, and newly retired. Despite his efforts to the contrary, he found his focus intermittently interrupted by thoughts of the Axman site and the quickly approaching date posted thereon – June 26. The coded date had been posted after his original retirement announcement, whereupon he had responded by re-posting his statement of retirement. He couldn't help but wonder if there had since been some recognition of his retirement declaration, or if it was still ignored like the proclamation of a reformed lifestyle coming from another Hollywood starlet gone bad. He finally realized that he'd never stop thinking about it if he didn't check to see, so late in the evening of the 22nd he used a proxy server to log onto the Axman site from his home computer once again. He consciously felt his anxiety heighten simply by the decision to log in to the page that he had visited consistently over the past decade.

The homepage remained inexorably unchanged and Stryker spent no time there before redirecting his screen to the discussion blog. Scrolling backward through the blog he surprisingly found multiple entries from multiple bloggers since his latest retirement posting. The discussion activity exceeded by far anything from the last ten years and Stryker's curiosity surged like an electric charge up his spine. He traced the postings back to his second retirement announcement and read them in chronological order. The names caught his attention first, but soon the discussion itself gained intrigue.

Hatchet: "Seeing the word retired posted here makes me think. Anybody have any idea how long executioners generally stayed on the job? Obviously, life expectancies then weren't anything like they are today, but I'm curious if anyone has any information on the 'career' side of our medieval friends."

Castleman: "I haven't heard or read anything specifically, but just thinking about it I can't imagine it was a job that men simply dropped into for a while to see if they'd like it. It had to be a long-term career choice."

Guillotine-lover: "Maybe a 'long-term' career choice, but I'm sure they wouldn't let anybody too young take the job to start with. They had to look for some sort of maturity or life experience. Given the shorter life expectancies, that wouldn't necessarily mean a very long career."

Castleman: "Obviously, you can expect that there'd be lots of variation based on individual people and circumstances. Maybe even from one town or community to another. What I wonder about though, is how they'd go about replacing an experienced executioner once he was finished. Did they hold auditions?"

Hatchet: "Your comment takes me back to my original question about retirement, Castleman. Obviously, if an executioner died, the community wouldn't have any choice but to find a replacement as best they could. But what if he simply retired? What if he didn't want to work anymore but they couldn't find anyone to replace him? Certainly they wouldn't suspend all executions simply because they lost their guy, right? Even so, it was obviously a very unique and specialized job, right? I assume they're not just going to grab the local butcher and have him fill in till they could find someone else."

Castleman: "I agree. My guess is that an executioner couldn't really retire until they had a satisfactory replacement. I suppose he could retire, but if his services were needed before they filled the spot, I'm sure he'd agree to 'come out of retirement' to do a single job if the community required it. He was, after all, a public servant."

Guillotine-lover: "I think it's all moot. I don't think anyone in the middle ages, executioner or not, retired. I think they all worked full time until they died or were too sick or disabled to work – even on a part-time basis."

Hatchet: "You're probably right, Guillotine. Good thing too, because I can't imagine it would be too easy to replace an executioner. They may have had an apprentice position, but if they didn't, or if the executioner died or for some reason couldn't do the job anymore before they had an apprentice in place, they were just screwed."

Castleman: "I don't know. I could see an executioner leaving the job before death. Maybe he'd move or maybe he'd just get tired of the job and wanted to do something else. I'm certain though, that if there were one final job that he was needed for, and the community was DESPERATE, that even a retired executioner would answer the call and fulfill his duties one last time. Regardless of the reasons for his retirement. It would certainly be easier for him than for anyone else they might come up with."

Hatchet: "I agree. If they were 'DESPERATE' as you say and if they made it very clear to the executioner that they would not ask again, no matter what happened – so that it was genuinely one last job only – then I think he would temporarily un-retire to help out. As you say, he was a public servant and I'm sure he wouldn't leave his community high and dry."

Guillotine-lover: "Well, assuming you guys are right, I'm sure they'd have to pay him something significant. He certainly would have his reasons for retiring and if he agreed to do one last job in spite of those reasons, the community would have to compensate him to make it worth his while. In other words, if he asked for more than his normal pay, they'd have to agree to it if they really needed his services."

Castleman: "Can't argue with that."

Hatchet: "Agreed. If they really wanted his services, they'd have to be willing to pay. Who knows, maybe that's why he'd retire in the first place."

Castleman: "No. I still think these guys were dedicated public servants. It might take the extra pay to bring him out of retirement, but he wouldn't retire just to try to force a pay raise."

Hatchet: "Sounds reasonable. And remember, the situation presented was for that one final job. They'd make it very clear that they'd never ask again."

The discussion blog ended there with Stryker feeling the pressure of the arguments that were clearly focused directly at him. He, or they, clearly acknowledged his retirement announcement and they seemed to be willing to accept it. At the same time they, or he, apparently were prepared to go ahead with the posting on the 26th with the promise that it would be the last one. Stryker logged off with the excitement of retirement nowhere evident in his immediate vicinity. Why had he ever logged back on to the site in the first place, he wondered.

He sat quietly for a few minutes with his head bowed toward his lap and his hands rubbing his eyes and temples. He replayed the discussion blog in his thoughts next to his plans for retirement. He finally walked away from the computer and ended up at his living room window staring out at the world that remained free from the drama of execution websites. He reminded himself that retirement remained completely in his hands, but that he could at least look at the posting to see about the job. He always had the option of ignoring it if he wanted. If he decided to take it, as one last job, it would be his choice. He had no doubt about one thing, however – the 26th would be his last ever visit to the Axman website.

Four days later Stryker sat down at his computer at 4:20 on a cool, overcast afternoon. The discussion thread on the Axman site remained unchanged except for one addition. It read: "Silvis Walker. Independence, Missouri." The one final job referenced in the discussion exchange. Stryker immediately recognized some familiarity in the name, but he couldn't place it. Time to do some research, he thought.

He logged off the Axman site for what he assumed would be the last time, and entered a general Internet search for the name Silvis Walker and came up with thousands of hits. The story had made national headlines over the past winter and spring, and Stryker quickly recognized the case and remembered many of the details as soon as he began reading the first entry.

Walker had been the prime suspect in dozens of rape, mutilation and murder cases over a number of years from across the state of Missouri. Eventually Walker made a mistake as he left alive a victim named Marciella Mendez. After a lengthy recovery from her near-death state she identified Walker and helped put together the final pieces of the case needed by prosecutors. Walker faced charges in twenty-two separate attacks, twenty-one of which ended in the death of the victim. News reports stated that Marciella Mendez, the twenty-second victim and the only known survivor, made a compelling and credible witness, and stood as the lynchpin to the prosecution's case to support their significant circumstantial evidence in all of the other charges.

Controversy surrounded the trial from the outset. Many legal experts questioned the tactic of combining all twenty-two cases together rather than bringing the strongest case, that of Mendez, first and separately. Speculation held that the Independence prosecutor hoped to make a significant splash with the full-scale prosecution as he faced a tough re-election campaign in the fall.

Both in pre-trial motions and once the trial began, it seemed to many that the judge made virtually every tight ruling against the prosecution. Some argued that her goal was to eliminate any possible grounds for appeal following conviction, but others questioned whether something else might be afoot. Walker never took the stand in his own defense but sat quietly and calmly throughout the proceedings. After more than three weeks of testimony and evidence, the eight man, four woman jury deliberated for seventeen hours before returning a verdict of not guilty on all counts. Marciella Mendez collapsed in the courtroom, observers were horrified, and news reporters reflected the widespread shock and disbelief of the community. Silvis Walker strode confidently from the courtroom with a humorless smile on his face.

Jurors were polled and all pointed at the circumstantial nature of most of the prosecution's evidence. They also claimed to have been swayed by expert testimony about the inherent unreliability of eyewitness testimony from a witness under extreme duress – Marciella Mendez. Each expressed the belief that they had returned the only verdict legally possible given the "beyond a reasonable doubt" standard faced by the prosecution.

Millions of people across the nation had joined in the shock and outrage of the Independence community at what most believed to have been an extreme miscarriage of justice resulting in the release of a certain murderer and public menace. The prosecutor faced widespread vilification for the acquittal following his decision to try all the cases together and subsequently dropped out of the race for re-election. In the weeks following the verdict, rumors and speculation of jury tampering circulated, but no supporting evidence had come forth and the rumors had died away. Recently, however, rumors spread about the possibility of Walker writing his memoirs, which would include details on many of the crimes for which he now enjoyed constitutional protections from the reach of the law.

Stryker shut down his computer after nearly an hour of reading about Walker and the trial. One last assignment? he asked himself. This one felt somewhat different from the prior cases that had come from the Axman site in that Silvis Walker couldn't be considered a national level figure or threat. Nonetheless, he clearly fit the profile of someone who had succeeded in evading justice and who deserved a different fate.

One last assignment? Stryker hadn't realized how much he looked forward to retirement until he announced it and thought it had begun. Now it seemed as though it would have to wait just a little bit longer. Stryker smiled wryly at his apparent fate. One more assignment. This wasn't the first time for things to turn out in a significantly different way from what he planned and expected.

26 YEARS AGO

CHAPTER TWENTY-ONE

Fifteen nervous teenage runners bounced, stretched and glanced around at their competitors at the starting line for the class 4A state championship mile race about to be run in Columbus, Ohio. The sixteenth runner, Thorne Stryker, stood perfectly still with his eyes focused on the track ahead of him as he calmly pictured the race unfolding in his mind. He forcibly dipped his shoulders and rolled his neck. The starter gave the same instructions the runners had heard dozens of times before and then stepped back to give the commands to start the race. The runners took off quickly at the gun, driven by nerves and a sudden surge of adrenaline. Sixty-one seconds later they crossed the starting line to complete their first lap, faster than most of them had run all season, but the entire group of sixteen moved as a single living entity in their competitive fury and confident enthusiasm. Veteran observers pointed out that the field would stretch from front to back on the second and third laps when the torrid early pace took its toll on the overtaxed young muscles and lungs.

A light breeze helped to cool the runners on the otherwise blistering late May afternoon. A momentary lull in the field events allowed the entire attention of the crowd to focus intently on the sixteen youthful milers. On the backstretch of the second lap paces began to change within the tight-knit group, which led to some bumping and jostling for position. Hands pushed and fought for space and safety in the tight crowd until the slowing of one runner caused another to clip his heel and before anyone could tell what had happened, three of the runners went from vertical and moving forward to horizontal and sprawled unmoving on the hard, unforgiving oval. Two of the three, Zachary Milford and Thorne Stryker were among the pre-race favorites.

The large, sun-baked crowd gasped in unison as the falling runners disrupted the smooth movement of the highly anticipated race. Zach Milford stayed on the ground in prone disbelief at his bad luck, watching the field run away from him like a group of young kids playing “ditch Zach”. Theo Williams and Thorne Stryker immediately rolled to their feet and took off after the lucky thirteen with two and a half laps to run. They ran together for 200 yards until Williams gave up hope for the chase and dropped back, resigned to the position forced upon him by the fates of misfortune. Stryker, however, locked his eyes on the back of the nearest runner and drove himself forward with a smooth stride carrying the valiant effort of a noble, but certainly lost cause.

At the halfway point of the race, most sets of eyes in the stadium focused on the tail end of the group of milers where Stryker had moved up on the field of competitors who had remained upright. As the runners moved to the backstretch of the third lap, the crowd moved together to their feet. Stryker strode past half the racers by the end of the third lap so that he sat in seventh place at the start of the fourth and final circuit of the track. So focused was the attention of everyone in the stadium that no one noticed a female high jumper setting a new meet record. The noise in the crowd grew with each runner he passed, but with three-fourths of a lap remaining until the finish, Stryker's confidence wavered. His throat burned as his lungs heaved too little oxygen in and out as fast as possible. His legs moved without feeling, as if entirely on their own, but his forearms and shoulders ached from the effort and his stomach began to feel nauseous. Even so, he willed himself onward and the runners finished the backstretch of the final lap and moved through the last turn with Stryker in fourth place and with fans across the stadium cheering wildly for the gutsy, even heroic performance.

The fall and the subsequent effort to make up lost ground had taken everything from Stryker's energy reserves. He became slightly light-headed from oxygen debt and he struggled to maintain focus and form. His legs now seemed heavier than tree trunks and mechanical in their motion and he was sure that they would stop working at any moment. And still, he refused to give in. The runners hit the final straightaway in a tight group of four with the finish line in sight. Fans who had never before seen Stryker jumped up and down and yelled to urge him onward in his unbelievable quest. Stryker's stomach fully joined in the agony of his muscles and lungs as he fought to retain some semblance of fluidity and reach the impossibly distant finish line. Those who stood nearest the track marveled afterward at the calmness evident on Stryker's stoic face throughout the final frantic yards to the finishing tape.

After crossing the line, Stryker refused to allow himself to collapse to the track despite the insistence of every body part he could still feel. His head pounded from a lack of oxygen as his blood flowed to his exhausted legs and arms. He rested his hands on his knees while searching desperately for air and valiantly fighting the urge to throw up. He felt pats on his back and shoulders and finally hands grabbed his arms and gently moved him forward with steps as uncertain as his first ones, seventeen years earlier. Eventually he found the strength to lift his head and he was shocked to see and hear people across the stadium still on their feet and cheering more than a minute after the race ended. Stryker finished in second place in what many veteran track fans described as the most remarkable and courageous race they had ever witnessed.

Three weeks following the Ohio State High School Track Championships, and two weeks after Throne Stryker's eighteenth birthday, James G. Garfield High School held its graduation ceremony for 417 seniors. Cameras flashed as smiles beamed equally from the audience and from those wearing caps and gowns. Encouraging speeches about limitless futures worked more to fill time than to inspire, but the general sense of giddiness could not be squelched. Nearly half of the graduates left immediately from the ceremony for a bus ride that took them to the S.S. Holiday for a parent organized all-night graduation party on Lake Erie. Stryker boarded the boat in a jubilant mood with two of his best friends. His elation and relief at the end of high school were tempered somewhat by the realization that he might never again see some of his fellow students with whom he had shared the last thirteen years of public education.

"Oh man, I can't believe we've finally done it!" gushed Simon Getz with a skip in his step as he eagerly checked out the amenities of the boat. At 5'5", Getz looked up to almost all of his male classmates, but remained one of the most outgoing. His longish hair highlighted his hawkish features, but couldn't hide the piercing brightness of his green eyes. He aggressively threw his arms around both Stryker and Jeff Stepanik. "We're out baby! No more Garfield. No more old man Ank. No more six mindless periods a day. We're free!"

"Feels good, don't it," agreed Stepanik, the largest and generally quietest of the three. "It's all been amazingly fast here at the end though. I still can't believe we're actually finished."

Getz frowned for the first time in hours. "What the hell are you talking about? Fast? Man I thought we'd never get outta there." He shook his head in disbelief and disengaged his arms from the nearby shoulders. "I bet this night'll go fast, though."

"Oh yeah," Stepanik agreed while stepping to the side of the boat to look out at the receding shoreline. "And did you see Kate the Great when we got on? Wow! Graduation sure didn't do her any harm."

"Hey, just calm down there Romeo," Getz kidded his friend with a nudge to the ribs. "And what's up with Stryk over here. A little quiet are we? Maybe his name isn't the only thing that's thorny tonight. You in a bad mood, bro?"

Stryker's thoughts came back to the present from someplace far away. "No, I'm good. Just gotta . . . . I don't know. Definitely glad to be away from the cameras and all the smiling, though. How many pictures do they need, huh?"

Getz laughed. "Your mom's always been that way. I bet she took a picture of you every day you went off to school for the past twelve years, right?" He pushed Stryker on the shoulder and winked at Stepanik. "I guarantee you they'll be waitin' when we get back tomorrow morning to get a picture of their golden boy as he steps off the boat. Right golden boy?"

Stryker ignored the jab, which he realized wasn't all that far off the mark. His parents always had been more than a bit obsessive over their only child. It didn't bother him for the most part, but he hadn't really realized that their doting nature had caught the attention of others. "Yeah, they'll take a picture of me," he said in feigned resignation, "but they're really hoping they can sneak a few shots of you in there."

"What about it, Stryk?" Stepanik interrupted semi-seriously as he turned his attention away from Kate. "What're your folks gonna do when you head off to California in the fall? Spend all day looking at pictures of their boy?"

"I bet they tried to talk you out of that meaningless scholarship, huh?" teased Getz. "Probably told you that a full ride to Stanford to play defensive back and study engineering wasn't that big a deal, right? Cleveland State would be just as good."

"Hey, there's nothing wrong with Cleveland State," offered Stepanik in a mock defensive tone and a push of the smaller Getz. "Seriously, though. Aren't they bummed about you moving across the country?"

"They're not nearly as upset as Getz is," Stryker nodded to his left. "Who's gonna help him with his homework after the second day of class?"

"Yeah, right," Getz shot back. "I carried you for the past four years and everyone at Garfield knows it. In fact, I heard some people talkin' during the ceremony saying they couldn't believe you were takin' the scholarship when I was the one who really earned it. You know, you really might need to take me along just to make sure you keep your head above water, buddy."

"Yeah, I'll miss ya all right," Stryker responded, "but not as much as I'll miss Mom. Or Kate. Or Anderson. Or Winger. Or Putziel. Or Ank. Or. . ."

"All right, all right," Getz interrupted. "I get it. Go ahead and go off to Stanford with all the blond chicks and brainiacs. You'll see how much you like it."

With laughs and hand slaps all around, the three friends turned their backs on the water and waded into the middle of the large, decorated party boat with plans and hopes for a memorable night with their classmates.

CHAPTER TWENTY-TWO

The SS Holiday arrived back at shore at just before 8:00 on a dry, brisk Sunday morning with a load of teenage passengers who were tired, but still wired with excitement. The adult chaperones were merely tired. Other than two incidents of drinking and three of seasickness, the night had been relatively problem free and ideally memorable for all. Both hugs and tears shared the stage as the trip came to an end, bringing with it the reality of the conclusion of a longer journey as well.

Thorne Stryker stepped off the boat, happily arm in arm with Simon Getz, toward the throng of parents waiting to pick up their graduates and move them onward toward the next stage of their lives. The eyes of both Stryker and Getz scoured the landing looking for Stryker's mother and her ubiquitous camera they had joked about earlier. It didn't take long for them to spot Getz's mother, but neither of Stryker's parents, generally at the front of the crowd, appeared among the greeters.

"Looks like you've been stood up, buddy," Getz kidded his friend. "Maybe now that you're a graduate heading for California the folks are ready to drop you like a hot potato."

"More likely they saw me walking off with you so they went to hide," Stryker shot back as his eyes continued to scan the crowd.

"Yeah, right. You're mom loves me and you know it. Truth be told," Getz patted Stryker sympathetically on the back; "they probably never really liked you all that much, and now they just don't have to pretend anymore."

"I suppose you're probably right," Stryker nodded in agreement at the jab. He smiled but in fact was a bit puzzled at his inability to find his parents in the crowd. They had clearly stated their plan to pick him up, as was obviously the case with most others on the boat and their parents. Even so, they didn't seem to be there.

Stryker and Getz walked up to Mrs. Getz who greeted each of them with a vigorous hug, much stronger than might be expected for a woman of her diminutive stature. "Did you have a good time?" she inquired cheerily.

"Yeah, it was great," Getz replied. "Lots of food, lots of girls, lots of alcohol. How could we not have a good time?"

"Simon!" she slapped him on the shoulder. "I can never get a straight answer from you. Thorne?"

"It was a lot of fun, Mrs. Getz," Stryker smiled at her. "And I kept Simon away from the alcohol after the first three hours. He'll be fine by noon I'd guess."

"Oh, you're both impossible!" she chided as she slapped Stryker's shoulder this time. "Your parents are coming, aren't they Thorne?" she asked in concern as she looked around.

"We decided they don't like him anymore," Getz offered.

"Well, I thought so," responded Stryker still scanning the faces in search of those most familiar to him. "But I don't see them. I take it you haven't seen them either?"

"No, I haven't seen them at all," Mrs. Getz's voice immediately morphed from playful to concerned. "You can certainly ride with us, or if you want to find a phone and call them, we'll wait for you."

"Umm, maybe you guys could wait for just a minute or so. If they don't show up, I'll ride home with you. No sense calling I don't think."

"Okay, that's fine," agreed Mrs. Getz with concern furrowed in her narrow forehead. "This certainly isn't like Tom and Marla, though."

"No, I'd have to agree with that," chuckled Stryker without humor. "They don't forget things very often."

"I already told you," Getz chimed in, refusing to let go of the opportunity. "They didn't forget anything. They just decided not to come. You're leaving them to go to Stanford – they've decided they're done with you too."

Mrs. Getz slapped him on the shoulder again and all three of them looked expectantly toward the parking lot.

Within ten minutes the boat had emptied and all but a few stragglers were gone from the landing. Mr. and Mrs. Stryker had not come rushing up out of breath and apologetic, as each of them believed was certain to happen. Stryker tried to erase the worry from his mind as he accepted the fact that they weren't going to show up.

"Well honey," Mrs. Getz broke the silence, "why don't we take you home. I'm sure there's a perfectly good reason for why they're not here." She gave a stern look at her son letting him know that more of his jokes were not welcome.

"Okay, thanks," Stryker agreed. "Sorry to trouble you, but I guess I don't have a lot of options right now."

"You know it's no trouble at all, Thorne," Mrs. Getz assured him. "I'm sure you boys must be tired though, so let's get going."

The Stryker home looked the same as it had the day before when they'd left for the graduation ceremony. Simon Getz fought a losing battle against sleep and Stryker insisted that he and his mother didn't need to wait around while he found out about his parents. He waved cheerfully goodbye and walked up the stone path to his front porch. As he approached the door his attention turned, as always, to the beginning of letters carved in the wood near the bottom left corner. The decade old vandalism brought more sadness than usual for the young graduate who forced his attention away from the gouging. The locked door rejected his entry attempt so Stryker grabbed the key from under a faded ceramic flowerpot on the porch to let himself in. He turned to wave once again to Mrs. Getz who then drove off after a final hesitation.

Cold and quiet enveloped Stryker as soon as he closed the door and stepped into his family's living room. "Mom?" he called out. "Dad? Anyone home?" The feel of the house already provided his answer, but he still asked once again. "Mom? Dad?!"

A puzzled Stryker looked quickly in the kitchen, family room and bedrooms only to reaffirm the answer that didn't come from his calls. No one was home. Worry quickly coalesced in the pit of Stryker's stomach and a surge in adrenaline removed any fatigue he carried from the all night party. Explanations for his parents' absence flashed through his head, but none that provided any comfort or relief from the quickly building anxiety. An accident? Severe illness? Heart attack? A crisis at his father's company? A problem with friends that demanded their immediate abandonment of everything else? Stryker knew his parents, and that knowledge carried with it the certainty that their failure to show up at the boat and their absence from home now carried ominous messages. He did not know, however, what that meant for his best immediate course of action.

Stryker started with the phone. He called his father's office and the company's main number. He received no answer as was to be expected on a weekend. He felt badly about calling any homes on a Sunday morning, but his worry outweighed his trepidation. Half a dozen calls to his parents' friends added to the number of puzzled and anxious people in town, but provided Stryker with no meaningful information.

He hung up the phone and wracked his brain for explanations and possible next steps. He guessed that phone calls to the police and hospitals should come next but he desperately wanted to exhaust all other possibilities before making those calls. Stumped, he sat next to the phone with his hands pressed together, forefingers against his lips, until his head jerked upward at the ringing of the doorbell. Stryker jumped up and bolted to the door to let in his parents who had forgotten their keys. Instead, he instantly felt a twenty-pound weight hit his stomach as he opened the door to see two uniformed police officers standing on the sun-drenched front porch.

"Thorne Stryker?" asked the Hispanic woman who was the younger and shorter of the two officers. She held her hat across her stomach with her left hand while her right hand hung loosely over the pistol on her hip.

"Yeah, what happened?" Stryker demanded immediately looking first at the woman and then at the male officer who held his hat tucked under his right elbow. Both carried grim but otherwise expressionless faces. "Is this about my Mom and Dad? Tell me what's going on?" Stryker couldn't hide his impatience even though he hadn't given either officer the time to answer.

"I'm Officer Perez and this is my partner Officer Day. May we come in for a minute?" the female officer asked politely as she nodded to the room over Stryker's shoulder. Day's attention appeared to focus on the impeccable shine of his black shoes.

Stryker tried ineffectively to calm himself and to hide his exasperation over the appearance of the worst of all possible visitors to his home. "Uh, yeah, sure. But please tell me. Is this about my parents?" He looked to both officers as they stepped quietly into the house and gently closed the door behind them.

"Yes, I'm afraid it is," responded Perez who glanced at her partner who had not yet spoken. "We have some bad news." Perez held her hat in her hands crossed in front of her as she tried to find a standing position that would ease the awkwardness that she felt. She failed, but did her best to hide her discomfort.

Stryker remained standing and kept his eyes focused on Perez while he felt the blood drain from his face. His fingers tingled and he unconsciously separated his feet to shoulder width to provide a solid foundation. "What is it?" he asked, somewhat surprised that his voice responded to the mental command.

Perez looked again at Day who remained motionless but physically relaxed and made no offer to step in and help out. She sighed while she fidgeted slightly and looked back to Stryker. "There's been an accident."

"My parents?" Stryker jumped in quickly. "They were supposed to pick me up this morning but they never showed up. I haven't been able to reach them since I got home. What happened? Are they hurt?"

"I'm afraid it's worse than that, son," Perez offered unwillingly in a softly compassionate voice. "Their car was hit late last night by a tanker truck." She paused and looked at the floor as though she would find an excuse to not have to continue. Seeing nothing, she looked back up at the eighteen-year-old graduate. "They were both killed instantly."

Stryker heard the words but the processing of their meaning was far from instantaneous. An accident. Tanker truck. Killed instantly. His parents weren't home. His parents weren't coming home. Dead.

"I'm sorry Thorne," Perez began again with wide eyes that revealed the pain she felt in her role as the messenger of death. "Is there someone else we should be talking to as well? Someone that you can talk to?" She reached out her hand to lightly touch Stryker's forearm.

Stryker continued staring out the window before finally offering his limited response. “Umm, no. I’m an only child.”

“Well, someone else?” Perez probed with sincere sympathy. “Aunts or uncles? Any other relatives nearby?”

“No,” Stryker responded matter-of-factly. “Both my parents are only-children too. Were,” he corrected. “No grandparents.”

The pain showed more strongly on Perez’s face. Day remained still and silent as he watched the drama unfold with detached interest. Perez clearly detested her role but finally spoke again. “How about some friends or neighbors? Is there someplace we can take you for now so that you’re not alone?”

“Ah, yeah, well, I’ll go,” Stryker responded as best he could although his focus was not on her question. “I’ll go in a bit. You don’t need to . . .” his gaze returned to the window although his eyes took nothing in.

“I’d really feel better if we took you somewhere,” Perez offered in the same quiet voice. “We can wait outside for a few minutes if you want.”

“Where?” asked Stryker.

“Just out in our car,” responded a confused Perez.

“No, the accident. Where was the accident?” Stryker asked.

“Oh,” Perez scolded herself internally. “They were on Route 11 coming into town. It was sometime after midnight.”

“Are you sure?” Stryker responded quickly with sudden energy and a hint of optimism in his voice. “I mean, are you sure it was them? Could there be some kind of mistake?”

“I’m sorry, son,” Perez softened once again. “It was your father’s car and we found identification with them. Also, the police chief was a friend of your father’s and he positively identified both of them. I’m sorry.”

Stryker nodded in acceptance but said nothing more. Day shuffled his feet in quiet discomfort.

"Um, so, someplace we can take you for now?" Perez asked once again with another gentle touch on Stryker's arm.

Stryker shook his head. "No thanks," he said in a near whisper. "I'm just gonna stay here for now. I'll be fine."

Stryker's stoic demeanor hid the most natural reactions, but Perez worried about the emotional shock for the young man so she persisted in her efforts. "It's really no trouble and we're actually under orders to not leave you here alone," she fibbed. "You can take some time before we leave, but we really need to take you somewhere for now. It's standard procedure in cases like this."

Stryker looked away from the window to glance at Day before settling his hard eyes on Perez, giving the officer the feeling that he was much older than his teenage years. "I'll go later," he said calmly but forcefully. "Thank you for coming by, but I'm going to stay here for now. I have places I can go and I will later on, but not right now." His eyes never wavered from Perez. "You can go now."

Perez looked at Day who merely shrugged before turning slightly toward the door. Perez shook her head and dropped her shoulders. "Here's my card," she extended her hand toward Stryker. "I'll check in with you later, but you can call me anytime."

Stryker took the card and moved across the room with the officers. Day opened the door and Stryker held it open. Perez turned to say something else but thought better of it and merely offered a sympathetic smile. The two officers walked slowly away from the house while Stryker closed the door on life as he'd known it.

CHAPTER TWENTY-THREE

In the month after the death of his parents, Stryker found that the individual days seemed to drag on interminably, but somehow the weeks passed quickly. He sat home alone on a stiflingly hot Sunday afternoon that marked four weeks since the return from the graduation night boat party. Four weeks from learning about the death of his entire family. Four weeks since instant adulthood. He sat with the windows open and a baseball game on TV but if he were asked which teams were playing, he wouldn't have been able to answer Cleveland and the Chicago White Sox without looking closely at the screen.

Stryker jumped slightly from his chair and from his mindless staring at the TV with an unexpected and loud knock on the front door. His natural instinct told him to ignore it until he looked up to see the face of Simon Getz peering at him through a window next to the door. Without getting up from his chair, Stryker waved to Simon to come in and then reached over to turn off the baseball game.

"Hey, buddy, how 'ya doing? Nice door," Getz greeted cheerfully as he plopped himself down on the sofa opposite Stryker's chair. Getz's hair trailing out from under his Cincinnati Reds baseball cap and over his collar was longer and more unkempt than Stryker had ever seen it in their years growing up together. Getz had refused to cut his hair since well before graduation and now he promised to let it go at least until Christmas, although he threatened a full year. Stryker thought it looked silly but didn't verbalize his opinion.

"Uh, okay. Hot." Stryker shrugged with his mouth and eyes and nodded toward the outside. "Yeah, I just replaced the door," he paused briefly, recognizing the awkwardness of his words. "So, what's up with you?"

"Not much with me. Mom is off to some family deal in Toledo and wanted to drag me along too, but I told her I wanted to see you instead. She was all over that, so thanks for the excuse." Getz smiled and offered a palms up, 'I couldn't help it,' look. "Haven't seen you much lately, though Stryk. Been kinda worried. You sure you're doing okay?"

Stryker nodded seven times without saying anything before he finally looked up and out the window beyond Getz's shoulder. The brightness of the sunshine revealed streak marks on the glass that his mother surely would have responded to instantly. Stryker pictured his mother standing on a chair to clean every inch of the windows, before bringing himself back to the present. "Uh, thanks, but yeah. I'm actually doing okay." He finally looked away from the window back at his friend who tried to hide a worried look. "It's actually been pretty busy, even since the funeral. I've been doing a ton of stuff with my dad's lawyer trying to sort things out with the estate. He's been really good, going over everything. I'd be in a mess without him. Brinkston Phell's his name."

"*Brinkston*? What the hell kind of a name is Brinkston?" Getz laughed and shook his head. "I don't know what anyone could possibly do *besides* become a lawyer with a name like Brinkston. That's almost as bad as Thorne."

"Yeah, thanks, Simon *Churringson*."

"Family name, and you know it. That means it doesn't count," smiled Getz as he played with the red hat he now held in his hands. "Besides, lots of people have weird middle names. It's the off-the-wall first names that always get me."

Stryker smiled slightly and looked back out the window but despite the effort, he couldn't readily conjure up the picture of his mother again. He looked again at Getz and smiled more genuinely than he had in some time. It was true that he hadn't seen much of his friends since graduation and it felt good simply to have Simon around.

"So, what kind of stuff is old *Brinkston* helping with anyway?" Getz broke back into the silence. "I mean, I assume it's okay to ask, right?"

"Oh yeah," Stryker assured him. "Just money stuff mostly. My parents both had life insurance policies that he helped me deal with and he's working on getting things transferred into my name. Just stuff like that, you know. It has to be done, but I'd really rather not do it. And, I wouldn't really know how either. So, like I said, he's been good."

"Hmmm. I guess I hadn't thought about you owning the house and everything else," responded Getz honestly with a look around the living room. "That means payments and bills and stuff too, right?"

"Well, I guess," agreed Stryker. "But the house is paid off so that would be the biggest thing. I'm just now getting a handle on everything though, so I'm still kinda clueless about a lot." He offered a semi-apologetic smile. "Anyway, it's all been pretty busy and taking time – that's why I haven't seen much of you lately. No offense, right?"

"Of course not, man," said Getz quickly. "I haven't been pushing it cause, you know, I wanted to give you your space if you needed it. As long as you know, me and mom are both here for you if you need anything at all. Okay?"

"Yeah, I know," responded Stryker with a thankful nod. "It's coming together."

"So, I hadn't really thought about it, but now that you mention it, what're you gonna do with the house? I mean, Stanford starts in early September, right? You can't just leave it here empty all year, can you? You gonna try to rent it out?"

Stryker hesitated momentarily before answering. "Actually, that's something else I'm going to have old *Brinkston* help me out with. I think I'm going to sell the house." It felt odd to Stryker to say the words for the first time and the pending reality made him feel guilty. It wasn't something he could hide very easily, however, with a "For Sale" sign soon to be up in the front lawn.

"No way, man! You're gonna sell it?" Getz yelped in disbelief. "You've lived here your whole life. I feel like I practically grew up here too."

"Well, you spent a lot of time here, I'm not sure about the growing up part though," Stryker kidded for the first time in quite a while. "Really, though, it's too big a house for me and I'm not gonna be here anyway, so it makes sense to sell it. I mean, I can't say I'm thrilled about it, but I'm not sure what else to do."

"Yeah, I guess," agreed Getz. "But what about when you come home for vacations and stuff? Actually," he paused as he considered the prospect, "I guess you could stay with us. I know mom would love it."

"Thanks, but we don't need to worry about that now," Stryker offered in newly practiced avoidance. "We can deal with that later." He paused and looked back outside where he could see the heat radiating off the street in shimmering waves. "You wanna go out for a Coke or something?"

Getz brightened immediately. "Yeah, let's go to Rackers. I'll buy you a burger."

"I'm in," said Stryker as he hopped out of his chair and headed for the newly installed door for one of the last times.

The following day, Stryker showed up at the law offices of Brinkston Phell a few minutes late for his 10:00 meeting. Phell's secretary led Stryker into the lawyer's office where Stryker waited patiently for Phell to finish a phone conversation that seemed to offer more counseling advice than legal advice.

"So, good to see you this morning Thorne," Phell began pleasantly after hanging up the phone. "I hope the weekend was good for you, as hot as it was."

"Yeah," Stryker replied. "I actually spent a little time with a friend so it was nice." He paused and looked over the impressive shelves of law books that gathered dust on the far wall. "I got the papers about the house title last week. Thanks."

"Oh, sure, that wasn't too difficult. We've also processed the insurance claims. I'd expect we'll see the checks in three or four weeks. I'll let you know."

"No problem." Stryker felt guilty even talking about the insurance money. He'd explained to Phell earlier that it didn't seem right that he should be getting money because his parents died. It felt dirty to think about taking the money. Phell had carefully explained that the purpose of the insurance was to provide for loved ones in just a situation such as his, but it still felt awful. He was glad that the money wouldn't arrive for a few more weeks.

Phell could tell the course of Stryker's thoughts, but chose not to address the issue again. "So, college isn't too far off. The biggest thing right now is to decide what you're going to do about the house come September. Any thoughts?"

Stryker expected the question and nodded confidently. "Yes. I've decided to sell it. Now. Is there someone you'd recommend for me to work with?"

Phell was caught off guard at Stryker's decisiveness. "Well, I know that selling it may make sense for now, but that's a pretty big one-way step. Are you sure you want to take that step right away? You could sell it just as easily in the fall, if that's what you wanted to do, but then you'd have more time to think about it." He looked for signs of uncertainty in Stryker's eyes but saw none. He continued nonetheless. "With the insurance money coming in you obviously won't need money from the house. Might make sense to wait a bit."

"No, I want to do it now. The sooner the better, actually. In an ideal world, I'd get it sold before the end of summer, but as you say, it's not a big deal if it ends up going into the fall. Either way, I want to list it now to get the process going." Stryker's voice remained firm and resolute to match his words.

"Are you sure you don't want to talk about options?" Phell inquired as he pondered the impetus for the young man's apparently firm position.

"Nope. I'm good," Stryker responded decisively.

"Okay," Phell relented with evident hesitation. He reached into his desk and pulled out a grayish business card with raised lettering that he handed to his young client. "Bonita Ainsley is as good as anyone and she usually gets pretty quick results. Here's her card. If you want me to go over the closing documents, or anything else, you know I'm here to help, right?"

"Thanks," said Stryker as he took the card and stood up from his chair. "Anything else I need to be concerned about right now?"

"Not right now," replied Phell who stood up from behind his desk. "As I said, I'll let you know when the insurance comes in.

And you be sure to let me know if you need any help with the house, okay?"

"You bet," Stryker shook the lawyer's hand. "Thanks again. I really appreciate all your help already."

With that, Stryker left the office of Brinkston Phell, never to return again.

CHAPTER TWENTY-FOUR

Thorne Stryker sat in front of Simon Getz's house under an August sun that burned the grass dry and his skin wet. The sun reflected brightly off the windows and recently applied white paint of the two-story house. Spending much of the summer in the sun left Stryker darkly tanned and oblivious to the sweat running down the middle of his back and beading up on his forehead. Getz came back from the house with two oversized glasses of pink lemonade on ice, courtesy of his ever-watchful mother, and handed one to Stryker.

"I don't know how you can sit there in the sun," marveled Getz with a touch of disgust as he plopped down ten feet from Stryker in grass that was darkened and cooled by the welcoming shade of a slightly bent oak tree. He took a lengthy drink from his glass. "It's too damn hot out here just in the shade."

"It's all about mind over matter, buddy," Stryker smiled over the top of his glass. "You know what they say – if you don't mind, it don't matter."

"Yeah, well I mind," admitted Getz with minor exasperation. "I don't know why it can't just stay in the low 80s. How come it's got to go to 95 or higher all the time?" He wiped his forehead with the back of his hand and looked at Stryker as if he actually expected an answer to his question. With one more drink only ice cubes remained in his glass and Getz then rolled the cool glass across his wet brow. Stryker had only sipped a bit from his lemonade.

Stryker merely shrugged at Getz's whining and stared intently at the dry but green grass in front of him. "You ready to head off to Columbus?" he asked. Getz was starting at Ohio State University in September.

"Gee, I dunno," Getz shook his head in exaggerated uncertainty and fear. "Columbus is a long ways away."

"Well, maybe not, but it'll still be different," Stryker assured him. "Living on campus and all. It seems like it's close, but it'll be a completely different world."

"I suppose," Getz conceded. "Still seems kinda lame compared to California. There's gonna be so many people from Garfield there – sometimes I'm sure it'll be just like high school only in a different place."

"Hmmph," snorted Stryker as he gazed into his lemonade glass. "There's so many students there you could probably walk the campus for weeks and never see another Garfield person. Besides, it'll be nice to be close enough to come home easily for vacations."

"Well, maybe," said an unconvinced Getz. "I still say Stanford's a ton more exciting, and not nearly as damn HOT," he exclaimed with a hint of anger as he looked up through the oak leaves at the bright sky. No snow in the winter, either."

Stryker's only response was a laugh and a sip from his lemonade glass.

"So, when's the closing on the house?" Getz asked in a calmer voice. "Didn't you say it was going to be this week?"

"Yeah. I got lucky and it sold the day after it was listed. All the closing stuff takes time, but they say it should be finalized in the next two or three days." Stryker tried to remove the wistfulness from his voice. "It's gonna be weird since I've lived there my whole life – but, I'm still happy it's done."

Getz nodded in agreement with a longing look at his empty glass. "It'll be weird alright, having someone else living there. It won't be quite so weird though since you're not gonna be here anyway. Mr. California man. Coming home for vacations will feel strange though." Getz motioned at Stryker's glass but Stryker declined the implied offer of a refill. "So, you've been working out a lot. You feel ready for football? That must start pretty soon, right?" Getz cocked his head and scrunched his eyebrows. "Come to think of it, when exactly are you leaving?"

"Actually, pretty quick now if nothing gets held up with the closing of the house." Stryker shrugged as if he hadn't really thought about it either. "I guess I could be gone by next weekend."

Getz still looked puzzled. "Don't they have a set time when you're supposed to be there? I mean . . ."

"Oh yeah," Stryker responded. "I told them about my parents though, and the house and all, and I'm pretty much okay to show up when it works for me. I'm sure they expect me by the time classes start in September, but I've got plenty of time for that. Football starts earlier, but they know what's going on."

Getz started to raise another question but decided against it. Instead he lay back in the cool, shaded grass and looked up again through the tree limbs to the crystal clear blue sky. "It's gonna be weird man. It's gonna be weird."

Five days later, a somewhat anxious Stryker walked into the offices of Merrill Lynch where, based on a referral call from Brinkston Phell, Stryker had an appointment with a broker named Julius Zarmi. Stryker arrived on time and was immediately escorted to

Zarmi's office, snuggled in among numerous others in a byzantine puzzle of corporate America. Stryker looked at all the well-dressed bodies in cubical after cubical after office and wondered about the engaging and important activities that kept them all serious and busy day after day.

Zarmi adeptly hid his surprise at Stryker's age, a factor that Phell hadn't referenced in his phone call. "Thorne? Nice to meet you. Julius Zarmi." He offered his hand and then pointed to a chair. Brinkston Phell tells me you're looking for a broker."

Stryker admired the classy simplicity of the office before he sat in the offered chair opposite Zarmi's large and slightly cluttered desk. "Yes I am," Stryker nodded while forgetting the office and keeping his eyes locked on Zarmi's. Stryker hadn't really thought about what a broker should look like, but he assumed that Zarmi fit the bill with thick eyebrows hovering between glasses and a balding head. Stryker guessed that the broker topped out at 140 pounds after a hefty Thanksgiving meal, but his slight frame didn't detract from his serious, intelligent and intent look. "I need to do some investing now and I need to make provisions for some future investing as well."

"That's what we're here for," Zarmi smiled and pulled out the paperwork necessary for opening a new account and arranged space in front of him on the desk. "Do you have any investing experience?"

"Umm, not directly," Stryker admitted. "Learned a bit about the stock market in school and my dad had some investments, that's about it."

"Oh yes, Brinkston told me about your parents. I'm very sorry," Zarmi offered with his hands folded on top of the papers.

"Thanks."

A moment of awkward silence followed before Zarmi began again. "So, do you have an idea of how you'd like to get started in the market?"

"Yep, but I'm not really thinking about 'getting started' if that implies easing into things slowly," Stryker responded with confidence as he continued his unrelenting eye contact across the desk. "Circumstances kind of necessitate that I jump in pretty much with both feet right off the bat. That's okay for you, right?"

"Well, yes, it's not really a problem for me," Zarmi said. He held up his hand and shook his head over Stryker's shoulder at a young clerk who poked her head in his office. He returned his attention to Stryker. "We always try to be a bit cautious with new investors, however. I want to make sure you know what we're doing – what you're doing – before we do too much."

Stryker nodded but his face didn't share in the agreement. "Like I said, circumstances don't really allow for a slow process right now. So, can we still move forward?"

"Um, yes, I mean, there are a number of forms for us to fill out and sign, but it's up to you what you want to do with your money. So tell me, what are you thinking about?"

"Ah, well, stocks," Stryker replied matter-of-factly. "I have some specific ones in mind but I'd be interested in your suggestions too. Overall, I want to be half invested in stable, consistent dividend paying stocks and half in growth stocks." He looked closely to read Zarmi's face, but wasn't sure exactly what he saw under the eyebrows.

"That's pretty aggressive, you know," Zarmi stated. "Full investment right now? And no bonds of any kind? You're obviously very young, but I'd still recommend something a little different than 100% common stocks."

"Well, I want to keep it simple," Stryker explained. "Now, before we talk specific stocks, I have two other questions."

"Shoot."

"For the dividend paying companies, I don't really want to deal with quarterly cash payments. Can I set it up so that all of the dividends are just reinvested in the company paying the dividend? Without me having to do anything, I mean?"

"Sure, we can do that. You'd still have to pay taxes on the dividends, even though you wouldn't actually receive the cash," Zarmi explained.

"No problem," assured Stryker. "I expected that."

"Okay," Zarmi prodded with evident uncertainty. "What's the other question?

"Once we're set up, can I send money monthly or maybe quarterly for you to continue to invest? I'd like to keep new money in the same fifty-fifty ratio, dividends and growth. Can we do that easily? It won't be a significant amount of money, but it will be steady."

"Sure, that's not a problem either."

"Okay, good," Stryker's appreciation of Zarmi's flexibility showed clearly on his face. He had expected more argument and reasoning about why things couldn't be done the way he wanted them. "Oh, one other thing. For the future investments, can I give you authority to choose what stocks the new money goes toward? It may not be practical for me to send specific instructions with the money each month."

Zarmi blew air noisily out of his mouth and looked down at the papers in front of him. "Well, we can set up the account for broker discretion, but it's not really advisable. It's your money after all, and we can't guarantee how your investments will perform." Zarmi looked down as he drummed his fingers on the desk. "Bottom line, we don't want our customers upset if we make choices for them and then they aren't happy with the results. I can certainly make recommendations, but ultimately, you should be making the choices. Especially with the aggressive investment plan that you propose." He gave a look of fatherly experience across his desk.

"Well, I'm not worried about that," Stryker assured him despite the look. "We can put it in writing however you want to make it work for both of us. Okay?"

"If that's what you want," Zarmi agreed reluctantly and with a touch of disbelief.

Stryker continued despite Zarmi's evident concern. "Great. So can we talk about specific stocks?"

"We've got the account paperwork to do, but sure, we need to talk about stocks too. May as well get started." Zarmi shuffled papers on his desk and then looked back at his newest and youngest client. "First, how much money are you talking about investing?"

"Well, like I said, I'll keep adding each month, but here's what I have right now," Stryker reached into his pocket for checks he brought along to sign over. "My parents were somewhat obsessive about insurance. For now, between the insurance money and the sale of the house and other things, I've got $950,000."

"Let's get started," Zarmi smiled.

One week later, with $800 in the bank and $950,000 invested in stocks of a variety of companies, Stryker sat eating in a McDonalds restaurant with Simon Getz and Jeff Stepanik. They playfully talked about school experiences dating back to first grade until Stepanik pushed them in another direction.

"So Stryk, what's up that you're just dying to share with us?" Stepanik probed with the right side of his mouth upturned slyly.

"Whadya mean?" asked Stryker innocently with Getz stuffing fries in his mouth while looking inquisitively at both of them.

"You know exactly what I mean," Stepanik accused. "You demand that we all get together for lunch and then you sit there quieter than anybody with this faraway look on your cute little face. Something's on your mind and it's high time you told us what it is."

Getz looked from Stryker to Stepanik and back again. "What?"

Stryker shrugged as he finished chewing a mouthful of cheeseburger. "Yeah, you're right," he admitted with a heavy sigh. "I do have a bit of news to share."

"What is it?" Getz and Stepanik asked in unison with eyes locked onto Stryker. Both put down their food as they focused across the table.

"Well, I called yesterday to tell Stanford that I'm not going," Stryker stated with immediate relief at having the decision out in the open for the first time.

"What?!"

"Yep. I turned down the scholarship and said that I wouldn't be showing up." Stryker slowly twirled his drink cup on the table.

Nobody said anything or ate anything for a moment as Getz and Stepanik were both stunned into silence. Stryker took a swallow of his drink and conveyed his sincerity with the seriousness of his eyes and mouth.

Getz finally responded. "But, no way man. I mean, Stanford's always been your dream. You've talked about going there since we were freshmen. How can you turn it down now?"

"He's right Stryk, you can't do this," Stepanik chimed in. "School's about to start. What, what're you gonna do if you don't go?"

"Well, I've already done it," Stryker responded. "I called them, but I also put it in writing and mailed it yesterday. It's done."

"Okay, but, so what about it," Getz sputtered. "It's too late to go someplace else, right? You gonna sit out a year? What are you gonna do?"

"Actually, that's why I wanted to get together with you guys today," Stryker started to explain but then hesitated while looking at his two friends. "I um, I leave tomorrow."

"Huh?" Stepanik questioned while Getz merely stared.

"I leave tomorrow," Stryker repeated. "I joined the Army."

CHAPTER TWENTY-FIVE

The large pastoral setting and relative quiet of the surrounding isolation gave Fort Benning the feel of summer camp prior to the arrival of hundreds of urban kids ready to be let loose upon the grounds. Stryker couldn't be sure, however, as he'd never joined the flocks of kids at summer camp. He'd never been to Georgia before, either, but it would now be his home for at least the next three months.

Stryker's official reporting date was on Sunday, but his enlistment information indicated that he could arrive any time on Saturday. Thus, he walked through the gate at 10:00 Saturday morning ready to take on the military commitment he had chosen instead of college. The reception period provided Stryker with a new, extremely low maintenance haircut along with uniforms and personal gear issued by his new employer. He also endured an extensive physical examination and an initial physical fitness test. Stryker found the medical exam at the hands of the Army doctors to be more trying that the relatively low-key fitness testing. Finally, he received an assignment for barracks space and plenty of regulations regarding upkeep of his uniform, barracks and gear. The overall regimentation and control felt good to Stryker, although he had no doubt that just six months earlier he would have found it stifling and unbearable.

Stryker's "Red" platoon consisted of thirty new recruits who shared a barracks and made up one fourth of their overall company. The other three platoons in the company received the creative monikers of Yellow, Blue and Green. The daily life of every platoon member answered to the whim of the platoon's drill sergeant – Peter Wick for Stryker's Red Platoon. For the recruits, however, Wick had only one name, and that was Drill Sergeant. Most often his name was Yes Drill Sergeant, occasionally it was No Drill Sergeant, but it was always Drill Sergeant.

For the past twenty-four years Wick wore an Army uniform, the last three of those years as a Basic Training instructor. His fighting days were now a part of his past, but given the changing nature of combat, he felt no great remorse over his current training assignment. He actually enjoyed the process of molding novice recruits, although he would never admit the fact to anyone other than his wife. He maintained a fit and trim 178 pounds on his 5' 11" frame, and his face remained youthfully unlined. Sunglasses or a perpetual squint hid his black eyes, though most believed that no recruit had ever looked directly into those eyes to verify their actual existence. His hair sported the first flecks of gray, but the tight cut, which he wouldn't have changed outside the Army, hid his only physical sign of age.

Peter Wick introduced himself to Red Platoon at 4:30 am on day one of the first phase of their Basic Combat Training. The thirty recruits had universally, though quietly, groaned the day before with the introductory explanation that wake up time was 5:00 am, with fall in time at 5:30 on the company grounds. Nobody hesitated, however, when Wick rousted the unconscious group with instructions to be on the grounds in twenty minutes.

They scrambled to shave, dress and secure their bunks in the allotted time. At 4:50 am, thirty men, ages 18-20, stood at attention before their drill sergeant.

"Do you know what time it is?" Wick demanded loudly in the intimidated face of Max Pearson, a recent high school graduate from a small town in western Maryland.

"No sir," Pearson responded quickly while remaining taut at attention and staring straight ahead. Stryker inwardly grimaced at the answer.

"Goddammit!" Wick bellowed in instant anger that surprised most of the platoon both for its volume and for the quickness of the evident volatility. "What are you, stupid or something? Did you already forget what you learned at reception?"

"No sir," Pearson answered a bit more timidly while still carefully avoiding the eyes of Peter Wick, and remaining perfectly still.

"I think you did," Wick shouted. "I think you're an idiot, that's what I think." Wick moved in front of Isaac West who stood three men over from Pearson. "What about you soldier?" Wick demanded, his face very close to West's. "Are you an idiot too?"

"No sir," West shouted his reply with confidence that belied his underlying fear.

"Goddammit I was right!" Wick yelled with spittle flying from his mouth onto West's shoulder. "You're all a bunch of idiots! Why I always get stuck with the losers I'll never know. Jesus Christ this is gonna be Goddamn impossible." Every man stood completely motionless while Wick ranted and moved down the line. He finally stopped in front of Benjamin Stone who stood rigidly next to Stryker. "What about you boy?" he brought his nose within inches of Stone's. "Do you know what goddamn time it is?"

"No Drill Sergeant!" Stone shouted his reply to Stryker's relief.

"That's goddamn right," exhorted Wick. "You the smart boy of the group Stone?" he asked looking at the name taped onto Stone's uniform.

"No Drill Sergeant!" Stone answered.

"At least he knows one thing," Wick spoke to the entire group as he walked away from Stone. "He knows my name and that's 'Drill Sergeant'. You morons got that? If I ask you a question your answer is 'yes drill sergeant' or 'no drill sergeant'. You got that?" he approached Marcus Johnson at the end of the line.

"Yes si. . ., er, Yes Drill Sergeant!" Johnson caught himself.

Wick shook his head and quickly walked so that he stood five feet in front of the motionless group. "Morons," he muttered loudly. "Now, do you know what time it is?" he yelled his question to the platoon in general.

Half the men responded, "No Drill Sergeant," in semi-unison.

Wick looked down at the ground and stretched his leathery neck before trying again. "I said, do you know what time it is!?"

This time the entire platoon responded together, "No Drill Sergeant!"

"It's 0455," Wick explained in his continued bellow, pronouncing the zero as the letter O. "Every other new recruit in this company is still cuddled up in his cot, sleeping away and won't be out here for another thirty five minutes." Wick motioned to the barracks on his left. "But, since I've got a bunch of morons in this platoon, we need a head start or you're never gonna learn anything." He looked carefully, hoping to see any visible form of protest, but no one providing him with the opening. "Now, everybody on the ground!"

With minor hesitations, some of the men went prone on the ground, some went to one knee, and a few sat. "Goddammit!" Wick began again. "When I tell you to hit the deck we're not sitting around the damn campfire roasting marshmallows. We're doing pushups!" he aggressively nudged one of the sitting men with the toe of his glistening black boot.

With every man on his stomach in the dirt, Wick resumed instructions. "Everybody up for pushups. Now, when I tell you to go down, you go down. When I tell you to go up, you go up.

You don't move without me telling you and you goddamn well better not be the first one to stop. Now, down!" He paused momentarily while walking among the men, inspecting their form. "Up!" The pauses and pacing continued. "Down! Don't you dare quit on me, soldier. Up!" Stryker could already see a quiver in the arms of Earl Michaels next to him.

"Down!" Wick continued. "Up! Goddammit get that ass down and your back flat," he yelled at someone distant from Stryker. "You're not humping the fat lady at the circus! Get that ass down! Everybody down!"

Stryker heard a groan and a flop behind him as one of the men gave up. Another immediately joined him.

"You goddamn sissies" Wick yelled. "What's that, five push-ups? Up! You had to do more than that in Reception. Down! A little isometric hold too tough for you candy asses? Up!" Others dropped out. "Don't goddamn lie there on the ground if you're quittin' on me. Down! Get your ass up and run in place while we see who's got some guts here! Up!"

Stryker heard more of his comrades drop out and join the jogging brigade, but he refused to turn his head to assess the platoon overall. He knew that Stone was still going on his right, but he had no clue about anyone else. Stryker's shoulders ached and he struggled to hold the down position and then push himself up again. Holding the upright position with locked elbows provided a relatively welcome relief.

As they went down once again, Stryker was physically finished, but he willed himself to not give in. When Wick finally yelled 'up', Stryker's arms shook, but he fought gravity and fatigue to slowly move his body back to the plank position. Stone struggled also, but didn't make it up. Stryker held himself up, but ready to call it quits at the next 'down' command.

"Fall in!" Wick instructed. Stryker struggled to his feet while others stopped jogging and resumed their places in line. Wick walked over to eyeball Stone and Stryker but said nothing to them individually. "Left face!" he commanded.

Stryker desperately wanted to rub his shoulders but resisted the urge. He was on his way to becoming a soldier, he thought to himself.

CHAPTER TWENTY-SIX

On the fourth day of Basic Combat Training, Stryker awoke with his platoon at 4:55 am slightly groggy, but still eager for his next day of training. He lay still for a moment, thoughts focused on the day ahead until he got up to find his locker open. Inside he found scuffed boots under his crumpled uniform on the floor of the locker. On closer inspection, he found a tear on the collar of his uniform, and he could not locate his belt at all. His stomach dropped off a cliff with fear gripping him instantly as he thought about falling in for inspection before Drill Sergeant Wick. He looked around at others crawling and jumping out of bed and preparing themselves for the day, but nobody seemed to be paying him any attention. Bile moved up his throat in panic before Stryker fought it back and took action.

His facial hair grew slowly so he hoped that he could get away with not shaving that morning. Instead, he grabbed his shoe polish and set to work on his boots as quickly as he could, still glancing around to gauge any reactions or visible interest from his platoon mates.

"What the hell are you doing, man?" asked James Martinez who bunked next to Stryker. "I thought you cleaned those last night?"

"So did I," responded Stryker without losing focus on the job at hand.

"You need anything? Can I help?" offered Martinez.

"No way, man," responded Stryker. "Just get yourself ready – no use two of us getting into it with the Drill Sergeant."

Martinez exhaled in relief at being let off the hook, but he still made up Stryker's bed before returning to his own preparation for the day.

Stryker looked in and around his bunk and locker for the missing belt when Wick's voice boomed through the barracks as if projected by giant speakers. "You boys better be quick this morning. Fall in for inspection at 0520 today. You need extra parade ground time so get your asses moving! You've got three minutes."

Stryker put on his uniform and his newly polished boots. He looked desperately for a spare belt, but knew that there was none to be found. He checked the status of his bed and closed his locker only to find streaks of what looked like nail polish on the locker door. Stryker swore under his breath and ran out to join his platoon for inspection.

Wick's mood seemed uglier than it had been on prior days as he reamed the platoon as a whole for their lack of military promise, and selected individuals for various minor transgressions. Ed Stanovsky drew Wick's ire until a sideways glance at Stryker stopped Wick in mid-scream. Instantly, his face buried itself against Stryker's with the smell of coffee bursting from his mouth with every angry syllable.

"Do NOT tell me that you're standing here for inspection with a wrinkled uniform and without a belt!" Wick's intimidating presence made everything else in the world virtually disappear for Stryker except for Wick's facial features that were exaggerated by their uncomfortable closeness to Stryker. "Drop and give me twenty!"

Stryker quickly performed the directed pushups and then resumed his position of attention and said nothing.

"Where the hell is your belt Stryker?" Wick's nose bumped against Stryker's and pulsating veins popped from his forehead.

"I don't know, Drill Sergeant," responded Stryker in a quieter voice than he intended.

"You don't know!?" Wick screamed incredulously. "Your government gives you a belt to wear and you lose it in less than a week!? I suppose you'd lose your rifle while in combat too, wouldn't you? Why don't you just lose your way out of here and quit this man's army if you're gonna be so goddamn careless!?"

Stryker stared straight ahead and kept silent.

"Go find your belt now while everyone else does pushups for you!" Wick directed. "Everyone hit the ground."

Stryker ran back to the barracks and looked once more around his bunk and locker but saw nothing. He didn't have time to look in every other locker but he scanned the rest of the room and looked under bunks with an increasing sense of dread. He was about to return to the grounds when he noticed something out of place in one corner of the barracks. He ran over and picked up a belt that he assumed to be his and he slipped it on while running back to his platoon.

Wick called the men to attention as Stryker returned and immediately locked his nose onto Stryker's once again. "I see you found your belt, soldier."

"Yes Drill Sergeant."

"Were you too busy wrinkling the rest of your uniform this morning to show up properly for inspection?" Wick asked in a mocking voice.

"No Drill Sergeant."

"Then what the hell are you doing on my grounds out of uniform!?" the volume increased with each word.

"I must have misplaced it Drill Sergeant."

"Misplaced it!? Goddammit I've got a whole platoon of morons here and you're the biggest moron of all! You're an embarrassment to the Army. What the hell is your problem?" Wick's voice contained anger of a different tone, which Stryker took to be real rather than affected for the sake of new recruits. Wick's face remained inches from Stryker's and the close-up distortion enhanced the magnitude of the anger.

Stryker tried desperately not to cower and he remained silently at attention while his mind wondered who had set him up in this way and what would set off Wick next.

It was the collar of his uniform. Stryker had attempted to tuck the tear into invisibility but his hurry for the belt had apparently exposed the damage to the collar. Wick was turning disgustedly away from Stryker when he caught sight of the collar and turned back to grab Stryker by the front of his uniform. By the time the haranguing was finished, Stryker looked forward to the two weeks of latrine duty during his personal time, as imposed by the Drill Sergeant, as well as a docking of his pay to purchase a new uniform.

In week two of Basic Combat Training, week one of latrine cleaning for Stryker, the platoon members sat one morning for three hours of basic intelligence and skills testing. It was the third year of a three year pilot program for the Army to determine if recruits could be directed more effectively to specialty training choices by assessing their innate abilities and incoming knowledge. Many training officers expressed skepticism, but they universally enjoyed the existence of one more reason to berate the ineptitude of the prospective soldiers. Sergeant Wick withheld no vigor in communicating his expectations to the Red Platoon.

Stryker had always enjoyed both the challenge and the stimulation of testing and he took on the task with energy and enthusiasm. He completed the test with more than thirty minutes of the allotted time remaining, then confidently closed his test booklet and remained quietly in his seat. Wick looked at his watch, shook his head, and muttered under his breath. He then motioned for Stryker to come forward whereupon he led Stryker into the hallway outside the testing room.

"What the hell are you doing now, Stryker," Wick asked in the closest approximation to yelling that was possible in a whisper.

"Nothing Drill Sergeant," came the innocent reply.

"Damn right nothing," Wick's voice rose was a bit louder. "Why the hell aren't you working on that test like everyone else?"

"I finished Drill Sergeant," Stryker explained calmly.

"Finished!? Goddammit soldier, if you half-assed your way through that test without trying I'll have your whole ass on latrine duty for the rest of your natural life!" Wick no longer even attempted to whisper. "I don't know what your problem is soldier, but I don't like your attitude and I don't like you screwing up my platoon!"

Stryker thought about his effort on the test and was certain that he had performed well. He had even double-checked most of his answers. He knew better than to argue with Wick, however, so he remained completely still and said nothing.

"Get your ass back in there!" Wick commanded without the accompanying threats that Stryker expected. Stryker took his seat and waited while the others completed the three hours of testing. Wick remained in a rotten mood the remainder of the day as he ran Red Platoon through more exercise and detailed training than normal and warned the soldiers about the test scores coming back the next day. Stryker enjoyed the running and physical training as much as he had the previous days, but numerous glares and comments came his way from the other recruits who clearly identified him as the sole cause of Wick's latest rage. Stryker ignored them as best he could while easily outdistancing the rest of the platoon in a fifty minute run.

Wick prepared to release the platoon for personal time, or cleaning time in Stryker's case, as he finished up his final rampage for the day at 8:30 pm. The men continued to disappoint Wick in their physical performance, their learning, and their potential as soldiers, but for the time being he fixated on their testing from the morning.

"This is the third year of administering this test," he explained for the third time that day. "The average scores of my soldiers have never been worse than second among the four platoons. I'll see the scores tomorrow, and if you morons break that streak," he glared at Stryker, "I'll work your asses so hard you'll be praying for easy days like today. Maybe it's time for some of you to figure out that you're just not Army material." He moved away from Stryker and paced to the other end of the lineup. "Now, get the hell out of my face," he ordered.

Back in the barracks before lights out, a few men played cards, a few wrote letters, and the rest spread out on their bunks in exhaustion. The exception was Stryker who cleaned and polished the fixtures and floor in the latrine. He moved as quickly as he could while taking care to be diligent and thorough. He had no intention of giving Wick any more ammunition for tomorrow's assault. He worked on the floor around one of the urinals when Ben Stone came in noisily beside him. Stryker looked up and moved to work on one of the sinks.

"What's your problem, Stryker?" Stone asked quietly but in a firmly accusatory tone.

"I've got no problem," Stryker responded a bit put off, but determined to ignore the jibe. "Just doing my volunteer work."

"Just getting the whole platoon in trouble, that's what you're doing." Stone hissed. "You're either screwing up or making everyone else look bad and either way, Wick comes down on all of us. Ever heard of being a team player?"

"Hey, look," Stryker replied defensively. "My only screw ups were someone else's doing, not mine. And if I'm making you look bad, then maybe you need to work a little harder. I'm not . . . hey, what the hell are you doing!?" Stryker interrupted himself as he saw Stone peeing on the floor with no attempt to hit the urinal.

"What? Oh gee, sorry about that," Stone grinned without humor. "The DS ain't gonna be too happy when he shows up for inspection in a couple of minutes." Stone stepped away from the urinal and faced Stryker. "Have fun, asshole."

Stryker flipped a sponge at Stone's face. "Clean it up yourself, jerk!"

Stone slapped at the sponge as it came toward him and stepped forward with a push to Stryker's chest. Stryker held his ground and locked eyes with Stone. Stone pushed again, harder this time and Stryker took a half step back to maintain his balance. The next movement from Stone was a fist flying toward Stryker's chin.

Stryker partially deflected the punch so that it glanced off the side of his head. He reached to grab the off-balance Stone but received a hard elbow to the stomach for his efforts. Stone spun around and threw another hard punch at Stryker's head. Stryker dodged the punch and responded with a short right to Stone's jaw. Stone's head jerked back, but then his whole body flew forward with a roar as he grabbed Stryker and wrestled him to the floor. The two men's arms were too fully engaged to throw any punches, but Stone managed to drive a knee into Stryker's thigh while his fingers tore at Stryker's neck. In another moment the latrine was full of men yelling and pulling Stone and Stryker away from each other and trying to restore order.

Suddenly, all was quieted by the dreaded booming voice of Drill Sergeant Wick. "What in the goddamn hell is going on in here!?" he questioned as he pushed through the excited crowd of soldiers.

"We're good, Drill Sergeant," responded Isaac West quickly. "Just playing around."

Wick quickly determined Stone and Stryker to be the focal point of attention and noted their red faces and the bright red streaks on the left side of Stryker's neck. "Goddamn playing around, huh?" he glared at Stryker for the umpteenth time that day. "Who the hell started this mess?" He looked briefly at Stone and then back at Stryker, neither of whom responded. "The rest of you get outta here," Wick commanded loudly.

Stryker and Stone stood at attention facing Wick while the other men moved out of the latrine, but stayed in listening range. Stryker calmed his breathing and his emotions as he contemplated his immediate options.

"I asked you who started this," Wick looked from one man to the other before settling his eyes on Stryker. "Is this your doing?"

Stryker hesitated only for a moment. "Yes Drill Sergeant," he responded through heavy breaths.

"Yes? What the hell's your problem, Stryker?" Wick demanded as he stepped menacingly closer to his quarry.

Stryker pursed his lips and shook his head but didn't otherwise respond.

"Two more weeks of latrine duty, soldier," Wick directed in a low voice. "And I want you on the parade ground at 0500 tomorrow for extra running before fall-in at 0530. You've obviously got some extra energy you don't need." Wick turned to leave but then stopped in his tracks. "And this latrine is a goddamn mess. Now get to work."

Stone followed Wick out and Stryker returned to cleaning. He ran nearly five miles in the morning before 0530 inspection.

The platoon stood at attention, ready to be released for dinner at 1700, or 5:00 pm, the next day when Wick brought up the looming issue of the test scores. Stomachs clenched in fear as the soldiers tried to imagine the tortures that would emanate from Wick in a worse mood than he'd already exhibited.

"I've seen the goddamn test scores from yesterday," he growled while the majority of the platoon refused to breathe. "You just barely beat out Blue Platoon," he hesitated and turned in his pacing, "but Yellow and Green were even worse. Now, go get some dinner."

The soldiers sorted through the words to determine their meaning, but quickly dispersed to the safety of the dining hall. As they moved away, however, Wick called out one more time.

"Stryker, stay here," he commanded.

Once everyone had cleared the area, Wick addressed Stryker directly. "What the hell are you doing here?"

"You called me here, Drill Sergeant," Stryker responded in confusion.

"No, what are you doing here in the Army," Wick demanded.

"Uh, learning to be a soldier, Drill Sergeant," Stryker's confusion remained unabated, but now complimented with a sense of dread.

"Drop the 'Drill Sergeant for a minute," Wick directed unexpectedly, "this is just man to man." He paused and assessed Stryker as if he'd find the answers hidden somewhere on the young man's face. "So tell me, what are you doing here in the Army?"

Stryker hesitated. "I'm not sure what you're asking, Sir."

"What about college?" Wick tried again. "Why the Army and not college?"

Stryker nodded. "I thought about college, Sir, but I decided the Army was the best place for me right now."

"Did you apply to college?"

"Uh, yes Sir."

"I assume you were accepted." He saw Stryker nod. "Where?"

"I'm not really sure why you're asking me this, Sir," Stryker responded.

"Where?" Wick remained undeterred.

"Ohio State and Stanford," came the reply.

"Scholarships?"

"Yes, Sir."

"But not West Point." Wick's voice remained calmer than Stryker had ever heard it. "So, I ask you once more. What are you doing in the Army?"

Stryker hesitated again, but Wick waited. "I wasn't ready for college, Sir. I thought the Army might be good for me and I wanted to serve my country."

Wick looked skeptical but withheld comment. "You know you aced that test yesterday," he stated without making it a question.

"I thought it was pretty straight-forward Sir."

"Highest score anyone's gotten in three years," Wick informed him. "But here you are screwing up inspection and getting in fights." Wick shook his head as if he didn't know where to go next. Finally he looked back at Stryker with a softer look than Stryker believed him capable. "I see that you're registered for Infantry School for your Advanced Individual Training?" AIT came after Basic Combat Training and provided soldiers the opportunity to receive specialized training in the field of their choice.

"Yes, Sir," Stryker admitted. "I was thinking about Intelligence, or maybe Military Police, but Infantry School seemed like the best general option since I didn't really know for sure what I wanted to pursue."

Wick nodded. "Well, it's probably a good choice for now. We'll have to see how things go, but what would you think about Ranger training?"

"Uh, I don't know," Stryker admitted. The Army Rangers had cross his mind briefly, but never as a serious consideration.

"Think about it. I'd be willing to give my recommendation, and it might be a good option for you. Now, go get your dinner."

"Yes, Drill Sergeant. Thank you, Sir." Stryker saluted and ran off to the dining room with all sorts of thoughts jumbled in his head. Two months later he began Infantry School, which lasted another six months. With acceptance into the Rangers, he then undertook Airborne School as the youngest in a recruiting class of twenty for the start of Army Ranger training.

CHAPTER TWENTY-SEVEN

Upon completion and graduation from Airborne School, Stryker was officially assigned to the 75th Ranger Regiment to begin the Ranger Indoctrination Program. Each of Stryker's training schools seemed to provide a significant step forward in both the physical and mental demands placed upon the soldiers. The Ranger Indoctrination Program, or RIP, added a final steep incline in the training intensity. For many soldiers, the acronym aptly depicted the near deadly nature of the undertaking.

As with every other level of training, Stryker excelled at both the learning requirements and the physical challenges. He enjoyed the patience and mathematical precision required by the sniper rifle just a much as he reveled in the pain and soreness that resulted from hand-to-hand combat. On numerous occasions he believed that he had reached the limits of his endurance, only to persevere and to find that virtually everyone else had broken before him. The occasional thoughts about classes and football at Stanford that popped up months ago were now long gone. Stryker knew without further question that he had made the right choice in pursuing the Army in general and the Rangers specifically. All the while, he rarely spent much money, so each month he sent at least half of his pay to Julius Zarmi at Merrill Lynch to add to his existing investment portfolio.

Throughout RIP training, Stryker felt certain at times that eyes beyond those of his instructors and fellow trainees were watching him. At times he learned, at times he trained, at times he simply endured, but the underlying feeling persisted that a greater evaluation process existed, beyond the successful completion of his Ranger training. Stryker's suspicions found confirmation in the final two weeks before achieving full Ranger status when a Major Dodd approached him for the first time. Stryker had seen Dodd once in a while, but Dodd had never conducted any trainings directly, nor had he ever spoken to Stryker or any of the other prospective Rangers. That changed when Stryker left the dining hall to return to his barracks one evening.

"Stryker, isn't it?" Dodd asked. "Major Dodd." Dodd's overweight softness did not represent his entire military career and the accumulation of years certainly contributed to the many creases on his forehead as well. Stryker marveled at the smallness of his eyes and briefly thought that Dodd would never be shot if the enemy operated under the order to wait until they saw the whites of his eyes. He didn't appear to have any.

Stryker saluted and stood smartly at attention. "Yes, Sir."

"At ease soldier," he commanded as Stryker relaxed, but only slightly. "In fact, I'd like for you to take a walk with me."

"Sir, I'm expected in Night Navigation class in five minutes," Stryker explained while wondering about the odd request. Being asked to go for a walk simply didn't happen in the Army, and certainly not with a major he'd never met before.

"Yes," Dodd responded, "I've already spoken to Lieutenant Sanchez. You're excused from class for this evening. In fact, Sanchez says you won't really miss anything at all. Says you could be teaching the class just as well as him. Is that true Stryker?" Dodd began to walk away from the dining hall and Stryker hesitantly stepped forward to walk beside him.

Stryker felt incredibly uncomfortable and glanced around with paranoia to see if anyone noticed him walking with the major. After a moment's self-conscious uncertainty, he responded to Dodd's question. "Uh, no Sir. Lieutenant Sanchez is miles ahead of me in nighttime navigation." Stryker didn't look at the major, but was dying to read his face to help him find answers to the questions he didn't dare ask.

"So," began the major as he walked with a swagger in the form of a side-to-side roll with each step, "I understand that you don't have any immediate family, is that right soldier?"

"Yes, Sir, that's right." Stryker puzzled over the nature of the question, but also over the entire conversation.

"Any relatives or close friends who served in the Army?" the major asked.

"No, Sir. My father spent two years in the Air Force, but no one in the Army."

"Air Force, right. I know from what I see and hear that you're excelling in all aspects of your training. What do you think about it though, Stryker?" the Major paused for a moment. "What I mean is, is everything going okay from your perspective? Any second thoughts about your decision to join the Rangers?"

"Not at all, Sir," Stryker responded quickly, but without further explanation. His training had taught him to respond directly and concisely to his superiors. Explanation and expansive detail were not part of the military code of communication, and certainly not when communicating up the chain of command.

Dodd immediately recognized the limitations imposed by Stryker's perspective. "I want you to speak freely right now, Stryker. This entire conversation will be informal and off-the-record. Please, remember that."

"Yes, Sir," was the only response Stryker could come up with.

"Yes. Well, I'll ask again – any reservations or second thoughts about your decision now that you're almost through with training?"

"Honestly, no Sir." Stryker fought the urge to stop there as he felt as though the major was compelling him to say more. "It's been challenging, of course Sir, but I expected that coming in. Nothing's changed about my view on becoming a Ranger."

"Good, good. So tell me, through all the training you've certainly thought about using that training in combat right?"

"Sure. I guess we all do."

"So, you've thought about killing another man when the time comes," the major stated without making it a question.

"Yes, I suppose so, Sir."

"Will you be ready?"

Stryker thought about the strangeness of the question. The entire purpose of the training over the past year was to make soldiers ready to use the skills they were taught. Ultimately, that meant killing. The question of readiness or doubt had never been breached. Soldiers were also taught to follow orders without question. Thus, the major's query seemed odd. Who could possibly go through this training and NOT be ready to kill when the time came. To him, the question itself was nonsensical, but he kept that opinion to himself and instead responded courteously. "Of course, Sir."

"I assumed as much," the major explained, "but you'd be surprised at how often men aren't prepared, regardless of the training they've received. It's been a long time since my training," he mused more to himself than to Stryker. "They do a great job with you boys here though. Nothing but the best."

They walked toward the sunset for a minute in a silence that Stryker wasn't going to take the initiative to break as he still wondered what he was doing out there in the first place. Based on the major's questions, Stryker worried that he had done something to raise concerns or to shake the confidence of his trainers about his ultimate ability to be a Ranger.

Finally, Dodd spoke again in a very calm and measured voice. "When you finish here, week after next, you're not going to be assigned to one of the three Ranger Battalions."

"Excuse me, Sir?" Stryker questioned in immediate panic as he swallowed hard. Had it been decided that he couldn't do it? Were they about drop him from the Rangers after months of strenuous, but successful training? He stopped walking and turned to look directly at the major who was now three steps ahead of him. Stryker's heart rate jumped up dramatically and he felt the muscles tense in his back and his neck.

Dodd stopped as well and turned to motion Stryker forward. "It's fine, Stryker. You're not in any kind of trouble. In fact, just the opposite."

"I'm sorry, Sir, but I don't get it," Stryker stated honestly as he reluctantly rejoined the major in their aimless walking. "If I've done anything to . . ."

"The Rangers are the best of the best, right?" Dodd interrupted.

"Yes, Sir," Stryker agreed immediately.

"And better than that?" Dodd asked mysteriously with a slight grin on his face. "What about the best of the Rangers?"

"I . . ., I don't know what you mean sir."

"As you know, the Rangers are the best that the Army has to offer. The most highly trained and highly skilled. The most elite and effective fighting force in the U.S. Army, and thus of any army in the world. Even so, the Rangers have their limitations. Sometimes it's bureaucracy, sometimes the media, sometimes the other Armed Forces." A hint of frustration entered the major's voice, but he quelled it before continuing. "Over the years, we've found that even the Rangers have more limits than we'd like for some of the actions that are needed for the good of the country." Stryker wondered about the "we" but chose to say nothing. "In any event," Dodd continued, "the Rangers are the best of the best, but they're not the only option we have."

Stryker cocked his head to look at the major, but realized he had nothing to add to the major's comments at the moment.

"Ever heard of Omega Operations Stryker?"

"Ah, no Sir,"

"I didn't think so," said the major. "You're not supposed to. Omega Operations, otherwise known as Double O is your new outfit. Welcome Stryker."

"But, I'm a Ranger, Sir. Or I'm about to become a Ranger. That's what I've trained to be and that's what I want to be."

"Oh you're still a Ranger, Stryker," explained Dodd. "Only now you're among the elite of the elite. Omega Ops is small, specialized and almost completely off the books. As far as anyone back home is concerned, you'll simply tell them you're a Ranger. For people within the Army who may know more specifics, you're a Ranger on special assignment. You'll meet your team, and your new commander, Major MacAfee, as soon as you finish here next week."

"It seems like I should have lots of questions," Stryker stated as his stride slowed momentarily. "I'm sure I do, or I will, but right now I don't know what to ask."

Dodd stepped in to help him out. "The Omega team does everything that you've been training for as a Ranger. They can, however, often do it more quickly and completely independently of other operations. Sometimes they're able to take actions that are essential, but that we couldn't get authorized through formal channels. You'll be on the front line of action and the great thing for you is, you'll be more productive for the protection of this country than any other man you've been training with. You can make a difference.

"Well, that sounds good sir, and the action part does too," Stryker agreed. "I'm a little leery about the 'off the books' stuff though."

"Understandable," said Dodd. "Really though, it's more about efficiency and avoiding bureaucracy than anything else. And, there are some benefits for you."

"Okay." Stryker waited for more explanation.

"As I said, you'll see more action and you'll do more productive work for the U.S. than you ever would otherwise. Being mostly 'off the books' however, also means that you don't get a regular paycheck. Instead, all of your expenses are paid, including spending money, and you receive one annual check for $50,000. You get your first check as soon as you get started. You do what you want with that money – family, investment, whatever – because all your other needs will be taken care of. All we ask of you is that you do your job and do it while protecting the confidentiality of the unit."

Stryker smiled as he thought of sending $50,000 to Zarmi, but then his thoughts turned back to his current situation. "Why me, Sir?" he asked.

Dodd nodded as though he'd been expecting the question for some time. "As I said, Omega Operations, or Double O, consists of the best of the best and your training and performance easily put you at the head of the class. Also, all of your training officers, going back to Sergeant Wick give you the highest marks for integrity and personal responsibility. And, to be candid, your lack of family is a plus at this point as well." Dodd paused and looked to Stryker for a reaction that didn't come. "You're younger than anyone we've ever brought on board, but overall, you're exactly what we're looking for. You're a member of the Omega team, Stryker, and you should be proud. I know that you'll make us proud."

"Thank you, Sir," was all that Stryker could say. He had no idea how much he was going to love the team that he was about to join. Omega Operations provided Stryker's work, home, and family for the next fifteen years.

PRESENT DAY

CHAPTER TWENTY-EIGHT

Silvis Walker. Independence, Missouri. Stryker already hated the name and only partly because of the horrible deeds perpetrated by Walker. The real hatred stemmed from the combination of Walker's crimes and the fact that his named appeared on the Axman website. Now, therefore, he had become Stryker's problem and Stryker hated him for it. It may be only one final job, Stryker thought to himself, but it was one more job than he intended on taking. Silvis Walker. Independence, Missouri. What a blot on the name of humanity. Damn him, Stryker thought.

Stryker ran through the downtown waterfront to Myrtle Edwards Park, which snaked along the shore of Puget Sound for nearly two miles between the Seattle business district and the Magnolia residential neighborhood north of downtown. The sun reflected brightly off the water and a mild breeze ruffled the leaves of the trees that lined the middle of the park with pedestrian paths on both sides. Numerous walkers and joggers moved through the park in solitude, but with a sense of community grounded in their shared activity. Each runner or walker that crossed paths with Stryker offered a greeting, a wave, or a nod, but Stryker couldn't find the mood needed to respond. He moved swiftly through the park and out onto the streets toward the Magnolia Bridge, which climbed high above the park to the bluff that looked out over the Sound. He enjoyed being out on the streets and bridge where the pedestrian population mirrored that of vehicles in the park.

As Stryker ran, he thought about Walker and about the trip, or trips, he would need to make to Missouri. He knew little about the man's current movements or habits, which meant that a traditional research job lay ahead of him. Even without any real information, he thought about past jobs and played out possible options and scenarios in his head. He found his focus continually interrupted, however, by thoughts of simply ignoring the job and returning to the life of retirement that he had yet to begin. He resented the job, and with almost equal fervor, he resented the fact that he resented the job. He could do it, of course. He should do it. But at the same time, he wanted to be finished. He chased away the thoughts of ignoring the posting and refusing the job, only to have them re-emerge as soon as he focused on performance once again. He needed to get his mind right, he thought, or he'd be in no position to do either – the job or retirement – very well.

After finishing his run/internal debate, Stryker met LJ Perkins for a late breakfast at the Phinney Ridge Café in the Greenwood area in the north end of Seattle. Snuggled into a crowded neighborhood without any pretentious signs, the café was easy to miss, but consistently entertained large crowds for weekend breakfast. Phinney Ridge served sizeable, tasty omelets with crispy hash browns, but its true claim to fame came from the huge, gooey cinnamon rolls that its customers packed away in sufficient numbers to keep local heart surgeons struggling to find room in their calendars to schedule vacations. Perkins wallowed in gastronomical heaven the moment they walked in the door. Stryker avoided the cinnamon roll chaser, figuring that he was doing enough damage to his arteries with the sausage and cheese omelet alone.

Patrons waiting to be seated were tortured by the intoxicating smell of cinnamon rolls that loomed so strong it even carried out to the street and parking lot. Stomachs growled from customers in line who looked greedily from table to table in search of empty plates being carted away. Stryker and Perkins ignored those around them while they ate and talked food and sports for a while until Stryker suddenly got serious.

"I've taken another job," he said through a mouthful of delicious potatoes.

"What do you mean?" Perkins inquired with minimal enthusiasm and the majority of his focus concentrated on his plate. "A real job?"

"I wish," Stryker lamented as he set down his fork. "There was another posting," he said matter-of-factly.

"What?" demanded an incredulous Perkins who actually stopped chewing momentarily. "I thought you retired, man. That Axman stuff's supposed to be all over with. How can there be another posting?"

Stryker explained the discussion thread about retirement that followed his announcement, and the eventual posting identifying Silvis Walker. He found the details painful and he tried to remove the defensive tone from his voice.

"Yeah, yeah, I get all that," Perkins sputtered through a large bite of cinnamon roll, "but what the hell were you doing going to the site in the first place? I thought the point of retirement was that you didn't look for postings any more. You were done. How'd you let yourself get sucked back in?" Perkins stared at Stryker with disbelief written everywhere on his face.

"I don't know," Stryker shook his head in personal disappointment. "Ego I guess. I thought there might have been some sort of comment or acknowledgement of my retirement. Instead, the date was posted. Once I saw that, I had to go back just to see what was going to show up, and the name was there. Now, I don't know." He turned his palms up in surrender as he looked across the table at his friend.

Perkins looked exasperated as he set down his fork. "Well, so what? You've turned down posted names before. And that's when you were still officially on the job. Well, never 'officially,' but you know what I mean. Anyway, if you could ignore names before, why not now when you're supposed to be retired anyway?" Perkins' tone made it abundantly clear that he really didn't see any semblance of a dilemma.

"Yeah, I know," Stryker agreed. "I've been thinking the same thing. But this Walker guy is one bad dude, and he's gonna walk free and clear as far as the law goes. If I don't take the job, then what?"

"Not your problem man," Perkins mumbled through another bite as he'd succumbed to temptation and returned partial attention to his plate. "There's always gonna be someone like Walker out there whether you're on the job or not. Did you really think that all the bad guys would just disappear once you retired? No way man. If you're gonna retire, you're gonna have to accept the fact that guys like Walker'll be out there. You can't deal with all of 'em." He paused and made sure he had Stryker's full attention before continuing. "You've done enough already. Just walk away like you planned and forget about it."

"Yeah, I could," Stryker lamented, "if I hadn't gone back to the site. Now that I've seen the posting though, and I know about Walker, it's not so easy."

"What's hard?" Perkins asked with a note of frustration. "I know about Walker and I'm not feeling any compulsion to go kill the man. You knew about Walker from the news earlier and you weren't heading off to Missouri. Why is it now your obligation?"

"Cause it was posted for me," Stryker thought carefully as this was exactly the question that had been bothering him as well. "I know there are plenty of bad guys out there and I know that I can't deal with all of them. Wouldn't even want to try." He shook his head slightly. "Once it's posted for me though, it becomes my obligation. I mean, what if I don't take it and Walker goes back to what he's been doing. How can I ignore that?"

"Mr. 'Always Gotta Do the Right Thing' huh?" Perkins joined in the head shaking. "I know you've got your code, man, but . . . Hell, you aren't even getting' paid, and you know that's been buggin' me for years."

"Well you know money's never been a factor," Stryker argued. "In fact, it would only complicate things in terms of me remaining anonymous. Besides, who are you to talk? You've taken plenty of jobs without getting paid just to help people out. What about that street guy who was getting harassed just last month? You see a lot of money out of that case?"

"Not a lot," admitted Perkins. "But at least I knew who the guy was. You got no connection to Walker or any of the victims. Just a name out of the computer. That's what's weird man." Perkins paused and stared at Stryker for a moment. "You still think that whoever's posting the names doesn't know who you are?"

"Yeah, I've got no reason to think otherwise. I can't imagine MacAfee telling anyone." Stryker felt a bit awkward talking about this in the restaurant, but their voices were low and nobody nearby seemed to be paying them any attention. "Obviously he told someone about the site and the code, but there wouldn't be any reason to tell them about me. Besides, there's been nothing over the years other than the postings on the site. You'd think I'd get some sort of contact if anyone knew who I was."

"I suppose" Perkins agreed. "It seems more odd though when you want to quit but they basically won't let you. Wouldn't be so bad if you knew who 'they' are and you knew who you're working for. The way it is, it's just kinda weird to not retire because you're being talked into staying on the job, you don't know who's doing the talking."

"Well, I resigned myself to that a long time ago. Besides, I never really felt like I was working just for whoever posted the names. They were more like just a spoke in the wheel. I always figured I was working for me, and the country I guess." Stryker's voice became quieter than it had been during the entire conversation, almost as though he were really just speaking to himself, and Perkins strained slightly to hear the words.

"So, you're gonna do it?" Perkins asked although he already knew the answer.

Stryker nodded in acknowledgement before responding. "I guess so. Last one though. I won't ever go back to the site again, so this is it."

"You thought about when or how?"

"Not a bit," Stryker grunted. "Just finally decided to go through with it, so I haven't gone beyond that yet."

"When you get to that point, you want my help?" Once again Perkins asked a question to which he already knew the answer.

Stryker smiled and reached across the table with his fork to grab one of the final bites of Perkins' cinnamon roll. Perkins showed mock horror on his face, but didn't interfere with the theft. Stryker responded before putting the bite in his mouth. "Thanks Zip, but you know how this works. It's me and me alone. Especially since it's the last one. As far as anyone else might be concerned, you don't even know what the hell I'm doing. Right?"

"What you're doing about what?" Perkins smiled. "Just so you know – if you change your mind and decide you need some help, well, I guess you can tell me what you're doing."

CHAPTER TWENTY-NINE

Most major stocks swung violently in heavy trading on Friday morning amid news of possible military conflict between China and Taiwan. The Dow and most of its component companies began the trading day sharply up on reports of tame inflation and overall national job growth. The market turned instantly and dramatically downward, however, as soon as reports hit the airwaves regarding Chinese ships steaming across the Taiwan Straits toward Taiwan following a terrorist attack on Shanghai, which was allegedly perpetrated by an extremist Taiwanese group. The market volatility provided nothing new to seasoned stock traders, but it proved unsettling to Sam Wykovicz nonetheless. Ultimately, her job was to advise and then execute the wishes of her clients. Regardless of the extent to which those clients adhered to her advice, she couldn't help but feel responsible when things didn't go well for them. The one client from whom she'd never heard the slightest whisper of a complaint was Thorne Stryker.

When the market mercifully closed at 1:00 pm Seattle time, Sam watched after hours trades for a bit while catching up with her phone messages. She smiled and felt her shoulders relax for the first time in hours when she heard Stryker's voice asking if she might like to meet for an early, or late, or normal dinner that evening. She called him back immediately without listening to the remaining messages.

"So, you're desperate for a little Friday evening companionship, huh?" she began as soon as he answered the phone.

"Hello to you too," chuckled Stryker. "Actually, I was just curious about whether I had any money left after what I heard about the market today. I certainly hope you didn't panic and sell everything. Of course, I guess we could sell everything and invest in Chinese military stocks. Do they have any of those?"

"I'm sure they do," Sam replied, "but it doesn't really matter for you 'cause you were right the first time. You don't have any money left. On the bright side though, that means that I can buy you dinner tonight since miraculously, all of my investments turned out to be perfectly safe. Funny how that works, huh?"

"Funny, yeah. That's exactly the word I was thinking of," grunted Stryker. "So, if you're buying, does that mean pizza or a bucket of fried chicken?"

Sam gasped in mock horror. "I'm deeply offended. Neither pizza nor fried chicken ever crossed my mind. I was thinking about burgers."

"Mmmm, hard to beat that," said Stryker. "So, shall I pick you up or would you rather meet somewhere?"

"Well, actually, are you willing to pick me up here at the office?"

"Works for me," Stryker agreed, "assuming I don't have to sell my car this afternoon in order to pay the phone bill."

"I rode the bus downtown today," Sam explained, ignoring his comment. "If we go to dinner from here that'll save me a bus ride after work and then you could drop me at home afterward. If that's okay?"

"Like I said, it works for me. As you know my schedule's not especially tight, so give me a time and I'll be at your beck and call."

"Yeah, right. Somehow I don't see you at anyone's beck and call. Certainly not mine," responded Sam. "But if you're willing, I was hoping to be out of here by 5:00 today. Is that too early for dinner for you?"

"Five is great," agreed Stryker. "We'll just go somewhere with slow service. Call me if something comes up. Otherwise, your chariot will be warmed and ready to start your weekend off right. See you then."

Stryker hung up the phone, looked at his watch, and sat down at the computer to learn what he could about Independence, Missouri.

Stryker waited in the car rather than going into the Merrill Lynch offices and Sam wasn't ready to leave the office until 5:20. Stryker didn't mind the wait, but he did need to circle the block twice from his three-minute "Load/Unload Only" parking spot. The congestion of downtown traffic created a level of tension and competition that caused Stryker to wonder about the long-term effects on those who grappled with it on a daily basis. The horns seemed an inadequate substitute for the curses that surely echoed inside the surging and dodging cars that switched lanes abruptly and squeezed through red lights at the peril of pedestrians. Stryker enjoyed the calm quiet of his radio as he felt out of place among the real commuters in their cars and on the buses. Despite the evident tension all around, he still enjoyed the energy and vibrancy that emanated from the streets.

Sam alerted Stryker that she was on her way down from her office and he told her where she could find his car. Two minutes later she buckled herself into the passenger seat with a heavy sigh and Stryker moved the car north up Fourth Avenue.

"That was a pretty dramatic sigh. Tough day?" he asked.

"Oh. Well, I guess so. Busy. But then it usually is. It's not just today," she explained, "I'm just always exhausted at the end of the week." She looked over at Stryker with a sly smile. "And how was your day, honey?"

Stryker chuckled. "Just great, dear. Thanks for asking. Aunt Martha's got the kids so we have three whole hours all to ourselves."

"I'll be asleep in two and a half," responded Sam, "but that's okay." She looked out the window of the car to gauge their progress. "So, where are we going anyway?"

"Why are you asking me? I thought you were buying dinner, lady."

"Sure, I'm buying, but you're driving in case you forgot. So, where are you taking me to spend my hard-earned money?"

Stryker glanced at her before returning his attention to the road. "Local favorite. Great food. Unbeatable atmosphere. Might not quite be on the list of approved places for the movers and shakers of the brokerage business, but we can find a secluded booth so you won't be seen."

"Thanks for your concern. But you didn't tell me where."

Stryker smiled. "Red Robin, of course."

"You're kidding," Sam exclaimed loudly with an evident surge of energy. "Really?" She looked at Stryker and decided that he was serious. "I haven't been to Red Robin since my college days! Are we really going there?"

"Hey, nothing but the best. Besides, you were the one who said burgers. I'm just following orders."

Sam nodded approvingly. "You're alright Thorne. Definitely different. Surprising sometimes. But you're alright."

"You're not too bad yourself, lady. Now let's go eat."

The Red Robin restaurants were a chain of semi-upscale hamburger places in the Puget Sound area that had evolved from a single original location near the University of Washington. The restaurants were always full, always noisy, and always full of energy. Every two minutes the wait staff could be heard singing their own version of "Happy Birthday" to another smiling patron. "Red" himself walked around with his bright red plumage, oversized feet and yellow beak, handing out helium filled balloons to adoring children. Stryker and Sam parked at the original location just at the north end of Lake Union, and waited fifteen minutes before being led to a booth.

They ordered exotic burgers with fries and laughed and talked through their meal, and at one point, Stryker couldn't help but realize that he was enjoying it much more than he would a fancy, expensive restaurant. Maybe it was the company. When the waiter cleared their burger baskets they pondered the damage of adding dessert to their intake.

"You gotta have some kind of dessert," Stryker pleaded. "It's Friday night, you've only had a burger and fries, you *need* to finish off the meal properly."

"'*Only*' a burger and fries?" Sam asked incredulously. "I can only guess how many calories were in that burger. And I ate the whole thing! No way can I add dessert to that."

"We'll split one," Stryker bargained. "Just a sundae? Come on, it's good for you."

"Right," Sam laughed. "Good for me. Go ahead and order one and I'll have a few bites. Just to make you happy, of course."

As they ate the sundae, Stryker's tone turned serious. "By the way, I may be out of touch for a while," he began. Sam looked up intently at the combination of his tone and his words. "I'm gonna be traveling for a bit."

"Oh," Sam responded nonchalantly. "Where are you off to?"

"That's part of the problem. I don't really know yet. I'm helping out LJ with another case," Stryker lied, "and he says it's probably gonna send me out of town for a while. That's why he needs my help – he's got other cases here he's working on. It's all pretty vague right now, though. He's not really sure when or where."

"Well, that's good that you can help him out, I guess," Sam said quietly.

"Yeah. I'd just as soon not, but I can't leave him hanging. Like I said though, I'm not sure when or where. So, if I suddenly disappear and you don't know where I am, I'll be off doing LJ stuff." Stryker's resentment over the Axman assignment reasserted itself as he hated misleading Sam. At the same time he wondered what was developing between them that he felt the need to explain his absence to her. He'd never done it before and it hadn't seemed like a problem. Now, however, he felt he couldn't just disappear without some explanation for her. He wasn't sure he liked that either.

"Well, if you find out more you can let me know," Sam said coolly. "Otherwise, you can let me know when you get back and we can set up your next quarterly review."

"Well, I'm sure I'll be back well before that," Stryker smiled. "And who knows, you may be hungry for a burger again."

Sam finally offered a half smile again. "Maybe pizza."

"Done deal," Stryker agreed.

"For now though, I'm stuffed and I'm bushed," Sam sighed. "Friday. You still willing to provide taxi service?"

"Only if the tip's good," Stryker said as he wiped his hands on his napkin and got up from the table.

Stryker followed Sam's directions to drive her home where he got out of the car to walk her to the front door. As he said goodnight, Sam stretched up and kissed him lightly on the lips. Stryker drove home thinking that the tip was just perfect.

CHAPTER THIRTY

Stryker spent most of the next two days reading about Silvis Walker and researching Independence, Missouri. He accessed the official city website, merchant pages, realty company sites and online map services. He learned a great deal about the city – its streets, schools, parks, neighborhoods, restaurants, businesses, and places of interest – but ultimately he knew that it would take boots on the ground to formulate any real plan. Unfortunately, Stryker thought, they needed to be his boots and he'd have to come up with the plan. Looking at the computer seemed a whole lot easier and less messy for a guy who had announced his retirement.

At the end of day two of Independence from afar, Perkins stopped by just as Stryker puzzled over his dinner options. The doorbell surprised Stryker, but the promise of distraction offered by Perkins proved to be a welcome capper to the day.

Perkins burst in loudly when Stryker opened the door. "Hey, buddy. Haven't heard from ya. Whadya been up to?"

"Pretty thrilling stuff," Stryker led Perkins into his living room. "Learning all about the great midwestern town of Independence. Kinda reminds me of working on a fifth grade social studies project – only we didn't have the Internet to use back then."

"Man, you're older than I thought," laughed Perkins. "You sure they even had schools back then?"

"Careful there Zip," Stryker offered back. "As I recall, you've got a couple of years on me."

"Yeah, but I came from an affluent neighborhood. We was way ahead of the times." Perkins raised his eyebrows and made a drinking gesture with his hand, which got Stryker moving to the kitchen. "So, you learn anything significant?"

"Not really," said Stryker as he handed Perkins a can of Diet Coke. "I mean, I learned a lot about the town, but I need to get there and see for myself. You remember how it was from mission reports we'd work with before we went in somewhere. Nothing's ever exactly as you expect it, and some things aren't even close. I've got the lay of the land, but I'm not sure how much more I'll get without being there."

Perkins looked disgustedly at the Coke can before finally opening it and drinking half of the can at once. He looked back at the can and shook his head. "So, how soon you going?"

Stryker hesitated as if he hadn't thought about the timing yet. "I don't know, really. Maybe a week. Maybe longer. There's not really a whole lot more to do here, but I still don't feel the urge to rush off right away. I dunno. I know I'm not going to change my mind now, but I'm still not in any hurry."

"What, you figure maybe Walker'll get struck by lightning or something if you wait long enough?"

"It happens," Stryker smiled.

"I still say, you don't gotta do it, man. Just let it go." Perkins finished off his Coke with a second attack on the can.

"We've been over that," reminded Stryker who wouldn't pursue the argument any further and thereby changed the subject. "So, you been working?"

"Yeah," said Perkins as he rested his feet on the coffee table in front of him. "It's actually been pretty steady for a while now. I might have to look into taking on a full time partner." He looked at Stryker but got no response. "I've got an insurance case right now – some guy making a bogus theft claim. He tacked on a personal property rider for $300,000 a month ago and now he's claiming he got robbed of a bunch of expensive jewelry. No receipts, of course. Claims it came from his parents." Perkins huffed through his nose to show his contempt. "Insurance cases are good money though. No complaints. Got another one of a divorced dad stalking his grade school daughter. Allegations of abuse before the divorce. Now dad's supposed to stay away, but mom doesn't think he is. I'm hoping that one doesn't get ugly."

"New client?" Stryker asked.

"Nah, I worked for her during the divorce," Perkins shook his head. "You remember – Cindy Tillis? Thought her husband was hiding assets? Lived up in Mukilteo?"

"Oh yeah," Stryker nodded. "I met her in your office. Nice lady."

"Yep. Great kid too," Perkins shook the empty can at Stryker. "Husband's a jerk though. Marvin. Real piece of work."

"By the way, I told Sam that I was going to be helping you out on a case that would probably take me out of town for a while," Stryker explained in resignation. "Told her I didn't know exactly when or where. Anyway, thought you should know just in case it comes up."

Perkins smiled. "Always like to have you on the team, man – whether it's real or just imaginary."

Stryker got up and took the empty can from Perkins back to the kitchen. This time he returned with a can and a bag of Cheetos. Perkins' eyes lit up. "You eat dinner yet?" Stryker asked.

"Nope," responded Perkins looking at his watch as if he hadn't realized it was dinnertime.

Stryker pulled back the offered bag of chips and returned to the kitchen. "Let's go eat then," he offered. "I'm starving."

"Works for me," agreed Perkins. "But that doesn't mean you gotta put the Cheetos away." He tried his best to look hurt.

"You'll live," Stryker laughed. "Let's go."

A stop the next day at a Bank of America branch with a visit to a safety deposit box yielded Stryker three complete sets of identification – driver's licenses, insurance cards, credit cards, and passports – although he left the passports behind. One set of identification he used to buy a round trip plane ticket from San Francisco to Kansas City, and then he mailed the cards to himself at a post office in San Francisco. He mailed the second set to a post office in Kansas City. The third set was used to buy a round trip plane ticket from Portland to San Francisco. Everything would be ready for Stryker to move within a few days. All that remained was a serious question of his commitment and mental preparation.

Late that same afternoon, Stryker found an upscale condominium complex in Lynnwood that held the current address for Marvin Tillis. He easily drove to the address, which took him into south Snohomish County, but couldn't find a parking place within two blocks of the building. The onset of evening brought cool shadows and increased activity, and Stryker enjoyed the walk from his car to Tillis' building. The condominiums looked to be relatively new with bright blue paint and a noticeably upbeat aura. The grounds were neatly kept and the balconies sported flowers and colorful wind chimes. A large, clean swimming pool sat unused in the middle of the three building complex.

The address for Tillis listed "Building C" which multiple signs clearly identified as the furthest to the right when approaching from the street. His unit was listed as C204 and the corresponding mailbox near the main entrance to the building offered confirmation with the name "Tillis, M." scribbled on a paper card just above the lock. Stryker used the stairs to access the second floor and found condominium 204 just two doors down the hallway from the stairwell. Two loud knocks on the door evoked no response from inside the unit. Stryker reversed his path on the stairwell and back out of the building.

Stryker had a phone number for Tillis, but because he hadn't wanted to announce his visit, he hadn't bothered to call before showing up at the apartment. He now questioned the wisdom of that decision. For all he knew, Tillis could be out of town for a week. Unlikely, of course, but there was still no guarantee that he'd be returning home directly from work. On the other hand, Stryker didn't have any immediate obligations for the rest of the day, and he wanted to deal with Tillis before leaving town to take on Silvis Walker. Thus, he would wait.

Stryker looked hopefully around the premises but didn't see any great place for waiting. He could hang out at the top of the stairwell near Tillis' door. He could stand around near the entrance to the building. He could circle the pool at a slow walk. He decided to wait in his car. While walking back, however, he did notice an open parking place near the entrance to the complex so he hurried to his car and moved it forward. He was now able to sit in the car and watch the entrance to Building C where Tillis would eventually arrive. He didn't know what Tillis looked like, but that seemed like a minor detail at best.

Stryker listened to a talk radio station as he waited. The host focused on a recent, highly publicized case of spousal abuse in which the victim had eventually hired a pair of street thugs to beat up the abusive husband. The abuser ended up dying as a result of the attack, which now had the victim-wife as the defendant in a murder-for-hire trial. The case created intense public interest and provided the talk show host with many effusive callers willing to debate the ideas of vigilante justice and murder victims who deserved their fate. The majority of callers wanted the defendant to walk away from the trial a free woman. Many expressed horror that the prosecution had brought the case to trial in the first place. Stryker found the arguments reassuring as he contemplated his pending job with Silvis Walker.

Two women entered Building C while Stryker watched. He felt fairly sure that neither was Marvin Tillis. A young man, young enough to also not be Marvin Tillis entered a bit later and an older man left the building. Stryker grew bored of the inaction and the repetition of arguments on the radio so he left the car once again to stretch his legs and share his boredom with the outside world. For the sake of thoroughness he retraced his steps up the stairwell in Tillis' building and knocked on the door of C204 once again.

"Who is it?" called a gruff voice from behind the door.

Momentarily startled, Stryker hesitated before responding. "Assistant to the manager. Got a message for you."

"Is this about the parking again?" Stryker heard movement behind the door to accompany the voice. "I told him I'd take care of it."

The door opened before Stryker felt the need to respond. He looked hard at Tillis standing in the doorway in pressed, unfaded jeans and a bright yellow Lacoste shirt. No shoes. "No, it isn't about the parking."

"What is it then?" Tillis looked troubled as if he sensed that Stryker's presence wasn't really on behalf of the manager. His brown hair was short, but still a bit messed up at the end of the day and it accompanied stubble on his face that indicated a man who didn't bother to shave daily. His shoulders were wide and firm and his forearms were the thick and rippled variety of a man who either worked out a lot or who spent his forty-hour weeks in demanding physical labor. His smooth hands, one on the doorknob and one on his chin, confirmed the absence of physical labor. Tillis' eyes were slightly bloodshot but alert as he assessed Stryker in the hallway.

Stryker assessed in return as he ignored the proffered question. Tillis clearly had strength and size, but free weight strength from the gym often didn't translate well into the real world. Stryker's strength and experience came from the real world. Tillis was about to be introduced.

"Whadya want?" Tillis asked again with his body and the door, connected by his left hand, blocking the entrance to the condo.

"I thought maybe you wanted to invite me in," Stryker smiled pleasantly.

"Who the hell are you and why would I want to invite you in?" Tillis sounded aggressive but the nervousness in his eyes revealed apprehension. His body remained unmoved.

"Who I am doesn't really matter to you. Why I'm here does," Stryker spoke evenly with his eyes locked on Tillis. "Let's go inside and talk about Cindy and Melissa."

"Get lost, as . . ." Tillis began to say as he moved the door closed. He was stopped abruptly, however, by Stryker's forearm thrust against the door, which knocked Tillis off balance back into his living room. Stryker followed the swinging door and stumbling man into the condo, then closed the door behind him.

"What the hell?" Tillis was clearly flustered and surprised, but he tried to hide his fear. "You can't come busting in here like that. Get out of my house. Now!"

"Not yet, Marvin," offered Stryker in the same calm voice. "As I said, we need to talk about Cindy and Melissa. Now, why don't you sit down quietly and not make this any tougher on yourself than it's going to be already."

Tillis stared at Stryker in disbelief and made no move to sit. His eyes flicked from left to right and then back to Stryker as he contemplated his options. Stryker expected a police threat to come next, but Tillis apparently decided to handle things on his own. "That bitch send you here?" he demanded.

Stryker shook his head. "Actually, no. Your ex-wife doesn't know me from Adam. But, I've heard about you from a friend of a friend, and I decided it was my business to intervene. Call it my good deed for the week. You like good deeds, don't you Marvin?"

"What I'd like is for you to leave, now." Tillis stood up from the couch he'd been leaning on. He crossed his arms in front of his chest in a manner that Stryker was certain was intended to be significant body language. Stryker wasn't listening.

"Oh I'm gonna leave alright, Marvin," Stryker continued to use his name in friendly familiarity, which he expected Tillis to find annoying, "but not until you and I come to an understanding. Now, *my* understanding is that you have no visitation rights with Melissa. You're supposed to stay away. I also understand that you're not following those rules too well. You've been harassing Cindy and stalking Melissa." Stryker looked hard at the man in front of him. "Please stop me if I'm getting anything wrong."

"What you're gettin' wrong is showing up here at all, and I'm sure as hell not listening to that crap from you. Now, get the hell out of here or I'm calling the police." Tillis remained standing with his arms crossed and his head tilted slightly to one side.

"You can call the police," Stryker offered as he walked toward the door. Tillis took a few steps behind him in hopeful anticipation. "In fact, that's probably what I should be doing because of your violation of court orders. But, I'm more of a do-it-yourself kind of guy so that's why I'm here." Stryker stopped and locked the door and engaged the safety chain as well. "Before you call though, let's make sure you've got something to call about." Stryker turned from the door to face Tillis who stopped his advance and swallowed hard.

"You like watching sports?" Stryker motioned to the oversized flat-screen TV on the side wall of the living room as he continued to move away from the door.

"Huh?" Tillis' response was not overly eloquent.

In a blur of motion, Stryker picked up a lamp off an end table by the couch and tossed it into the middle of the screen, sending ceramic from the lamp and glass from the TV crashing to the hardwood floor. Tillis' mouth dropped open in disbelief, but no words came out.

Stryker moved over to the stereo system that stood mounted in the corner next to where the TV had recently resided. He examined the components and then looked over his shoulder at Tillis who hadn't moved since Stryker locked the door. He yanked the CD player out, separating it violently from its wires, and threw it hard through the glass doors that enclosed a small fireplace on an adjoining wall.

Finally, Tillis reacted as he moved quickly to Stryker in an attempt to grab him and prevent further damage to his possessions. As he approached, he attempted to say something that Stryker didn't really hear. As he got close, Stryker wheeled around and swung his left elbow into Tillis' jaw, which sent the man instantly into a crumpled mass next to the shards of glass and plastic.

Shaken, but still conscious, Tillis didn't move for a few moments as he assessed the pain in his face. Finally, he looked up with fearful eyes at the apparent madman who seemed intent on wrecking his life.

Stryker stood over Tillis without moving until he finally kicked him lightly in the shin. "Get up," Stryker ordered. Tillis didn't move immediately, so Stryker kicked harder. "Get up," he repeated and Tillis moved to one knee and then to his feet. Stryker pointed him to the couch where Tillis reluctantly sat with one hand glued to his aching jaw.

"You and I need to come to an understanding Marvin." The calmness in Stryker's voice frightened Tillis almost as much as the violence that had preceded it.

Tillis stared at Stryker with wide eyes that desperately wanted to close to make everything go away. He continued to say nothing.

Stryker sat in a chair opposite Tillis. "Here's the deal," Stryker explained. "Your ex-wife doesn't know me, and she sure as hell doesn't know that anybody's here talking to you. We're gonna keep it that way. Right Marvin?" Tillis nodded almost without thought. "Good. Now, consider me an agent of the court. The court says you're to have no contact with Cindy or Melissa. Anything unclear about that to you?" Tillis shook his head without taking his eyes off Stryker. "Good again. As an unofficial agent of the court, I'm taking it upon myself to make sure that you follow the court orders. You haven't done that. Today, it's going to cost you some damage to some of your possessions here. You're going to have to live with that. If I end up back here again because you can't follow the court's orders, you're going to wish that the rest of your body felt as good as your jaw feels right now. Anything unclear to you about that?" Tillis dropped his hand from his jaw and shook his head once again.

Stryker got up from his chair and walked into the small dining area adjoining the living room. He picked up one of the four chairs surrounding the table and in the motion of chopping wood he broke off two of the legs against the floor. Tillis offered no response beyond a slight jump at the sound of the cracking wood. Stryker walked back to the living room and stood close behind Tillis who remained seated on the couch. Stryker leaned in close and spoke directly into Tillis right ear.

"You and I need to come to an understanding Marvin," he repeated quietly into Tillis' ear. Tillis nodded obediently. "I'm not the kind of man that you want to have upset with you. Right now, I'm upset with you. I'm also in a bad mood overall," he paused for a moment while he stepped away slightly and turned Tillis' head to face him. "I guarantee you though, I'll be in a much worse mood if I have to come back here again. And next time, I won't waste time on your TV or your furniture." Stryker looked with intense seriousness at the man in front of him who seemed to be shrinking by the second. "Now," he continued, "do you and I have an understanding Marvin?"

Tillis nodded while swallowing hard.

"Tell me what our understanding is, Marvin."

"I stay away from Cindy and Melissa." Tillis' voice shook slightly as he spoke for the first time in what seemed to him like hours.

"When, Marvin?"

"Huh?"

"When do you stay away from Cindy and Melissa?"

"Always."

"Very good, Marvin," Stryker complimented his quarry. "I'm glad we were able to reach this understanding. Now, the good thing is, you've still got all your fingers and they're not broken." Tillis glanced down at his hands with renewed fear. "I want you to use those fingers to get a piece of paper and write something down for me. Can you do that Marvin?"

Tillis nodded and quickly moved to the kitchen where he produced a paper and pen from a drawer. He looked at Stryker for instructions.

"We'll keep it short and simple Marvin. Write this – 'I hereby give up all interest in my possessions and in my physical being if I ever again bother my ex-wife Cindy, or my daughter Melissa.'" Stryker repeated the message twice until Tillis stopped writing. "Got it Marvin?" Tillis nodded. "Good. Then sign your name."

Stryker took the paper from Tillis and glanced at the writing before smiling with a slight nod. "Well," he offered, "you've got cause now if you want to call the police. Shall I do it for you Marvin?"

Tillis shook his head while setting the pen down on the countertop.

"Alright, if you're sure." Stryker glanced around the condo before looking back at Tillis. "Like I said, I'm in a bad mood, and part of me feels like breaking more stuff." Tillis' face fell as he swallowed hard once again. "That doesn't seem quite fair though since we've come to an agreement. Remember though Marvin, you *do not* want to see me again. Don't do anything stupid."

Tillis nodded at Stryker without saying anything further and then watched as Stryker turned and walked out of the condo. Tillis looked at his beloved flat-screen TV and shook his head with remorse. He thought briefly about what more could have happened before he shook those thoughts from his head. "I was thinking about asking for a transfer anyway," he thought to himself.

The next morning, Cindy Tillis found a plain white envelope tucked under the morning newspaper on her porch. Her brow crinkled in puzzlement as she read and re-read the brief note in her ex-husband's handwriting. She stepped back into her apartment and immediately called LJ Perkins. She read the note over the phone and asked Perkins what it meant.

"It means your problems with Marvin are over," Perkins explained. "If anything else happens, let me know, but you should be good from here on out."

"I don't understand," she questioned. "What did you do? How can I ever thank you?"

"Believe me, it was nothing," Perkins admitted. "Let's just consider it over."

"What about your bill?" she asked.

Perkins snorted a quick laugh. "Use the money to buy something nice for Melissa," he instructed. "Like I said though, let me know right away if anything else should happen."

As they hung up the phone, Cindy stared back at the note in perplexed optimism. Perkins smiled and shook his head, and wished he could have been there to witness the events that led to Tillis writing the note.

CHAPTER THIRTY-ONE

Stryker drove for just over three hours south from Seattle to Portland on Interstate 5. The drive provided stunning views of Mt. Rainier, Mt. St. Helens, and Mt. Adams along with car dealers, fast food restaurants, and farmland. Stryker generally maintained a very keen sense of his surroundings while also being caught up in the mindless monotony of the hypnotic flow of traffic. He enjoyed crossing into Oregon over the Columbia River where an uncountable number of logs filled the river and its banks for the nearby lumber mills. He contemplated how many toothpicks might be fashioned out of a single huge log and was certain that it had to be enough for the entire state of Oregon for at least a year. He also wondered if any of the wood might be lucky enough to be destined for the major leagues to face a 95 mph fastball. Then again, maybe a replacement chair for Marvin Tillis floated in the river below him.

Upon reaching Portland, Stryker drove directly to the airport where he left his car near the entrance of a long-term parking lot. He parked at the end of a row so that he had another car on only one side of his. He carried one small bag and his pre-printed boarding pass as he road the shuttle bus to his terminal a full ninety minutes before the departure of his plane. At the terminal he passed easily through security and walked directly to his gate where he sat and read the latest Newsweek magazine while waiting for the loading of his plane. The name on his ticket, Caleb Brooks, matched the Oregon driver's license and credit cards he carried in his wallet. He boarded the plane with his carry-on bag and enjoyed a quick, uneventful flight to the bay area.

When the plane arrived almost on time in San Francisco, Stryker immediately took a cab to a nearby post office on Standard Avenue. The small office presented two service windows, both of which were manned by middle aged women when Stryker walked in.

"I need to retrieve a package that was sent here to general delivery," he explained to the small Hispanic looking clerk once she gestured him to her window.

"What name?" she asked.

"Caleb Brooks," he offered as he pulled from his wallet the Oregon driver's license with his picture.

"Just one moment, please." She left the window and slipped behind a magic curtain. Stryker glanced at his watch to see that all was well with his schedule.

The clerk returned and handed Stryker the envelope that he had addressed and mailed himself. He thanked her and walked next door to a small stationary store where he purchased a similar envelope and then opened the one he received at the post office.

The envelope contained a California driver's license, credit cards and plane ticket to Kansas City in the name of Scott Densmore. The picture on the license was Stryker's. He removed the Densmore documents and placed them in his wallet and dropped the Caleb Brooks cards and return ticket to Portland into the new envelope which he then addressed to Densmore in care of general delivery at a post office branch in San Francisco, not far from the one he just left. He sealed the envelope, returned to the post office and mailed the Brooks documents to Densmore. He then took a cab back to the airport where, as Scott Densmore, he waited less than thirty minutes before boarding his nonstop flight to Missouri.

Stryker sat in an aisle seat in coach and spent most of the flight with his eyes on a magazine and his thoughts on Silvis Walker. As with any job, he would be careful and thorough in his preparation, but at the same time he wanted to minimize his time in Independence. Knowing with certainty that this would be his last job didn't leave Stryker with any sense of nostalgia or a need to embrace the moment. Rather, he wanted completion as quickly as possible. He cautioned himself about not allowing urgency to interfere with the need for care.

Stryker's research before leaving Seattle had left him with a few ideas about how he might complete the job. Despite the fact that nothing could be determined until he actually set foot in Missouri, he couldn't stop the options from ruminating in his mind. He weighed pros and cons and unknowns, then told himself it was useless until he got there and learned more. Then he weighed the pros and cons again. He tried to read the magazine, but couldn't focus on the words. He settled in and resigned himself to a long flight.

Next to Stryker in the middle of the row sat a woman named Mary Arndt who seemed completely untroubled by any murders in her immediate future. She held a paperback romance novel, but seemed much more interested in conversation than in reading. Unfortunately for Stryker, the young woman in the window seat quickly fell asleep, or at least pretended to do so, leaving him as the only available other half of Mary's conversation. Stryker's share of the conversation was actually much closer to ten percent, rather than half, and consisted primarily of a question followed by a few "hmmms" and "oh reallys".

Stryker estimated Mary Arndt's weight at ninety pounds, but he may have overestimated given the fact that she was sitting down. Her glasses were much too big for her small head and seemed unnaturally rigid on a face whose lines had been sagging longer than Stryker had been walking. Her veins exuded a deep blue at her temples and her hands and her fingers looked as frail and brittle as chicken bones left out in the desert sun for weeks. Stryker quickly reviewed his CPR skills when she coughed violently in reaction to taking a small drink from her cup of orange juice.

Mary stopped coughing before her body snapped in two and slapped herself hard on the chest. She then looked back at Stryker. "So," she said, "I haven't heard much about you, young man. What takes you to Kansas City? Is it a woman?"

"Actually, no," Stryker laughed. "I'm going to visit a friend from college. Nothing special, and not very long, but he invited me out and I decided to go."

Mary responded with a four-minute discourse about her best friend from school, now dead, with whom she'd shared many visits over the years. She ended with advice for Stryker. "Now I know you're young, and it seems like you've got forever in front of you," she patted him on the arm, "but take it from me, you never know what tomorrow's going to bring and the worst thing you can do is to have regrets about what you didn't do with friends and family. Now I don't know your friend at all, but I'm glad you're going to see him. God forbid he should die soon, but if he did, you'd be sorry that you didn't take the time to visit when you had the chance." She patted him on the arm once again. "You'll be happy you went," she assured him, "and so will your friend. After I visit my daughter in Kansas City, I'll be going home to Peru, Illinois. That's where I live. The first thing I'm going to do when I get home is to visit all my friends. In my case, you really don't know who might die tomorrow so I can't waste any time."

Stryker smiled inwardly about who might die tomorrow, or the next day, but then he was back to listening to Mary, now talking about her family. He couldn't help but to laugh to himself about this woman who, in many ways, was so unlike himself. And yet, he couldn't help but like her. He made a mental note to visit Mary Arndt of Peru, Illinois someday, or at least to send her a note. Just because. If she died and he hadn't done it, he'd feel badly about missing the opportunity. He didn't really care whether or not Silvis Walker had made all of his important visits, but he knew that Walker had little time left to do so.

Stryker left the Kansas City International Airport quickly as he had no checked luggage to retrieve. He took his sole carry-on bag and headed to the nearest taxi stand where he jumped in a cab and gave the driver a street address that was about two blocks away from a nearby post office. Stryker paid the driver and walked to the post office where he repeated his actions from San Francisco. This time, he used his current identification to obtain a package from general delivery addressed to Scott Densmore. He also bought a similar sized envelope.

He took the envelopes to a nearby coffee shop where he took a booth and ordered a sandwich with a Diet Pepsi. While he waited for his food, he opened the envelope addressed to Densmore and removed credit cards, an insurance card, and an Indiana driver's license in the name of Michael Carter. He addressed the new envelope to general delivery at a different post office in Kansas City, in care of Michael Carter, and inserted the Densmore license and credit cards. He placed the new cards in his wallet shortly before his food arrived. After eating, he would mail the new envelope and, as Michael Carter, he would leave Kansas City for nearby Independence.

CHAPTER THIRTY-TWO

Stryker stepped off the bus in Independence at just past 9:30 in the evening and walked nearly two miles to a Motel 6 where, as Michael Carter, he registered for three nights. He knew that he might choose to leave sooner, but he didn't expect that there would be any reason to do so. By 11:00, he lay sound asleep less than ten miles from where Silvis Walker quietly bedded down for one of the last times in his life.

The next morning dawned cool and clear, with a promise of warm temperatures by mid-afternoon. Stryker ran for nearly an hour on the streets with familiar names from his time spent with maps, and eventually worked his way through the trails of a large wooded park before showering and preparing himself for the day. His day would begin with a trip to a county library to read recent editions of the Independence Gazette. The library was within walking distance for Stryker, so he left the hotel on foot with plans to find some breakfast along the way, as he knew that the library didn't open until 9:00 am.

Breakfast consisted of hash browns, toast, and eggs scrambled with cheese, eaten with the morning Gazette opened on the table of his booth. The generic breakfast was difficult for a cook to screw up, but in this case Stryker found it especially good because of the crispness of the hash browns and the home-style thickness of the toast. He left a sizable tip and meandered slowly to the South Branch of the Independence Public Library to arrive by 9:15.

Stryker approached the information desk where he found the stereotypical librarian. Stereotypical first because she was a she. Her appearance also fit Stryker's prototype for a librarian. He guessed she was in her mid fifties with dark framed glasses perched on her nose, but secured with a decorative chain around her neck. Her earrings were modest and a wedding ring completed the entirety of her jewelry ensemble. She wore a blue cardigan sweater over a white blouse that was buttoned up to her throat. Her hair was cut short and trimmed neatly to the contours of her smallish head. Her eyes shined brightly behind her glasses as she looked up at Stryker.

"How can I help you this morning?" she asked in a friendly voice that wasn't nearly as quiet as Stryker expected from a librarian in the context of her work. Of course, for all he knew he could be her only customer so far this morning.

"Local newspapers," Stryker responded in his library voice. "The Gazette. I'd like to read everything for the past two or three weeks."

"Are you looking for something specific? I'd be happy to help you find it," she offered in her non-library voice once again.

"Actually no," said Stryker. "I've been out of town and I'd just want to go over past issues to see what I missed. I try to read the paper religiously, and I hate it when I miss out," he smiled at her as if surely she would understand.

Apparently she did, as she proffered no further questions. “The computers are right over there,” she pointed to Stryker’s right. “We normally limit our customers to thirty minutes, but as you can see, it’s very quiet right now. You should be able to use one for as long as you want. We get busy later in the afternoon, but not so much on weekday mornings.”

“Thanks,” Stryker nodded with pursed lips, “but I’m kind of an old-fashioned guy. I can use the computer if I need to, but I’d really prefer to read the hard copies. Any chance you have those around?”

She looked at him with glistening eyes as if she had just been reunited with a long lost twin. “Yes, yes of course!” she nearly yelled with excitement. “Today’s paper is right over there,” she pointed to a rack behind her. “I’ll go in back and bring out our other hard copies for you. How far back did you say you wanted?”

“Well, ideally three weeks,” Stryker winced as he said it. “That’s how long I’ve been gone. If you don’t have that many though, that’s okay. I’ll go online for the older ones.”

“No, no, we’ve got three weeks worth,” she hurriedly assured him as if she were afraid that he might leave if she couldn’t meet his needs perfectly. “We’ve got some nice reading chairs by the periodicals so you can find yourself a spot over there and I’ll be right out. Are you sure that three weeks is all you want?”

“Yeah, really, that’s perfect,” Stryker said. “It may even be a day or two more than I need, but that’s okay. I really appreciate your not making me read on the computer.”

“I know exactly how you feel, believe me,” she cooed at him. “Now go sit down and I’ll be right back.”

Stryker almost expected her to offer him tea and cookies. He would have accepted the cookies, but he made his way over to the reading area without them.

In less than two minutes she placed a stack of papers in front of him. "I've got them in chronological order," she explained as she smoothed out the stack with the loving and tender touch of a mother fixing the disheveled hair of a favorite child. "I assumed you'd want to read the older ones first so they're on top."

"Perfect," complimented Stryker with a pleasant smile. "Do we have a thirty minute limit on reading chairs as well?"

"We close at nine," she offered with a slight laugh. "That's your limit."

"I think that'll do," Stryker responded with a laugh of his own as he glanced at his watch. "Thanks for all your help."

"I'll be up at the front desk if there's anything else you need," she offered. "Don't hesitate to ask."

Stryker nodded a response as he picked the first paper from the pile. He knew that anything on Walker would be in the first section or the local section, so he could ignore sports, business, and arts. He also knew that he'd probably find nothing at all. Even so, it wouldn't take long to look and it was the most logical place to start.

Stryker worked all the way through the pile to the last paper, yesterday's edition, before striking pay dirt. The front page of the local section carried a daily column about celebrities and events of local interest, and the Monday column began with a brief diatribe about Silvis Walker calling a press conference for noon on Friday. Popular speculation seemed to be that he would be announcing a newly signed book deal, the thought of which left the columnist utterly disgusted as she expressed in numerous biting and caustic paragraphs. The press conference was to be held at the front of the Jackson County Courthouse– less than a half mile from where Stryker sat reading. Less than seventy-five hours away.

CHAPTER THIRTY-THREE

To take advantage of the public opportunity just three days off, Stryker knew that he would be incredibly busy. He took the stack of neatly reorganized newspapers back to the front desk and returned them to the librarian with effusive thanks. He then headed outside to walk the streets around the Courthouse building. Stryker knew most of the major streets from his time spent with city maps before his arrival in Independence. His morning run hadn't taken him downtown, so now he needed to see those streets for himself in order to formulate a plan.

From everything that Stryker had been able to discern, Walker had worked hard to keep a very low profile since his acquittal at trial. He successfully maintained such invisibility that some even argued that he had left town. From the newspaper column, however, he clearly remained part of the Independence landscape. For Stryker, that left only two options. He could make an attack at Walker's house, but the evidence gathering capabilities of forensic science made that an option of last resort. The press conference, on the other hand, gave him the much safer alternative of killing from a distance, if he could put together a workable plan in just three days.

Downtown Independence, significantly quieter than larger cities Stryker had known, displayed many of the characteristics of a typical midwestern city. Trees could still be found on many streets and the sidewalks exhibited the cleanliness of a town not too big to still care about such things. Few buildings stood taller than three stories and many of the older structures carried the date of their construction on the brick and stone exteriors. Traffic flowed smoothly without significant congestion and drivers seemed genuinely patient and courteous with others on the roads. Stryker found it difficult to imagine Silvis Walker hunting on these friendly and inviting streets.

The Jackson County Courthouse made its home in a classic red brick, two story building with four large white pillars at the main entrance and an open entry from the street through a very few trees and three wide steps. Stryker guessed that the building dated from the 1940s. Though less than fifteen miles from Kansas City, it seemed a world away in its small town charm. Stryker walked both sides of Lexington Avenue two times while focusing on the Courthouse building and imagining the location of Walker's planned press conference. He wondered about the negotiations with the city or county officials that resulted in the agreement to hold the press conference outdoors on government property. He guessed that the expected presence of national news agencies played into the decision. He tried to picture the now quiet and empty entrance to the building as it would look at noon on Friday when Walker faced the camera and microphones.

With the scene clearly in focus in his mind, Stryker began to ponder the options for someone who might want to permanently interrupt the pending press conference. For that, and with no security cameras evident, he took a seat on the steps of the Courthouse and scanned the nearby buildings to inventory his options.

Moderate traffic moved in both directions on Lexington Avenue with traffic lights at both ends of the block. Enough trees impeded the view from the east that no real option existed for Stryker from that side of the building. The building faced south, but without any prominent buildings in that direction. Thus, Stryker focused his attention toward the west where Lexington extended without any turns for at least six blocks. Something within a few blocks and on the south side of the street might work for an experienced sniper. Stryker walked west.

The corner of Lexington and Liberty offered a stoplight, left turn lanes and nothing of interest to tourist or sniper. Stryker crossed with the light, staying on the north side of Lexington but keeping his eyes focused across to the southern side of the street. The block after Liberty contained a bank on the corner next to an unremarkable office building, followed by a Teriyaki restaurant and another smaller office building. At the end of the block, on the corner of Osage Street, sat the offices of Merrill Lynch. Stryker quickly banished thoughts of Sam from his head.

No dramatic changes were evident as Stryker crossed Osage and continued on Lexington Avenue toward Spring Street. More buildings housing various businesses. All stood two to three stories. None offered anything remarkable. Stryker looked back toward City Hall, now over two blocks away, and began to ponder other options. Immediately, however, his heart jumped as he continued up the block and looked across the Spring Street intersection. On the corner stood a clothing store, 'Mendelson's' the window said, with blackened exterior walls. The building had suffered a recent fire and appeared to be waiting for much-needed repairs. Stryker's door of opportunity swung open widely.

Mendelson's sat on the corner of Lexington and Spring next to a dry cleaner. The building stood two stories tall and sported extensive street level windows on both streets. The second floor had fewer windows but much more evidence of the recent fire. Stryker walked past Mendelson's on Spring where he found an alleyway, containing mostly dumpsters, on the back side of the building and running parallel to Lexington Avenue. He walked past the alley to Kansas Avenue where he turned right to circle the block and approach Mendelson's from the opposite direction on Lexington. The remainder of the block seemed unaffected by the fire. How long ago the fire had occurred was not apparent, nor was the current situation inside the building. Stryker decided to return to the library.

This time, Stryker walked quietly to the bank of computers, more than half of which were unused, and looked up the Independence Gazette online. He typed in "fire" and "Mendelson's" as key words and found a handful of articles. Mendelson's recently celebrated its 50th year in business in the same location. The fire had hit the store just a week earlier, and while its origins were reported as unknown, the investigation identified the possibility of arson. In addition to the physical damage to much of the second floor of the building, the majority of the store's inventory had been damaged by smoke and water. The reports indicated that repairs would be delayed until the insurance company could sort out liability issues related to the cause of the fire. Mendelson's owners reportedly planned to re-open at a temporary location if it looked as though the building would be unusable for an extended period of time. For Stryker, the building seemed perfectly usable.

He left the library while carefully avoiding contact with the librarian and returned to the street to contemplate his options. He needed to see the inside of the Mendelson building and he needed to return to Kansas City to pick up packages that should be waiting for him at the post office. A glance at his watch told him it was still before noon. Kansas City sat a mere eleven miles away. Mendelson's sat a mere few blocks away. Might as well start with Mendelson's, he thought.

Stryker quickly decided that the easiest approach to Mendelson's would be in broad daylight. He hoped that anyone who saw him would assume that he belonged there – insurance adjustor, fire investigator, store employee, whatever. For anyone who might actually question him, he would offer simple innocent curiosity. Better than sneaking around at night when it would be impossible to mask his intentions. Thus, Kansas City could wait.

He walked three blocks past Mendelson's and was about to ask for help when he saw a hardware store on the opposite side of the street. Stryker crossed at the corner and entered the store with a bell ringing to announce his arrival.

"Morning," offered the clerk who turned toward the door from an array of rakes and shovels in need of organization near the main window of the store. "Help you find anything?" He peered at Stryker over the top of his glasses, which caused the light to reflect off his perfectly smooth and shiny head. He wore a nametag that announced him as Cyrus. Stryker sensed that he really hoped for a negative answer to his question, so Stryker happily complied.

"Not yet, thanks," replied Stryker. "I'll look around a bit and then let you know."

"Help yourself," Cyrus offered as he immediately returned to his work.

Stryker saw no one else in the store as he searched the small tools and accompanying pieces for the right combination that would allow him to pick a lock. He picked up a few more pieces than he likely needed, but he preferred to be over prepared as opposed to needing a return trip. He strode to the cash register with his disparate collection and stood patiently for a minute looking at the back of the hardware man engrossed in his window display. Stryker shuffled his feet a bit and cleared his throat, but to no avail. Finally, he walked over to the man.

“”Sorry to interrupt,” Stryker interrupted, “but I think I’ve got what I need.”

Cyrus turned as if surprised that anyone else was in the store with him. He looked at Stryker and then back at his work, shrugged, and walked with Stryker to the cash register.

“Sure this is all you need?” he asked as he looked at the tools Stryker laid on the counter. “Kind of an odd lot of items.”

“Yeah, I know,” Stryker agreed. “A couple of things I’ve been meaning to pick up for a long time and never got around to it. Then I needed something else. Finally, I decided just to put a list together and here I am.”

“Glad we had what you needed,” Cyrus took the cash offered by Stryker and gave him change. “Enjoy the rest of your day now.”

“Thanks,” smiled Stryker. “I may be back if it turns out I forgot something. I want to get all this done with today.”

“Open till six,” said Cyrus as he moved back to his display.

Stryker walked an indirect route to the alley at the back side of Mendelson’s. He used his newly acquired tools to quickly open the lock on the delivery entrance at the back of the store, and then walked in and through the building to unlock the front door. He wasted no time in retracing his steps out the back door, which he closed but also left unlocked. He circled the entire block and came back to the front entrance of Mendelson’s from the west on Lexington. When he got to the front door he opened it and walked in calmly as if he owned the building.

Once inside, Stryker headed directly for the second floor where the focus of the fire had been. Plywood boards covered some of the windows, including those on the northeast corner of the store, the corner that faced the Jackson County Courthouse.

At that corner Stryker saw, as expected that the boarding of the windows was very makeshift and clearly intended as short-term solution rather than permanent one. He looked easily through a space between two plywood sheets at an unobstructed view of the grounds in front of the Courthouse, not quite three blocks away. The site of Silvis Walker's press conference at noon on Friday. Stryker carefully inspected the surrounding buildings, but saw nothing of immediate concern. Because Mendelson's sat on the corner of the block, it had no immediate neighbors in the direction of the Courthouse. Traffic signals and street signs took up space above the street, but below Stryker's projected line of fire. He wasn't thrilled with the idea of shooting from within a building, but with a few days to create a diversion plan and multiple escape options, Stryker felt his confidence grow. He turned to leave the building, making mental notes of the layout for his escape plans. He walked back out the front door, which he closed behind him, still unlocked, and walked on Lexington Avenue away from the Courthouse looking for some lunch.

The next morning, Stryker – as Michael Carter – stepped off a bus in downtown Kansas City. He first stopped at a uniform rental/ purchase store he had found online and bought a generic work uniform that seemed appropriate for a janitorial service. He then walked to a Federal Express office where he retrieved three packages of varying size addressed to Michael Carter. With four packages in hand he would have preferred taking a taxi back to Independence, but he settled for the anonymity of the bus once again. At half past noon in his hotel room, he examined the parts of the previously unused, and completely untraceable, sniper rifle. Everything seemed to be in perfect working order, but Stryker couldn't be sure. He had plans for some test firing late that night in the woods on the outskirts of Independence.

For the time being, however, he disassembled the rifle and returned the parts to the three packages.

Stryker spent that afternoon completing more shopping. He bought a gym bag, a baseball cap, and oversized running shoes from a sporting goods store, while a grocery store yielded thin rubber gloves, disinfectant cleaner and a cell phone with pre-paid minutes. Finally, a local Goodwill store provided him with a t-shirt and a jacket. By dinnertime on Wednesday evening Stryker felt physically prepared for the job ahead. Thursday would be spent on mental preparation and planning. Friday he would complete his final Axman assignment.

Just before eating his dinner, Stryker used his newly purchased cell phone to call Sam Wykovicz.

"Hello?" she answered the phone with uncertainty.

"Hey Sam, it's Thorne Stryker. How are you this rainy evening?" The Weather Channel had confirmed a wet day in Seattle.

"Thorne, I'm great! Are you back in town?"

"Just got back," Stryker lied without a twinge of regret. "Always nice to be back home." Stryker coughed into the phone.

"So, where've you been? What've you been doing?" Sam asked quickly.

"Well, how about we . . ." Stryker coughed again. "Sorry. How about we talk over dinner tomorrow night? Any chance you're free at this late notice?" Another cough.

"You don't sound so good. Are you okay?" Sam asked with a voice cloaked in concern.

"Well, I may be coming down with something, but I'm sure I'll be fine." Stryker coughed one more time. "So, possible for dinner?"

"Ummm," Sam hesitated while she thought. "Yeah, I can do that. What time?"

"How about I pick you up at 7:30?" Stryker proposed before a final cough.

"Okay, if you're sure you're not going to die between now and then," Sam agreed.

"No plans to do that. See you at 7:30. Bye now." Stryker turned off the cell phone.

Thursday afternoon Stryker called Sam again with a gravelly, coughing voice to postpone the dinner plans. "We can try for tomorrow," he raspingly suggested, "but it may have to be Saturday. Is that going to mess you up badly?"

"No problem," agreed Sam, "But actually, I've already got plans for Friday, so why don't we just make it Saturday. That'll give you another day to recover, and it sounds like you could use it."

"Okay, thanks," coughed Stryker. "Pick you up at 7:30 on Saturday."

"Well, let me know if you're still not up to it," Sam offered. "Do you have what you need? Can I bring you anything?"

"No thanks," Stryker responded in a near whisper. "LJ brought me some soup and some of that nighttime cold medicine that always knocks me out."

"Okay," Sam said. "Take care of yourself."

"No problem," agreed Stryker. "I can already feel myself turning the corner. I'll be as good as new on Saturday. Guaranteed."

With that, Stryker resumed his final preparations for Friday morning, although he continued to look forward to the conclusion of the job and the immediate return to Seattle. It was time for the end of Axman.

CHAPTER THIRTY-FOUR

Stryker lay wide awake in bed in his hotel room at 4:00 Friday morning with his three escape routes tracing their way through his mind. He resisted the temptation of making a third trip down the alleyway behind Mendelson's to confirm that the rear door remained unlocked. He resisted the even greater temptation of looking ahead to the completion of the job. Now was the time for concerted focus and the avoidance of any mistakes.

He stepped from the shower at exactly 5:00 and dressed in his janitorial uniform pants with the t-shirt and jacket from Goodwill. He packed the uniform shirt along with his other clothes and the three rifle packages in the newly purchased gym bag. With everything packed, he then spent nearly thirty minutes thoroughly cleaning the surfaces of the room, although he had made a point of touching very little during his stay. He had no reason to think that the authorities would end up in his room, but he saw no reason to take any chances.

At 5:40 Stryker stood at the front desk in the waning minutes of the night clerk's shift for a quick and efficient checking out of the hotel. He then walked to a very quiet Lexington Avenue, slipped into the alleyway behind Mendelson's, and entered the rear door of the abandoned store. He left the door unlocked, in the event that he would have to explain his presence in the store, but walked through the store to lock the front door before proceeding to the empty second floor. Once there, Stryker put on the uniform shirt and baseball cap and stored the jacket in the bag, which he then carefully hid for the six-hour wait until noon. He took a spot on the dirty floor with his back against the wall and sat, unmoving and largely unblinking, while he thought about his return trip to Seattle by way of Kansas City, San Francisco, and Portland.

Street noises gradually increased in both volume and frequency until they became steady by 10:00. Stryker noted the time on his watch, and then began unwavering focus on the job at hand. He got up to peer through the cracks in the boards for a clear view of the entrance to the Courthouse. He moved from place to place to get an overall view of the streets and saw nothing to indicate unusual activity for a Friday morning. He sat back down, closed his eyes, and played out the upcoming scene in his head, concluding with the variations for his possible exit routes. He intentionally slowed his breathing and his heart rate as he willed his body into the calm dispassion he had known many times before. He repeated his visualization through deep, very slow breaths until he felt on the verge of falling asleep. At that point he stood up, looked at his watch, and began a constant surveillance through the cracks in the boards.

By 11:15, news cameras began to set up on the grounds in front of the Jackson County Courthouse. A few bystanders stopped, but most merely paused before walking past. By 11:45, however, at least 50 people gathered behind the cameras, which stood their vigil pointed toward the left side of the entrance to the building.

Stryker, wearing very thin rubber gloves, assembled the rifle and looked through the scope toward the gathered crowd. He stood back from the former windows far enough so that the tip of the rifle barrel remained within the space between the boards, none of it protruding to the exterior of the building. The morning was dry and calm with the air not yet warming excessively. Stryker rotated the rifle slightly to take in the street beyond the Courthouse, before returning his sight to the crowd. Three times he smoothly swiveled the rifle to focus on the crowd, and then on a late model silver Cadillac parked one block past the Courthouse and then back on the crowd. He glanced at his watch: 11:52. He continued his surveillance without the aid of the scope. Twice more he moved his sight from the Cadillac to the crowd. 11:55. Nothing changed. 11:57. Two protest signs emerged from the crowd. 11:58. A police officer moved people back a few steps from the building to the edge of the grass and the sidewalk. 11:59. Stryker resumed his observation with 100% concentration through the scope of his rifle. Once again he rotated his view to the Cadillac and back again.

Two minutes later Silvis Walker stepped from the back seat of a blue Ford Explorer and circled the edge of the crowd to face the cameras with his back to the Courthouse building. Stryker viewed Walker's face clearly through the scope, while his index finger rested on the trigger of the rifle. He breathed very slowly and deeply and his heart rate dropped below fifty beats per minute. He then swiveled the rifle to the Cadillac and fired a single shot into the trunk of the defenseless vehicle. Without waiting to see the result of the shot, he instantly swung the rifle barrel back slightly to the left and set his sight on Walker. The crowd turned as one to the cracking sound to the east, which was followed immediately by the bleeping of the Cadillac's car alarm. Collectively they turned their heads back toward the Courthouse, but Walker was nowhere to be seen. He lay unmoving on the ground with a reddening hole just above his left eye.

Stryker pulled back from the window and set the rifle on the floor in front of him. He rose up, ready to leave the building, when he was stopped short by the sickening feel of cold metal pressing against the back left side of his neck.

"Nice shot, Mr. Axman," said a deep, calm voice connected to the cold metal.

CHAPTER THIRTY-FIVE

Stryker's mind raced as quickly as his accelerated heart rate. Axman? Somebody referring to him as Mr. Axman? Clearly not a policeman who happened to stumble upon him, but how could anyone be here other than by chance? Axman?

"Don't even think about reaching back for that rifle," the voice instructed firmly. "Now, take two slow, very slow, steps backward away from the window."

Stryker found no familiarity in the voice as he weighed his options while simultaneously trying to determine who was behind him and how he got there. He also considered the urgency of movement in the passing seconds following the shooting of Walker. A harsh nudge of the gun into his neck prompted Stryker to comply with the request for slow backward movement. He still said nothing.

"Exactly how I would have done it," said the voice with a touch of self-admiration. "Assuming you were going to make the hit, which we knew you were, doing it as a sniper during his only public appearance would clearly be your preferred option," the voice nearly whispered into his left ear. "I approached the situation as if I were going to take the shot, and this is where I ended up. It was a bit cold spending the night here last night, but it was worth it when you came in this morning. What's it like to be so predictable Mr. Axman?"

Stryker offered nothing in response, but he silently cursed the evaporating escape opportunity with the inexorable ticking of his mental clock. The gun holder would surely want to be out of there without delay, other than the brief delay that would come from reveling in his deductive brilliance. That moment seemed to be winding down.

With his eyes briefly closed, Stryker slowed his breathing and internalized a hopeful wish as he moved his left hand slightly. His captor bit.

"Now, now, steady there," he commanded in the continued calm and confident voice of someone who held an undeniable position of control. "What say you raise those hands, slowly, before we say our goodbye?'

Wish granted. Stryker knew that the odds were against him, but he had two immediate advantages. First, his killer was standing right next to him with the gun pressed into his neck – presumably his ego demanded the close proximity. Had he been holding a gun across the room, Stryker would have had no chance at all. Second, the gun holder now expected movement with the command for the hands to be raised. Stryker breathed slowly while he prepared to try his only opportunity.

"Now," the voice commanded firmly with a nudge at Stryker's neck.

Stryker readied himself as he began to raise his hands while asking a question to provide further distraction. "So, can I guess who sent you to . . ." he began until his hands hit shoulder height. Then in mid-sentence and with all the quickness he could muster, knowing that his life depended on it, Stryker spun to his left exaggerating the movement of his neck away from the gun and his left forearm toward the gun. It could have been the last movement of his life, but the only thing that flashed through Stryker's mind was the action of following immediately with his left foot into the groin of his assailant.

During his sudden and violent move, Stryker heard but ignored the "phffft" sound of a silenced shot followed instantly with a thud as the bullet struck the wall to the right of the boarded windows. Stryker followed his own left arm, left foot movement with a continued spin in which his left fist struck crushingly down on the wrist that held the gun while his right knee drove upward as hard as he could into the face that had doubled over toward the floor. The man's body shot instantly backward into an unmoving heap on the floor. Stryker assumed that his neck had snapped, but he cared only to note that the man had stopped breathing. Stryker quickly checked through his pockets while mentally noting the passage of time.

The pockets yielded nothing more than a cell phone, which Stryker stuffed into his own pocket. The dead man appeared to be in his early thirties and generically white and indistinctive. Stryker guessed that almost two minutes had passed since the shooting, so he quickly grabbed the gym bag and moved to leave the building. He left the untraceable rifle along with the silenced pistol. Puzzling questions were sure to plague the local authorities once they ended up in the building. Puzzling questions if Stryker managed to escape.

He removed the glove on his left hand as he descended the stairs, but kept the right glove on until he relocked and closed the alleyway door behind him. He saw movement and commotion on Lexington Avenue, heading toward the Courthouse, as he walked calmly away from Lexington on Spring. Four blocks later he hopped on a city bus for a short ride to the west side of town. Once there, Stryker boarded another bus for a longer trip to Kansas City. He spent the entire ride expecting the bus to be stopped by a roadblock like in the 1940s police movies, and despite the fact that the distance was covered without interruption, it seemed liked a much longer trip than when Stryker had taken it two days earlier.

Stryker felt as though he breathed for the first time in hours when he stepped off the bus and into the anonymity of the crowded streets of Kansas City. He pondered the possibility of grabbing some food but decided to simply move forward with his travel plans as directly as possible. He made a quick visit to the post office to retrieve the Scott Densmore identification and credit cards and then jumped into a taxi for a ride to the airport for his flight to San Francisco. He chose not to eat in the airport either and was thrilled to find that his flight would leave at its scheduled time. With as much thinking as he had to do, Stryker knew that the two thousand mile flight would be quicker than the eleven mile bus ride.

CHAPTER THIRTY-SIX

From Kansas City to San Francisco and San Francisco to Portland by plane, and from Portland to Seattle by car, Stryker struggled to make sense of the unexpected turn of events. The key elements, as he saw them, began with the announcement of his retirement on the Axman website. The announcement had prompted the dialogue between 'Castleman,' 'Guillotine-lover,' and 'Hatchet' that clearly had been aimed at getting him to accept one last job. In accepting that job, Stryker had traveled to Independence and had taken advantage of the first real opportunity to take out Walker. While he planned and carried out that assignment, someone else had been mimicking his plan, not in competition to kill Walker, but for an opportunity to kill Stryker.

It seemed clear that the assassin didn't know Stryker's identity, although he knew about Axman and about the Walker assignment. Stryker's retirement announcement, followed by the online discussion, made it likely that Silvis Walker would be his last job. Apparently, whoever had posted the assignment wanted to make sure of the same thing. But why? That was the part that Stryker puzzled over for much of his trip home. Evidently, he posed a threat of some kind, but Stryker couldn't figure out how he could be a threat to anyone else without causing serious trouble for himself.

Another issue he pondered at great length – who was the man with the gun who had been sent to kill him? Was he operating from another website like Axman? Were there others? What did he know about Stryker beyond the Walker assignment? Stryker regretted the quick death that denied him the opportunity to question the assassin, but also realized that he hadn't had the time to question the man in any event. Which brought him back to thinking about who had sent the assassin in the first place. And why? He also found it interesting that the assassin had waited until after the shooting of Walker before preparing to kill Stryker. Again, the question was why.

By the time Stryker reached his condo in Seattle, at nearly 2:00 the morning after Walker's death, he had tossed around the facts as he knew them hundreds of times and had discovered no answers that were even remotely worthwhile. The assassin knew about the Axman site and the posting of Walker's name. The assassin said "we" knew that Stryker was going to make the hit. The assassin knew that Stryker would likely assume the role of sniper for the killing. The assassin showed up to kill Stryker, but not until after Stryker killed Walker. He knew that taking the Walker assignment had been a mistake.

That much Stryker knew, and from there he made some assumptions. He assumed that the assassin didn't know his identity since he addressed him as "Mr. Axman." He assumed that the "we" included whoever made the posting to the Axman website. He assumed that he posed some sort of threat to whoever controlled the Axman site. Finally, he assumed that whoever wanted him dead wouldn't be happy at the result of the events in Mendelson's store, and thus would try again to find him and kill him.

With the assumption that the assassin, and thereby the director of the assassin, didn't know Stryker's identity, Stryker wanted to assume that he would be safe merely by staying away from the Axman site and thus from any further jobs. He wasn't completely certain about the safety of that assumption, however. The more he thought about it, the more Stryker realized that he would need some very specific help. Help that he could get from Al Jeffries. Help that he'd relied on earlier in his Axman days.

6 YEARS AGO

CHAPTER THIRTY-SEVEN

His head throbbed. Blood continued to seep from Stryker's side as it had for the past twelve hours. The newspaper he pressed against the wound approached saturation and soon would need to be replaced once again, despite the fact that the cold temperatures surely slowed the flow of life from his body. Stryker had no real idea of how long he had lost consciousness after stumbling into the alleyway where he sat huddled, but he sensed that time was not working in his favor. His options weren't extensive either, but he knew that something had to be done despite the fact that any sort of extensive movement would accelerate the blood flow. He slowly inched his back up, pressing and scraping against the brick wall while compressing the newspaper as hard as he could bear with his left hand against the wound. Sweat immediately beaded on his forehead from the movement, despite the continued cold temperatures.

Three immediate problems faced Stryker as he readied himself to take affirmative steps toward survival. First, he couldn't travel far on foot, and even if he began, he didn't have a specific destination in mind. Second, he wasn't sure that he could avoid unwanted scrutiny from a cab driver or bus driver should he try to travel by those means. Third and most importantly, what he really needed was medical care, but whether on foot or by wheels, he couldn't go to a hospital or doctor without facing questions and reports that he needed to avoid. Bleed to death in the street? Deal with the wound and end up under investigation or arrest? Stryker found his immediate options to be less than enticing.

On the streets of Philadelphia. Injured and knowing no one in town. Unable to rest on simply self-reliance as he had so often in the past. He hated the feeling of helplessness, but he needed help. Al Jeffries in New York, he thought. Not a great option, but at least a chance.

Stryker moved cautiously into a convenience store with fresh newspaper as unobtrusive as possible against his side. He used cash to buy an energy bar, energy drink, and a cell phone with prepaid minutes. The clerk, apparently of some Eastern European descent, gave a momentary suspicious look at Stryker before dully returning to the bikini photos in his celebrity gossip magazine. Stryker stepped out of the store and into another alleyway where he leaned against the wall and powered up the phone. He called information in New York City and got the phone number for the central headquarters of the NYPD. He ate and drank a bit and mentally crossed his fingers before calling the number.

"NYPD. Sergeant Bishop. How can I direct your call?" The voice sounded bored and expressionless as Stryker tried to imagine a bland face over a dark blue uniform with a belly protruding on top of an overworked belt. Indiscernible noises mingled in the background.

"I'm not sure," Stryker began with a concerted effort to keep his voice as normal as possible. "I'm a neighbor trying to help out with a family emergency and I need to reach Al Jeffries. I know that he's a Detective with the NYPD, but I don't have a clue where he's stationed or how to locate him. It's an emergency."

"Hold on a second." Stryker listened to nothing on the line and hoped that he was merely on hold rather than disconnected. He waited expectantly and impatiently, and noted that his current newspaper looked more maroon than white.

He finally heard a clicking sound, followed by Sergeant Bishop's disinterested voice. "I can only tell you that he's working out of Precinct 14. You'll have to call there to track him down if you can't reach him at home."

"Fourteen. Thanks. Can you put me through to them, or do you have a number?" Stryker asked hopefully.

"You'll have to call them yourself," directed Bishop, who then proceeded to give Stryker the phone number.

Stryker's call to Precinct 14 could have been answered by Bishop's telephonic twin for all that Stryker could tell, except that he identified himself as Sergeant Kelly.

"Hey there," greeted Stryker. "I'm looking for Al Jeffries."

"Not here," replied Kelly with no evident inclination to help.

"Any clue where I can contact him?" Stryker tried to find the correct mix of urgency and detachment, although he doubted how closely the distracted Sergeant Kelly really listened. He had little doubt about how much Sergeant Kelly cared. "I need to track him down in connection with an out-of-town family emergency. I'm just a neighbor trying to help out and I don't have a home number for him. I just know that he works out of your precinct."

"Nothing I can do," said Kelly without apparent remorse. "Al's off today and tomorrow, and I'm not allowed to give out any phone numbers or personal information. Sorry."

"No, I know you can't," offered Stryker, "but I've really got to get in touch with him immediately and he doesn't have a listed home number." A quick but hard shiver ran through him and he winced with pain at the movement through his injury. He regained his breath quickly. "Umm, could I give you my name and number and have you get it to Detective Jeffries? I know he'll be really upset if he doesn't hear about this for two more days. He'll want to call me back right away. Could you do that without too much bother?"

"Yeah, okay," sighed Kelly dramatically with unenthusiastic resignation. "Give me the name and number."

Stryker gave his name and the number of the cell phone, then disconnected the call and waited with his fingers still crossed in his mind. His legs stretched out straight in from of him as he sat in his non-descript alley and remained as still as possible. The cold bit cruelly at his fingers and ears. A police siren screamed nearby, but rapidly faded away to the north.

The ringing of the phone twenty-five minutes later startled Stryker, despite the fact that he waited and hoped for the call for what seemed like two hours. It took him a moment to find the right button the answer the call. "Al?" he asked.

"Thorne Stryker? Is that really you?" Jeffries asked in a loud and jovial voice. "What's this crap about a family emergency?"

"If I can call myself family, then it's not a lie," Stryker began to explain. "I'm in Philadelphia and I need help badly. And quickly. And it's got to be under the radar." Stryker paused while he caught his breath. "I'm sorry to do this to you Al, but I'm desperate and I've got nowhere else to turn right now."

"Hey, you know I'll help you out if I can, Stryk," Jeffries responded with assurance. "What kind of trouble are you in and what do you need from me?"

Stryker hesitated, but quickly realized that the decision already had been made as soon as he called Jeffries in the first place. "I can't explain everything now, but I'm hurt, and I can't go to a hospital. I'm on the street in Philly and I'm not sure I can move much without drawing attention or making the injury worse. Or both."

"What the hell have you gotten yourself into Stryker? No, skip that for now," Jeffries reconsidered and then thought for a moment. "Ah, okay. I know a guy who does some off the books medical work. He owes me a favor. I'll grab him and come to you as quick as we can. Sounds like we should drive so that we can get you back here as well, so we're looking at maybe two and a half hours, maybe a little less, assuming I can find him right away. You okay for that long?"

"Yeah, I'll be here," Stryker felt relief at the simple prospect of Jeffries on his way to Philadelphia. "Call me when you get close and I'll tell you where I am."

"No problem. You just sit tight and I'll get the horses moving. Anything else I should bring along besides Doc and his gear?"

"A blanket might be good so we don't get blood all over your car," Stryker tried to laugh. "Thanks Al."

Jeffries gave Stryker his cell phone number and then scrambled into action. Stryker put the phone back in his pocket and snuggled next to the wall and dumpster in the alleyway where he hoped to be able to wait without moving. He sat quietly and lamented the mistakes that necessitated his call to Jeffries.

6 YEARS AGO – ABOUT 12 HOURS EARLIER

CHAPTER THIRTY-EIGHT

The streets themselves seemed to shiver in the bitter Philadelphia cold of late January and the nighttime darkness amplified the inescapable feeling of the freezing temperatures. Stryker worked to control his body against the stifling chill of the elements, but the cold penetrated with the ease of an ice pick falling point first on a marshmallow. He hated the shivering, which he associated with a lack of discipline, but the extended time in the wind and freezing air had taken its toll as he tried to huddle nearer the wall where he stood waiting. The building helped block some of the wind, but provided no soothing warmth.

The streets hosted few people that evening and those who had no choice but to brave the cold moved with the intent purpose of a heat-seeking missile, ignoring everything around them. This was not a night for lingering or for casual strolls in the evening air. Yet Stryker lingered, and shivered, but remained intently focused on his purpose.

Stryker waited across the street from the small but exclusive Mauricio's Restaurant where Abdi Hassan ate pasta heavy on garlic in a room heavy on Mediterranean atmosphere. The restaurant was heavy on comforting heat as well. Hassan dined alone in the nearly empty room while his ever-present bodyguard stood near the door, standing erect with his eyes never resting on one spot for more than two or three seconds. The bodyguard showed no signs of distraction from the tempting smells that permeated the small establishment, but his alert watchfulness heightened as he saw Hassan finishing off the last of his wine and pasta.

Hassan had lived in the United States for the past 11 years, during which time he had spent hundreds of thousands of dollars on travel, restaurants and hotels. U.S. citizenship never entered his thoughts, despite the fact that he thoroughly enjoyed the fruits of the American free enterprise system. He also planned to do his part to destroy that system. His current activities toward that end included recruiting and organizing dissident cells, although the eventual training was to be provided by others. He also worked actively and with increasing effectiveness in fund raising, and had become especially adept at moving and hiding large sums of money. His dinner at Mauricio's marked the successful completion of his latest recruiting and fund raising quotas. He hoped now to receive direction to move forward with a large-scale plan for the systematic poisoning of the water supply in a number of major east coast cities.

Hassan's name appeared on the Axman website less than a month earlier. Stryker's subsequent research revealed an overly cautious target, seemingly without friends or vices, who never stayed in any city for longer than six weeks. Hassan had just completed five weeks in Philadelphia and Stryker had no idea where he might be headed next. Because Hassan's restaurant trips marked his only consistent forays into the public, Stryker decided that he had no choice but to take advantage of an opportunity that might prove difficult to replicate. Thus he shivered in the relentless winter cold while waiting for the comfortable Hassan to finish his final meal.

Stryker had followed Hassan as his bodyguard drove from their hotel to the outrageously expensive restaurant. To Stryker's surprise, the bodyguard had parked their rental car in a lot one block east of Mauricio's, and the two walked together to the restaurant. Stryker could only assume that they would retrace their steps after Hassan finished eating, and their time on foot in the parking lot would give Stryker the opening he decided to use. From his vantage point across the street, Stryker could not see Hassan, but he maintained a clear view of the bodyguard's hulking presence near the door. His movement would trigger Stryker's move into position in the dimly lit parking lot. He would have preferred a situation without the bodyguard's presence, but his observations of Hassan made it clear that such an opportunity would not be forthcoming.

The movement of the bodyguard came at 10:25 pm with the streets outside no less cold and no less quiet than they had been throughout Stryker's vigil. The bodyguard moved away from the door, which signaled to Stryker that Hassan was getting up from his table and preparing to re-emerge onto the street from the cozily warm restaurant. Stryker moved away from the restaurant toward the parking lot and then skipped across the street before Hassan stepped out. A single beat up Honda Civic moved down the street, followed by a green taxi and then emptiness. Looking over his shoulder at the sidewalk in front of Mauricio's, Stryker stopped at the corner of the lot where Hassan's car sat in the back and middle of the lot, well off of the street. Stryker flexed his frozen fingers near the handle of the silenced pistol in his right jacket pocket and kept his eyes on the entrance of the restaurant. As soon as the bodyguard cleared the door, Stryker turned into the lot and moved to the brick wall at the far end of Hassan's car where he waited in the shadows. Although he no longer shivered, he vigorously rubbed his hands before blowing into them, then slipped on his thin leather gloves. He continued to flex his fingers on the warming handle of the pistol and looked in anticipation at the corner. He instantly lost all thoughts about the cold.

Thirty seconds later, Hassan and the bodyguard rounded the corner and walked toward the car where Stryker waited, unmoving in the darkness, with his right hand now out of his pocket and firmly gripping his silenced pistol. He waited. Hassan and the bodyguard, heads down and silent, both approached the driver's side of the car, presumably heading to the front and back seats. Once they moved within two steps of the car, Stryker stepped from the shadows.

"Hands up," he forcefully directed with a movement of the gun. He moved slightly to his right so that he had a clear view of Hassan past the bodyguard. Both men jerked quickly in surprise, but neither moved nor spoke. Hassan wore a fur-lined hat over his heavy topcoat. His hat, coat, gloves and shoes were limited variations of shades of black. The bodyguard's coat appeared thinner, but covered a body much bulkier. His head and hands braved the cold without reinforcement.

"I said, hands up," Stryker repeated with the gun more threateningly outstretched as he moved one step closer and to the right again. The bodyguard, at the front of the car, stood closer than Hassan to Stryker, but not directly between the two.

"You may have my wallet," offered Hassan as he raised his hands just above shoulder level. "I will give it to you."

Stryker ignored him. "You too," he gestured with the gun at the bodyguard who had not moved, but who now slowly raised his hands. "Now," he instructed the bodyguard with a nod and a wave of the pistol, "step away from the car and start walking back toward the street. I need to have a quick talk with your boss."

Hassan darted a worried glance at the bodyguard and then back at Stryker. The bodyguard remained unmoved with his eyes locked on the gun.

"Look," Stryker spoke to the bodyguard again, "this isn't about you. You've done your job, but now it's time for you to walk away. Slowly. Toward the street." He directed again with the gun and a nonchalant nod of his head that hid his mounting impatience. The bodyguard made no move to separate himself from the gun pointing at his chest.

Stryker tried again. "I really don't want to hurt you," he said honestly in a calm voice. "I need a few words with Mr. Hassan," he said not so honestly, "and I need to do it without you here. Now move," he demanded more forcefully.

The bodyguard moved, but as a man of dutiful commitment, he moved directly at Stryker. His quickness for his size surprised Stryker, as did his attack into the barrel of a pointed gun. Nonetheless, with the gun pointed directly at the bodyguard, Stryker had plenty of time to shoot. He didn't. He genuinely didn't want to hurt the man whom he viewed in the same role as an innocent bystander. His job was to kill Hassan, not the bodyguard.

The bodyguard charged with a bellowing roar and Stryker lifted the gun while keeping one eye on Hassan. He brought the butt of the gun down with crashing force just above the ear on the left side of the bodyguard's head as the bodyguard's right shoulder drove into Stryker's sternum. Stryker felt a burning sensation just below his left ribs as he fell hard to the ground with the full weight of the bodyguard on his chest. Stryker's head bounced numbingly off the pavement and stars blurred his vision momentarily. He regained his sight in time to see a curiously stunned Hassan turn to run from the unmoving pile of bodies. Stryker didn't attempt to free himself from the bodyguard, but instead fired three quick, silenced shots at the retreating figure who instantly pitched forward into his own private pile.

Stryker then moved to extricate himself from beneath the oversized bodyguard only to seize his breath in pain at the attempted exertion. The burning sensation intensified in his left side and made it impossible to lift that side in order to roll off the recently employed bodyguard. He winced again as he shifted his weight to push up with his right arm while trying to tuck his left side in tighter under the body he wore as a blanket. Through much pain and effort, he pushed the bodyguard off his now-agonizing left side where the body thumped to the ground with an accompanying clatter of metal. Stryker struggled to his knees where he saw the bodyguard's six-inch blade lying on the ground, covered in Stryker's blood. He pocketed his gun, picked up the knife, and then carefully stood up while holding tight to his warm and wet left abdomen. The bodyguard's chest moved up and down as he lay unconsciously on his back with closed eyes staring up at a few scattered flakes of snow.

Stryker walked slowly over to Hassan to verify his demise and then immediately left the parking lot by the back alleyway as he had planned for his exit. He walked for nearly a mile through cold dark alleys and quiet streets until he felt increasingly dizzy with a persistent throbbing at the back of his head. He finally stopped in an alley where he tried to disappear amongst a pile of stuffed black plastic garbage bags that were stacked without care next to a pair of overflowing dumpsters. With newspaper pressed against his side, Stryker struggled to slow his breathing and clear his vision. He lost the battle as he dropped into unconsciousness.

CHAPTER THIRTY-NINE

Stryker estimated that more than an hour had passed since he called Jeffries, but how much more, he couldn't be sure. He remained virtually invisible, wedged up against the dumpster and garbage bags in the dimly lit alleyway, and hoped that he could remain still until Jeffries called back. He was cold, weak, and highly annoyed at the feeling of vulnerability that he wasn't accustomed to enduring. He prepared himself to act drunk and slightly incoherent should anyone approach with unwanted curiosity. The slightly incoherent part wouldn't be much of a stretch.

He felt better at the certainty that the blood flow had slowed considerably, and maybe stopped entirely with the combination of the persistently cold temperatures, pressure on the wound, and his sustained lack of movement. Nonetheless, he knew that he had lost a considerable amount of blood and that the wound in his side needed immediate attention. He could only hope that Jeffries came through with the promised help. He glanced at the cell phone and willed it to ring, but the phone refused to cooperate.

While Stryker didn't hear the phone ring, he did hear voices approaching from his left in the alley. His stomach dropped at the thought of the potential difficulties that approached along with the voices. It sounded like at least two men, and other than reaching for the grip of his pistol, before remembering that he had already discarded the gun, Stryker remained motionless.

"Could you believe that chick comin' on to me like that?" Stryker heard. "How can someone that ugly have that much nerve?"

"I thought you two made a perfect couple," his companion laughed in a deep and gravelly voice coated with alcohol despite the morning hour. "She's probably still there if you wanna go back." The voices moved slowly, but drew closer and Stryker closed his eyes as much as possible while leaving enough of a slit between his eyelids to see the two men.

"Up yours," the first voice responded. "Unless you wanted to go back to see if she might be interested in you – now that I turned her down, that is." The voices were nearly right on top of Stryker who remained perfectly still.

"Hell, give her another hour and she'll end up out here tryin' to pick up this guy." Stryker saw the two men pause next to him and he readied himself for action. He had the advantage of their assumption that he was a harmless, passed-out drunk. He had the disadvantage of knowing that any quick movement would certainly start the blood flowing again. He also didn't know how much strength he could actually muster at the moment.

"Who?" the first voice asked. "Oh, geez, didn't even see him there." Stryker tensed in readiness. "Nah, even she wouldn't stoop that low." The two men remained stopped next to Stryker who wished he still had his gun.

"Let's get going before we catch some kind of disease," voice number two offered. "The Blue Box opens early. Let's head over there." The men started to move again. "Ain't nothin' but the best lookin' ladies there. Course, that might make it a little tough for you since that's not the kind that you attract, but you can at least enjoy watching me." He laughed as their voices receded from Stryker.

"Asshole," was the last thing Stryker heard from them as he finally relaxed again.

Twenty minutes later Stryker had dozed off until the ringing of the cell phone startled him back to consciousness. He reached again for the gun that wasn't there, then fumbled with the phone before flipping it open to answer the call.

"How ya doing, buddy?" came Jeffries voice on the other end of the call.

"Still here," responded Stryker without enthusiasm. "You getting close already?"

"Already?" questioned Jeffries. "It's taken longer than I hoped, but yeah, we're approaching the city now. Where are you?"

Stryker directed Jeffries to the south side of the city and identified the cross streets nearest his alley. "You got the doc with you?" he asked.

"He's here and thrilled about it," said Jeffries. "Nothing he'd rather be doing this afternoon," he paused. "So, I see where you are on my map here. Looks like we're no more than ten minutes from you. You okay till we get there?"

"Not going anywhere," answered Stryker. "So yeah, I'm okay. See you in a few." He closed the phone and returned it to his pocket with a wave of relief finally overcoming the helplessness he'd been feeling.

Stryker sat, somewhat prone, in the back of Jeffries' car while he enjoyed the heat emanating from the front. The doctor worked on his side. One of the first things the doctor had done was to give Stryker a shot of some kind, and Stryker found it odd how willingly he accepted an injection from a man he'd never seen before. The doctor had cleaned the wound and was applying temporary stitches, but confessed that he couldn't make any significant decisions until he could look at Stryker more carefully in his office. As soon as he finished with the stitches, Jeffries began the drive back to New York.

"How ya doing back there?" Jeffries called over his shoulder.

"Haven't felt better since yesterday," Stryker responded with half a smile. "Thanks for asking. And keep your eyes on the road."

"Oh yeah, you're one to be giving orders right now," Jeffries laughed. "You've got a lot of explaining to do son," he glanced over at the doctor sitting in the passenger seat next to him, "but we'll wait for that till we get back to New York. Why don't you get some sleep now." Stryker's eyes were already firmly closed.

When Stryker woke up again, he hid his initial confusion as he found himself lying in an unfamiliar bed with an equally unfamiliar dresser facing him. He started to get up from the bed before an immediate, searing pain in his side sent him rigidly back to the mattress. Gradually he remembered the back seat of the car with Jeffries driving, and he assumed he had awakened in New York. There was no sign of Jeffries or the doctor, but Stryker judiciously decided that patience would prove to be a virtue in his present circumstance, so he relaxed into the mattress with the plan of moving as little as possible.

When he awoke once again the pain in his side felt minor in comparison to his exploding bladder. Jeffries paced the floor and Stryker quickly called for assistance.

"Bathroom," Stryker mumbled through dry lips.

"No, the doctor's gone," replied Jeffries as he stopped at the foot of the bed.

"Bathroom!" Stryker repeated with more urgent clarity.

"Oh, yeah, let me help you," said Jeffries as he helped Stryker move from the bed to the bathroom and then back again.

"So, what did the Doc have to say?" asked Stryker in a more normal voice after his cautious return to the bed. He noticed the very visible scar on Jeffries' left ear that had been turned away from him in the car.

"Well, we went straight to his office once we got back to the city," explained Jeffries. "He checked you out pretty carefully and decided you were damn lucky in terms of internal organs. You lost a lot of blood, but he cleaned things up and stitched you up good. Says you'll be slowed down for a while, but no long term damage."

Stryker nodded in relief and gratitude as he looked around the room. Jeffries still stood next to the bed looking down on Stryker. His commanding presence always gave others the impression of size that he didn't really possess. He stood an even six feet tall and weighed the same 205 pounds that he carried when he was twenty. Stryker noticed flecks of gray at the temples of his otherwise dark, closely cropped hair. His nose angled a bit to one side and his cheeks carried an ever-present stubble of beard. His eyes remained constantly alert and intelligent under a forehead permanently marked with two deep, horizontal wrinkle lines.

"So," Jeffries went on with a quiet voice that was laced with mild exasperation, "you ready to tell me what the heck's going on? I haven't heard from you in what, five or six years? Next thing I know you're in an alley in Philadelphia with a major knife wound and you can't go to a hospital? Now I don't mind helping out – coming to get you to play taxi driver and then nursemaid – but I think I deserve a little explanation. Or rather, a lot of explanation. You ready to spill the beans instead of the blood?"

Stryker stared at the wing-shaped brackets attaching the handles to the dresser and thought that they looked like military insignias. He anticipated this moment, but he still didn't like it and he hesitated while focused on the dresser drawers. Eventually, he sighed heavily and responded, "Yeah, I guess so. Now?"

"Now works just fine for me," replied Jeffries with his arms crossed in front of his hard chest. "You're not going anywhere and I've got nowhere that I need to be right now. I could be entertained with a little story telling," he shrugged himself into a chair next to Stryker's bed. "I'm all ears, buddy."

Starting slowly and methodically, Stryker told Jeffries all about the initial contact with General MacAfee, the Axman website, the first killing in Los Angeles and the assignments he had undertaken over the ensuing years. He finished with the killing of Abdi Hassan. Jeffries nodded occasionally, but otherwise sat without saying a word until it was clear that Stryker had concluded his story. He waited for a moment for Stryker to finish it off with a 'just kidding' followed by a story of some trouble with the law and an unrelated street mugging, but it never came. Instead, Stryker finished talking and simply looked at Jeffries with serious eyes, waiting for a reaction.

"Are you even half serious?" demanded Jeffries after a momentary silence.

"More than half, I'm afraid," Stryker admitted with a direct look at his friend. "You really think I'd make all that up?"

"Well, one could hope," Jeffries laughed. "You do remember that I'm a policeman, right? The kind of guy who's out looking for Hassan's killer right now? The kind of guy that shouldn't be helping a fugitive? The kind of guy who'll be back hanging out with hundreds of other policemen on the job tomorrow?"

"Yeah, I know. That's why I figured you'd have the contacts to be able to help me." Stryker looked hard at the friend he hadn't seen in years. "And, I assumed that all of the negatives in this situation might be outweighed by Omega Operations. I hope I didn't assume wrong."

Jeffries didn't hesitate. "Of course you didn't assume wrong. You're here aren't you? I've just gotta extract a bit of guilt as payment if I can." He smiled broadly. "We've still got some significant talking to do, however. You up for a little food first?"

"You know, now that you bring it up, I'd kill for something to eat." He raised his eyebrows at Jeffries and followed it up with a smile. "Got any soup?"

"I'll be back in fifteen minutes," replied Jeffries as he walked to the door of the room. "Don't go anywhere."

Ten minutes later Stryker remained unmoved in the bed while he examined the attractively decorated room with curiosity. The windows were decorated with a colorful, flowered sash, and a lace pillow adorned the seat of the chair where Jeffries had sat. Two pictures on the wall were bright prints of Claude Monet flower paintings and the mirror over the dresser sat within an ornate, silver frame. Stryker tried to imagine Jeffries making the decorating choices, but decided that the apartment must have come furnished.

A third alternative presented itself when the door opened after a light knock to reveal a very pretty, petite woman carrying a serving tray with soup and bread.

"Al said you could use something to eat," she offered as she moved into the room, "but he didn't say what you'd like to drink. Coffee?"

"Umm, no thanks," he smiled in gratitude while hiding his surprise at the woman's unexpected appearance, "just a glass of water would be great."

"Of course, right away," she smiled in return. "I'm Amanda by the way." She wore a comfortable looking white sweater over a pale blue blouse and well-worn jeans. Her hair was tied up at the back of her head and she wore minimal makeup and jewelry. The friendly kindness she projected would have made her an ideal candidate for the nursing profession and Stryker wondered momentarily if Jeffries had hired her to help care for him.

"Thorne," he responded without asking the questions that ran through his mind. "Thorne Stryker."

"Yes, Al told me. From his Army days." She placed the tray on the end table next to the bed. "Here, you start eating and I'll have Al bring the water. Anything else you need?"

"No, thank you. It smells great."

"Al will be right in," she waved as she moved to the door. "Let him know if you need anything else."

Stryker began with the soup, beef barley, although he found it awkward to eat while moving as little as possible in the bed. Within a minute, Jeffries re-entered the room.

"Amanda, huh?" Stryker questioned after swallowing.

"Oh yeah, guess you didn't know," Jeffries laughed. "Been married just over four years now. Got a little boy too. Anthony. He'll be three this summer."

"Well, congratulations," Stryker offered with a smile from only the right side of his mouth. "Now I feel really lousy about calling you and getting you involved with my problems. You should have told me Al, or you should have just said 'no'."

"As you may recall, my good man, you didn't exactly let me know what I was getting myself into when you called. Remember that?" Stryker rubbed his eyes in frustration. "That said, it wouldn't have made any difference and you know that. Amanda's cool and she wants to help. If anything happens I can always say I was simply helping a friend, but I didn't know any more than that. Okay by you?"

"Yeah, thanks," Stryker grudgingly agreed. "It's not like I had a lot of options, I guess." He paused and looked down at the empty bowl. "Besides, Amanda makes a hell of a bowl of soup. Any chance there's any more?"

"You know, I'm sure there is, and I think I'm going to have to join you this time. It does smell good."

Thirty minutes later after some reminiscing and catching up on recent events, Jeffries turned serious. "So, let's talk about this website stuff."

"Axman," Stryker reminded him. "Okay."

"How many jobs have you taken?"

"Five total," Stryker responded without having to think about it. "The first one for MacAfee, almost four years ago, and then three others between then and Hassan yesterday. He was number five."

"And you really have no idea who's supplying the names now that the General's dead?" Jeffries questioned.

"None," admitted Stryker. "Obviously someone the General knew and presumably trusted, since he must have shared the information about the site and the code, but that doesn't really tell us much."

"And it doesn't bother you that you don't know who's on the other end of the assignments?" Jeffries quizzed. "Doesn't that seem odd?"

"Sure, it's kind of weird," agreed Stryker, "but like I said, it's clearly someone connected to MacAfee. Plus, I check out any assignment that's posted. There've been two that I decided not to take, different reasons for each, but the bottom line is, I have the final say on whether or not I take a job. Every assignment I've taken is someone who's avoided justice, who deserved to die – at least from my perspective. The kind of guys that you and your cop friends are trying to get off the streets in the first place. I use a different method, but we're working toward the same end. So, it doesn't really matter who's posting the names, does it?"

"Omega Operations in civilian clothes," Jeffries nodded slowly. "I get it. Still, it's a little awkward given my current line of work, you know?"

"Yeah," smiled Stryker, "but you've always been a man of subtlety and depth, right? A little convoluted morality play is right up your alley – assuming you can keep it between us without involving the beautiful Amanda."

"Well, Amanda doesn't know anything about Double O either," admitted Jeffries, "so she sure as hell isn't going to hear about your Axman activities." He held out his hand, which Stryker took in as firm a shake as he could muster. "So, we're good buddy. Let's just get you well enough to get you the hell out of my house, okay?" With a laugh he left the room and went to find Anthony.

CHAPTER FORTY

Two weeks later the Seattle sky loomed gray and threatening as the wind whipped through the air that for the moment remained free of raindrops. The temperature hovered near 40 degrees and little natural light remained despite the fact that the clock had just registered 3:00 in the afternoon. Stryker sat and looked out the window of his condo, fascinated at the visual texture brought to the sky by the heavy rain falling from the dark clouds he could see in the west.

Stryker had been home for a week, during which time he focused on physical recovery while he monitored the Philadelphia newspapers online and stayed in close contact with Jeffries. The dual sources confirmed that the Philadelphia police faced a dead end in their investigation of Hassan's death, and that no weapons or other persons had been found at the scene. Stryker wished for the best for the bodyguard, though he continued to lament the carelessness that had involved the bodyguard in the first place.

Following his discussions with Jeffries, Stryker had independently questioned his Axman activities and decided that everything he explained to Jeffries was genuine rather than simply forced justification for his actions. It honestly didn't bother him that the postings came from an unknown source since the original one from General MacAfee. His ability to accept or reject the jobs that were posted worked for his sensibilities and he truly felt that he had made a positive contribution to society by eliminating some of the baser elements that had eluded law enforcement. Nonetheless, he had not revisited the web site.

Jeffries himself brought a different revelation as Stryker found it surprising that he liked the fact that Jeffries was in on his Axman secret. Stryker had never felt the slightest temptation to tell anyone about the site or about his activities, but now he felt no remorse about the fact that Jeffries knew. The close call with Hassan's bodyguard had forced his hand to something he wouldn't have done otherwise, but now that the hand was played, Stryker felt comfort in the outcome. Partially he appreciated the fact that Jeffries didn't openly disapprove, and partially he recognized the fact that Jeffries knew only the outline without any specific details, other than Hassan. Overall, having someone he trusted with at least some knowledge of Axman brought Stryker an unexpected sense of calm rather than the anxiety he might have imagined.

Having accepted this unintended result, Stryker then found himself reassessing his Axman role from another perspective. He had no family and few close ties but a considerable amount of money. What if Hassan's bodyguard had killed him? Surely he wouldn't be widely missed in the world, but it still seemed as though there should be some means of closure if he were to die. Those thoughts led Stryker to two rather mundane issues he had never considered before. Writing a will and securing an executor for his estate should the need arise. The writing of the will would be easy enough and he vowed to do so immediately. The issue of an executor proved to be no more troublesome after a moment's thought. LJ Perkins. Perkins' local availability and general 'anything for a buddy' attitude meant that he wouldn't think twice about taking on the role. More importantly, however, Perkins was completely trustworthy, which led Stryker to his next revelation. It was time to tell Perkins about Axman. Sharing with Jeffries proved liberating and not the least bit threatening. Sharing with Perkins would be just as secure, but would allow Stryker to be completely honest with someone about what he was doing. He smiled broadly in anticipation of Perkins' reaction when he shared the whole story.

"Your executor, huh?" repeated Perkins with a hint of skepticism. "Well I don't know anything about it, but sure, I'd be honored. Have you been having morbid thoughts or something? What the heck brings this up now?" He sat back in a comfortable chair in Stryker's living room and took a long drink from a bottle of beer.

"Funny you should ask," Stryker smiled without real humor. "Fact is I came a bit closer to dying than I'd like a couple of weeks ago." He gingerly unbuttoned his shirt and revealed his bandaged side.

"What the hell you talking about, man?" Perkins leaned forward quickly and nearly splashed beer from his bottle. "I didn't hear nothin' about this. What happened? When? You got some serious explaining to do here buddy and I ain't moving till I get some serious answers. Now get started and give me the whole story."

For the second time in two weeks, and the second time in four years, Stryker told the story of MacAfee and the Axman site and his subsequent killings, ending with his problems with Hassan in Philadelphia and the help he received from Al Jeffries.

"So Al knows all about this?" Perkins questioned from the edge of his seat and with a twinge of hurt in his voice.

"Well, he does now. It all came out of the blue for him when I called him from Philadelphia," Stryker explained. "I was a more than a little desperate and I knew that I could trust him, as well as the fact that he could help me. I didn't have any choice but to explain everything to him. Once I did; once I wasn't the only one who knew what I was doing, it only made sense to tell you too." Stryker looked hard at his friend. "Like I said, I want you to be my executor, but I also want you to know what's going on in case something happens again like in Philly."

Perkins stared at Stryker across the room as he sat unmoving with thoughts swirling through his head. He leaned back in his chair and studied the ceiling before looking back at Stryker. Finally, he asked, "So, you gonna keep doing it? The Hatchetman stuff I mean?"

"Axman. Yeah, I guess so," Stryker acknowledged. "Well, all I do is check the site. If I find a posting, then I decide whether or not to take on the job. But, for now, yeah, I'm planning to keep checking the site to see what comes up."

"So, you want any help?" Perkins asked in all seriousness.

Stryker couldn't help but laugh that Perkins' first reaction was to join in. "No way, buddy," he responded with a firm shake of his head. "You've got a good, legitimate business here. And besides, I don't think Marlene would take it too well if she were to find out."

"Yeah, you've gotta have all the fun for yourself, don't you?" Perkins picked up his bottle and took another long drink. "Who knows though. Maybe the next one will be a perfect two-man job. We won't need to let Marlene in on it."

"Who knows," laughed Stryker. "Who knows." After sharing his secret with Perkins, he forgot all about his plan to execute a will.

CHAPTER FORTY-ONE

The room buzzed despite the subduing elegance of the ornate decorations. The women created much of the buzz with their animated conversation, while silently measuring themselves against every other woman in viewing distance. The men contributed to the buzz with their somewhat duller conversation, while silently picturing themselves at the sides of various women other than the one with whom they had arrived. The alcohol contributed to the buzz more than anything else, while slowly and silently creating a much more ugly morning after than all of its participants would like to believe possible.

The wealthy and influential gathered for the $200 a plate dinner to hear Julius Kinnard speak about his latest travels to the disappearing Amazonian rain forest and his pending muckraking book on the role of major American industries in the deplorable environmental devastation. The money raised at the dinner was destined for the purchase of rain forest acreage to guarantee its perpetual preservation. Some of the attendees actually cared about the rain forest and others at least knew the purpose of the dinner. For many, however, the status of attending the social event itself mattered above all else.

Thorne Stryker enjoyed the sociality of such occasions and appreciated the legitimizing effect they had on his place within the Seattle community. At the same time he believed in the importance of rain forest preservation and thus had made an additional $15,000 contribution beyond the cost of his place at the dinner. He sampled a number of the hors d'oeuvres, making multiple trips to the trays of deviled eggs, while not partaking in the alcohol. He tried to contribute to the buzz as much as possible while silently admiring many of the women present, although he attended the dinner without a companion.

"So, Mr. Stryker," the thirty-something redhead began with a tilt of her chin, "my husband tells me that you're a businessman." She nodded toward the tall, broad-shouldered man whose back retreated from them toward the far end of the large reception room. "Rather generic don't you think? It leaves me with two immediate questions. One, what sort of business? And two, is it all business and no pleasure?"

Stryker smiled as he sipped his Diet Pepsi disguised in a small tumbler. "I'm afraid he's being a bit generous with the 'businessman' description Mrs. Schuster. I invest in a variety of companies, but I don't really do anything worthwhile myself. If that makes me a businessman, I'm afraid it's an affront to many of our fellow guests here tonight."

"And?" she asked with her head back in the same flirtatious tilt with her thinly plucked eyebrows raised high. "All work and no play?"

"I certainly hope not," he responded with a touch of concern. "I'm here for a pleasant, non-business evening tonight, at least."

"Be sure to let me know if you need any help," she half whispered over her cocktail glass. "By the way, it's Veronica, but please call me Ronnie."

"Yes, of course," he looked over her shoulder in increasing nervousness. "Excuse me a moment, won't you?"

"I'll be right here," she offered with a light touch on his arm and her glass lightly kissing her lips.

Stryker didn't look back as he walked past, desperately seeking the rescue of a familiar face. He found one that was familiar and suddenly available, although the familiarity came only through the news. The face belonged to Stanton Reicks, CEO of Seattle Standard Trust, the largest bank headquartered west of the Mississippi and one that Reicks had recently taken public, much to his personal financial benefit.

"Stanton Reicks?" Stryker put forth his hand in greeting. "We've never met. My name's Thorne Stryker."

"My pleasure, Mr. Stryker," Reicks shook hands agreeably. "Enjoying our little shindig this evening?"

"Yes, it's very nice," Stryker nodded while making a show of looking around at the crowd, substantial both in size and in status. "And I wanted to thank you, or your bank I guess, for sponsoring the event. It's nice to see our locally based businesses taking the lead for the benefit of the larger community."

"Well, thanks for your support by attending," Reicks sipped his drink. "Are you involved in business here in town?"

"Umm, not directly," Stryker responded, "although I did buy a handful of shares of your bank at the Initial Public Offering. And, I spent some time in the Amazon during my years in the Army. So, I had sort of a dual interest in attending."

Reicks smiled. "Congratulations on your IPO purchase – we've been quite pleased with the way the public has responded. And I'm glad to see that there's someone here who may actually care about the Rain Forest, rather than simply the Rain Society here in town. Actually, I shouldn't say that. I'm sure many of our supporters are genuine in their environmental concerns. I've just been talking to a group, however, that couldn't tell the difference between the Rain Forest and Siberia. But, I guess their money will help as much as yours or mine."

"It will indeed," Stryker agreed with a nod and a tip of his glass. "So, I read that you're a big baseball fan. Is that true?"

"Of course – best game in the world," said Reicks with the boredom leaving his voice for the first time. "You too?"

"Oh yeah," confirmed Stryker. "For as long as I can remember. Listened on the radio all the time as a kid, but now I'll listen, watch, attend, or just follow. I agree with you – best game in the world."

"Ah, yes," Reicks stared off a bit nostalgically, "baseball on the radio. When I was growing up the Phillies were my team. Old Veterans Stadium, lots of bad teams, but I loved it on the radio. Have you ever been to Philadelphia Mr. Stryker?"

"Thorne, please," offered Stryker with practiced calm, "and yes but it's been awhile. Never been to a game there though. I've been to ballparks in quite a few cities around the country, but never Philadelphia."

"Lot of great history in the city Thorne," said Reicks, "but it's changed a lot over the years. Not necessarily for the better either. But it's still worth a trip for a ball game. So, you follow the local team now?"

"You bet," smiled Stryker. "Good or bad. Anyone can jump on the bandwagon of a winner and feel good about themselves, but there's nothing like the continuity over time as well as the day-to-day continuity of following the local team. I couldn't imagine living in a city without a team, just like I couldn't imagine following a team from another city. That makes me tried and true for the Mariners. You?"

"Have to agree with you," Reicks drank again from his glass. "I tried to stay a fan of the Phillies after moving away, but it got hard over time. Might be easier now with the Internet than it was earlier I suppose, but I agree it's not the same as backing the local team. So, yeah, I'm a Mariners guy. There'll be a lot more of us when they finally win something, but we'll know who the true fans are, right?"

"It'll make the winning that much more enjoyable to have suffered through the bad years. We're just paying our dues right now, but we'll get our reward," Stryker smiled over his glass. "I wouldn't mind if it were sooner rather than later, however."

"I hope you're right. 'When' is certainly the key question. Are you optimistic about the moves they're making now?"

The two men continued to talk baseball until the call came to move into dinner where they were seated far apart from one another. They agreed to attend a game together in the upcoming season. As Stryker found his place, he sighed in relief to find himself also far removed from Veronica Schuster.

When Stryker arrived home shortly after midnight he found a message waiting on his answering machine from Al Jeffries. He waited to call at a more reasonable morning time in New York and caught Jeffries just before he left for work.

"So, everything feeling okay?" Jeffries asked after hearing Stryker's voice on the line. "Doc didn't mess you up too badly?"

"Feeling great," Stryker declared. "Doc did a dandy job."

"Alright, good. I'd hate to think I was trying to help you out, but ended up causing more problems instead," Jeffries laughed.

"Nope, you saved my bacon Al," Stryker responded sincerely, "and I won't forget it. You let me know if you need anything from me, right?"

"Yeah sure," agreed Jeffries. "Next time I'm dying on the streets of Philadelphia." He paused. "Does this mean you're back in business?"

"Umm, not at the moment, but I suppose I could be in the future. We'll have to see how that goes," Stryker hesitated. "By the way, our old friend LJ Perkins heard about my trip your way – and everything that led up to it. Just so you know."

"Zip, huh?" mused Jeffries. "You mentioned he was in Seattle. Anyway, probably not a bad thing to have him on board. If the business continues, that is."

"Well, on board, but not with an active role," Stryker assured him. "It's still a sole proprietorship."

"Even so . . .," said Jeffries. "Well, I just wanted to check that you were doing okay. If you need anything in the future, you know you can call me. Of course, you could also just be in touch socially, you know. Nothing wrong with that."

"Thanks Al," Stryker smiled into the phone. "Hopefully socially only. Now, go get the bad guys okay?"

"Working on it," laughed Jeffries. "Sometimes it's a little hard to tell though, you know?"

PRESENT DAY

CHAPTER FORTY-TWO

Stryker slept until nearly noon on Saturday and immediately tried calling Al Jeffries as soon as he rejoined the conscious world. Jeffries was working mid-shift, however, and Stryker decided it would be best to wait until the end of that shift to catch Jeffries on his personal time, rather than while he was on duty. His next call went to Sam Wykovicz to confirm that he felt fully recovered from his illness and would pick her up at 7:30 for the dinner they had planned and postponed. Sam didn't suggest meeting at the restaurant this time, but willingly accepted his offer to stop by her house to pick her up. Stryker saw that as a good sign, although he wasn't entirely sure how much he was looking for good signs.

With little food in his kitchen after being gone for most of a week, Stryker faced the choice of eating out for lunch or making a trip to the grocery store. He quickly chose the grocery store given that he had eaten out consistently for the past week and would be going out with Sam later that evening. He headed out into a gray but pleasantly warm afternoon to shop at a Safeway store just over a mile away.

Stryker quickly gathered the items he wanted, plus a few things he hadn't intended to purchase and made his way to the check-out lines. Six lines were manned by cashiers, and each sported at least four customers waiting to be checked out. He sighed with resignation and joined the queue nearest him without any attempt to assess which line might be quickest. He had long ago learned that such efforts involved too many unpredictable variables so that the only consistent result seemed to be disappointment at choosing the line that stagnated immediately upon entry, while every other line flowed as smoothly as a deeply bedded stream running down a steep slope on a warm summer day.

He deposited himself in line and his competitive nature kicked in as he made a mental note of where he would have been in other lines so that he could gauge his relative progress. He fought the temptation to jump to the line immediately to his left when a voice addressed him from behind.

"Thorne? Thorne Stryker? What a surprise!" exclaimed a female voice that Stryker turned to connect to a body.

The voice and body both belonged to Dottie Parmienta whom Stryker had met on a number of social occasions. Her husband, Ted Parmienta, recently struck it rich through the sale of his Internet company that automatically sent merchant coupons by email to consumers based on their history of credit card and debit card purchases. Both consumers and merchants loved the service and a brief bidding war between two corporate giants resulted in an incredibly lucrative deal for Ted Parmienta and hence for Dottie as well.

Stryker smiled with a touch of surprise when he turned to see Dottie in line behind him. "Dottie, how nice to see you. You're not here tracking my spending patterns, are you?"

"Silly man," she laughed. "I could, I suppose, but I never really pictured you as someone who would use coupons."

"Never leave home without 'em," Stryker countered. "I have to say though, I never really pictured you doing your own shopping since you and Ted made the big sale. Just out here remembering what it used to be like?"

"No, we really haven't changed things much at all," she responded a bit defensively. "Besides, I always liked shopping. It wouldn't make sense to give up something you enjoy just because you don't have to do it anymore."

'Yeah, I guess you're right," he agreed as he moved forward in line. "Still washing your own cars too?"

"Okay," she laughed, "maybe a few things have changed."

"So, how's Ted doing?" Stryker inquired. "I don't think I've seen him since the Fifth Avenue auction."

"Really? Come to think of it, we didn't see you at the Marshall party last weekend did we?"

"Nope," agreed Stryker. "Not high enough on the Who's Who list to finagle an invitation to that one I'm afraid."

"Oh, I'm sure it was just a mistake if you weren't invited," Dottie tsked him. "But you know, Ted's putting together a golfing group for the week after next. I'm sure he'd love to have you join them. Can I tell him you're interested?"

"Well, the old swing might be a little rusty," Stryker made the motion of a golf swing next to his shopping cart. "But I'm always game. I don't want to force myself into anything though."

"No, no," Dottie assured him. "Ted was just asking this morning if I had any ideas for who else to invite. I can't believe I didn't think of you right away, but I'm sure he's already planning to invite you as it is. Anyway, I'll have him call you this evening." She motioned him to move forward so that he was the next in line to be checked out.

Stryker bought his items and said goodbye to Dottie Parmienta before moving to the exit of the store. As he walked away he wondered if he'd actually be able to golf next weekend or if the aftermath of Silvis Walker in Missouri would have him otherwise occupied. He reached his car with a touch of envy for Ted and Dottie and the enjoyment of a truly retired civilian life. To find out how closely that life awaited, he still needed to talk to Al Jeffries later that evening.

It was 9:15 pm in New York when Stryker looked at the clock on his computer at 6:15 pm in Seattle. He assumed that Jeffries' shift would be over by now and he needed to leave by 7:00 to pick up Sam for dinner. Thus, he had the perfect window of opportunity to call Jeffries who answered the phone on the second ring.

"Jeffries here," he greeted in a slightly subdued voice.

"Hey, Al. Thorne Stryker calling," greeted Stryker who spoke into a recently purchased, limited minutes, cell phone. "Any chance you've got a few minutes to chat?"

"Sure," agreed Jeffries, "but how about if I call you back in five minutes or so. I need to go down to the corner to pick up a few things, and I'll call you from a phone there. You got a number for me?"

Stryker gave it to him and disconnected the phone to wait for the return call. It came in less than five minutes.

"So, I assume this isn't just a social call, or did I find this pay phone for no reason?" Jeffries asked.

"My calls to you are always social," argued Stryker. "So tell me, how are Anthony and the beautiful Amanda?"

"They're just fine, you lying dog. Although they're probably wondering what I'm doing going out at this time after working all day. So tell me, what *am* I doing going out at this time?" Jeffries asked again.

"Well," Stryker began, "I'm not sure how much you keep up on news from the Midwest, but I just got back from there. A business trip. I was wondering if anything had come across your desk that might be of interest."

"The Midwest, huh?" Jeffries commented in immediate recognition. "There's been a lot of chatter the past day or two about a double murder in Missouri. An alleged infamous rapist-murderer was gunned down by a sniper and another body, possibly the sniper, was found dead a few blocks away in an abandoned building. Current speculation, though, is that the second dead guy wasn't the sniper, but was another victim of the sniper. His neck was snapped."

"Yeah, I heard something about the shooting. What else do you know?" Stryker prodded.

"Apparently, it's a big deal. It came across our desk because someone's initiated a nationwide manhunt effort for the killer. Asking for the assistance of law-enforcement agencies all over the country," Jeffries paused for a moment before adding a further detail. "They say that the killer is possibly involved in a number of vigilante style murders and someone wants him bad."

"Any descriptions or clues to go on?" Stryker asked with intense curiosity.

"Nope. But they mention a number of unsolved murders from the past few years that they say may be tied to the same killer," Jeffries explained. "Some cases that you and I have discussed in the past. They're looking for any connections they can find."

"And who are 'they'?" Stryker asked.

"Can't say for sure," Jeffries admitted. "Comes from Washington. D.C. that is. Don't know much more that that."

"Hmmmm," Stryker mused. "What about the second dead guy in Missouri? Anything come through on him?"

"Nothing that I've heard yet," said Jeffries. "Last report I saw listed him as a John Doe. No ID and no claims to him yet. I'll let you know if I hear anything different."

"Okay, thanks," Stryker pondered the significance of the lack of identity. "I'd appreciate any other information that happens to cross your desk as well. If you can, that is."

"Oh, I'm sure I can manage it," Jeffries laughed. "I just hope there's nothing too significant, if you know what I mean."

"Me too. Might help to know more specifically about where this is coming from in Washington. Don't know if that's possible, but if you hear anything . . ."

"I'll keep my ears open."

"By the way," Stryker offered, "don't know if you heard about my retirement."

"Well," Jeffries began, "I know you've been talking about it, but I assumed you'd changed your mind."

"No, not really" Stryker explained. "Unfortunately, I did get talked into delaying it for a bit, but it's fully in effect now. Some interesting circumstances about the delay that have me wondering about ulterior motives on the part of my employer, however. It seems more and more certain that they may not have my best interests at heart."

"And who are 'they'"? Jeffries echoed the question.

"Interesting point," agreed Stryker. "I know we've had this conversation before. Maybe I should have listened to you then."

"Maybe indeed," Jeffries said quietly into the phone.

The two men set specific times for contact over the next few days and then concluded their call. Stryker pondered the assassin who tried to kill him in Independence, along with the current "nation-wide manhunt". Somebody quite seriously wanted to take him out of the picture.

CHAPTER FORTY-THREE

After hanging up the phone with Jeffries, Stryker looked at the clock on the wall that had the numbers printed on the face in reverse order, and decided that he had twenty minutes before he needed to leave to pick up Sam. He was dressed and ready to leave for dinner, so he picked up the phone again to check in with LJ Perkins. A lot had happened that Perkins should know about, and Stryker wanted to at least initiate that conversation before the passing of another day. He called Perkins at the office of Discreet Inquiries.

Perkins answered on the third ring with a mumbled greeting that sounded as though it were fighting to get through the food stuffed into Perkins' mouth.

"That's a very professional telephone manner you've got there." Stryker commented. "Catch you at a bad time?"

Perkins swallowed hard on the other end of the call. "No man, no. Just catching a little snack here while I catch up on some paperwork. I should be a fisherman as much 'catching' as I'm doing right now." Perkins laughed lightly.

"Well, I'm heading out to pick up Sam for dinner," Stryker explained. "I'll be passing near your office and I've got about twenty minutes to spare. Can I bug you for that long, just to get something off my chest?"

Perkins immediately took on a more serious tone at the sound of the request. "Sure, I'll be here. I assume you'd rather talk in person?"

"That'd be my preference. I'll be there in a few." Stryker disconnected the call and with a needless scan of his condo he grabbed his keys and stepped out to his car. Discreet Inquiries sat slightly out of the way, but he still figured he had plenty of time before picking up Sam.

Perkins stood waiting at the entrance to his outer office when Stryker pulled up outside. "Come on in, man," Perkins welcomed and then closed the door behind them.

"Like I said on the phone, I've only got a few minutes," Stryker glanced at his watch in confirmation, "but I wanted to get you in the loop sooner rather than later."

"Problems, huh?" Perkins questioned knowingly.

"Problems," Stryker confirmed. "And beyond. I still haven't sorted everything out, but I figure I may be asking for your help sooner or later. So, here I am."

"Works for me. So what's up?" Perkins inquired again.

"Someone's trying to kill me," Stryker said bluntly.

Perkins' eyebrows furrowed in an instant look of questioning concern. "What? One of the cases you worked on for me?" he asked.

"I wish," Stryker sighed with a shake of his head. "That'd be a whole lot simpler. No, this is Axman."

"Uh oh. I assume this is tied to Missouri?"

"Yeah, but bigger than just that job," Stryker sat on the edge of the desk and told Perkins about the fire damaged shooting spot in Independence and the arrival of the assassin at the completion of the job.

"And he called you 'Mr. Axman'?" Perkins questioned in disbelief. "So he not only knew you were going to be there to kill Walter, but he knew about the assignment coming from the website too."

"Walker," Stryker corrected him. "And yeah, he didn't know me specifically, but he certainly knew about the Axman job and he was there, very specifically, to kill whomever was carrying out the Axman assignment."

"Which means that he was sent by whoever posted the job in the first place," Perkins stated the obvious conclusion. "Didn't I tell you that it was weird not knowing who was posting the jobs that you were taking? I told you that when you first told me about this Axman stuff years ago. Now do you believe me?" He shook his head with the confirming certainty of hindsight. "The thing I can't figure out though, is why they'd want to take you out, whoever 'they' is. Or are."

"I don't know either," Stryker agreed, flipping in his hand a pen he picked up off the desk. "I never got the chance to question the guy who tried to kill me. The only thing I can figure is that it's tied to my retirement announcement. Maybe it's like the Mafia where they won't let you out once you're on the inside," he smiled.

"So, you should have just stopped taking jobs and never said anything about retiring," Perkins reasoned.

"I guess," Stryker agreed as he flipped the pen once again, "In retrospect, at least. But I assumed that I was communicating to someone who was on the same team as me. I wasn't thinking of them as a problem or a threat."

"Time to change your thinking, partner," Perkins said gravely. "So, now what?"

"Can't say for sure," admitted Stryker glancing at his watch. "Right now I've got a dinner date though, so I'm gonna head out. Just wanted you to know what was up."

"Appreciate it. You said you might be asking for my help. Just let me know, man. Anything, anytime." Perkins held out his hand, which Stryker shook without really thinking. "Jeffries in on this too?"

"Yep. You two guys are the only ones who know about Axman. From my end at least. I'm sorry to bring this on both of you, but . . ." Stryker didn't finish.

"Go enjoy your dinner, man," Perkins directed. "We'll talk about it tomorrow."

"I'm going," Stryker looked at his watch again. "But you know you don't have to be any part of this, right? I mean, I wanted you to know what happened so you'll have a clue about what's going on if something happens in the future. Fact is though, this isn't your deal and I don't want you to get caught up in something if I can help it."

"Uh huh," Perkins nodded with a slight smile. "And if the situation was reversed and I just told you about someone trying to kill me, you'd just back away and say 'whatever you do, don't get me involved', right?"

Stryker didn't respond but pursed his lips and looked directly at his friend with soft eyes of gratitude.

"That's what I thought," said Perkins with a light push of Stryker's shoulder off the desk and toward the door. "Now get the hell out of my office and get to dinner before someone takes a shot at you here and ruins my fancy décor. And don't steal my pen."

"By the way," Stryker explained as he set down the pen and moved toward the door. "I was supposed to have this dinner on Thursday but I was sick and needed to postpone it till tonight.

Thanks for the soup and Nyquil that you brought over yesterday morning. They both helped a lot."

"My pleasure, buddy. Glad I could help."

Stryker gave a quick wave over his shoulder as he trotted to his car to return to the normal world of dinner with a lady.

CHAPTER FORTY-FOUR

A typically steady but not especially heavy Seattle rain had started to fall by the time Stryker arrived at Sam's apartment at 7:29. He cursed himself under his breath for being what he considered to be late, while he dialed her number on his cell phone to let her know that he had arrived outside. She responded that she'd be down in a minute or two and didn't invite him up.

Twenty minutes later Sam walked briskly out the door with a light step and a breezy aura about her. She held her coat up tented over her head to ward off the rain and Stryker jumped out of the car as soon as he saw her and moved quickly around the front end to open the passenger door. Sam slipped into the seat with the smooth ease of a well-trained athlete and offered Stryker a cheery smile as he took his place behind the wheel.

"Sorry I took a little longer than I thought," Sam apologized with a pat of her hand on Stryker's leg.

He greedily breathed in her scent and returned the welcoming smile. "I didn't even notice," he fibbed. "I was kind of mesmerized enjoying the rain on the windshield. So, Italian okay with you?" he asked as he reached for the ignition.

"Exactly what I was thinking!" Sam exuded energy and excitement. "But can we stop at a Starbucks on the way?"

Stryker gave her a puzzled look with the thought that she certainly didn't seem to need any caffeine, but readily agreed to stop nonetheless. "Is there one nearby?" he asked.

"This is Seattle, Thorne. Is there any place in town where there isn't one nearby?" she kidded him in response.

"You've got a point there," he agreed. "But still, there aren't as many as there used to be. Who knows, someday they could be a relic of the past."

"Somehow I doubt it," Sam responded. "But if that happens, it better be after I die. Anyway, go up three blocks and turn right, there's one just a block down," she instructed as Stryker moved the car from the curb and turned on the windshield wipers. "It's close enough that I walk there a lot on weekends."

"We'll be there momentarily, M'Lady. I hope you won't be offended though if I don't join you."

Sam laughed and shook her head. "I really can't understand how you can not drink coffee every chance you get, but I really didn't expect you to change now." She pointed ahead as Stryker turned the corner as instructed. "We can just go through the drive-thru."

"Ah, no, we'll go in," Stryker disagreed as he pulled into one of the many available parking spaces.

Sam gave him a puzzled look. "But there aren't any cars in line, and it's raining. Come on," she urged, "the drive-thru's easier."

"Easier doesn't make it better. If you want your coffee, you're going to have to go inside," said Stryker as he turned off the motor.

"You're kidding, right?" asked Sam who hadn't reached to remove her seatbelt. "You're going to walk into the store instead of using the drive-thru? I don't get it."

Stryker remained seated next to her with keys in his hand. "You said you walk here on weekends, right?"

"Well, sure," Sam agreed. "But that's when I'm on foot from my apartment. Whenever I'm in my car I always use the drive-thru. It's way quicker and easier than finding a parking place, getting in and out of the car, locking and unlocking, etc.. Besides, it's raining."

Stryker put his hand on the door handle. "Well, we've got a parking spot, and I'll handle the locking and unlocking part. Now let's go get your coffee so we can move on to the restaurant. I'm getting hungry."

"You're serious, aren't you? You're really going to walk in the store when the drive-thru's wide open," Sam stated in marginal disbelief.

"Don't believe in 'em," Stryker stated matter-of-factly as he opened the door and stepped out into the light rain. He walked around to the passenger's side where Sam remained unmoved and opened the door for her. "Come on, lady. Coffee's waiting."

Sam stepped from the car with her head shaking under the coat she raised in tented fashion once again. "Don't believe in them?" she questioned as they walked to the door of the store. "As in, you don't think they exist?"

"Nope, just don't believe in using them," Stryker stated without explanation as he held open the door for Sam to enter.

"Okay, so I'm here. Now explain exactly what it is that you don't believe in," Sam demanded as she dropped her coat to her shoulders.

"Go ahead and order first," Stryker directed. "Dinner's waiting."

After a complicated order that Stryker didn't fully understand, Sam looked back at him while waiting for the order to be filled. "Well?"

"It's really not a big deal, and it's not difficult to understand," Stryker explained. "I'm just against the idea of things that promote laziness and waste under the guise of modern efficiency. Now, this certainly doesn't apply to you, but everyone knows that we're a nation of increasing weight and health problems, right?" Sam shrugged in acknowledgement. "And yet we won't even get out of our cars and walk a hundred feet into a store or a bank if we can stay seated in our cars instead."

"You don't use the drive-thru at the bank either?" Sam asked in incredulity.

"Afraid not," Stryker smiled. "To be honest with you, the idea just bugs me. I mean, think about the people who complain that they don't have time to work out, and then drive incessantly around a parking lot looking for a place close to the doors so they can walk the fewest steps possible. It just doesn't make sense."

"Yeah I get that," agreed Sam as she looked to check on the progress of her order. "But you're not one of those people. You exercise all the time. You are in shape. So why should you avoid the drive-thru?"

"Just principle, I guess," said Stryker as he pointed to her completed coffee. "Can't give in to the pervasive weakening of society. You know, got to draw the line somewhere, right?"

Sam shook her head as they moved out the door and back to the car. She settled in to her seat and sipped her coffee while Stryker started the car and backed out of the parking space. "You're kinda weird, Thorne," she laughed. "Have you got any other strange ideas like this drive-thru business?"

"Lots of 'em," Stryker admitted with a laugh of his own. "But I think we better wait until you know me better before we talk about those."

"I can hardly wait," responded Sam with a tone of skeptical interest. "I can hardly imagine."

An hour later they had food in front of them at a corner booth of an Italian restaurant with the walls covered with paintings of Venice and bottles of wine. Sam sampled her steaming tortellini while Stryker dug into his traditional, very cheesy, lasagna. The pasta matched the quality of the bread they had greedily devoured while waiting for the entrees.

After spending time on a variety of different topics, Sam turned the conversation from the stock market to Stryker's recent week. "You seem like you're feeling a lot better," she questioned in the form of a comment through a final bite of pasta.

"Yeah, I am," he acknowledged. "I was pretty miserable for a couple of days, but I was feeling a lot better by last night."

"I tried to call yesterday to check on you, but you weren't answering."

"No. LJ brought some stuff by for me in the morning, then I slept most of the day. Turned my phone off. Sorry to have missed your call though. I'm sure it would have helped make me feel better," he said with a smile.

"That reminds me," she stated as she set down her fork, "what kind of work do you do for LJ anyway? You were out of town for him recently. What did he have you doing?"

"Oh, it's always something different. You know. Whatever he needs on a given case at any given time." Stryker looked away as he drank from his water glass.

"No, I don't know," Sam followed. "That's why I was asking. I'm curious about the kinds of things that you do."

Stryker swallowed. "Well, it's nothing too exciting, believe me. Some investigating. Sometimes it's court records or county filings. Lots of times it's asking people questions. I'm usually just helping out on some legwork while LJ handles the case overall. I don't even know sometimes what the big picture is. I just get the information he needs and then leave it at that. Like I said – not too exciting." Stryker took another drink from his water glass. "LJ just gets busy sometimes and needs an extra hand for a day or two."

"Okay, but I really am curious," Sam persisted. "Tell me about the most recent case. Where did you go? What sort of non-exciting stuff were you doing there?"

Stryker looked down at the floor and then back at Sam across the table. He didn't want to lie to her, but he didn't know how evasive he could be. "Well, I can't give any real specifics, but LJ was hired to sort out a case of industrial theft and possible sabotage. To find out what he needed he worked at the company full time for a while. Between working nine hours a day at the factory and tailing some guys at night, it didn't leave him much time for anything else. So, I followed up on some related things outside the company. It mostly ended up as dead ends for me, but LJ found the guy responsible and turned him over to the boss. I ended up being no real help at all." He tried to read her reaction to his explanation, but without success. "Like I said, nothing too exciting."

Sam's face turned cool, which helped Stryker gauge her lack of satisfaction. "Well, I didn't mean to pry," she said without emotion before picking up her water glass for a lengthy drink and then looking at her watch.

"Sorry I can't give you more details," Stryker attempted an appeasement, "but even if I could, there really wouldn't be much to tell in this case. Like I said, LJ ended up doing most everything on his own after all."

"In that case," Sam began, "oh, forget it." She looked at her watch again. "You know, you may be feeling better, but I'm really not feeling all that great. I think maybe I ought to just go home before I start going downhill. You don't mind do you?"

“No, that’s fine,” agreed Stryker as he reached for the bill. “I’m not sure I’m really up for a late night either.”

They spoke little in the car on the way back to Sam’s apartment, despite Stryker’s attempts at questions and small talk. When they arrived at the building Sam quickly opened the passenger door and said that she could see herself inside. She thanked Stryker for the dinner and reminded him of his upcoming quarterly review. She then closed the door and strode off to her building without looking back. Stryker watched until the building door closed behind her and then drove off, wondering if he’d just witnessed another Axman casualty.

CHAPTER FORTY-FIVE

Stryker arrived at the downtown Seattle offices of Stanley, Jacobs, and Utterhuis at 9:20 am for his 9:30 appointment. The receptionist, with the ubiquitous headset – earpiece connected to a thin wire bringing the mouthpiece to her right cheek – greeted him and directed him to a couch were he could wait comfortably. He politely refused the offer of coffee and felt a touch of déjà vu. Stryker gazed around the professional but understated surroundings until an elderly man in a crisp white shirt adorned with a classic conservatively striped tie strolled casually through the lobby with a brief hand wave to the receptionist and a friendly nod and smile at Stryker. Stryker wondered whether Stanley, Jacobs, or Utterhuis ever crossed the threshold of the lobby any more and whether he might have just exchanged greetings with one of them. He decided to ask.

"I'm sorry," he interrupted the receptionist and gained her attention, "who was that who just walked through here?"

"Hmmm?" she glanced across the lobby at the receding back. "Oh, that was Mr. Nielsen, one of the senior partners. Did you need something?"

"Oh no," Stryker assured her. "He just looked familiar to me, but I guess I must have been mistaken. Sorry to bother you."

"No bother at all," she assured him and returned to her work.

The one person at the firm that Stryker actually knew appeared in the lobby less than a minute later. "Thorne, how good to see you," greeted Karmody Fenn with a warm handshake. "Won't you come back to my office?"

Stryker got up from his seat and smiled at the receptionist as he followed Karmody away from the lobby. She pointed out the view through the glass doors of a conference room, and made a meaningless inquiry about how Stryker was doing while they walked three-fourths of the way down a hallway to her office, which shared the same view of Puget Sound as that of the conference room. She directed Stryker to a chair in front of her desk while she closed the office door and then moved to sit in her own chair behind the desk. He admired the view and noticed that the two paintings on the walls depicted water scenes as well. Her lone bookshelf held neatly organized files, but none of the ubiquitous casebooks that he expected in a lawyer's office.

She folded her hands on her impressively clean desk and smiled at Stryker. She wore a light pink blouse over a gray pinstriped skirt. Her jewelry consisted of diamond earrings and a subtle gold necklace. She wore no rings. "So, I was a bit surprised to get your call," she began. "You haven't had any issues with Allen, have you?"

Stryker hadn't expected the question, but quickly realized the logic of it from her perspective. "No, no. Have you?"

She laughed pleasantly. "Oh, good, I was nervous when I got your call for an appointment. But to answer your question, no, not a word from him. Thanks to you. I was a bit skeptical at first, but he seems to have moved on to greener pastures. Anyway, you did very well with that, thank you again," she paused and leaned back in her chair toward the credenza on the back wall of her office which stood as neat and clean as her desk. "If Allen's not an issue though, I'm curious about why you called to see me."

"Well, you see," he began with a straight face, "I've got this old girlfriend who keeps harassing me and she won't accept the fact that we're broken up. I was wondering if you might be able to help me."

"What?" she exclaimed in disbelief as she leaned forward into the desk.

"Just kidding," Stryker smiled as Karmody sat back in her chair. "I am, however, looking for legal services, and you're the first lawyer I thought of. Would you care to take me on as a client?"

Karmody looked a little surprised, but maintained her professional demeanor. "Sure. I mean, that's what we do is represent clients. The nature of your legal issues will make a difference, however. We all have some area of specialty and I may have to direct you to someone else in the firm depending on what you need," she looked at Stryker who merely nodded without comment so she continued. "Our firm handles a bit of everything, of course, but I don't deal with any family law or criminal law, for instance. Most of my clients are corporate clients as I handle primarily contracts and business issues."

"So, I look like a criminal to you?" Stryker stated in mock offense. "Or a cheating husband looking for a quick divorce?"

Karmody blanched instantly and backpedaled quickly. "No, no, my goodness. I was just giving examples of the possible limitations. You know, bankruptcy would be another example. A very specialized field that most lawyers don't delve into."

"Oh, so now I'm a deadbeat, huh"? Stryker questioned in private enjoyment at Karmody's discomfort.

She hesitated for a moment before continuing with a note of minor exasperation. "Look, I'm not trying to guess what your legal issues are, so let's start over. Why don't you tell me what you need so I can tell you whether I can help, or whether I need to direct you to someone else in the firm. Does that work for you?"

"Sounds like a most reasonable idea," he agreed with a smile. "But I was just teasing you a bit. Sorry."

"You're forgiven," Karmody offered with a return of the smile. "So, why don't you tell me what's up?"

"Well, despite what you just said, I first want to make one thing clear," Stryker began with an earnest tone. "I don't know anyone else in your firm and I won't choose to work with anyone else in your firm. I understand the specialization of the legal world today, but I'm an old fashioned kind of guy. And, as an old fashioned guy, the idea of a client and a lawyer working together on whatever issues arise, appeals to me. The idea of a client and an entire firm doesn't resonate the same way. So, you're free to send me out the door if you'd like, but I want to be clear up front. I want to hire *you*, not Stanley and Utterhuis, and whoever else."

"I appreciate the implicit vote of confidence," Karmody began in response, "but it's not really practical in the legal world today. The fact is, there are hundreds of branches of law and I can't fairly pretend to represent you in most of them. That's why we develop different specialties within the firm," she sighed and leaned back in her chair once again. "That still brings us back to the fact that you haven't told me what it is you actually need. It's possible that this whole discussion is moot. I mean, maybe I can do whatever it is that you want. So, let's go back to the beginning and you can tell me what you need."

Stryker pursed his lips and nodded before starting in once again. "Actually, we are at the beginning, and we'll get to my specific issue in just a minute. Let's deal with an example first – assume you're working on a contract for me – would you do all of the work yourself?"

"Possibly, I guess," Karmody answered with her palms gesturing toward the ceiling. "But I don't get your point."

"Well, if you *might* do all the work yourself," he explained, "then I assume you might also farm out some of the work to a clerk or a paralegal or an associate, yes?"

"Sure," Karmody agreed. "That's the way large firms work."

"Okay, and that's just fine with me," Stryker held up his hands in surrender. "I would trust your judgment on that and I would let you work within your firm as you see fit. From my side of things, however, I want to hire you as my attorney. For now and for the foreseeable future. You, not your firm. For me, that means the old fashioned relationship where I come to you with whatever issue I need. If you need to work with others, that's up to you, but as far as I'm concerned, I talk to you and only to you. Is that workable for you?"

Karmody shrugged and chuckled lightly before responding. "Yeah, I guess. Sure. You may change your mind down the road, but we can start with that. So, do you want to tell me what you need now, or should we talk about my rates?"

"Let's not worry about the rates," Stryker shook his head. "Charge me whatever you normally would charge any of your clients and we'll be fine. So, does this mean that you're officially my attorney?"

"If you're hiring me, I'm accepting the job," Karmody agreed and held out her hand across the desk. "So yes, I'm officially your attorney."

"Thanks," he smiled while rising to shake her hand. "And that also means that all of our legal communications are privileged, right?"

Karmody raised her eyebrows and thrust her lower lip slightly forward before responding. "Yes, that's correct. But now you've got me a bit worried. Let's get to the issue at hand, shall we?"

"Absolutely," said Stryker agreeably. "I need a will."

"A will?" Karmody repeated in disbelief. "All this talk about lawyer-client relationships, and you're here for a will?"

"Yes ma'am. I thought about one a long time ago, but I never followed through with it. I want to do it now."

"Okay, but I'm still confused," Karmody admitted. "Of course I can help you with a will, but you know they don't have to be very complicated. I'm sure you can do it on your own quite easily in fact."

"Yeah, I'm sure that's true," he nodded. "But I'd feel better if you did it, and besides, I'd like for you to be the executor as well. Is that okay?"

"Um, sure," Karmody agreed.

"The other thing is that while I need a will right now, it's very possible I'm going to need other legal services in the near future. So, the whole 'attorney-client relationship' thing is more about the big picture than about today's issue."

Karmody nodded in acceptance. "Of course, that makes sense." Karmody looked at the clock on the wall. "Well, we've got about thirty minutes right now till I've got another appointment. Shall we get started?"

"Works for me," Stryker agreed as she pulled a pad of paper out of a desk drawer to provide clutter to her barren desktop. She also took up a sleek dark pen in her left hand.

"Okay, so you said you thought about a will before, but didn't do it. I assume that means that you don't have an existing will?" Karmody began.

"That's right."

"Okay, that makes things easier," she stated as she wrote his name and the day's date on the legal pad. "It's a good idea to have a will, of course, but can I ask what prompted you to finally create one now?"

"Sure," he agreed. "My assets are reasonable in size and I don't have any family. So, I'd like to direct where my assets go rather than having the state do it." Karmody nodded politely. "And, circumstances are such that something may happen and I may not be living much longer," Stryker said matter-of-factly.

Karmody dropped her pen on the pad and stared across the desk. "What?"

"Sorry," Stryker said. "That part of it we'll need to get into later. But, that's the honest answer to your question. For now, let's just get the will in place, and then we can deal with other issues. Okay?"

"Now wait a minute," Karmody started until she quickly recognized the unrelenting look in the face sitting across from her. "Well, okay," she agreed with some hesitation as she gathered herself. "So then, what kind of assets are we talking about?"

It took less than thirty minutes for Stryker to share the pertinent information about his assets and his intended beneficiaries. In the absence of a trust instrument or minor heirs, Karmody assured him that the will would prove to be quite generic and thereby easy to draft and execute.

As Fenn finished her immediate questions and notes, she looked at the clock and thought briefly about postponing her pending meeting. Instead, she set down her pen and again broached the subject that hadn't left her mind since Stryker had mentioned it. "So, I may have to follow up by phone, but we've got enough to go on and I've got a few more minutes. I don't mean to pry, but you've got me a bit worried right now. Would you care to talk about this premonition of death that you mentioned? You're not sick are you?"

"No, I'm not sick, and yes, I probably want to talk to you about it," he shrugged slightly, "but not right now. It's a bit more complicated than a simple premonition and I still need to grapple a bit with the confidentiality of our relationship. Trust me, I'm really not trying to be a jerk. I'm just not quite ready right now. We're okay with that, right?"

"You're the boss," she stated simply. "Anyway, the will's pretty simple so I can have it drawn up for you to review and potentially sign within a day or two. Shall we set up a follow-up appointment now?"

"Yeah, the sooner the better."

"Okay, I'll have you check with my secretary on the way out and she'll find a time that works for you." Karmody buzzed her secretary and then stood and held out her hand once again for a firm shake. "Welcome aboard, Thorne. I look forward to a long and interesting attorney-client relationship."

"I'll just settle for long," Stryker laughed as he turned to head out the door.

CHAPTER FORTY-SIX

A come-from-behind victory for the Mariners the previous evening made the morning newspaper infinitely more enjoyable to read with a light breakfast. Coupled with a gorgeous start to what was predicted to be an equally gorgeous 80-degree day and Stryker found it hard to imagine a more brightly painted picture of his prospects. Except for the cloud of being the target of a nationwide manhunt, that is.

Stryker looked forward to running in some sunshine and heat so he purposefully put off his run until later in the day. He had a 10:00 appointment with Karmody Fenn for the signing of his will, but had planned to stay around home before that. His phone rang at 8:40 with an unknown caller identified. Stryker waited for the answering machine to kick in, but then picked up the phone in his bedroom when he heard the voice of Al Jeffries.

"Screening your calls, huh?" Jeffries began after Stryker's greeting interrupted Jeffries' message.

"Gotta keep the east coast riff raff out," Stryker kidded. "So, what's up? You got the day off today, Al?"

"Actually, just grabbing an early lunch. Spending most of the day following up on some earlier cases," Jeffries explained. "Lots of leg work and nothing too exciting, so I thought I'd take a minute to update you on the latest – though it's not much right now."

"Thanks, and I'm all ears," said Stryker. "What's the word?"

"Well, our office is getting pushed hard for information on a case dating back quite a few years. Killings here in New York of two guys suspected of organizing a group that kidnapped young girls here in the northeast, smuggled them into Canada, then sold them to overseas buyers. When we found the bodies, we also found enough evidence to make lots of arrests and shut down the entire operation. We didn't get anywhere on tracking down the killer of the two guys, however, and it's been quiet in our cold case file for some time." Jeffries paused. "You remember hearing anything about the case?"

"Yeah, I guess it rings a bell," Stryker admitted. "Anyway, why the push now and who's doing the pushing?"

"Well, why the push now is clear," Jeffries went on. "We're being told the case is tied to the recent murders in Independence, Missouri. As for who is doing the pushing, that's less clear. We're getting calls from the FBI, but also from Homeland Security and apparently from the Justice Department. One of our guys also had a talk with Military Intelligence. Seems odd, but also seems like a lot of different groups all looking for the same thing. It's definitely not normal, and it sure seems to me like the strings are being pulled by someone with a lot of pulling power."

"Hmmm," Stryker thought for a moment. "Anything helpful coming out of New York?"

"Nope. We turned over all of our files, but there wasn't much in them. Whoever pulled off the job here was a real pro."

"Okay. Anything else?"

"Just the rumor that whoever's doing the pushing is doing it in lots of different places at the same time. Lots of shovels out doing lots of digging."

"Thanks, Al. Everything good at home?" Stryker changed the tone of the call.

"Yeah, great," Jeffries' voice picked up. "Got Anthony catching a ball like an all-star. The kid's a natural."

"He gets it from his mom, I'm sure," Stryker responded. "Anyway, I gotta run, Al. Thanks for the call. Oh, and by the way, LJ's in on the recent developments. Just so you know."

"I figured as much. Take care buddy," Jeffries offered in a serious voice. "Call me if you need anything."

"Thanks, but I won't plan to," Stryker stated. "Gotta do my best to keep you on the right side of things, big guy."

"Always have been," Jeffries said before hanging up the phone.

Stryker looked at a clock on the wall and decided to make another call. Rather than a digital clock, it was of the old fashioned variety with hands. The face of the clock displayed no numbers, however, and thus simply showed two hands reaching into space with no context except each other. Stryker pondered the clock for a moment and tried to decipher some symbolic meaning behind the fact that he purchased it. He also thought about the clock in his living room with the numbers printed in reverse order. He came up empty and reached for the phone.

"Sam Wykovicz please," he requested in response to the query from the other end. "Thorne Stryker." It pleased him that at least during working hours, his brokerage company had not yet succumbed to automated answering with a menu of options. He wondered how long they would hold out. He listened to subdued music while he waited patiently on hold.

"Thorne?" Sam asked when the music disappeared.

"Yeah, hi. Sorry to interrupt things," Stryker began, "but I'm heading downtown in a bit and I thought I'd check to see if you were available for lunch."

"Today?" Sam asked. "What brings you downtown?"

"Actually, I've got an appointment with my lawyer," Stryker responded with a touch of pride in making the verbal declaration for the first time. "It shouldn't take too long though, so I thought while I was down there . . ."

"I didn't know you had a lawyer," Sam stated in a way that made it a question.

"Well, I didn't until recently," Stryker admitted. "Seemed like time though – part of growing up I guess. Anyway, we've got a short meeting this morning, then I'm free for awhile if you want to hook up for lunch."

"Growing up, huh? Uh, never mind," Sam paused momentarily but Stryker didn't step into the sound void. "So," she continued, "I'm afraid I'm booked all day. I'm not even sure I'll get to snack on anything at my desk. In any event, there's no way I can get away for lunch."

"Oh, well, no problem. Maybe in a day or two," Stryker offered.

"Well, you can try," Sam replied in a tone that offered little hope, "but it's looking like it's going to be a killer week or two. I'm just getting ready to hunker down and wade through everything I've got coming. I don't think I'm going to see much of the outside world for awhile."

"Bummer. Sorry about the schedule," Stryker said. "Sounds like you're going to be earning your money these days so I'll stay out of your hair for now."

"You mean I usually don't earn my money?" Sam replied haughtily. "This is some kind of exception?"

Stryker thought desperately for a way to get off the phone. "No, no. I didn't mean that. Just an expression acknowledging how busy you are. You know. Look, I've got to run now and obviously you've got a lot on your plate. I'll check back with you later, okay?"

"Bye," was the only thing Stryker heard before the dial tone buzzed in his ear.

Bad choice on making that call, he thought to himself. Really screwed up something somewhere. The hands on the anonymously faced clock told him he had just a few minutes left before he needed to head downtown to meet with Karmody Fenn. He spent those few minutes carefully avoiding the phone.

The signing and witnessing of the will took but a few minutes. Karmody gave Stryker a copy to take home, while keeping the original to be held at the firm. Once the witnesses and notary left her office, Karmody closed the door and sat behind her desk facing Stryker as she had a few days earlier.

"Well," she began, "you definitely made a good move in executing a will. You've got a fair amount of wealth, and with no family and no will, the state would have taken a sizeable chunk on your death. Things will be much smoother and better for your estate now, although hopefully that will be a long ways off." She paused and looked down at her hands before looking back at Stryker. "Anything else you need for the time being? Legal help or advice?"

"You guys offering any specials that I haven't heard about? File one lawsuit, get a second at half price?" Stryker smiled across at her.

"Half price divorces are all we've got right now," she smiled back. "You'd have to get married first, however."

"I guess we can skip that then," Stryker stated while smoothing a wrinkle in his polo shirt. "Although I'm always looking for a good deal."

"Nothing else, huh?" Karmody inspected her hands once again as if she hadn't had the chance to clean them properly. "I'm still a little concerned about that comment you made last time about not living too much longer. You're sure there's nothing we need to deal with?"

"Soon, I'm sure," Stryker assured her as best he could. "You are my lawyer, after all." Stryker looked out the window at a ferry crossing the Sound through water that glistened in the sun. "I've got a few things that I need to check on, then we may need to talk again. Can we plan to meet again in about two weeks?"

"I'll be here," Karmody nodded. "I'll have you make an appointment with my secretary on your way out again," she reached for the phone and gave a brief instruction after punching only one button. "Just don't get yourself into any trouble between now and then, okay?" she directed with a single raised eyebrow as she set down the phone.

"Choirboy all the way," Stryker promised with the three-fingered salute of the Boy Scouts. He picked up his copy of the will and left the office without further delay. Karmody watched with curiosity as he walked out the door.

Stryker began his run in the early afternoon with thoughts of Independence, Washington D.C., Sam, and his will all jumbled in his mind. He enjoyed the penetrating warmth of the sun that quickly brought beads of sweat to his forehead. After a few of miles at about seven minute mile pace, darkened v-shapes of sweat had formed on both his back and chest and the sweat flowed freely down his face. By the four mile mark, he didn't realize that he wasn't thinking about any of his recent issues. He simply ran, a little faster, and enjoyed the sunshine and his surroundings. His thoughts focused on his breathing and keeping his shoulders loose. He took off his shirt and when he finished after nearly an hour, his shorts were soaked from the sweat that had run off his chest and back. He felt tired and fabulous.

Stryker cooled off leisurely and then showered quickly. He dressed in shorts and a t-shirt and called Perkins at his office.

LJ answered on the second ring. "Discreet Inquiries."

"My cat's stuck in a tree, can you PLEEEEASE help me," Stryker pleaded in his best grandmotherly voice.

"Sorry," Perkins responded, "that's superhero kind of work. We're just regular folk around here."

"Well, Mr. Regular Folk, you up for a quick trip to Vegas?" Stryker asked.

"Vegas? When you talking about going, man?"

"Oh, I don't know. This evening maybe. What's the case load look like?"

Perkins laughed lightly. "You notice how quickly I answered the phone? I was mostly happy to hear that it still worked."

"So, you in?"

"May as well. What's up though? You just got the itch for some table time, or is it something serious?"

"I've always got the itch for a little gambling," Stryker chuckled. "You know that. While we're there though, I thought I might do a little website surfing as well."

"Sounds like a plan," Perkins agreed.

"Pick you up in an hour," Stryker instructed before hanging up the phone.

CHAPTER FORTY-SEVEN

Stryker and Perkins used false identification to fly to Phoenix where they rented a car and proceeded to drive six hours north to Las Vegas. Once in Vegas Stryker used a different ID and credit card to secure a large room at the Bellagio Hotel and Casino. Fatigue had set in once they claimed their room, but they still managed to rally up enough energy to walk the Strip for an hour before an hour of uneventful and unproductive blackjack play at Caesars Casino. Perkins looked at Stryker and nodded, at which time the two men got up from the table and wound their way through the slot machines to find the exit that took them back to the Bellagio and their room. Within fifteen minutes a duet of heavy breathing reverberated off the walls.

Perkins remained asleep the next morning when Stryker left the room and strode out through the abnormally quiet casino to the sunshine that so few Vegas visitors ever encountered. The streets echoed the emptiness of the casino and Stryker easily navigated his way to an Internet coffee shop not far off Las Vegas Boulevard. The shop operated under the name 'Caffeine

Online' and had a relatively small front window below a neon sign announcing its presence. The employee at the desk, a large man who looked to be in his early twenties with a neck that melded perfectly into his jawbone, looked incredibly bored for 8:00 in the morning and Stryker wondered if the locals spent late nights at the poker tables or roulette just like the tourists. Stryker asked about accessing a computer and the clerk used his neck-chin to point to the rates posted on the wall behind him. Stryker handed him the same credit card that had secured the room at the Bellagio and the clerk said nothing as he swiped the card to pay for 30 minutes of Internet time. He handed back the credit card along with an Internet use agreement that Stryker signed without reading. He remained silent as he exchanged the signed agreement for a paper with a printed access password. Stryker looked over his shoulder and then back at the clerk who simply shrugged and used his neck to point to the rows of empty computers. Stryker understood the gesture to mean 'take your pick' so he sat down at a computer in the corner and entered the password. He glanced back at the clerk to see him leaning back in his chair with his eyes already half closed. He assumed that the clerk was dreaming of an uninterrupted remainder of the morning, which would suit Stryker just fine. The chances of being interrupted at all seemed miniscule in light of the fact that Stryker was amazed that such establishments still existed given that everyone seemed to have the ability to use cell phones to search the internet.

He logged on to the Axman website, half expecting alarms to go off while dozens of armed men charged in off the street. Instead the shop remained free of alarms and Stryker's only companion in the shop remained immobile behind his counter. The main page of the website popped up the same as it had many times before, although Stryker looked at it more than usual to verify its familiarity. Seeing nothing different, he hit the tab for the discussion blog and waited while the screen changed before him. Again he checked the clerk with a feeling of paranoia, but then directed his attention back to the computer. The discussion blog appeared with three recent entries, each under the name "Bullet-Blogger," and each without pretense of discussion about medieval executioners.

The oldest of the three, posted two days after the death of Silvis Walker read: "Aware of recent problems. What happened? Can help."

The next posting followed the same thread: "You are compromised. Help is waiting. When and where?"

The most recent of the three blurbs offered little different: "Want to help. You need help. Use established method to post meeting time and place. Don't try to go it alone."

The link to log in and post a comment stared at Stryker in defiant temptation. He certainly wasn't going to ask for help, but he felt a strong temptation to set up a meeting just to see who would show up. Maybe later, he thought. For now he couldn't see any advantage gained for him by any sort of response so he logged off the site and then erased the 'history' listing on the Internet entry window. Finally, he quickly visited a few random news sites before quitting out of the computer and leaving the shop. Stryker had no real concept of the limits of technology, but he made assumptions about the theoretical idea that someone with enough knowledge and desire could track the computers logged on to a website at any given time. If that were in fact technologically possible, Stryker had no intention of sitting at the guilty computer when the men in black showed up. Instead, he would be ready.

Stryker called Perkins at the hotel room. "It's time," was all that Stryker said when Perkins answered the phone.

"That was fast," acknowledged Perkins. "Where?"

Stryker gave him the cross streets of an intersection.

"See you in thirty," Perkins replied and then hung up the phone.

Stryker removed the glasses, hat and wig that he had also worn in the Bellagio and dropped them into a nearly full dumpster while he watched the shop and awaited Perkins' arrival.

Twenty-nine minutes later Perkins strode up to Stryker who leaned up against a white stucco building.

"Where are we?" Stryker asked.

"Canals in the middle of the desert. 2312 at the beautiful Venetian," Perkins identified the new hotel room that now housed their small bags under the name of Perkins false identification. "So, what's the plan, boss?"

"I figure it's worth a couple of hours, if that's okay with you," Stryker responded with a nod down the street toward Caffeine Online. "Like I said it's just a hunch, but I'm assuming they can monitor the site, and if they are, I wouldn't be surprised if they could get boots on the ground pretty quickly. If not, then we wasted a couple of hours in the morning in Vegas. No big deal, right?"

"Hey, as long as we get to the show tonight and I get a little table time in somewhere, I'm all good man. You're payin' for the trip, so what've I got to worry about?" Perkins smiled his satisfaction with life in general. "So, where do we hang out for these couple of hours?"

Stryker shrugged slightly. "We'll take turns walking the street and hanging out where there's good visibility. More and more people out now so we'll be able to blend in pretty easily. Just make sure you keep your eyes on the Internet place but don't get too near it." He looked at Perkins pocket. "Got your cell phone handy?"

"Yep," Perkins confirmed. "If you don't mind I'll walk first. Need to see a bit of what's around anyway." He looked both directions on both streets before turning back to Stryker. "If they show up, I don't suppose they'll come in wearing signs that say 'bad guy' will they?"

"No, I don't suppose," Stryker smiled. "I'm hoping they'll stand out though. Well, actually I'm hoping they don't show up at all. But, you never know."

Perkins tipped the hat he wasn't wearing and walked away just behind an elderly couple wearing real hats.

They definitely stood out when they showed up. Less than twenty minutes after Stryker and Perkins parted, Stryker called Perkins' cell phone to tell him they had arrived. 'They' were two thirty-something white men wearing sport coats over jeans and button-down shirts. Each had tightly cut hair and both sported solid bodies on frames just over six feet. They paused, scanning the street outside Caffeine Online, and then moved with athletic precision into the store. Stryker watched with fascination and wished desperately to be inside the walls with them.

Perkins quickly joined Stryker and together they watched the shop from a corner arcade of kiosks just down the street. Stryker looked at his watch and informed Perkins that the men had been in the shop for about three minutes.

"You sure it's them?" Perkins asked.

"Well, I didn't get the chance to interview them, but yeah, I'm sure," Stryker nodded in resignation. "It's a little disturbing that they got here as quickly as they did, but I guess we were prepared for that."

"You suppose they've got anyone else out here watching the outside like we're doing?" Perkins glanced around the streets, not really knowing what he was looking for.

"Nah, I doubt it," Stryker said with relative confidence. "They came on the run to track down a lead. There's no way they would think that we're on to them."

"You hope," Perkins replied.

They continued to watch the shop for another ten minutes, during which time no one entered or exited the doors. Stryker pictured their activities in his mind – talking to the clerk, checking the computer, questioning the clerk some more, tracing the credit card number, then leaving the clerk with vague warnings and a contact phone number. He pictured the clerk sweating with his day ruined, as he would likely not return to his half-conscious bliss. Stryker looked at his watch again and then down the street in vague paranoia over Perkins' question about others outside.

Perkins nudged Stryker's side as the two men emerged from Caffeine Online and stood on the street outside the door. One of the men immediately placed a call on a cell phone and talked for about two minutes while they remained unmoving on the sidewalk. When he put the phone back in his pocket, he gestured up the street to his partner and the two men walked back toward Las Vegas Boulevard. Stryker and Perkins, on the opposite side of the street, slowly followed their westward progress.

More pedestrians on both sides of the street made it relatively easy for Stryker and Perkins to blend in as they moved toward the strip. The two men in sport coats crossed the boulevard and took up positions leaning against a metal railing and watching the foot traffic around them. Stryker crossed Las Vegas Boulevard and found a spot to watch from across Washington Way. Perkins crossed Washington and stepped into a lobby from which he could see the men across the boulevard. The four men remained sedentary while everyone around them moved from the disappointment of wherever they'd just been to the hope of wherever they were going. Stryker worried about his visibility, but the two men never looked in his direction.

In just over five minutes, the man who had placed the earlier phone call reached into his pocket and removed his cell phone once again, but this time to receive a call as he punched no numbers into the phone. After a fifteen second conversation he placed the phone back in his pocket and gestured to his companion. They began moving north up Las Vegas Boulevard. Stryker and Perkins followed on opposite sides of the street.

At the next corner the two men crossed from Stryker's side to Perkins' side, just as Stryker expected. Stryker remained on his side of the strip, although the two men walked purposefully forward without so much as a glance behind them. After another block, they turned right to enter the Bellagio Hotel.

Stryker crossed the street to meet up with Perkins. "Well," he said, "no surprise there, I guess."

"Credit card records, huh?" Perkins noted more than he asked. "Pretty quick turnaround from the Internet shop."

"Yeah, gotta like the efficiency," Stryker smiled. "Pretty quick getting here in the first place and then pretty quick tracking their information."

"So, who are they?" Perkins questioned.

"My guess is FBI. They've got people here locally and they can respond as fast as anybody." He rubbed his chin briefly while keeping his eyes on the entrance to the hotel/casino. "My guess is they don't know anything about Axman, though. Probably just doing the legwork at the direction of someone else. Al said lots of heat out of Washington, but it could be anybody."

"So, what now?" Perkins asked. "Do we follow them when they leave here?"

"Nope," responded Stryker as he began to walk past the hotel entrance with Perkins in tow. "They're at a dead end now so they've got nothing left to do. We found out what we wanted – they, whoever 'they' may be, are monitoring access to the site and they've got the ability to respond quickly. At this point, I don't know that there's much else for them to go on, however. If I stay off the site and don't do anything else stupid, I'm not sure there's any more they can do to follow up. So," he looked over at Perkins as they walked, "you wanted a little more table time before we hit the show this evening?"

"Now you're talkin, man," Perkins bumped him with a forearm as he skipped slightly over the sidewalk. "Where should we play?"

"I'll let you choose that," Stryker shrugged, "but we need to hit the Bellagio lobby in about an hour."

"Huh?"

"We'll let those two guys clear out, and then I need to log onto the site one last time." Stryker rubbed his hands as they walked. "We'll use one of the computers in the lobby that they've got for guests to check in for their plane flights."

"You just said you'd stay off the site," Perkins complained without vehemence.

"After one final posting," Stryker said.

"They've got cameras in the lobby," Perkins noted.

"I'll avoid them like we did before," Stryker assured him. "It'll be very quick. I feel a bit sorry for those two guys who are going to be sent right back out here again. But, not much we can do about that, I guess."

An hour later Stryker logged onto the Axman website and clicked on the discussion blog. Nothing had been added since the three posts offering assistance. He logged in as 'Axman' and posted a message that read: "Thanks for offering to help, but we really don't need it. Not a big deal if we lose one guy. It's happened before. Keep us informed." With that, Stryker logged off and left the hotel to join Perkins for some blackjack playing at the New York New York Casino. The next day they flew back to Seattle with plans to take in a Mariner game over the weekend. Stryker relaxed with the thought that his Axman days were now truly behind him.

CHAPTER FORTY-EIGHT

Stryker lay in bed for twenty minutes after waking early without the prompting of an alarm clock. Random thoughts ran through his head without any real focus as he simply enjoyed the warmth and comfort of his queen sized bed and his commitment free future. He finally pulled himself from the cozy confines and repeated the habit from the army of carefully making up the bed before doing anything else to begin his day. He spent fifteen minutes scanning the newspaper and made mental notes of articles that warranted a return visit later on. He then slipped into running shorts, a tank top and running shoes and stepped from his condo for an hour on the roads of sunny Seattle. Rather than stretching before he ran, Stryker began at an easy, comfortable pace while his muscles warmed and loosened. Before long his pace had dropped considerably and he ran with few thoughts beyond his breathing and his stride. He nodded or waved a slight acknowledgement at a few fellow runners, but ignored bikers, cars and most walkers. He breathed hard, sweated heavily, and loved every minute of it.

At the finish of his run he stood outside on his deck and stretched a bit while he cooled off and drank cold water. He ignored the ringing of the telephone inside the condo and couldn't tell whether or not the caller left a message. He didn't really care. Before long, the water glass held no more liquid and his stretching was complete, but Stryker remained on the deck looking at nothing and thinking about even less.

Eventually he made his way back inside for a shower followed by breakfast of juice and cereal and a return to the newspaper. As he walked toward the bathroom and the awaiting shower, he didn't bother to look for a possible message on his phone until it rang and he noticed that the message light was not blinking. Stryker contemplated ignoring the call once again, but decided at the last second to answer.

"Hello," he spoke into the mouthpiece without enthusiasm.

"Good morning sir, is this Thorne Stryker that I'm speaking with?" asked a strong female voice with an accent from Virginia or North Carolina.

"Yes it is," Stryker responded with a touch of reluctance in his voice.

He then confirmed his military ID number and his prior status as a lieutenant in the Army while his curiosity rose.

"Thank you Lieutenant Stryker," the voice offered through the phone. "This is Captain Rosalie Tapp in Washington D.C. with the Department of Defense. We're updating and upgrading our database of inactive military personnel in an effort to provide services to our retirees and to help with future recruiting efforts. Could you help me out with a little information? It'll only take five minutes of your time."

"I guess that'll depend on the information you're looking for, Captain Tapp," Stryker responded.

"Fair enough, Lieutenant. You certainly don't need to answer any of our questions if you find them objectionable in any way."

Her tone was friendly and non-threatening, but Stryker felt a threat nonetheless. "Now, we have your date and place of birth, your induction and release dates from the Army, and your current address and phone number. You also show no living relatives, is that correct?"

"That's correct," Stryker confirmed.

"Not married?" she asked.

"Not married."

"And we don't show any other addresses for you besides the one in Seattle, is that correct?" she asked as though she were referring to an information sheet.

"Yep," Stryker acknowledged. "I've lived here in Seattle ever since I left the Army."

"Alright," Tapp paused as she presumably checked the list of questions in front of her. "Now, have there been any issues for you regarding your pension?"

It was now Stryker's turn to pause. "Ah, I don't receive a pension, Captain. As you noted, I was in active service for fifteen years. Thus, no pension."

"Of course, my mistake," Tapp apologized. "We've got this generic list of questions we're asking everybody. Sorry about that. Okay, let's move on. Would you ever consider rejoining active service?"

"No," Stryker responded matter-of-factly.

"Would you be available to help with Army recruiting efforts in your geographic area?"

"No."

"Oh, okay. I guess we can skip the follow up questions there. Umm, let's see. What adjustment issues did you have in your transfer from the Army to civilian life? Was there any major issue?"

"Clothes," Stryker answered.

"Excuse me?" Tapp asked with uncertainty.

"Clothes," Stryker repeated. "I had trouble adjusting to wearing civilian clothes in place of a uniform."

"Are you being serious, or are you pulling my leg?"

"Completely serious," Stryker confirmed. "I didn't have any real adjustment problems other than the issue of clothes."

"Okay, then. What sort of employment history have you held since you left the Army?"

"Nothing steady," replied Stryker.

"Are you currently employed?" Tapp asked.

"Nope."

"Umm, okay," Tapp seemed a bit confused and unsure how to proceed. "So, have you remained in contact with military personnel since you left the Army?"

"Sure," was all that Stryker said.

"People still in uniform or others who are ex-military?"

"Both, I suppose," Stryker replied. "It's been quite a few years now since I left the Army." He paused for a moment but stepped in again before Tapp asked her next question. "About how much longer will this take?"

"Oh, ah, not very long, a lot of the questions are pretty quick and easy," she promised. "Now, let's see, do you have a passport?"

"I'm not sure how that can be of any interest to the Army at this time, but yes, I do."

"And do you travel frequently from your home in Seattle?"

"Sorry, but I'm still not seeing the relevance for any database you might be trying to build," Stryker stated with an effort to avoid sounding defensive.

"Oh, well I can't really say," Tapp replied. "I'm just asking the questions, not coming up with them. But it's not a problem, we can skip that one. Umm, let's see, do you own your own home?"

"Yes, a condominium."

"Okay, and do you own a cell phone?"

Stryker thought for a moment, but decided there was no use in avoiding a question to which most anyone could easily find the answer. "Yes," he said.

"And what about a computer, do you own a computer?"

Interesting, Stryker thought. "Yes, I do," he responded. "I've had one almost the entire time since I left the Army."

"Great," Tapp looked to her next question. "And what about a gun? Do you own a gun?"

"I don't know any ex-soldier who doesn't," Stryker responded somewhat evasively.

"Can I get any detail on that?" Tapp asked.

"Nope."

"Okay then," Tapp began again. "Are you a member of any clubs or organizations?"

"Nope." Stryker found that he liked the answer more each time he gave it.

"Well, that almost finishes up for us," Tapp said. "Just a couple of final questions where you can give us a number from one to five, five being very satisfied and one being very unsatisfied. Is that clear?"

"Got it," Stryker responded with a bit of impatience.

"Good, so, first, how would you rate your training experience in the Army?"

"Four," Stryker responded without hesitation.

"And your overall rating of the officers under whom you worked during your time in uniform?"

"Four."

"And how would you rate your overall experience in the Army?"

"Four."

"You're very consistent, Mr. Stryker. How would you rate your relations with the Army since your retirement?"

"Four."

"Okay. And finally, how would you rate your satisfaction with civilian life since your retirement from the Army?"

"How about four and a half," Stryker responded. "It would be a five, but for the darn clothes issue."

"Right. Well, thank you for your cooperation, Lieutenant Stryker," Tapp said by way of ending the survey. "We're just beginning this survey process, so may we contact you again if we have follow-up questions?"

Stryker hesitated slightly, "Ah, I guess so. As long as you'll be the one asking the questions Captain Tapp."

"Well, thank you for your time. Goodbye."

Stryker disconnected the phone and thought about the circumstances of this rather odd survey coming at the same time as the Axman manhunt. He didn't like the coincidence and decided to get Perkins' perspective but couldn't get LJ to answer his phone. He headed for the shower with many possibilities swirling in his mind.

Stryker didn't talk to Perkins until after dinner that evening when Perkins responded to a message left much earlier in the day. "Hey, man, what's up?" Perkins greeted when Stryker answered the phone.

"Just missing you buddy, you know how it is," Stryker replied. "You got a few minutes to grab some nachos or something?"

"You're speaking my language. Where and when?"

They met at a relatively quiet bar and grill where they ordered an extra large plate of nachos along with a beer for Perkins and a Diet Pepsi for Stryker. They talked about nothing for a few minutes while waiting for their order to arrive.

Finally, Stryker looked at Perkins with a raised eyebrow. "So, I had an interesting phone call this morning."

"You too?" Perkins said to Stryker's surprise. "I answered a lot of questions from a lovely sounding Captain Tapp this morning. That wouldn't mean anything to you, would it?"

"I don't know about the 'lovely sounding' part," Stryker chuckled, "but I did spend some time on the phone with the Captain. Did you answer all her questions?"

"Yeah, most of 'em," Perkins acknowledged. "Said it was for some kind of Army database update. I was a little hesitant just because of your deal, but I figured it was better to answer than to not answer. Didn't seem like anything too dangerous."

"Yeah, I answered too," Stryker told him. "Maybe I'm a bit paranoid right now, but I thought it was interesting that she asked about travel and passports, as well as whether I had a computer and a cell phone. I wasn't sure how some of the questions would be pertinent for any kind of Army database, but I was like you, I answered the questions."

"Passport, computer and cell phone?" Perkins repeated with surprise in his voice. "She didn't ask me any of that stuff."

"What?" Stryker replied in alarm. "What did she ask you?"

"Just kidding, man," Perkins laughed. "Sounds like we got the same questions."

"Funny guy," Stryker smiled across the table. "Well, I'm not sure I'm buying any thought of coincidence regarding the timing of these calls. I'm betting it's the groundwork being laid for the investigation that's underway. I'm not sure exactly what they were looking for, but like I said, probably not a coincidence."

"Probably a fair guess," Perkins acknowledged. "So, what do we do now?"

"That's exactly what I've been thinking about," replied Stryker as he grabbed an extra-cheesy chip to the disappointment of Perkins. "Unfortunately, I don't have any great answers. I'm a bit thrown by the call, I guess. It's probably the most contact I've had with the Army in ten years. More than I planned on ever having either."

"Yeah, I know you figured those days were past," Perkins said with semi-serious sympathy. "I guess I did too, but I've got regular contact 'cause I'm at least drawing my pension. You left too early for that."

"So I did," said Stryker. "So I did."

TEN YEARS AGO

CHAPTER FORTY-NINE

Jose Fernandez sat leaning against a shaded wall and stared aimlessly from the same position on Faraz Plaza that he had occupied virtually non-stop for the past three days. His feet, covered by worn sandals were tucked up under his legs most of the time, only occasionally appearing when he stretched his legs. His torn white pants carried dirt from weeks of wear without washing and his oversized white t-shirt showed darkened sweat spots under the arms and below the throat. He held his hand out to passers-by, but without any real enthusiasm or optimism. Shoppers, walkers, and all others on the street entirely ignored Fernandez, except for two nearby shopkeepers, each of whom individually plotted ways in which they could get the beggar to take up residence further from their doors and customers.

At the same time, Fernandez was the focus of unrelenting watchfulness from eyes in an apartment window across the street and to his right, and in a clothing store across the street in the opposite direction. The watching eyes changed frequently among the other eight members of Fernandez's nine man team.

Fernandez himself watched the street intently while masterfully appearing semi-conscious and completely disengaged from his surroundings. He also focused on the cell phone in his pocket that would vibrate to warn him of an awaited approach.

Fernandez sat on the main shopping street for the local inhabitants of downtown Kabul, Afghanistan, which was located just five blocks from the true center of the city. Those few blocks separated different worlds. Within the narrow radius of the city center, which began just one block west of where Fernandez sat, the streets were clogged with hotels, banks, restaurants, fancy clothing stores, coffee shops, and policemen. On those streets, French and English could be heard as frequently as Arabic, and Fernandez would never have been allowed to take up residence against the side of a building.

Faraz Plaza marked the beginnings of traditional Kabul and remained the most popular gathering place for shopping and socializing. The shops were small but neat, hotels were non-existent, and rarely could a trained ear hear anything other than Arabic from the frequently loud voices.

Broken pieces of disparate conversations drifted in and out of Fernandez's ear from people on the street. He heard snippets about a problem child, a trip to Europe, an upsetting phone call, a suspected infidelity, a recent purchase, as well as comments on the weather, politics, and seasonal fruit. He took it all in, but cared about none of it as he fought the loss of focus brought on by monotony. He hid his reaction of surprise and guilt as an elderly woman dropped two coins into his outstretched hand.

Thorne Stryker stood in the apartment window across the street and shifted his watch from Fernandez to the street approaching Fernandez from the north and back again. He also glanced repeatedly at the radio transmitter on the table next to him to verify that the power button sat in the "on" position. Each time he looked at it, its status remained unchanged, but it also remained quiet. After three days of repeated nothingness Stryker tried to will the radio to offer up some indication of activity, but his will proved insufficient to accomplish the feat. He looked again to make sure that radio power button was turned on.

Fernandez, Stryker, and seven other members of their Omega team waited in Kabul for the expected appearance of Ibrahim Khan, the leader of Jaish Ansar or 'The Army of Partisans'. Jaish Ansar worked to destabilize the Middle East in an effort to create turmoil leading to the eventual destruction of Israel. In addition, they focused many of their terrorist efforts toward the goal of preventing Middle Eastern oil from reaching the United States and other western nations that supported Israel. The group did not seek out headlines, like many of their counterpart groups, but had become increasingly effective and influential nonetheless.

Khan led the group's quick rise to prominence and had achieved cult hero status throughout Afghanistan. His name and fame slowly spread to neighboring nations as well, and increasing numbers of recruits sought out membership in Jaish Ansar for the glory they would find within its swelling ranks. Only recently had he come to the attention of American military forces.

Khan had done everything possible to maintain his anonymity, but the success of his organization made those efforts increasingly futile. As a result, Khan isolated himself with his closest followers in the safety of the hills to the north of Kabul, never making public appearances or venturing far from his ever-moving camp.

Rumor circulated, however, that this week was to be an exception. Khan's favorite niece, Sakeena Aziz, the daughter of his dead sister, his only sibling, was to be married in Kabul in two days. Whispers rapidly spread the word that the great Khan himself would venture to the city to give his personal blessing to the marriage. Some believed he would give the niece away at the ceremony while others argued that he would simply meet with the bride and groom before or after the blessed day. Others offered knowing assurances that Khan was much too important and busy to concern himself with a marriage, even of his niece.

Word of his possible appearance had reached American ears and resulted in the deployment of two Omega teams to Kabul. Alpha Team watched the house and the movements of Khan's niece, while Delta Team watched Faraz Plaza in the heart of ancient Kabul where Khan had spent many years as a youth. Both teams grew anxious with the wedding approaching and four days of nothingness already sapping their energy and focus.

On day five, Alpha Team members discreetly followed Sakeena Aziz and her entourage to the northern edge of Faraz Plaza, while communication of the movement to Delta Team created a surge of energy at the prospect of action. Stryker left the apartment with a tingle of excitement as he joined the moving street reconnaissance below. He walked slowly away from Fernandez, stopping at shops and open market stands with an intense level of alertness. He felt that he could see and hear everything, but constantly feared that he would miss something as he did his best to appear casual and aloof. He had walked the streets enough in the past week to lose the feeling of conspicuousness, but he still tasted the edginess brought on by paranoia. He stopped to inspect the offerings of vendors while working his way to a street-side café offering bread and juice.

A voice in Stryker's nearly invisible earpiece informed him and other team members that Sakeena Aziz had stepped off Faraz Plaza into a closed restaurant three blocks north of where Fernandez remained seated. Two members of her group remained standing immediately outside the door of the restaurant while two more stood blatantly visible across the street.

Adrenaline pumped through the veins of every member of Delta Team with the possibility that the intelligence regarding Ibrahim Kahn might prove to be correct. Nine pairs of eyes closely watched Faraz Plaza from the center to the south while Alpha Team members watched the restaurant and the northern end of the Plaza.

Stryker saw the crowd at the exact moment his earpiece announced the arrival of Ibrahim Khan on the Plaza four blocks south of Fernandez. Stryker observed the crowd moving slowing northward along the Plaza with Khan leading the group, but flanked closely on both sides and behind by a veritable army of protective bodies. Stryker paused and watched as well-wishers approached Khan with reverence for a word or a handshake. Khan didn't have the long hair and long beard that Stryker expected, but instead his beard was neatly trimmed and his hair displayed western styling with a cut above the ears. He appeared to receive more than his share of the bright sunlight as he reveled in the attention he received following his lengthy seclusion. He radiated a constant smile while he nodded, shook hands, and smiled some more, but the high alert status of those around him could not be hidden.

The group continued to move north, presumably to the restaurant where Khan's niece waited. Stryker's ear heard orders given in accordance with one of the many plans that Omega Operations had prepared for this moment. He pictured the movements in conjunction with those orders as Khan and his followers continued their progress past his position. His breathing grew shallower and his heart rate increased as Khan approached the corner where Fernandez sat with his hand outstretched.

At the moment Khan reached Fernandez, a commotion broke out in the street just ahead of them. Stryker looked and saw two men circling each other with knives thrust outward toward the other, then he immediately turned his attention back toward Khan. Khan stopped and his followers closed in around him with all eyes focused on the street fight. Numerous people yelled, a woman screamed, and everyone seemed to behave like magnets – either drawn toward the fight or repelled away from it. Shouts calling for police officers could be heard along with whistles blowing from the northern end of the Plaza.

With Khan and his group stopped, and the eyes on the street directed at the knife fighters, Fernandez scooted quickly toward Khan, mumbling softly in Arabic his pleas for charity, and keeping his hand outstretched in front of him. It wasn't until Fernandez gently rubbed the white cloak, or thobe, of Khan that the terrorist leader's followers noticed the beggar looking up humbly, but with slightly distracted eyes. Khan himself noticed at the same time as he felt the slight pull on his thobe. Two of Khan's followers yelled at Fernandez and quickly moved to push him away, but Khan held up one hand in a signal for them to be gentle. He patted Fernandez lightly on the shoulder and instructed one of his men to give some money, which the man grudgingly obliged. Fernandez then scurried back to his wall to resume his well-practiced sitting position.

The knife fighters suddenly ran off in opposite directions as the whistling police officers reached the crowd. Bystanders began to disperse as well and the commotion died away almost as quickly as it had started. The two police officers split up in pursuit of the fleeing fighters. With a word from Khan, his group began moving up the street again, but this time with a greater sense of purpose that forced the people on the street to back away. Within minutes they left the street to enter the restaurant where his niece waited.

Stryker walked back to the apartment overlooking the street where he regrouped with the Delta Team members, other than Fernandez who remained on the street with his head down and his hand outstretched. They quickly assembled their gear and cleaned up the apartment while Max Tan communicated with Colonel MacAfee on their status. The men dispersed to leave the city individually, but then met up with Alpha Team at a tiny airstrip about ten miles outside of Kabul. The soldiers rested briefly while preparations were put in place to implement the next stage of Assignment Khan.

CHAPTER FIFTY

Colonel MacAfee of Omega Operations received constant updates about the movements of Ibrahim Khan who had spent just over two hours in Kabul before moving back out of the city to the mountainous region to the west and north. MacAfee immediately assembled the soldiers from three Omega teams for a final briefing on the action they had prepared and planned for over the past several weeks. The twenty seven soldiers squeezed together to face MacAfee in a makeshift meeting room at the back of a maintenance hanger near the equally makeshift airstrip. The airstrip served no regular traffic, but carried numerous high-tech safeguards against any possible electronic surveillance.

Thorne Stryker looked approvingly at the other soldiers in the room as they waited for the Colonel to begin. Over the course of his fifteen years in Omega Operations, Stryker had worked constantly with some of the men, less frequently with others, but he trusted the skills and abilities of every man in the room without question. The history of their successes supported his faith, but for Stryker it was more a question of character than résumé. Omega successes stemmed largely from the unwavering commitment of every man in the room. Stryker actually smiled to himself at the good fortune he felt simply serving as a member of this elite group.

MacAfee's voice interrupted Stryker's thoughts. "Gentlemen," he began, "we don't have any time to waste as the hard part of our operation is about to begin. The hard part, but the mission we've been preparing for." He turned to the map of Afghanistan on the wall behind him. "We've tracked Khan's position here," he pointed at the map, "in the mountains about 100 miles northwest of Kabul. Thanks to the tracker placed expertly by Lieutenant Fernandez." He nodded at Fernandez but addressed the entire group. "Nice job to everyone in Kabul, but now we've got to move quickly before the tracker is discovered, as unlikely as that may be. All three teams will be going in simultaneously and everyone needs to be ready to move at 2230," he glanced at his watch. "I'll explain the specifics for each of the teams, but before we begin with that, let me restate our objective as clearly as I can so that we eliminate any possible confusion." He paused and surveyed every face in the room carefully before continuing. "Our objective is to take Ibrahim Khan out alive. We'll use whatever steps are necessary with anyone else at his camp, but Khan is not to be killed. Everyone clear on that?"

Multiple nods accompanied a handful of 'Yes, Sir's.'

"Alright then," MacAfee turned back to the map. "Let's get started."

At twenty minutes before midnight, twenty seven Rangers making up three Omega Operations teams stepped from their transport plane nearly ten miles south of their target. The plane immediately took off again leaving the soldiers with light gear seemingly in the middle of nowhere in the darkness of the Afghan desert. Alpha team quickly split off to the west while Beta team members moved east. The nine soldiers of Delta team gathered briefly and split into three groups of three for their movement directly north to Khan's compound. They checked their radios for team communication, while the Delta Team leader for the mission, Max Tan, checked on his contact with the other two teams. Within minutes, the soldiers moved with quick and quiet efficiency.

Max Tan remained in the center with Carl Bedovski and TC Webb. Approximately one hundred yards to the left of Tan's group the threesome of Steven Bond, Bo Coolidge and Jose Fernandez moved silently toward their target. Thorne Stryker moved with Al Jeffries and Zach Gold at the same one hundred yard distance on Tan's right. The three groups stayed remarkably parallel with each other as they jogged through the darkness with their night vision goggles. They had just over three hours to cover the ten miles that waited between them and their 3:00 am rendezvous spot outside of Khan's compound. During the daytime, the trek would have been laughably easy for the intensely trained soldiers, but the darkness added a minor challenge to the endeavor. Even so, their pace merely needed to be steady, not overly fast.

Stryker took the lead for his trio with his eyes darting constantly to both sides while he listened intently as well. Jeffries and Gold, equally alert, flared slightly behind him with Jeffries offset to the left and Gold to the right. They moved noiselessly and in unison with Stryker checking the compass on his wrist to keep them perfectly on target. They walked for five minutes after every thirty minutes of consistent jogging, but otherwise never stopped nor slowed. None of the three even thought about taking a water break. They would finish their trek well before their mandated time of 0300, and would drink only after they had secured their position.

Stryker's constant movement and mental focus allowed him to ignore the coldness of the nighttime desert. He tripped once on a rock his goggle-aided vision missed, but otherwise he felt smooth and fluid as he jogged over the slightly up-sloping landscape. He could hear Jeffries and Gold behind him, but he kept his eyes focused ahead. They said nothing. Stryker didn't worry about the fact that they covered ground more quickly than they needed. An early arrival would simply give them time to rest and prepare for the job that waited at their destination.

The trio slowed to a consistent walk when Stryker's GPS watch indicated that they had traveled nine and a half miles toward their destination. They continued unwavering on their compass course. Tan checked in by radio and Stryker responded by confirming that his group had reached the rendezvous point. In less than five minutes, the nine members of Delta Team regrouped and settled in to wait out the remaining time until their 0430 assault.

Tan communicated with the other two teams although he knew that double checking was no more than a formality with every Omega member in place and ready to do his job. While they waited, they scanned the ground in front of them where they could see occasional movement in the compound that was built strategically into the hillside behind it. Stryker admired the ingenuity of the camouflaging that worked effectively to hide the camp from unsuspecting eyes.

The nine men of Delta Team prepared with M16 rifles draped over shoulders as backup weapons only. Each man carried a matching pair of sixteen-shot Glock 22 silenced handguns for the initial assault, and every one of the eighteen battle-tested guns displayed the immaculate cleanliness and perfect working condition of brand new weapons. Each man was also armed with confidence in his role in the attack.

At exactly 0430, Tan, Bedovski, Gold and Coolidge moved in unison with four men from each of the other teams. They moved silently and swiftly toward the compound and the tracker that continued to lead them to Khan. Immediately after the groups of four, Stryker and Jeffries moved to the very edge of the compound without entering. Two men from Alpha and Beta teams did the same. Webb, Bond and Fernandez held their positions, keeping careful eyes and deadly guns waiting for any enemy targets.

As soon as Tan and his team entered the compound, Stryker and Jeffries began setting explosives near the main entrance to the terrorist hideout. They knew that identical actions were underway to their left and right, but they kept their focus on their immediate job. Jeffries armed the explosives while Stryker watched and listened for any movement.

The inside teams had been out of sight for nearly a minute, but for the anxious men outside it seemed much longer. Stryker glanced at Jeffries to see that he was almost finished, but resisted the temptation to look at his watch. Three quick flashes from Stryker's right heightened his anxiety, although he knew it meant the presence of two or three fewer enemy soldiers.

Stryker and Jeffries both froze at the sound of muffled voices approaching from inside the compound. Jeffries grabbed his gun, but remained crouched over the explosives while Stryker willed himself to blend into the makeshift wall that he stood against. Two men emerged from the compound just to the left of Stryker and Jeffries, with one of the two about to light a cigarette. He never finished the action as Stryker instantly put a silenced bullet in the back of each man's head. Jeffries stood up and nodded to indicate his completion. Stryker quickly dragged one of the two men and rolled him up against the wall, then repeated the action with the other man while Jeffries stood watch. Nothing moved that they could see or hear.

After what seemed like much too long a time, the transmitter in Stryker's ear told him that Khan was being moved outside. He remained calm despite the tense level of his alert status. Fifteen seconds later, the twelve Omega team members emerged from the compound with Ibrahim Khan in their midst. They quickly moved two hundred yards from the encampment where they planned to regroup with all three Omega teams for the exit stage of the operation. Stryker and Jeffries followed the larger group closely, while keeping their focus on the encampment behind them. Jeffries held securely to the detonator.

The twenty seven soldiers of the three teams assembled briefly to begin their movement toward the pickup point, just over a mile away from the camp in a slightly southwesterly direction. Alpha Team divided so that five team members took responsibility for the point position, while the remaining four moved just behind them with Khan. Beta Team split with five soldiers guarding the left flank, while the other four watched the right side. Taking up the defensive positions in the rear were the nine members of Delta Team.

Alpha and Beta teams moved out first as Tan radioed to confirm their pickup schedule. Delta Team prepared to follow, but saw frenzied movement from the compound before beginning their retreat. They all removed their night vision goggles before Jeffries, Webb and Bond triggered the detonators for the three sets of explosives rigged at the edge of the compound. The blasts brought momentary daylight to the scene and revealed dozens of armed men scrambling in an effort to decide which way to move. Delta Team used the chaos created by the blasts to begin their move as the rear-guard for Alpha Team.

As they moved, a succession of six flares ignited overhead and on both sides basking the Omega soldiers in unwanted light. Flashes from rifles near the compound immediately augmented the overhead illumination. Bullets plunked in the ground and whistled through the air around the Delta Team members as they moved away from the source. They selectively returned fire, but primarily focused on making sure that no one from the compound made significant gains on their position.

As Stryker moved, one of the bullets plunked with a different sound than the others, immediately followed by Bo Coolidge seizing his breath and tumbling to the ground. Stryker kept his attention on the compound.

"I'm hit in the leg," yelled Coolidge as he struggled to get up.

"TC, Carl, grab him," ordered Max Tan. "You guys move on ahead as fast as you can, we'll cover back here." Webb and Bedovski immediately took up positions on either side of Bo Coolidge and began moving in the direction of Alpha Team in front of them.

Tan radioed ahead to share a status report, then gave orders to the remaining Delta Team members. "Listen up, we're gonna leap frog up in three teams of two. Thirty seconds at a time. Stryker, you and Jeffries stay back first," he nodded in the breaking light. "Blanket anything you see moving with heavy fire for thirty seconds, then high tail it to the front of the line. Zack and I will move up from here and be next in line. Bond and Jose will move farther up and be next in line. Once the next pair passes you, do your job for thirty seconds and then move up," he checked the magazine on his M-16. "We've got to keep those assholes back, but we've also got to be right on Alpha Team's tail when they hit the pickup location. Okay, let's do it."

Tan, Gold, Bond and Fernandez all moved quickly ahead while Stryker and Jeffries took aim to the rear. Jeffries looked at his watch for their starting time. They no longer needed the night vision enhancement to see continued chaotic movement from the north and they both unleashed a volley of shots. Jeffries emptied first and quickly moved to replace his magazine when a body flew in from his right side and knocked him to the ground.

The attacker screamed incomprehensively with his teeth bared like a wolf attacking a much larger prey. Jeffries struggled on the ground with both hands working desperately to hold off the knife that came at him from above. The anger-driven strength behind the attacker's right arm proved too much however, as the eight-inch blade drove directly to Jeffries' left eye, seemingly in the same instant that the attacker was upon him. The only thing Jeffries could do was to jerk his head to the side at the last second so that the knife sliced through his left ear before imbedding in the ground.

Stryker turned instantly and fired his M-16. He had no doubt that his only remaining shot hit his target cleanly, but it seemed to have no effect on the crazed attacker. Jeffries drove his right fist into the throat and chin of his assailant whose only response was to scream louder with eyes wider than seemed humanly possible. He jerked the knife back from the ground to re-position it in Jeffries' face when Stryker drove the butt of his M-16 into the side of the man's head with enough force to crush the skull holding the fanatical brain. The blow knocked the man off balance and stopped the movement of the deathblow from the blade, but it didn't quiet the quell the screams and spittle spewing from his mouth.

Stryker drew back to deliver another blow when simultaneous shots grazed his right thigh and his left elbow. The next shot blew out the back of the attacker's head. Stryker's attack with the butt of his rifle had allowed Jeffries to reach his Glock, which he immediately fired into the wild face above his own. The knife remained hovering in the air momentarily until it followed the back of the attacker's head and the rest of his body back and off of Jeffries.

Jeffries quickly rolled over and the two of them took off in a low crouch toward their comrades. They said nothing as they passed Tan and Gold and then Bond and Fernandez. Judging a similar distance toward their target, they dropped and waited for their next turn, which came in less than a minute. While they waited, the blood flowed from Jeffries' ear to mingle with the attacker's blood that caked his uniform shirt from the single shot fired by Stryker. Stryker's leg and elbow wounds stung noticeably, but didn't bleed nearly as much as the sliced ear. The only comment on the attack came non-verbally as Jeffries shook his head in disbelief. Stryker patted him on the back while keeping his eyes focused on the ground behind them.

Stryker and Jeffries repeated the drill twice more until they could see the connected trio of one injured and two helping Delta Team members ahead, along with the Alpha Team group with Ibrahim Khan, less than two minutes from their destination. The pursuers had dropped back significantly under the deadly fire and the last rotation for each pair had yielded only one short burst of gunfire. As Stryker and Jeffries moved up one last time, Stryker could hear the whipping blades of two helicopters just ahead – precisely on time and exactly in the right place.

Stryker, Jeffries, Bond and Fernandez stood protectively with their backs to the helicopters while everyone else boarded. Both Bond and Fernandez stared momentarily at the blood covering their two teammates, but they asked no questions. At the sound of a whistle, the final four jumped aboard and the helicopters lifted in unison off the Afghan desert. Stryker, Jeffries and Coolidge all received brief medical attention, but few questions, during the short flight across the border into northern Pakistan where two planes waited with engines warmed and ready to go. One plane quickly took off with Khan in the hands of new handlers while the other plane whisked the Omega soldiers to Delhi, India where they quickly debriefed and split up into separate teams.

The following day, Delta Team members flew to London to enjoy some time off while awaiting word of their next mission.

Bo Coolidge took a lot of ribbing about the gunshot wound that was somewhat higher than his description of a "leg" wound, but he looked forward to a quick recovery. Jeffries wore a conspicuous bandage on his left ear, but he swore it would be off within two days. Stryker's wounds were minor and he reveled in the adrenaline high that he always experienced at the end of a mission. Successful teamwork, minimal damage, a win for the country. What could be better, he thought.

CHAPTER FIFTY-ONE

Stryker's salivary glands kicked into high production mode as the extra large waitress set the extra large cheeseburger down in front of him. The waitress stared briefly at Jeffries' ear as she delivered him the same order. Jose Fernandez waited for his fish and chips. Two large beers and an extra large glass of water were already partially consumed as well as a plate of deep-fried onions with melted cheese. They sat at a dark-stained table in a lively pub in the east end of London. No one paid much attention to the threesome, although out of habit they each remained constantly watchful and alert.

"We oughta take one of these burgers to Cool," said Jeffries as he gestured with the oversized offering in his right hand. "Gotta take the man's mind off his ass."

"I don't know," replied Fernandez. "First of all, this is London so fish and chips is the only way to go. Besides as greasy as those things are it's likely to run right through him so he'd spend the rest of the day on the toilet. That wouldn't be too good for the old Purple Heart remnant he's dealing with." He paused as he took another large helping of the cheesy onions. "Not that he's ever gonna see that Purple Heart," he added through a full mouth.

"Yeah, the ugly downside of Omega Operations," commented Stryker as he picked up the burger for the first time. "Lots of action, good pay, little accountability, but no damn medals. Of course there's also the issue of the company you've got to keep. Between that and the medals, it's a wonder I've lasted this long."

Jeffries grunted loudly. "You're never going anywhere Stryk, and you know it. Double O's the only thing you've ever known. Besides, much as I hate to admit it, you're not bad at what we do. What else are you gonna do, drive a cab?"

"Well, if I drove one in New York it might be a lot like what we do, huh?" Stryker responded before turning to his burger with anticipation. "What would you do if you weren't in Double O?" he asked Jeffries seriously.

"Already planning it," Jeffries responded to Stryker's surprise. "I'm coming up on twenty years and I've been looking into law enforcement options – in case I decide to get out. I know a guy in New York, speaking of which, who's ready to *grease* the wheels for me." He emphasized the word 'grease' with a tip of his burger.

"You got twenty years in?" asked Fernandez in genuine surprise. "No way man. This is my fourth and sometimes it seems like twenty. I can't imagine actually having a full twenty years in the books." He took a drink from his beer. "What about you Stryk. How long you been in?"

"Ah, I guess it's been about fifteen for me," Stryker acknowledged. "Seems more like five though. It's gone by awful fast."

Fernandez shook his head in a combination of disbelief and semi-disgust. "You guys are crazy man."

"Hey, that reminds me," said Jeffries between bites. "I talked to Zip Perkins the other day. He's wanting to use me as a credit reference, if you can believe that," Jeffries laughed. "I guess he's setting up some kind of business in Seattle."

"Really? He doing okay?" asked Stryker.

"Seemed to be," Jeffries replied without a lot of thought. "We didn't talk long, but yeah, I got the sense that he was doing just fine."

"Well then," Stryker mumbled through a mouthful of cheeseburger, "if Zip can start a business in Seattle, I could drive a cab in New York. It wouldn't be so hard. I could even come up with an unintelligible accent."

"No way buddy," chimed in Fernandez. "There's no way it's as easy as you think. We're all good at what we do, but we've all done something else as well – at least in the Army. We're all Omega, but you were born Omega. Know what I mean?"

Stryker shook his head and held up his water glass to toast the two nearly empty beers. They all laughed, ate, ordered more drinks, and shared stories of Zip Perkins that they'd all heard many times before.

A formal meeting of the Delta Team in London was highly unusual. Each Omega team had its own city for a home base where the men lived, trained, and relaxed between missions. Teams changed cities every four months, and Delta Team's London assignment was only beginning its second month. Typically, the only formal meetings of the team occurred at the air base when they were about to be shipped off for their next assignment. Thus, Stryker's surprise came tinged with paranoia when he received orders to report for an official team meeting at the Tudor Mill on the outskirts of the city. He checked quickly with Jeffries and Fernandez to verify that they had received the same orders through the same team code. Even with that confirmation, however, his sense of uncertainty and unease remained strong.

Stryker, Jeffries and Fernandez arrived first for the meeting and stood around waiting to sit in the first row of chairs, as was their custom. Max Tan arrived next.

"Hey Max, you know what's up?" asked Fernandez on behalf of the trio.

Tan shrugged his shoulders while raising his eyebrows. "I was hoping you guys would tell me."

"You really got no clue?" Jeffries followed up.

"Nothing," confirmed Tan. "It better be good though. I had to break a date I've been trying for weeks to set up." Two others joined them in their waiting.

"Maybe we got a job here in town?" Fernandez speculated. "We're not meeting at the base cause they're not sending us anywhere."

"No chance," Stryker piped up. "They'd never give us a job where we've been living. Not even decision-makers would be that stupid. It's weird though. Other than our triads, we're never together here except when we meet at the base."

The conversation stopped as Colonel MacAfee stepped into the room and gestured the men to their seats. Stryker noticed that the other team members had arrived so that nine men sat in the small room facing MacAfee who stood before them. The room held seven rows of six chairs each, but the last five rows remained empty. The day outside unfolded with typical London coolness, but the room felt stuffy and uncomfortably warm. Stryker fidgeted in his seat trying to find comfort in the hard wooden chair while MacAfee focused on a sheet of paper in front of him.

Finally, MacAfee cleared his throat and looked at each individual face in front of him. "Delta Team," he began in his usual deep resonance as he crossed his hands behind his waist, "I know that it's highly unusual to convene the entire team here in London and I'm sure there's a great deal of speculation regarding the nature of this meeting. Nothing for you guys to worry about, however. Suffice it to say that we're here entirely as a favor to me. I wanted the opportunity to personally say goodbye to you."

He paused and cleared his throat again while the nine motionless men pondered the significance of the unexpected words. Sideways glances, raised eyebrows and shaking heads took the place of any verbal response from MacAfee's audience.

"I've been promoted," the colonel continued. "I'm about to become a General. With the star on the shoulder comes a job in Washington." A few quiet murmurs could be heard in the room, but immediately dissipated once MacAfee started up again. "Anyway, I ship back across the pond in less than an hour. Like I said, however, I wanted to say goodbye personally. You men have been a great team and you're a credit to the Army and to your country. I thank you for your work, and I want you to feel free to contact me if you need anything in the future."

"Sir," began Steven Bond.

"Wait a minute, Bond," MacAfee interrupted. "Your new commander is Major Atkinson. He's coming in on the same plane that's taking me out, so you guys will wait here and meet him when he arrives. I expect you to work with him as well as you've worked with me."

MacAfee paused for a moment, so Bond jumped in once again. "Sir, I take it you weren't looking for this *promotion*?" he said the word with a clear tone of disdain.

"An officer is always looking for a promotion," MacAfee responded unconvincingly. "A desk job will take a bit of adjustment, but I'm ready for it."

"Come on Sir," Gold jumped in. "It's not too late to turn it down is it? You don't want to be a desk jockey."

MacAfee stared at him for a minute. "I never considered turning it down. And, as I said, my plane leaves in just a few minutes."

"What do you know about Atkinson, Sir?" asked Bedovski looking forward with a soldier's acceptance of the situation over which he had no control. "Where's he from?"

"I'll let Major Atkinson handle his own introduction," MacAfee deferred with an awkward glance at his watch. "I know that he's a hard-ass though. And he's sure to keep you boys from getting too lazy over here."

"Any truth to the rumor, Sir, that Double O is being shut down or scaled back?" asked Tan. "Is that what's behind this move?" Stryker looked with interest at Tan, having not heard any such rumor previously.

"Not a chance soldier," MacAfee answered confidently with his hands opened before him as if to reinforce the point that he had nothing to hide. "If that were the case, they'd keep an old guy like me on board instead of sending in someone new."

Tan nodded at the logic of the response and appeared ready to speak again but held back instead.

Stryker finally spoke into the temporary void. "Well Sir, I know that I speak for everyone in this room when I say that you're going to be missed around here. You've been a great leader and we appreciate your command."

MacAfee swallowed in evident discomfort and he looked once again at his watch for a moment's distraction. "Well," he spoke firmly, "I came here to thank you men and now I've got to make some final arrangements so this will be it. Goodbye gentlemen, and good luck to you."

Fernandez immediately jumped up and offered his hand to MacAfee for a shake. Everyone else quickly followed suit and within two minutes, MacAfee was gone and the room was quiet, but somehow colder and not nearly as stuffy as it had felt just ten minutes earlier.

CHAPTER FIFTY-TWO

Major Teague Atkinson walked into the room with a mild, well-practiced sneer on his face. Stryker anticipated the "I chew nails for breakfast" speech that invariably came from every new commanding officer. Even in the Rangers. Atkinson wasn't far off the mark. He stood with his thumbs tucked into the waistband of his pants and he tapped his right foot lightly while assessing the nine men seated in the room.

"My name's Atkinson," he began, "you can call me Major." He looked with apparent disappointment at each man in front of him. "I understand that you men have been consistently operational, but your training has been a little lax, to say the least. That changes today. Before you leave, each Triad will receive a training schedule that kicks in right away. You'll also undergo immediate situational and strategic tests as well as individual meetings with me." He paused and rubbed his pointed chin vigorously as if he were trying to make it even more pointed. "We're going to pick up our productivity while we eliminate some sloppiness. We will not take avoidable casualties like you did on your last mission. That was just plain sloppy and it's time to sharpen up." He paused once again and went back to work on his chin "That'll be all."

The nine members of Delta Team got up to leave while Atkinson stood immobile. As they began to file out of the room, Atkinson called out loudly, "Stryker?"

Stryker stopped abruptly in surprise and looked back toward the major. "Yes Sir?" he responded with a minor hesitation.

"Wait here a minute," Atkinson directed.

Stryker glanced at Jeffries who raised his eyebrows in a non-verbal question. Stryker shrugged lightly and nodded at Jeffries to wait for him outside. Jeffries stepped out with the rest of the team and closed the door behind him. Stryker looked back at Atkinson and waited.

"MacAfee says you're the leader of this team," Atkinson asserted with his lips moving as little as possible as if to conserve energy.

"No Sir," Stryker responded immediately, a bit taken back by the statement. "I've been around longer than a lot of the guys," he acknowledged, "but Delta Team operates without any established leaders within the team. Someone usually takes the lead on any given mission, but overall, we operate as equal team members."

Atkinson smiled without warmth while continuing to conserve energy in his mouth. He looked down at the floor before addressing Stryker again. "I'm fully aware of the Double O command structure, soldier," he chided. The minimal projection of his voice matched the minimal movement of his lips. His eyes looked cold and dark through eyelids that narrowed without appearing to squint. "I assume that MacAfee was talking about perceived leadership in a team of equals. So, are you the leader of this team, Stryker?"

Stryker paused for a moment to seriously consider the question that he had never thought about before. The thought also flashed through his mind about the possibility that a trap lay waiting behind the query. There was no way of telling about Atkinson's motivation behind the question, but Stryker would have answered the same way regardless. "No Sir," he stated firmly without elaboration.

Atkinson nodded but decided not to pursue the issue further. "I guess we'll soon see," he commented. "Make sure your guys are scheduled for training before you leave," he gestured toward the door and turned away from Stryker.

"Yes Sir," Stryker affirmed as he moved quickly and thankfully out of the room to find Jeffries and Fernandez waiting for him. "We signed up?" Stryker asked though he already knew the answer.

"Yeah, we're starting tomorrow," responded Fernandez as they walked together toward the exit. "What was that about?" he nodded back toward the room with Atkinson. "He asking you out for drinks? I thought he was eyeing you kinda funny when we were all in there."

They stepped outside into a light mist that seemed to hover more than it fell. The few nearby lights reflected brightly off the wet pavement and appeared to flicker as their footsteps disturbed the gathering puddles.

"Weird," Stryker finally offered as they approached their car. "He was asking about leadership within the team even though he knew the way we operate. I'm not sure what he was really asking, or why."

"Maybe he's just looking for a buddy," Fernandez opined. "You know, his pipeline into the hearts and minds of the troops."

"Yeah, well, he'll have a little trouble with the minds of this mindless group," Stryker laughed. "Either way, I don't see Atkinson trying to forge relationships with the troops. Not likely his M-O."

"Well, as long as he keeps us operational and not wasting all our time with a lot of bullshit exercises," Fernandez commented with his words filled with anticipatory resentment. "I don't like anybody wasting my time."

"No shortage of time, buddy," Jeffries chimed in. "We've got lots of time."

"Angola, gentlemen," said Atkinson in a voice somewhat louder than needed. "You've read your briefing notes and I know that you've been studying on your own. I'd like to be able to call it the armpit of Africa but so much of the rest of the continent is screwed up that it might actually be better than a lot of places." Stryker thought he could almost detect a smile on the major's ever-placid face. "The civil war there's been going on for years because that's all that the damn Africans seem to be able to do is kill each other. Our job is to tip the balance in the ongoing revolution. We're going in as representatives of PEFA, Peace Envoy For Africa. We'll take out our target and be back to civilization before the sun ruins your delicate skin. No other teams on this one – just Delta." He stopped for a moment and Stryker thought he sensed excitement coming from Atkinson as if this were his first mission ever, not just his first with his current team. "Testing tomorrow at 0700," Atkinson continued. "Geography, culture, and specifics on the cities of Luanda and Luena. The scores had better be perfect. Any questions?" His pause could not have been shorter before he concluded. "Good, now get out of here."

Stryker, Jeffries and Fernandez sat in their apartment and watched the raindrops roll down the windows. Each man felt fully prepared for testing on Angola, but they had put off talking about the pending mission.

Jeffries finally broke the silence. "You guys still getting a weird feeling about Atkinson?" he asked while staring at the window.

"I don't know," responded Stryker. "He's not someone that I'd choose to spend leave time with, but I'd say the same thing about most officers I've ever known. Other than that, he doesn't seem that different to me."

"I don't like the guy," said Fernandez bluntly. "Haven't liked him since he first walked off the plane. The guy's a jerk."

"I don't know about that," replied Jeffries who seemed to be thinking aloud. "He just strikes me as kinda odd. Maybe it's just 'cause he's different from MacAfee. I don't know."

"I say give the guy a break," offered Stryker as he got up and moved toward the refrigerator. We haven't seen him outside of his training sessions yet. You guys want anything?" he pointed at the refrigerator. Jeffries held up a hand for Stryker to toss him a bottle of beer.

"You just like him cause he thinks you're the leader," chided Fernandez while turning down the offer of a drink. "The guy turned you in his favor on day one."

"I guess you're right," smiled Stryker. "He's almost agreed to transfer you back to the grunts as well. Then I'll know for sure that he's an alright guy." Despite his joking words, Stryker was less than certain about their new commander.

CHAPTER FIFTY-THREE

Luanda, Angola proved to be a much busier city than Stryker had pictured. The population had increased dramatically over the past few years as people sought the relative safety of the city from the constant warfare that tormented the majority of the country. The residents of the city now numbered four million and the infrastructure had not kept pace with the population growth. Thus, it seemed as though half of those four million filled the streets throughout the day and night.

The air temperature never seemed to drop much, but it remained bearable for Stryker and his teammates. They intended to spend two days in Luanda, wearing their PEFA shirts constantly, before venturing into the countryside for their mission. The mission required them to assassinate Buddu Gaddim, the leader of a rebel group responsible for terrorizing villages with attacks of rape, murder and mutilation. Gaddim's group roamed freely through the countryside for the past ten years and proudly claimed responsibility for over 200,000 deaths and for the complete destruction of dozens of villages of rival groups.

Stryker and Jeffries spent their first day in Luanda meeting with local officials on behalf of the Peace Envoy For Africa. They consistently heard pleas for the deployment of United Nations peacekeeping forces to bring an end to the devastating bloodshed in the country. They listened politely, but offered no promises.

On the second day in Luanda, Delta Team met early to hear the details of their mission outside of the city to eliminate Gaddim. Atkinson clearly enjoyed his position of authority as he made the team wait for nearly fifteen minutes while he intently studied papers and maps laid out on a desk in front of him. Max Tan shook his head in disbelief and impatience at the obvious power play, but all nine men waited quietly pursuant to their training.

Finally, Atkinson shuffled the papers into a pile and got up from the desk to address the assembled team. Even then, he cleared his throat, tucked his thumbs into his waistband, and waited longer than necessary to begin his instructions. When he was certain that he held the undivided attention of every man, he walked to the enlarged, very white map on the side wall and pointed to a desolate area about thirty-five miles northeast of Luanda. He annoyingly tapped the wooden pointer against the map several times before he began speaking.

"Our intelligence tells us that Gaddim and his troops are holed up here," he tapped the map once again, "but are likely headed north within the next few days. So, we move out at 0300 tomorrow. This is going to be a sniper operation, and we'll have three teams in place by 0500. I'll give you the individual positions as soon as we're finished here." Atkinson turned from the map and used the pointer to add visual vehemence to his instructions. "For the rest of today, you're still operating as members of the Peace Envoy. We're set to fly out as early as 0700 tomorrow, and we'll communicate as things play out, but regardless of how it happens, we need to be out before noon. So, as soon as the job's done, we meet back here for immediate boarding." He set down the pointer and wiped his forehead with the back of his right hand while he looked at a paper in his right hand. "Two of the teams will travel in one vehicle while the third will travel separately. Team A will have Webb shooting, Bedovski spotting, and Coolidge in the vehicle. Teams B and C will travel together with Tan driving. Team B will have Fernandez on the trigger and Gold spotting. Team C will be Bond shooting and Jeffries spotting. Stryker will be with me."

"Sir?" Steven Bond blurted out immediately. "Stryker's the best sniper we've got sir. There's no way I should be on the rifle instead of him."

Half the men quickly nodded in agreement while Atkinson ignored them and glared at Bond. "I've given the orders, soldier," he stated coldly, "now we'll set up specific locations for each of the teams."

"Excuse me Sir," began TC Webb, "but Bond's right. Stryker's better than anyone on the sniper rifle. Even if we've got three in place, he should be on one of them. He always does our major rifle work, Sir."

Atkinson's face turned harder than Delta Team had seen it before. The pointed chin seemed almost dangerous and a dark aura emanated from his eyes. He picked up the pointer and squeezed it in his hands as though he were trying to force the life out of the wood. He swallowed hard before speaking in a near whisper. "I'm not sure how this team has worked in the past, but I can tell you how it's going to work now. I'm going to give the orders and you're going to follow the orders. I don't give a shit what you think or what you've done before. You got that?" He didn't wait for a reply. "Now, for your positions. Webb, Bedovski, Coolidge."

The three men stood and walked to the front of the room to receive their specific instructions and were gruffly then dismissed from the room. The other two teams followed suit while Stryker remained seated, silent and slightly perturbed. When only he and Atkinson remained in the room, Stryker stood and walked slowly toward his commander. Atkinson stared intently at the map in front of him and seemed dead set on ignoring Stryker.

Stryker finally spoke. "The guys were right, Sir," he began in a carefully measured tone. "I am the best of the team with the sniper rifle. Is there some reason you don't have me on one of the shooting teams?"

Atkinson stiffened noticeably while keeping his focus on the map. Finally he looked up with his lips pursed tightly together and his eyes sharp and challenging. "Like I just said, I give the orders and you follow the orders. You got a problem with that Stryker?"

"Not as a general rule, Sir," Stryker said in as close to a statement of defiance as he'd ever given a superior officer. "The situation's just a bit unclear in this case. It's just got the guys wondering what's up." Stryker looked directly at Atkinson but tried to do so with the same calmness he projected in his voice. No sense in completely setting off the major at the outset of their first mission under his command.

Atkinson's seething was evident, but he displayed more restraint than Stryker had given him credit for. "That's just because none of you know the whole picture," he stated. "That's simply the way things work sometimes. In any event, I'm fully aware of your skills as a sniper, and that's the very reason you're *not* on one of those three teams," he stated only to add to Stryker's confusion. "You see," he explained smugly, "we actually have two targets tomorrow. The second is here in the city, but will also be a sniper action. Because it's here, we want to minimize the number of bodies involved. Thus, it's just you and me. Since you're the best with the rifle, you'll be taking this shot solo," he smiled in self-congratulation. "I certainly don't feel the need to explain everything to the team, but now does it all make sense to you?"

"Yes, Sir," Stryker answered a bit sheepishly. "Sorry for the questions."

"We'll forget it this time," offered Atkinson with a hint of a threat as he looked back at the map. "Now, as I said, our target is here in the city and we're on the same time frame as the other action. We should have a shot sometime between 0530 and 0630 so we'll be ready to ship out with the rest of the team by 0700. Our target's here," he pointed at the St. Regis Hotel on the map of the city, "and he goes out for a walk early each morning. Intelligence tells us he walks the same route every day," he traced streets on the map with his finger, "so we'll pick out the best shooting option and be in place by 0500. We'll also need to plan our return to the base, of course, but that'll be relatively easy. Shall we get to work?"

Stryker stared at the map considering options and problems, and never thought to ask any details about the second target.

At just past 2:30 in the morning, the nine members of Delta Team carefully checked their weapons before a final review of plans and the loading of their vehicles. Jeffries shot a silent question at Stryker who merely shrugged and mouthed "later". With a final check of their communication equipment, three men loaded into one PEFA truck while five others piled into a twin truck. The two trucks moved out at exactly 3:00 am, leaving Stryker and Atkinson behind in the dark but warm city.

Stryker finished checking his rifle and re-packed it into a lightweight Peace Envoy For Africa briefcase. Atkinson carried an identical briefcase with maps and a radio. The two men set off on foot just after the trucks left. The city was shut down but far from quiet even at the early hour, and Atkinson and Stryker stayed on the main streets while working their way to their chosen shooting spot a mile and a quarter away. Neither spoke a word as they walked.

At the end of their trek they reached the outer edge of the southern side of the city, which Atkinson had said marked the turning point of the morning walk of their target. Stryker was amazed at how instantly the city turned into the nothingness of the countryside, as if walking off the edge of a movie set dropped into the middle of nowhere. As the city street ended and became a dirt road heading out toward the villages of the south, a small hillside rose on the eastern side of the road. The hill served as the home of a very old cemetery that hosted little recent business with the current popularity of cremation for the dearly departed. The cemetery on the hill would serve as the shooting spot for Stryker.

The sun had not yet made an appearance when Stryker and Atkinson settled into position near the middle of the cemetery. Their elevated position gave them clear sight of the final three blocks of the street before it reached the edge of the city, providing plenty of time to assess the target and make the shot as the target began his return to his hotel.

As they settled in and surveyed the lightening surroundings, Stryker finally inquired about the purpose of their mission. "So," he asked as he scanned the road below them and then looked over at Atkinson, "the other guys are taking out Gaddim, who've we got?"

A cheerless smile slowly took over Atkinson's face as he nodded at Stryker. "Ah yes," his face appeared unusually pale and drawn as his eyes scanned the makeshift pale and worn headstones. "We get to stir things up a bit this morning. In about an hour and a half, Jonathan Bimidi will come walking up that street to the edge of the road. When we take him out, the Peace Envoy For Africa representatives will have no choice but to leave the country as this place is going to explode."

"Bimidi?" Stryker questioned in instant disbelief. "Isn't he set to win the elections next week? He's the one who's going to bring democracy and some stability to the country. Isn't that why we're taking out Gaddim? To help Bimidi turn things around here?"

Atkinson blew breath out of his nose in a quasi laugh. He talked without looking at Stryker. "Well, the U.S. isn't thrilled with Gaddim and his actions, but we're not necessarily thrilled about the idea of a stable democracy, either. Turns out the civil war here works in the interests of a number of American businesses. Not so bad for us in the military either, as I understand." He peered down the road and looked at his watch once again as if out of sheer habit. "Anyway, Gaddim and Bimidi both go down this morning and then we get the hell out of Dodge while everything falls into the stinkin' crapper."

Stryker remained silent and unmoving for a moment while he considered his distaste for Atkinson in relation to the information that Atkinson had just shared. When he spoke, the words came out slowly and quietly. "Since when are we interested in killing democratically elected leaders who are in a position to improve things for their country?"

"He ain't elected yet," Atkinson laughed. "Doesn't matter though. Our job is to fulfill the mission so that we can get out of here and wait for the next assignment." He kept his focus on the road rather than looking at Stryker.

"Who sent the order?" Stryker asked.

"What?" Atkinson's response clearly communicated his incredulity at hearing the question. Stryker remained unmoved by the tone.

"I asked whose order it was," Stryker repeated.

"What the hell kind of question is that?" Atkinson demanded without expecting a response. "Whose order? It's Washington's order to give and it's ours to carry out. What the hell difference does it make who gave the order?" Atkinson's voice rose with an equal balance of disdain and disbelief.

"I've been with this team for fifteen years and we've just never had this kind of assignment before, is all," Stryker stated semi-defensively. "Gaddim makes sense, but not Bimidi.

"Oh well," Atkinson responded derisively. "You can take it up with the boys at the Pentagon next time you're back in the states."

Stryker's mind worked feverishly ruminating on the situation and the possibilities. Eight men sent out to kill Gaddim while he alone stayed behind with Atkinson. Atkinson saying nothing about the second target until after the others had left. Jonathan Bimidi, the first realistic hope for the country in decades, as the target. Stryker as the shooter. The orders coming through Atkinson, whom he neither knew well, nor liked much. Did he trust him? Stryker now mimicked Atkinson by looking at his watch before returning his eyes to the road below. Just over an hour until the beginning of the appearance window for the target.

Atkinson looked at Stryker in the silence while he prepared to reassert command. "Go ahead and assemble and check your rifle while I check the radio," he ordered. He then pulled the radio from his briefcase and switched it to the agreed upon frequency. "Home to A Team," he spoke into the handset, "green here."

A moment's static preceded the reply. "A Team green," came the voice that Stryker recognized as Webb's.

Atkinson repeated the communication with the other vehicle before turning back to Stryker. "I said assemble and check your weapon Stryker." His voice projected hardness though it was little more than a whisper in the relative coolness of the cemetery. He looked back toward the road while Stryker reached for his briefcase.

"May I see the map, Sir?" Stryker asked somewhat out of the blue.

"The map?" repeated Atkinson. "What the hell for?"

"Routine, Sir," Stryker explained. "I always double check the primary escape route as well as possible options before any engagement. I'm not expecting trouble, but it's always when you're not prepared that something happens." He reached out his hand for the map.

Atkinson shrugged and handed Stryker the city map from his briefcase.

"You got a pen, Sir?" Stryker asked.

Atkinson sighed in annoyance and pulled a pen from his briefcase. He handed the pen to Stryker before turning his attention back to the road. "We've been over everything multiple times, Stryker," Atkinson stated with another sigh. "I guess we've got time though."

Stryker rearranged the map before him and scribbled on it momentarily before partially refolding the paper. He then closed his briefcase and stood up.

"What the hell are you doing?" demanded Atkinson as he swiveled fully around without standing to face Stryker.

"Heading back to the base," Stryker replied evenly. "I'll wait for the rest of the team to return and then we'll leave as planned."

Atkinson shook his head in a mixture of confusion and anger. "We've got a job to do, soldier. Now assemble your weapon and get ready. That's an order."

"No," said Stryker simply.

"No?! No?!" Atkinson stood up as his anger easily outdistanced his confusion. "I gave you a goddamn order Stryker. Now get the hell back down there and get your head screwed on right before you screw up your career."

"No," Stryker repeated calmly with his eyes focused clearly on Atkinson's. "I'm not sure where you got the order to kill Bimidi, but I'm not going to do it." He drew his shoulders back slightly as he stood at attention.

Atkinson stared without responding for a moment as he weighed his options. When he spoke his voice came out significantly quieter than Stryker expected. "You know you'll be facing a court-martial if you refuse to follow orders. We can forget about this now, but don't let it go any further." Stryker found himself respecting the self-control that Atkinson exhibited. It was more than Stryker expected, but it wasn't to last.

"Once again I have to say no," Stryker's demeanor matched Atkinson's apparent calm. "I also assume that we can avoid the court-martial since I'm no longer a member of the Army. I resigned just a few minutes ago." He handed Atkinson the map on which Stryker had written his formal resignation.

Atkinson glanced at the writing on the map and then threw it on the ground. The sky continued to lighten and Atkinson looked at his watch in increasing agitation. He looked at the road and then back at Stryker who remained unmoved. "This is your last chance, Stryker," he warned. "Get that goddamned rifle out before it's too late. Too late for the assignment, and too late for your future."

Stryker simply shook his head with pursed lips. His body tensed as his mind raced.

Atkinson reached with his left hand for Stryker's briefcase, but Stryker pulled it back from his grasp. At the same time, Atkinson used his right hand to pull his 9mm pistol from the side of his belt. He pointed the gun at Stryker with a full-scale sneer on his face. "Your options just changed, asshole," he declared coldly. "Either you complete the job and face the music afterward, or I report you as KIA by enemy fire. Your choice."

"Enemy fire, huh?' replied Stryker. "I guess that wouldn't be far from wrong."

Stryker considered his options when movement on the road below drew Atkinson's attention for just a moment. Without thought, Stryker jumped at the opportunity to knock down the hand that held the gun. He followed the blow immediately with a devastating strike at the front inside of Atkinson's right shoulder, which worked to momentarily paralyze that arm. The gun dropped from Atkinson's right hand as his left hand, now a fist, shot toward Stryker's jaw. The punch was weak, no doubt hampered by the pain in his opposite shoulder, and Stryker easily deflected the blow.

Atkinson attempted to raise his right arm but it wasn't ready to cooperate just yet. Frustrated, he let out a growl as he threw another left-handed jab that Stryker knocked harmlessly away once again. Finally, Atkinson threw himself at Stryker but his disabled right side kept the threat minimal. Stryker stepped to his left and simply used Atkinson's momentum to push him by without the ability to grab Stryker as he intended. Atkinson stumbled and fell to one knee. Stryker reached down and picked up the pistol off the ground and also grabbed his briefcase with the sniper rifle inside.

Atkinson remained on one knee but turned to face Stryker once again. He shook his right arm as it slowly regained feeling. His face glowed a deep red and pulsing veins protruded from both temples, not from exertion, but from pure rage. He finally spoke as he stood up, still shaking his right arm. "Get the hell out of here Stryker, and don't even think that you can stay with Double O after this," his voice came out guttural and shaking. "Even if you never put on a uniform again I'll still have you court-martialed. You make me sick." He spit on the ground at Stryker's feet but said nothing further. Stryker turned and walked away with the gun and the briefcase.

The Delta Team members returned to Luanda at 8:15 am just over an hour after Gaddim's death by a sniper's bullet. They drove directly to the airbase where their plane and Major Atkinson awaited them. Despite the fact that they'd already communicated by radio, Webb signaled Atkinson with a thumb up as he stepped out of the truck.

The men immediately loaded their gear into the plane and began to board when Jeffries stopped short. "Where's Stryker?" he asked to no one in particular. Hearing no reply he directed the question specifically to Atkinson. "Major? Where's Stryker?" he repeated.

"He's not going with us," Atkinson replied bluntly as he pointed with his thumb for the men to continue boarding the plane.

Everyone stopped instantly and Fernandez spoke next. "Not going with us? What the hell does that mean? What else is he gonna do?"

"I have no idea," said Atkinson coldly as he handed the partly folded map to Jeffries. "He refused to carry out his assignment and he resigned this morning," he nodded at the map. "The son of a bitch'll be court-martialed if I have anything to say about it. Either way, he's not part of the team anymore. He took his gear and he left about an hour ago. Now get on the plane and let's get the hell out of here."

"We can't leave him here, Major," Jeffries argued. "Stryker wouldn't just resign like that in the middle of an operation. Something's not right."

Atkinson pointed at the map in innocent naiveté. "You see it right there. Like I said, he refused to do his job, he resigned and he walked out. There's nothing you or I can do about that.

He's not an Omega guy anymore. Now, get the hell on that plane and let's get wheels off the ground before we're too late."

Jeffries examined Stryker's clear resignation once again before eight bewildered soldiers reluctantly boarded the plane. They sat in silence during the first half of the flight as they contemplated what had just taken place, and then talked quietly for the duration of the trip, but without agreement on a reasonable explanation. Other than a few limited and unrevealing conversations with Al Jeffries, none of them had any contact with Thorne Stryker for nearly two years.

PRESENT DAY

CHAPTER FIFTY-FOUR

Nearly two weeks passed following the information gathering phone call for the Army "database", with no other contact so much as hinting at the investigation that Jeffries confirmed as ongoing within the various law enforcement groups. Stryker sometimes found himself going two whole hours without thinking about Axman or the incident in Independence or the continuing manhunt. Were it not for the current seven game losing streak for the Mariners, Stryker might have begun to enjoy a blissful Seattle summer as a relatively well-to-do retiree. Might have, were it not for a Friday morning phone call from LJ Perkins.

"Stryk," Perkins jumped in as soon as Stryker answered the phone, "did you forget we were meeting for a run? Discovery Park. Like ten minutes ago. Right?"

"Ahh," Stryker stalled for a moment while he assessed the question. He knew full well that he hadn't missed a running appointment, and certainly not with Perkins who never ran a step unless it got him to the front of the line at a buffet table.

"Come on, man," Perkins jumped into the void. "Get your butt moving."

"Sorry, buddy," Stryker offered. "On my way."

Two minutes later in shorts, t-shirt and running shoes, Stryker jumped into his car and drove directly to Discovery Park in the Magnolia neighborhood of Seattle. The park provided trails, beaches, trees and open space on over 500 acres overlooking the Puget Sound. Upon arriving in the main parking lot he stepped out of his car to find Perkins waiting on the edge of the grass.

Stryker smiled at seeing Perkins in running shoes and lime-green shorts. "What's this, some sort of summertime resolution I didn't hear about?" Stryker asked as he approached from the parking lot. "I assume something's up, but it must be a huge deal if it's got you out here ready to run."

"Big enough," Perkins acknowledged. "Let's jog a bit before I come to my senses and change my mind."

"You're the boss," Stryker laughed as he joined in step with the slowly moving Perkins. "You better start talking though, cause in a quarter mile or so you're going to be breathing too hard to say anything."

"Just don't be thinking you're gonna get lucky and be the one to give me mouth-to-mouth," Perkins countered while he clasped his hand over his heart. "Anyway, I thought you might want to know that this morning I had a visit from two DOD investigators." Stryker almost stopped completely as he stared at Perkins without saying anything. "Lots of questions about the Army, my work, travel, stuff like that," Perkins continued. "They didn't come out and say it, but it was pretty obvious to me that they're part of the search for that maniacal vigilante been running around the country for awhile."

"Defense Department, huh?" Stryker asked without really asking. "They didn't tell you what they were investigating?"

"Just said a criminal matter possibly involving ex-military," Perkins explained. "Didn't ask nothing about specific crimes – just seemed like they were getting the lay of the land, you know, eliminating possibilities, or whatever. Who knows what brought them to a nice, clean cut, law-abiding vet like me."

"So, I've got to assume they'll be talking to me too while they're in town," Stryker speculated.

"Don't know why not," Perkins agreed. "You're a hell of a lot more suspicious than me." His breathing picked up as they moved further into the park. "Anyway, I thought you might want a heads up before they showed up at your door."

"Thanks, I appreciate it," Stryker responded while assessing the situation. "Don't know that I'll do anything differently, but it's nice to not be surprised. When you get home, write down as many specific questions as you can, will you? It might be good to compare to get a sense if they're targeting anything in particular." Stryker took a moment to admire the brilliantly snow-capped Olympic Mountains that appeared through a clearing over the crystal blue water of the Sound. "Shall we?" He pointed over his shoulder with his thumb to see if Perkins was ready to turn around, but Perkins shook his head and continued forward. "The truth is," Stryker continued, "they probably won't show up to talk to me at all. They're just checking on the scary guys like you."

"Yeah, you're probably right," nodded Perkins. "Not that you couldn't be a killer, of course. But they'd figure there's no way you'd be smart enough to use a computer like you'd need to. I'm sure you're safe."

Twenty minutes later they returned to their cars with Perkins breathing hard and in a full sweat while Stryker felt ready to begin a workout. As his drove away from the park, he realized that the upcoming workout might not be a physical one.

The knock on Stryker's door came just five minutes after he stepped from the shower. He finished slipping a light gray t-shirt over his head just before he opened the door to see two men that he assumed were the ones that Perkins had told him about. Both stood about the same height as Stryker, or a shade shorter, but one must have weighed 235 pounds while the other couldn't have been over 175.

"Thorne Stryker?" asked the larger of the two men. He sported sandy blond hair with green eyes. He could have been an NFL tight end thought Stryker, but with another thirty years and thirty pounds he'd be a great department store Santa.

"Yep," Stryker acknowledged with the door opened wide.

The speaker held up an impressive looking badge in his right hand while Stryker looked back and forth at the two men. "We're investigators from the Department of Defense," the man offered. "I'm Captain Ehlo and this is Captain Gutierrez," he nodded at his companion. "We need to ask you a few questions."

"Well," Stryker looked at Gutierrez and then back at Ehlo. "Let me ask you two questions first. One, what's this about? And two, should I call my lawyer?" Stryker knew exactly how Ehlo would respond, but the questions seemed appropriate nonetheless. He remained standing in the open doorway and noticed Gutierrez looking with curiosity over his shoulder.

"This is about an ongoing investigation," said Ehlo as the evident spokesman of the duo, "and we're looking into former military men for possible connections." The answer proved more forthright than Stryker expected. "You're certainly welcome to have a lawyer present, but you're not charged with anything or even suspected of anything. We're simply checking names off a list and gathering information." Ehlo hesitated to see how his answers played out. In the absence of an immediate response from Stryker, he jumped in again with a repetition of his original request. "May we come in and ask you a few questions?"

"Tell you what," replied Stryker congenially. "I'd be more than happy to answer your questions, but I'm starved and I was just heading out to grab something to eat. Why don't you guys come along, and you can ask your questions over a little breakfast. It's just up the block," Stryker pointed to his right.

"This really won't take very long, Mr. Stryker," Ehlo argued. "If we could just ask our questions here, then you could have your breakfast and go about the rest of your day." He nodded once over Stryker's shoulder.

"Nope," said Stryker amiably as he stepped out of the condo and closed the door behind him. "Besides, Gutierrez here looks hungry. I think you've been working him too hard. Right Gutierrez?" Stryker smiled at the unspeaking member of the team who looked calmly out of nearly black eyes. His overall slightly sallow appearance made Stryker think of a wild coyote in wintertime.

"I could use a little breakfast," Gutierrez offered in a surprisingly deep voice. "Let's go with him, Jay."

"Waste of time," Ehlo commented in resigned frustration as they began walking away from Stryker's door.

"Hey, a good breakfast's never a waste of time," Stryker said happily. "And you're gonna love the hash browns at this place."

Stryker sat on one side of their booth while Ehlo and Gutierrez uncomfortably filled the opposite bench. They talked a bit about Seattle and the Army while deciding what to eat. Once the waitress left the table with their orders, Ehlo opened the questioning while Gutierrez produced a tape recorder and a pad of paper for taking notes. He looked at Stryker who shrugged his consent. The one booth immediately next to them sat empty, but an elderly couple at a nearby table looked with curiosity at the tape recorder before pretending not to notice.

"So, we know your general military background, Stryker," Ehlo began in a low tone. "We're interested in your life after the military. You're not employed, is that right?"

"That's right," Stryker confirmed.

"And how are you working that, if I may ask? You don't seem to be doing too badly."

"No real secret," Stryker shrugged. "I came into some money when I was young and I've invested fairly productively since then."

"How much are we talking about?" Ehlo delved.

"None of your business," Stryker smiled.

"No, you're right of course," Ehlo held up his hands. "More just my own curiosity. Anyway, when's the last time you traveled out of the state?"

"I'm not really sure," Stryker evaded. "Nothing too recent, I guess."

"You own any weapons?" Ehlo asked while Gutierrez scribbled on his paper.

"Yep, I've got a .44 automatic at home. Fully registered."

"No others."

"Nope."

Ehlo drank from his water glass before continuing. "You ever been to Missouri?"

"I was there a few years ago on a baseball trip. Went to games for both the Cardinals and the Royals, mostly just to see the stadiums. I think that was four summers ago." Stryker looked directly at Ehlo while Gutierrez stared at Stryker.

"You go alone?" Ehlo asked.

"Part of the time I was there with a friend from the Army, LJ Perkins. He left before I did though, so part of the time I was there by myself."

"Do you know the name Silvis Walker?" Ehlo put extra emphasis on the last name.

"I've heard it in the news with his killing a few weeks ago. Heard about him earlier with his trial also." Stryker had reached for his water glass but hesitated as he started to pick it up. "Is that what this is about? Walker's death?"

"We'll ask the questions, Stryker. You can . . ." Ehlo stopped as the waitress appeared with their food. Gutierrez smiled at her arrival while Ehlo seemed less pleased. She set down their plates and walked away while Stryker reached for the salt and Gutierrez dug in with his fork. Ehlo continued looking at Stryker.

"Eat up, it's good stuff," Stryker encouraged with a nonchalant smile.

Ehlo picked up his fork and poked at his hash browns with the energy of a child in his first encounter with broccoli. "Do you use credit cards, Stryker?"

"Yeah, sure," Stryker acknowledged as he swallowed. "I've got a couple of them that I use quite a bit. I'm not sure that I get the line of questions though. What are you guys after?"

Ehlo ignored the question and glanced instead at Gutierrez who seemed to be enjoying his meal. Ehlo looked back across the table. "You seem like a good guy, Stryker. Good record in the Army, although you left rather abruptly. No trouble since you've been out. You hiding something from us?"

Stryker couldn't help but laugh. "I'm sure I'm hiding a lot from you guys. I'll answer your questions, but I'm not interested in opening up my whole life to two guys I've never met before – regardless of what your badges say. So, eat your breakfast and let's finish with your questions so I can get on with my day. Lots of important things to do, you know."

Ehlo and Gutierrez exchanged looks and Gutierrez offered his opinion in the form of raised eyebrows and a shrug. Both went back to their breakfasts without immediate comment until Ehlo reached across the table and turned off the tape recorder. "We're good with the questions for now," he said after wiping the corners of his mouth with a napkin. "We'll let you know if we need to follow up with anything else, but I doubt it. So, off the record, is Seattle really as nice a place to live as everyone says?"

"Yep," Stryker nodded. "Not nearly as rainy either." He looked at both men across from him in the booth. "As long as we're off the record, who the heck are you guys working for?"

"We told you," Ehlo sat up a little straighter in his seat. "Department of Defense."

"Yeah, I know," responded Stryker. "But what's the DOD doing with investigators out here in Seattle asking questions of somebody who hasn't been in the Army for over a decade? It still doesn't make any sense."

"Hey, you know the way the military works," Gutierrez surprised Stryker by jumping in ahead of Ehlo. "We just do what we're told. 'Ours is not to question why, . . .' Right?"

"Well, that's as good a reason as any to be ex-Army in my book," Stryker shook his head. "Sorry you guys are wasting your time – if you are, that is. I'll get the check," he offered as he reached across his empty plate for the bill.

"See ya, Stryker," nodded Ehlo as all three men stood up and shook hands.

Hopefully not, thought Stryker as he watched the two investigators walk away. I certainly hope not.

CHAPTER FIFTY-FIVE

Stryker sat comfortably in a reading chair on a misty Thursday morning and stared at the gleaming silver telephone. The newspaper lay next to the phone fully read, and thus demanded no further attention and provided no distraction from the phone. Stryker stared at the phone thinking that it might bring a call from Perkins in need of his assistance on a newly troublesome case. The phone remained silent. He stared at the phone thinking that a follow-up contact from Ehlo and Gutierrez, or someone else from the DOD, might be imminent. The phone remained silent. Stryker stared at the phone thinking that Sam Wykovicz might use it to suggest a lunch or dinner date that had been put off for too long. The phone remained silent. He stared at the phone thinking that he might use it to call Sam to apologize and to set up a meeting. Stryker remained motionless. Neither he nor the phone budged in their battle of wills as his condominium remained quiet and still.

Eventually Stryker gave in, but he left the phone alone. Instead, he took the action that he often found comforting when all else failed – he went out for a run. Stryker found the mist pleasant rather than annoying, and he set off for a long, easy paced run over the top of Capitol Hill and down to the shores of Lake Washington. Few runners or bikers graced the road on a wet weekday morning, and Stryker remained largely oblivious to the vehicle traffic as he ran through the city with a relaxed stride in his gray shirt and shorts that complimented the skies. He crossed intersections with little regard for traffic lights or pedestrian signals and received belligerent honks from an over-sized pickup truck and an older model Toyota. Stryker ignored the temptation of responding to them with a single finger wave.

Thirty minutes into his run Stryker continued moving further away from his home. He found himself moving closer to the answers he sought, however. He fully realized that his current frustration came from two different, but connected angles. The first angle pertained to his retirement and the fact that someone unknown sought to interfere with that retirement through Stryker's death or arrest. Certainly not the retirement that Stryker had envisioned, and Stryker didn't deal well with disappointment.

The second angle, or rather a second part of the same angle was the fact that Stryker found himself playing the role of the hunted. After twenty-five years of hunting, Stryker didn't take well to the role reversal and every future he could see remained fringed with uncertainty because of the danger of that hunt. Thus far, he had no definite indication that the hunters knew specifically that he was the target. The fact that he was on the list, however, didn't sit well. Stryker couldn't imagine simply waiting to see how the hunt might continue and how it might involve him. He finally turned to head for home once he reached a decision. It was time to take a more active role to learn more about the manhunt for the Axman. Stryker retraced his steps over Capitol Hill, continuing to ignore the traffic, but doing so with a quicker stride that reflected an improving mood.

Three years earlier LJ Perkins had been hired to provide legwork for NetSecure, a technology company that was employed to help three local banks with the problem of a computer hacker. Stryker actually provided most of the legwork, but he found the job fascinating in that he learned how much he didn't know about computers and how much was possible by someone who knew a great deal about the machines that had come to dominate the modern age. The hacker, a wizard at nineteen named Hadley Dygard, possessed more knowledge than Stryker deemed imaginable.

Dygard went by "Had" and he enjoyed telling people that Had was short for "Hack All Day". He did, in fact, spend most of his days on the computer seeing where he could go and what he could learn. Stryker followed up numerous leads from NetSecure, one of which led to Dygard, stereotypically ensconced in the basement of his parents' house where he sat surrounded by electronic equipment and magazines.

Stryker had approached Dygard quickly and quietly, prepared to strong-arm a confession before turning him over to the police to deal with. Instead, Dygard had immediately admitted to the hacking and then spent the next two hours showing an enthralled Stryker some of his hacking practices and secrets. Stryker determined that Dygard's hacking into the banks stemmed from curiosity and a sense of challenge, but was completely free from malice. Thus, Stryker extracted a promise from Dygard that he would never visit the bank sites again, while reporting to NetSecure that all the leads fell through.

Before long, Dygard moved out on his own, continued his hacking, and became an indebted friend of Thorne Stryker.

Stryker now prepared to call upon that debt to help with his current predicament.

Stryker called Dygard but as he expected, the phone went unanswered, so Stryker drove to Dygard's house in West Seattle. The smallish house with faded yellow paint appeared old and worn on the outside with dirty windows and a broken gutter, but Stryker knew that it contained nothing but the newest and best on the inside. A small patch of grass that now consisted of weeds and dirt patches as much as grass fronted the house. Two newspapers lay rolled up on the front porch, but Stryker never doubted that Dygard breathed behind the paint chipped walls.

He opened the rickety screen-door and knocked loudly on the smooth cream-colored wood door. He waited briefly and knocked again before trying the doorknob. The door opened readily and Stryker stepped into the overly dark and lifeless living room that looked largely unchanged from the last time he had visited. Evidence of the recent presence of Dygard's mother came in the form of three potted plants that Stryker saw wilting on a table near a window with the blinds drawn. He opened the blinds and poured some water on the plants before moving to the stairs that led to the cool basement where Dygard worked on his computers and spent ninety percent of his time. He called down the stairs but received no response.

Stryker descended the stairs behind Dygard who sat leaning back in his chair with his hands on the keyboard and headphones over his ears. Dygard's toothpick ghost-like arms at the keyboard mirrored his equally thin frame that barely made a dent in his soft chair. The headphones covered partly disheveled hair, but his face shone smoothly from a close shave. Stryker couldn't see the pale, gray eyes, but he knew well the intense focus they carried. He decided to approach from the side into Dygard's peripheral vision rather than directly from behind, but Dygard still jumped noticeably when he realized he wasn't alone in his lair. He removed the headphones with his left hand while placing his right hand dramatically over his chest and his Pokémon t-shirt.

Dygard gave out a heavily audible sigh. "Jesus, you gave me a heart attack, man. Don't do that to me."

"Sorry buddy," Stryker offered sincerely. "But you didn't answer the door and I guess you didn't hear me when I yelled for you," Stryker nodded toward the stairs. "You probably should lock your door, you know."

"I thought I did," said Dygard as he pushed himself away from the keyboard. Stryker guessed it was the first time in hours that he'd looked away from the screen. "So, what brings you slumming today?"

"Thought you might want to go out for some lunch," Stryker smiled. "That and maybe I've got a question or two for you." Dygard looked apprehensively and lovingly back to the computer that he clearly had reservations about leaving and was about to offer an excuse when Stryker preempted him. "Hey, come on, HD. I bet you haven't eaten all day. Even computer geeks have to eat sometime, right?"

Dygard's hand moved to his invisible stomach. "Probably more like two days," he acknowledged. "Except for Coke and Wheat Thins." Stryker noticed dozens of empty red cans but saw no evidence of the Wheat Thins. "Okay. I guess I could use a little break." Dygard relented and got up from the chair. "Where we going?"

"Aren't you going to shut things down?" Stryker looked toward the equipment behind Dygard.

"Nah. It'll all shut down automatically as soon as I leave." Dygard walked toward the stairs. "So, where to?"

"You're the starving one," Stryker laughed as he moved behind Dygard. "You pick the place and I'll pick up the bill."

Twenty minutes later they took opposite sides in a booth at an International House of Pancakes restaurant. Stryker realized that he hadn't set foot in an IHOP since he left the Army, but he took up a menu with certainty that the offerings would be largely the same. After they caught up a bit and ordered their pancakes, Stryker got down to business.

"So, as you might guess, I'm looking for some advice regarding my running and weight-lifting training. Can you help?" Stryker looked across the table with pleading eyes.

Dygard smirked a silent response before looking longingly toward the kitchen.

"No?" Stryker began again. "Okay, well maybe I need some help with some computer issues."

"How did I know that? Did you bring it along?" asked Dygard in clear hope that he wouldn't be asked to venture so far as Stryker's home.

"No, not a problem with my actual computer. I need some help with covering my tracks over some Internet use," he explained. "Both past and future."

"Details?" Dygard asked with arched eyebrows.

"Probably best you didn't know," replied Stryker with a long look at his thin, sharp looking companion. "You know I'll tell you if you really want to know, but I'd prefer not to."

Dygard waved his hand at Stryker while turning his head toward the window. "No skin off my back. Besides, I've got enough issues to worry about already." He paused for a moment before looking back from the window. "So, past use is no problem. The options vary depending on the level of your concern. We can erase all kinds of stuff pretty easily, but if someone is good and they really care, they can still find out a lot despite the erasing. If that's an issue, we could always simply swap out your hard drive for a new one. Along with a couple other quick clean up procedures, that will eliminate all your existing footsteps."

Stryker nodded at the anticipated answer. "Okay. I think that's what I'll probably do. Is it very difficult?"

Dygard rolled his eyes at the question he found offensive. "For you or for me?" he asked snidely. "Bring it by and I'll have you out the door in ten minutes." He looked impatiently for their waitress but saw no sign of her or their food. "Now," he turned back in disappointment, "it's good to think about future use, but if someone does come looking, you'll want to have a history of use on the machine, rather than a brand new hard drive. Might look a little suspicious, right? So, if you swap out the hard drive now, you'll take care of your past use, but you'll still want a history as well as a clean record going forward." He stopped and looked at Stryker with a gleam in his eye. "You going bank snooping or is this some kind of government deal? You in trouble with the Feds?"

Stryker merely smiled without a response.

"Yeah, I know," Dygard continued. "I told you I didn't care what it was. Anyway, I assume you're concerned primarily about someone searching your machine right?"

Stryker alternated between nodding and shaking his head. "Actually yes, but I also need to go to a website and I'm fairly sure they're tracking visitors to that site. I'm not really sure how someone might do that, but I think it's being done."

Dygard jumped in eagerly as he forgot about the absent waitress. "Hey it's easy," he offered with excitement. "All you need to do is to set up . . ."

"Wait, wait, wait," Stryker interrupted. "You know that I'm fascinated with the things you can do on a computer, but for my sake we've got to keep this focused right now. Okay?"

Dygard looked momentarily disappointed, but lightened up quickly as the waitress brought their food. After pouring half a container of blueberry syrup over his steaming pancakes so that the syrup nearly overflowed off his plate, Dygard took three quick bites before looking up at Stryker once again.

"Okay," he mumbled through a mouthful of syrup, "I've got what you need." He added another forkful to his mouth before continuing. "There's a number of sites that I use for stuff like this. You can use one called HiJinxxx." He smiled, clearly pleased with himself, as he spelled it out for Stryker. "It's a porn site so be careful that you don't let yourself get distracted." Stryker shook his head but said nothing. "The site has a search mode," Dygard began again as he momentarily stopped his attack on the plate of food, "but if you start your search request with a dot, you know, a period, it takes your search out to the Net in general. Then, and this is the great part," his eyes sparked with excitement, "the search is tied to Facebook." He stopped and looked at Stryker in momentary alarm. "You do know what Facebook is, don't you old man?"

"Can't say I've ever used it," Stryker admitted as he watched Dygard's fork move quickly over his plate, "but yeah, I do know what it is. A little different from when my dad used to tell me to get my face in a book. Anyway, go on please."

"Okay, so, the search connects to current logins on Facebook. Then, it randomly jumps from one login to another every ten seconds. You see? If anyone's watching a particular site to see who's visiting, they get bounced between random Facebook users, none of whom are actually on the watched site, every ten seconds. As long as you're logged on through the HiJinxxx search mode, there's no connection back to you." Dygard smiled at the deceptive intricacies. "And the last thing is, your computer records will show you logging on to HiJinxxx, but nothing about where you go through the searches on that sight. It's perfect, man."

"Sounds exactly like what I need, HD. You're a stud," Stryker smiled at him while noticing that somehow Dygard had been doing the talking, but still managed to eat twice as much off his plate as Stryker had off his. Stryker took a bite to try to keep up. "So, any tricks to using the site besides the dot thing at the start of the search request?"

"Easy man," said Dygard as he reached for more syrup. "Even a 19th century guy like you can do it."

"Thanks for the vote of confidence," Stryker laughed. "You want another plate?" he offered as Dygard finished his last soggy bite.

Dygard leaned back as if to stretch his stomach. "Well," he began hesitantly, "ah, what the hell. Sure. Let's do it again."

"There's no 'us' here Kimosabe," laughed Stryker as he waved to the waitress. "You're on your own with that, but I will have fun watching."

After the waitress cleared their plates and took Dygard's second order, he continued with his instruction. "Now, the HiJinxxx site will keep you clear from any real-time tracking. However, access to the site itself is gonna show up if someone comes to check on your computer down the road, right? Now, all they're gonna see is a porn site, but it's gonna show up at exactly the times that someone accessed the site they're watching, right?"

"Yeah, I guess so," agreed Stryker as he pondered the implications.

"So, that just means you gotta be smart," smiled Dygard. "Log on to the site frequently without using the search mode. Also, when you do go on to make a search, log on for a while first, and stay logged on after you're done. That should cover you pretty well." He stopped for a moment as the waitress brought his second plate of pancakes. "You'll look like a pervert, but you'll keep the red flags from going up." He smiled as he reached for the new dispenser of syrup dropped off by the waitress. You're not going to be accessing the watched site a lot are you?"

"I don't think so," Stryker responded. "A couple of times at most."

"You should be good then," said Dygard as he emptied the syrup bottle on his fresh and hot stack of cakes. He nodded and then offered another thought. "As an extra precaution, why don't you use HiJinxxx to make your first logon before we swap out your hard drive. As soon as you've done it, bring your computer by and we'll swap out for a new hard drive. I'll have it ready, and I'll make sure it's got some existing history, including access to HiJinxxx before we install it for you. That way, you'll be even more clear if you do end up with an on site inspection."

"Sounds perfect," Stryker praised him. "Anything else I need to worry about?"

"Bad guys with guns?"

"Hopefully not. So, I could use HiJinxxx from any computer right?"

"Theoretically, sure," Dygard acknowledged. "It does show up as a porn site, however, so you'd have trouble with lots of workplace or public computers since most have blockers on them to keep people from accessing sites like HiJinxxx. Other than that, though . . ."

"Alright then," said a satisfied Stryker as he reached for the bill. "I'll be bringing my computer by for a new hard drive tomorrow. Say about 10:00 am. Is that too soon for you?"

"I'm ready right now, my man. I'm always ready." Dygard licked the remaining syrup from his fork and got up to leave the restaurant. "Thanks for the breakfast and lunch, Stryker. Now I can get some real work done."

Two hours later Stryker turned on his computer with a twinge of excitement at his newfound knowledge and the sense of power that went along with it. Even so, he delayed momentarily while he checked out the latest news and a Seattle Mariners blog. Eventually, he typed in the web address for HiJinxxx and stared at the screen momentarily as a variety of pornographic video options appeared before him. In the upper left hand corner of the page he found a white rectangular search box where he clicked his mouse and typed the address of the Mariners blog with a dot in front of it. After a brief hesitation, Stryker's screen showed the site he had just visited while his Internet address box still showed the HiJinxxx address. He smiled, offered a silent thanks to Hadley Dygard, and logged off the Internet.

A few minutes later Stryker was back at the HiJinxxx site where he searched for the Axman address. When it showed up, he went to the discussion blog and saw the previous postings offering help.

One additional posting appeared at the end of the link under the name 'Execute': "In the absence of assistance, a retired executioner should stay inactive, quiet and out of sight."

Stryker logged in as Axman and posted his reply: "Sedentary, dumb and blind." Momentarily satisfied, he then shut down the computer while awaiting its new hard drive the next morning.

CHAPTER FIFTY-SIX

"Hey there, buddy. Broken any significant commandments lately?" Al Jeffries' deep voice boomed through the phone much too loudly for the early morning hours.

"Hey yourself. Nice to hear from you," Stryker responded. He began pacing as soon as he heard the familiar voice on the line. "And to answer your question, only the one about 'Thou Shalt Not Mock Police Officers' or however it goes."

"That must be part (b) of the one about taking the Lord's name in vain," came Jeffries' retort. "Anyway, how's it going on the left coast? Got any sunshine out there?"

"You know it's always beautiful in Seattle," Stryker laughed as he looked out the window at a gray and uninviting Seattle morning that at least promised to improve later in the day. "It's only when people are thinking about moving here that we talk about the rain. But no, things have been good. Pretty quiet actually."

"Glad to hear it 'cause we're still sensing the heat here. I mean, not really for me directly, but it's clear that the pressure's still being applied. Someone really wants this thing to crack open and everyone knows that after this much time that's not too likely. Even so, everyone gets to feel the frustration of whoever it is calling the shots."

"Still no insight about who that is?" Stryker inquired with muted pessimism.

"Nada," Jeffries admitted. "It's clear that the pressure's coming from Washington, but nobody here wants to admit that someone else is making decisions and yanking them around. So, they talk about 'interagency cooperation' and crap like that. Make it sound like we're doing our part to help out our buddies in blue – but everyone knows it's more than that."

"You directly involved at all?"

"Nope, and that makes it hard too. I try to keep my ear to the ground, but I'm not really in a position to ask many questions. From what I can tell, they're not getting anywhere. But I guess that could change if they keep looking deeper in more places." Jeffries paused and breathed audibly into the phone. "So, how's retirement treating you? Ready to get married and settle down? Join the real world after all these years?"

"Well, I'd think about it," Stryker responded with a thoughtful pause, "but Amanda's already taken. Unfortunately for her, she probably really did get taken in that deal, but that still leaves me without a lot of options."

"Funny guy," Jeffries snorted a laugh. "What about your stockbroker lady. I thought you two were spending more time together?"

"Yeah well, I think she wanted things a bit more open and honest than I was capable of. You know how women are that way. You suddenly disappear without any notice for a week or two and they always want to know where you were, what you were doing, who you were with, blah, blah, blah." Stryker's tone tinged of sarcasm but it rang hollow in his own ears. "Anyway, I haven't felt very retired yet. Hopefully that will all change pretty darn soon."

"Well, if you need a getaway vacation, head on out to the big city any time," Jeffries invited. "You could even go to a real stadium and see some real baseball out here."

"Hey, now you're treading in my wheelhouse buddy, so back off before you get yourself in trouble. You've never even been to a ball game out here."

"Phht. Minors."

"Alright, well sometime soon I'll pick the straw out of my hair and take you up on that offer. We'll pick a time when the Mariners are in town so we can see at least one good team for the price of a ticket." Stryker waited a moment for a rejoinder but Jeffries offered none. "Anyway, thanks for the update. I'll let you know if anything changes out here."

"Do that. And don't give up on the stock lady. She may yet decide that you're okay as a retired guy."

"I guess you never know," smiled Stryker as he hung up the phone. There seem to be lots of things that I don't know, he thought to himself.

After a run and a late lunch, Stryker sat with a novel in his favorite reading chair when an unexpected knock came to his door. He considered ignoring it but a second and louder knock quickly followed to clearly communicate a sense of urgency. Stryker's feeling tended more toward anxiety than urgency, but he pushed himself out of the chair and walked to the door with his book still in hand. Waiting outside the door were two faces he had hoped to never see again – Ehlo and Gutierrez from the Department of Defense. A third man stood just behind them and easily looked over their heads as Stryker estimated his height to be at least six feet, seven inches. He stood ramrod straight but with a forward thrust of his neck to accentuate a sharply defined chin.

"Stryker, glad we caught you at home," greeted Ehlo while Gutierrez maintained his customary silence. Stryker glanced at the two, but looked harder at the wild card in the form of the third man. "Mind if we come in?"

"Uh, sure," Stryker stepped back from the door while the three men in nearly identical blue suits crossed the threshold. "More off the wall questions?"

"Actually, no," said Ehlo with a slight apologetic tone in his voice. "We need to look around a bit."

"'Look around a bit'? As in search?" Stryker stiffened in both voice and body.

"Yeah," Ehlo offered in the same 'don't take offense' tone. "You seem like a good guy Stryker, and I'm sure you've got nothing to hide, but – orders you know. Just hoops we've got to jump through."

"Well, I agree that I'm a good guy," Stryker smiled without any genuine warmth, "and I'm sure I don't have much to hide, but I'm still not thrilled with the idea of a search. You guys are gonna have to get a warrant for that."

"We've got it," Ehlo pulled a paper from his briefcase. "Just one of a stack we've got to go through, but we've still got to do it." He handed the paper to Stryker but none of the three men moved to begin their search.

Stryker looked at the warrant to see that it was issued from a federal court in Washington D.C. "D.C.?" he asked incredulously. "A D.C. warrant here in Seattle?"

Ehlo merely shrugged while the other two waited.

"I think I want my attorney to look at this," Stryker stated as he reached for his cell phone and punched in the number of Karmody Fenn's office.

"Feel free," offered Ehlo, "but we're not obligated to wait."

"Yeah, just give me a minute," Stryker said as he listened to the phone ring. He was surprised and relieved when Karmody immediately picked up her phone after he asked the receptionist to speak to her. "Karmody, Thorne Stryker here," he greeted without delay. "Say, I've got a couple of acquaintances here with a warrant wanting to search my home. I've got no clue if the warrant's valid, but either way, I'd sure like to have my attorney present. What's your afternoon look like?"

"Nothing I can't massage," Karmody offered as Stryker could hear her moving in her office. "I can be there in twenty minutes, tops."

"Thanks. We'll be here." Stryker disconnected the call and turned back to Ehlo. "She's on her way. Twenty minutes."

Ehlo looked at his watch as he considered his options. "Well, we'll start slowly, but we are going to start."

Stryker nodded but then delayed with another question. "What's with your friend here?" he pointed at the very tall, thin member of the trio that he hadn't met before. "Is this a three man job or is he here just to learn from your expertise?"

A ringing had all four men looking at their cell phones. Once Gutierrez opened his phone, Ehlo responded. "Sorry. Zack Fogtree. Electronics guy."

Stryker nodded and shook Fogtree's hand while Gutierrez moved toward the door. Fogtree looked at Stryker with extreme disinterest while his sinewy fingers wrapped nearly completely around Stryker's hand.

"Yes sir," Gutierrez spoke into the phone. "Yes sir. Stryker. Thorne Stryker. Yes sir." He stepped out the door and closed it behind him. Stryker wanted to follow him outside to continue eavesdropping as the closed door cut off his end of the conversation.

"So, Fogtree will start with the computer if you can show him where that is. I'll look around here," Ehlo explained.

Stryker looked at the clock on the wall and silently urged Karmody onward. Then he waved a finger at Fogtree who moved with him carrying his briefcase. Stryker walked Fogtree into the room he used as his office and pointed to the computer while he wondered about the history provided on the week old hard drive from Dygard.

Fogtree moved to the chair in front of the computer when the deep voice of Gutierrez said, "Let's go" from the front room.

Stryker looked around the corner as Ehlo looked a question at Gutierrez.

"Zack, come on," Gutierrez called. "We've got other orders for now," Gutierrez explained to Ehlo. "Besides, the boss says Stryker's a waste of time." Stryker tried to hide his curiosity while he saw Gutierrez smile for the first time. "Let's go."

Ehlo reached for the warrant and placed it back in his briefcase on top of what looked like similar papers. Fogtree joined them and all three strode to the door. "Sorry for the trouble," Ehlo offered without hiding his frustration. "Hopefully we won't be back." He shook Stryker's hand and walked out behind Gutierrez and Fogtree. Stryker closed the door behind them to puzzle at the unexpected turn of events.

Karmody Fenn arrived at Stryker's door with a light knock just ten minutes after the three investigators walked out. Stryker's surprise at the abrupt disruption of the search and departure of Ehlo and his companions had caused him to forget that his lawyer was racing to his rescue. She walked in with an aura of forceful authority, but stopped short when she saw no one with Stryker in the living room of his condo. She looked around and began moving toward the adjoining rooms when Stryker stopped her with a quick touch on her arm

"They're gone," he said with an unexpected feeling of remorse. "Sorry." He wasn't sure if her look of confusion came from the fact that there was no one for her to battle, or from the fact that he apologized for it.

She adjusted the collar of her thin black sweater, although it needed no adjustment, and Stryker caught a hint of her subtle perfume. The combative authority she exuded remained despite the absence of a foe. "Gone? What did they take?" she asked.

"Nothing, actually. I called you – they heard your name and that you were on your way – they left." Stryker smiled. "I knew I hired a good lawyer."

"Okay. So, what really happened?" she returned the smile that showed a retreat from her belligerent high.

"One of them got a call that sent them somewhere else. I suppose they could be back, but who knows."

"What were they searching for? Did you look closely at the warrant?" Karmody asked with a tilt of her head and her eyes slightly squinted.

"I didn't look closely," Stryker admitted, "and they didn't say. One of them was about to start with my computer when the call came, but . . ." He raised his palms in a display of ignorance.

"Well, I'll brush up on my search and seizure law, but there's not much more we can do for now, then," she looked carefully at the calm look on Stryker's face. "Anything else you need to tell me? Remember, as your lawyer everything you share with me is confidential, as long as it doesn't pertain to a future crime."

"I guess not right now. But I gotta say, it was really cool to have a lawyer to call as 'my lawyer'. Thanks. You'll be sure to bill me, right?"

Fenn laughed as she took Stryker's proffered hand. "Trust me," she said, "there's no need to worry about that. If they show up again, call me right away, but if I'm not available, ask for Marshall Pye. He's probably the best in the firm for dealing with something like this." She saw the skeptical look on Stryker's face and placed her hand on his forearm. "Only if I'm not available. After all, I am your attorney, right?"

"And a darn good one at that," replied Stryker as he let her out the door. "Here's hoping I won't be calling soon."

Stryker sat back down in his reading chair but instead of returning to his book, he pondered the significance of the near search. He knew that nothing would be found, but he wondered if the search itself meant that other evidence pointed them in his direction. Ehlo mentioned other warrants, so maybe bureaucratic overkill was in operation, but Stryker still felt unsettled. The feeling remained until it got worse three days later.

CHAPTER FIFTY-SEVEN

Shortly after his lawyer's departure, Stryker called Perkins to let him know about the reappearance of the DOD investigators. The following day Ehlo, Gutierrez and Fogtree showed up at Perkins' office for a search that seemed half-hearted and that netted nothing. Stryker and Perkins met for a pizza dinner the following evening.

They ordered a large pizza with everything on it from Magellan's Pizzeria near Greenlake and took the pizza to a bench by the lake. They devoured the pizza while they watched the joggers and walkers burn off calories along the path circling the lake. Neither noticed any incongruity in their circumstances.

With the pizza nearly half gone, Stryker turned the attention away from the legs of the women passing by. "So, how long did they spend at your place?"

"I don't know. Two hours maybe? A bit of shuffling around by the Ehlo and Garcia guys, but it seemed like they were mostly interested in the computer."

"Gutierrez," corrected Stryker.

"Whatever. Anyway, nothing for them to find and they didn't seem too surprised by that. I just don't look like the criminal type, you know?" Perkins reached for another heavily loaded slice of pizza. "Now you, I'm surprised they didn't show up directly with an arrest warrant." He paused while washing pizza down with a lengthy drink of beer. "Seriously though, any idea why they left your place without searching?"

"Like I said, a phone call came in sending them somewhere else. It was weird though," Stryker stared off at the lake while he remembered the conversation. "After Gutierrez said they needed to leave, after the phone call, he also said, 'the boss says Stryker's a waste of time.' Weird huh? I mean, who's the boss and why would he say that searching my place is a waste of time?"

Perkins swallowed before responding. "Maybe we're jumping the gun here making assumptions. I mean, who says that Ehlo and Gonzalez have got anything to do with Axman in the first place? It makes sense that they do, but maybe they're involved with something else altogether. You never know."

"Well, that'd be quite a coincidence if they were to show up with questions and search warrants right now and to not have anything to do with the search that we know is going on." Stryker shook his head with conviction. "No, I don't buy it. But, and I'm not complaining mind you, I still don't know why they'd say that I'm a waste of time."

"You really shouldn't leave yourself wide open like that, man," Perkins laughed. "But I won't take advantage. Anyway, what's that saying about gift horses?"

"I don't know, but right now I'm thinking about the end opposite the horse's mouth," Stryker smiled before a drink of Diet Pepsi. "You finished?" he nodded at the pizza box.

"I guess so, unless we're going to order another one," said Perkins as he patted his full stomach.

"Let's go then, and watch the end of the game at my place," suggested Stryker as he looked at his watch. Perkins looked longingly at the empty box, but eventually joined Stryker in a walk back to Stryker's car.

They watched two innings of a quick moving Mariners' game before Stryker's phone rang. Never a huge fan of the telephone to begin with, he readily ignored the call when his caller ID showed an "Unidentified Caller." Less than ten minutes later the phone rang again with the same anonymity on the other end. Perkins shot a look of annoyance at Stryker as he continued to ignore the ringing. When the interruption came a third time, just five minutes later, Perkins rolled his eyes and pointed at the phone directing Stryker to answer. He finally complied under the assumption that the caller's persistence would outlast his patience.

"Hello," he greeted in a tone not intended to conceal his exasperation.

"Is this Stryker?" asked the muffled male voice on the other end of the call.

"Yeah. Who's this?" he asked without enthusiasm.

"A friend," the voice responded with sarcasm. "Now listen carefully cause we've got your lady stockbroker friend here and we'd hate to see anything happen to her."

"What!? What the hell are you talking about?" Stryker demanded as he stood up quickly from his chair.

"I'm talking about you listening and then doing what I say. Starting now or I hurt the lady. Say hello to your boyfriend, lady."

"Thorne, it's me. I'm . . ."

Stryker recognized the voice and his face reddened as his hand gripped the phone more tightly. At the same time, he motioned Perkins to listen in on the call.

"So, here's what you do," said the muffled voice once again as Perkins jumped up to Stryker's side. "You're going to drive to the employee parking lot at the Boeing plant in Everett. You're going to come alone. The parking lot is huge and it's wide open so we'll see if anyone else is with you. You're going to be here in forty-five minutes or the stock lady gets hurt. When you show up, we'll have a little chat and the lady will walk away untouched."

"What do you want?" Stryker tried to conceal the anxiety in his voice while wishing he could jump through the phone to the other end. "Why did you . . ."

"Clock's ticking Stryker," the voice interrupted until it was replaced by a dial tone.

Stryker put down the phone and looked at Perkins through firmly set eyes. "No time to set up a sniper play," he reasoned as he moved to pick up two handguns and accompanying ammunition. "We'll have to play this one on the fly."

"Let's go, man," replied Perkins with a jolt of energy. "We'll figure out a plan on the way up there."

Stryker drove past the entrance to the spacious lot with eyes carefully peeled before he pulled up next to the fence that encircled the parking area and turned off the quiet running BMW. He could see four figures in the middle of the lot with one of the four much shorter than the other three. He also saw his 9mm automatic on the seat next to him as he hesitated before opening the door. The pistol remained unmoved as Stryker exited the car and lightly closed the door behind him. He took his eyes off the middle of the lot to scan the fence line where, thirty feet to his right, he saw a pedestrian S-gate. After another moment's pause he moved slowly but steadily to the opening that provided entry to the field of battle.

Stryker passed through the gate and into the parking lot where it became clear that the shortest of the four figures was Sam Wykovicz on her knees. Two of the three standing figures moved toward Stryker as he approached, while the third remained directly behind Sam. Stryker raised his hands to shoulder height as he continued his deliberately slow walk. The two men walking toward Stryker were both solidly built, although one looked to be less than five feet, six inches, while the other stood nearly a foot taller than that. Both had closely cropped hair and wore similar versions of leather aviator jackets. As they drew closer, Stryker noticed a large, dark tattoo on the left side of the neck of the shorter man. The taller one pushed up his sleeves to reveal a thick, silver studded leather bracelet on his right wrist, then looked over his shoulder to see the same thing that Stryker looked at – Sam still on her knees with the third man standing over her.

"Just in time, Stryker," hissed tattoo-neck as he stopped walking about two yards from Stryker who stopped as well. "Hate to have to mess up the lady on your account."

"That would be a bad mistake on your part," said Stryker in a soft and calm voice as he assessed the two men. "This is against my better judgment, but you guys can walk away now and we'll forget this meeting ever happened."

The taller man laughed instantly and looked at his shorter companion. "Gee, he's gonna let us walk away," he said in deep sarcasm. "Can you believe that?" He turned back to Stryker without laughing any further. "We're gonna walk away all right, believe me, but I'm not so sure about you."

The shorter man dropped a baseball bat and a steel pipe and pushed his sleeves up to match his partner. Both arms showed more ink than the front page of the New York Times. "Somebody doesn't like you much, Stryker," he said in his continued hiss. "Says he owes you a debt, and we're here to pay off." He nodded to his partner. "Don't think you're gonna like collecting though," he hissed out a laugh.

Stryker made his confusion clearly visible while dropping his hands to his sides. "Someone hired you to pay off an old debt? Who?"

"That don't matter much to you, Stryker," said the taller man as he stepped into the gap separating them. "You just get to collect while the lady back there watches."

Stryker stiffened his body as he saw the blow coming to his midsection. The punch hit harder than he expected but did no real damage as it landed on ribs and muscle. Still, Stryker made a point of spewing forth an exaggerated grunt and doubling over in pain before struggling to slowly stand back up again.

Leather bracelet grinned and blew on his fist before giving it a mock shining against his jacket. "That's right Stryker. You'd better just take what's coming to you."

Stryker made no move to respond as the emboldened shorter man stepped forward and threw a punch upward at Stryker's head. At the last moment, Stryker turned slightly away from the punch so that it caught the back of his head, just behind his left ear. The punch stung and brought a ringing to his ear, but Stryker again made a point of overplaying his reaction in the mode of a silent movie actor. He cringed and grabbed at his head as he again doubled over and sharply drew in his breath.

The puncher reacted even more strongly however. "Damn it!" he yelled as he jumped up and down briefly while grabbing his right hand in his left. "I knew we should have used the bat. God damn it!" He shook his hand but otherwise regained his composure as he picked up the bat and approached Stryker once again. "Like I said, somebody don't like you much Stryker." He jabbed the barrel of the bat like a poker into Stryker's stomach with more force than the earlier punch. It hurt badly despite the fact that Stryker had prepared for the contact, but he still embellished his reaction with as much drama as he could muster. Tattoo-neck laughed and gave up the bat to the eager hand of his taller compatriot.

This time the bat was drawn back for a traditional baseball swing and the eyes of the shorter onlooker widened in anticipation. Now, however, Stryker saw over the shoulders of his attackers the moment he had been waiting for as the distracted third man hit the pavement following a heavy blow to the back of his head delivered by LJ Perkins. Without further worry about Sam, Stryker jumped quickly inside the arc of the swinging bat, engulfed the taller attacker in his arms and delivered a crushing head-butt to the nose of his surprised adversary. The unconscious man with the shattered nose collapsed instantly with his body laying over his silver-studded leather, and the bat clattering to the ground.

The smaller man's look of glee turned to instant confusion before he reached down for the bat. Stryker kicked the bat away and delivered a near lethal punch to the middle of the tattoo on the man's neck. The attacker yelped in agony and dropped to one knee while he struggled to maintain his vision. He started to stand back up when Stryker delivered another shot to the same spot on his neck. He cried out again and dropped to both knees. His leather-banded companion remained unmoving on the ground.

Stryker breathed hard with fire in his cheeks as Perkins drew closer. Sam remained a few steps behind Perkins, but continued to inch forward as well. Stryker drew in a deep calming breath and offered a nod of appreciation to Perkins before once again turning his attention to the gasping man on his knees.

"I gave you the opportunity to leave," he reminded the pained assailant. "You should have listened. Now, what's your name?"

The man shook his head and stared at the pavement two feet from his face while he grasped his tattoo as if it fear that it might run away.

Stryker nodded to Perkins who quickly, and without resistance, frisked the man until he pulled out a worn leather wallet. Perkins carefully opened the wallet and removed the driver's license, then threw the wallet on the ground. "Larry," he said.

"Alright, Larry," said Stryker as he knelt down, "we've only got a few minutes and you need to tell me who hired you and why. It's very simple. You tell me, and we go away." Larry continued staring at the ground and continued saying nothing. "No need to be a hero, Larry," Stryker offered. "I guarantee you that whoever hired you wouldn't hesitate to give you up if the situation were reversed. Look who's in the bad position now."

"I got nothing," Larry muttered in less of a hiss than before. Stryker shook his head and looked up at Perkins who shrugged his response.

Stryker reached in quickly, grabbed Larry's left hand, and immediately bent the little finger as far back as it would naturally go. "This is going to be very painful compared to your neck," Stryker warned, "but that's up to you. Now, who hired you and why?"

Larry shook his head once again and Stryker instantly snapped the finger back so that the nail touched Larry's wrist. Larry screamed and pulled hard but Stryker retained a firm grip just above his wrist. Sam gasped and threw her hand to her mouth as she fought a surge of nausea.

"Who hired you?" Stryker asked again as he grabbed the ring finger next to the now-dangling pinkie. He pulled the finger back to the point of pressure as terror gripped the eyes that frequently had been rubbed by the endangered hand.

"No, no. Stop!" Larry pleaded as Stryker slightly released the pressure on the finger. "I don't know the guy. None of us did." He spoke quickly without taking his eyes off his hand. "We got into some trouble at the base – Fort Lewis – some guy contacted Jarvis and said he could make it all go away, plus we'd get three hundred bucks apiece," the words flowed easily in building relief. "Said all we had to do was rough up some guy named Stryker," he looked up for the first time to gauge the future of his fingers.

"Who was he?" Stryker asked calmly.

"I have no idea, I swear," Larry pleaded once again. "None of us did. We got the money up front so we figured we'd come out ahead either way even if we didn't get the help on the charges. Not a big deal beating somebody up, right?" he looked hopefully at Stryker.

"What did he look like?" Stryker probed without much optimism.

"Never saw him," Larry replied readily with desperation evident in his voice for answers that he knew Stryker wouldn't like. "None of us did, I swear. He talked to Jarvis on the phone and the money showed up right away in an envelope."

"When was this?"

"Yesterday. Guy said he wanted it done right away, so we did," Larry's voice was calmer but his eyes still communicated fear. "That's all I know, I swear. Oh, and he said you were due a beating for a long time. That's it."

Stryker believed the story, but felt disappointment at not learning more. He looked up at Perkins and saw Sam standing with her hand over her mouth. He looked back at Larry. "What about her?" he asked with renewed venom in his voice.

Larry's eyes widened in the realization that he'd left something out. He reacted quickly to rectify the error and remove the anger from Stryker's voice. "Yeah, yeah. The guy gave Jarvis her name. Said you were a dangerous guy, but if we had her, you'd be easy to deal with." His face begged for mercy. "That's all I know man. You gotta believe me. We got nothing against you or her. Just doing a job."

Stryker released the wrist and looked hard into Larry's face. "If you ever go near her again," he offered in a menacing whisper, "you'll wish I'd broken every finger right now compared with what'll happen then. You got that?" He pondered demanding that Larry let him know if they had any further contact from the mysterious employer, but decided it was probably a waste of time. "You'll need to get a new license, Larry. We'll keep this one." He stood up and faced Perkins and Sam. "Take care of your friends," he directed before walking over to Sam. "You okay?" he asked quietly.

Sam merely nodded while still looking at the two men on the ground in front of her.

"Let's go," urged Stryker with a light touch on her shoulder.

They retreated to Stryker's car and drove away with Perkins at the wheel and Stryker feeling like a taxi passenger as he and Sam occupied the back seat. Sam remained silent until they neared Seattle and she insisted on going home. Alone. She'd be fine, she assured them.

"Well, you can certainly sleep alone," said Stryker softly, "but you're not staying alone in your apartment after tonight." He noticed a tightening in the corners of Sam's mouth as he spoke. "No way, lady. I'll sit all night in the hallway, if you insist, but I'd prefer to hang out in your living room."

"I'm not a child," Sam insisted while looking out the side window. "It was scary, but nothing happened. I'll be fine."

Perkins glanced in the rear-view mirror, but offered nothing to the quiet argument.

"Of course you'll be fine," Stryker agreed in the same quiet tone. "I'm staying for me. I won't sleep a wink if I leave you alone tonight, so I may as well stay and make myself feel better. You're not going to deny me that, are you?"

Sam sighed heavily and looked at her hands in her lap. "There's really no need," she offered without much enthusiasm. "I know how stubborn you are, though, and I really don't want to hanging out in the hallway all night." She paused but didn't look up. "Alright. The living room is yours."

Stryker nodded and looked up at Perkins. "You take the car and come back in the morning, will you?" he asked. "There won't be any trouble, but keep your phone nearby. I may need you during the night if Sam changes her mind."

Sam shook her head slightly, but offered nothing. Perkins pulled up in front of her apartment building and kept the motor running while they stepped out onto the street. Stryker nodded at him, but said nothing.

"You a brave lady," Perkins offered as they walked away. "Having that guy in your apartment all night." He hoped that she may have smiled, but only saw a slight wave as they walked away from the car.

After a fitful night of dozing on a too-small couch, Stryker heard Sam moving in her bedroom at 5:45 am. He sat quietly and waited until she stepped into the living room, dressed in a light green sweater over a white blouse and dark skirt. She smoothed back her hair and spoke before Stryker could open his mouth.

"Thanks for staying, but please don't argue about today. I'm going to work." She looked at him with serious eyes that helped hide the lack of sleep. "I've got a ton of things to do, and there's no way I'm sitting around here all day. So, there's no sense arguing." Her hands grasped her hips while her left footed jutted forward slightly in a stance that spoke of both defiance and determination. She raised her chin in expectation of the argument to come. It didn't.

"No, no, I agree, "offered Stryker with his hands up in anticipatory surrender. "Like I said, staying here last night was simply for my own good. You won't have any trouble today." He looked for a softening in her body and features, but a slight dropping of the chin is all that she was willing to give. "I'll call LJ to pick me up. How about if we give you a ride to work?"

Sam looked at her watch and he could see her fighting back the urge to argue about something else. "Sure," she finally agreed as her hands dropped and she walked toward her kitchen. "Orange juice?"

After walking Sam to the front door of Merrill, Lynch, Stryker returned to the car and peered at Perkins. “So, what do you think about last night?” he asked.

Perkins rubbed his jaw. “Axman search. Ehlo and Guatemala. Now this, and these guys knew about Sam. Too much to be a coincidence.”

“That’s what I was thinking,” agreed Stryker, “and it’s starting to piss me off.”

“I kinda figured that,” smiled Perkins. “So, should we go grab some breakfast, and chat about it?”

“Nothing I’d rather do than buy you some eggs, my friend,” Stryker smiled in return. “Maybe we can even find some decent coffee to go along with a cinnamon roll.”

“Now you’re talking, man,” Perkins bounced in his seat behind the wheal. “At least about the cinnamon roll. Let’s go.”

CHAPTER FIFTY-EIGHT

The next day, Stryker showed up ten minutes early for his quarterly meeting with Sam Wykovicz at the offices of Merrill Lynch. He then waited twenty minutes past his meeting time before Sam walked into the lobby with a closed mouth smile. She wore her traditional office conservative black pants suit with a white blouse, but her scarf added more color to the top of the outfit while the shoes carried a more sedate, lower heel than usual at the other end. Stryker tipped his imaginary hat to Linda the smiling receptionist and followed Sam to her office and wondered about the combination of scarf and heels. The lack of significant movement in the overall market obviated the need for any real portfolio shifting and Sam's discretionary trades had been lighter than in many quarters. Sam reported that Stryker's dividend stocks maintained their steadily growing performance through dividend reinvestment. Stryker listened politely, but frequently stared out the window in relative disinterest at the gray clouds that moved from south to north.

After the standard portfolio review and a few perfunctory questions, Sam closed up her file of papers and clasped her relatively small hands in front of her. "So," she began with a long pause wherein she appeared to talk herself into continuing despite her better judgment to the contrary, "do you care to explain about the other night?"

Stryker forgot about the literal clouds outside and pondered the figurative ones building within the walls of Sam's office. He exhaled deeply as he held Sam's eyes with his and opened his hands briefly in front of him before dropping them back to his lap. "I'm not sure I can explain any more than I have," he offered as he leaned back slightly in his comfortably deep chair. "You heard the guy out there at Boeing. Someone with an old grudge hired them to beat me up. They didn't know who it was."

"And you don't know either?" she challenged with a hint of skepticism.

"Believe me, I wish I did," he replied sincerely.

"You broke his finger like it was nothing," she stated without evident emotion. "And the other guy's face was bleeding really badly."

Stryker could think of no meaningful response and decided that a flippant one wasn't a wise idea, so he simply nodded with pursed lips.

"I was really scared," she admitted, although the confession wasn't necessary. "I almost threw up."

"Look," Stryker began as he moved to the edge of the chair with a mixture of anger and genuine sympathy; "I hate the fact that they pulled you into this. Especially since I don't know who's behind it in the first place. I guarantee you though," he continued earnestly, "that nothing's going to happen. LJ and I will make sure of that."

Sam nodded but didn't convey a strong level of confidence in his assurances. She looked at Stryker with more detachment than he had seen in years as she adjusted her chair and glanced down at the file folder in front of her. He knew that her real fear had less to do with her personal safety and more to do with his personal conduct and character. "We should schedule your next quarterly review," she instructed, "but I don't think I should see you before that." She looked slightly guilty as she forced out the words and fiddled with her scarf.

Stryker resisted the urge to argue and instead nodded as he got up from his chair. "Sure, sure. But if something comes up, if you need anything, don't hesitate to call, alright?" He didn't wait for a response and quietly closed the office door behind him as he left.

Later that same Tuesday evening, Perkins responded to the phone call invitation by driving to Stryker's condo. A cold beer stood waiting for him as he entered and Stryker offered up a plate of pastrami sandwiches on wheat bread with cheese and heavy mustard.

"Starting with the bribes right off, huh?" Perkins laughed as he reached for a sandwich. "Works for me."

"Appeal to the stomach, buddy. Works every time." Stryker took a sandwich for himself and moved to a chair opposite the couch now occupied by Perkins. Half of Perkins sandwich had disappeared by the time Stryker sat down. "I need a bit of cover, just in case," he jumped right in without hesitation. "It won't be perfect, but if everything pans out, I'm going for a four day hike at Mount Rainier. Need you to drop me off and pick me up if you will."

"And where might you be going for your Mount Rainier hike?" Perkins asked knowingly while pondering whether he needed a drink before his next bite of sandwich.

"D.C. hopefully," Stryker acknowledged. "I'm going to try to set it up tonight. Looking at three days out. I just got off the phone with Al Jeffries and he's got time off and he's ready to meet me there if you can help cover me on this end."

"Oh sure, Al gets the fun stuff," Perkins complained through a mouthful of pastrami. "I get to babysit your shadow."

"Thanks, pal. I appreciate it," Stryker stated as he set down his sandwich and opened his laptop. "Shall we do a little fishing?"

"I'm hooked," smiled Perkins as he got up to look over Stryker's shoulder. "What's the plan?"

"I'm looking to set up a meeting," Stryker explained as the computer awakened to the Internet site he had logged on to earlier. "See who shows up and take it from there."

"Just what I was thinking," said Perkins as he looked at Stryker's screen. "Whoa! What the hell?" Perkins leaned forward at the HiJinxxx site in full view. "What kind of meeting are you looking to set up?"

Stryker laughed and directed the cursor to the search box. "Sir Hadley's idea for protecting me from online predators," he explained. "Makes me look like a pervert if anyone searches my computer, but it hides any tracks of sites that I really visit. Pretty ingenious, actually." He typed the Axman URL, preceded by a dot, and watched the familiar page replace the porn offerings. He moved directly to the discussion blog where he found no new entries, and logged in as "Axman." Perkins watched in silent fascination.

"Axman being hunted," he typed slowly. "Pressure building. Help still available?" After a minute's hesitation while he considered the message, he clicked to add the posting and then logged off the site.

"Now what?" Perkins asked as he gave up his viewing position to walk back to the coffee table to pick up a second sandwich. Stryker had prepared four, knowing that Perkins would eat at least two, if not three. "We wait for the flashing lights to appear?"

"Hopefully we don't have to worry about that," said Stryker with a tilt of his head. "If they're monitoring the site, as we assume they are, we should see a response pretty quickly. Once that happens, we'll see if they'll agree to a meet."

"Whoever 'they' are," Perkins stated between chews.

"Exactly the point," agreed Stryker as he reached for the remote control and turned on SportsCenter. "Exactly the point."

Stryker paid little attention to the daily sports news, but even so he noticed when he began to see a repeat of stories on SportsCenter after thirty minutes. He returned to the computer with the tension of unspoken anticipation. He accessed the Axman discussion blog through HiJinxxx as before and saw the entry he'd hoped for.

The entry came under the name "Red Cross" and simply said: "Ready to help."

"Got it!" Stryker immediately logged on as Axman and posted the message he had planned. "Meet at 1:15 pm on Thursday. Far east end of the Vietnam Memorial Wall." He stayed logged on to the site with a gleam of excitement and an immediate sense of frustration that three days felt like a long ways off. He returned to SportsCenter with Perkins who didn't seem to mind the recycling of stories as he sat with his feet up and his eyes glued to the flat screen.

"Well?" Perkins asked without looking away from the baseball highlights as they counted down the best defensive plays of the day.

"I put the offer out," Stryker responded. "I'll check back again in a few minutes. If it works, I'll fly out in the morning so I can get things set up. I'd appreciate that ride to Mount Rainier if you're willing."

"Let me know what time," Perkins spoke to the television screen. "Got a nice quiet day tomorrow."

Perkins remained unmoved and apparently free of worry as Stryker checked back for the third time. The latest blog entry read: "Help will be there."

He then deleted his entries and shut down the computer. "We're on," he said to Perkins before picking up the phone to call Al Jeffries. We are on indeed, he thought as he willed himself to the same calm dispassion he felt with the sniper rifle in his hands.

CHAPTER FIFTY-NINE

Stryker stared intently at his toast with his mind lost in thought, but not focused on anything in particular. He didn't see the blackberry jelly that he had spread carefully and evenly to cover the entire exposed surface of the wheat bread, yet that was all he saw. He repeatedly pressed and released his right forefinger against the adjoining thumb as his forearm rested on the rounded edge of the speckled table. While oblivious to everything else, he was somehow conscious of a black fly walking upward on the window next to the table.

"You okay?" Jeffries asked quietly.

Stryker looked up from nothing and raised a single eyebrow at his unusual pensiveness. "Sure." He sat up a little straighter and reached for the compelling toast. "Everything's ready. We just need to see what develops. We're good, right?"

"I'm ready. Phones are charged. You've got the earpiece. We've got our places. Piece of cake," Jeffries turned his palms to the ceiling. "As long as they don't nail us."

Stryker took a bite of his toast that could just as easily have been codfish and nodded his head in agreement as he dabbed a touch of blackberry from the corner of his mouth with his napkin. "As long as they don't nail us. Yeah. I hadn't thought about that part." He sat back as the plain, middle-aged waitress refilled their water glasses and poured more steaming, heavily caffeinated coffee into sturdy, ceramic cups. She walked away with an exaggerated swivel of her hips. "We know they're gonna get there early. Probably there right now in fact," he speculated as he looked at his watch. "So, the earlier we are, the greater the likelihood they spot us. That gives us five hours to kill."

"You confident the flowers will still be there?" asked Jeffries before he took his turn checking the time.

"Yeah, I think so," assured Stryker. "Not much we can do about it if they're not. So, anything you want to do before one?"

"The Smithsonian opens at nine," replied Jeffries. "We should be able to kill at least a couple of hours there," he laughed.

Stryker picked up the bill and slid out of the booth. "Let's go."

At 1:00 in the afternoon, Stryker sat on the grass under an aging, beautifully proportioned oak tree about forty yards from the east end of the Vietnam Memorial. He wore charcoal gray shorts and a white tank top with his running shoes, but also had a t-shirt, light sweatshirt, and cargo pants on the ground next to him. The sweatshirt and tank top both advertised Georgetown University in blue letters. Stryker leaned against the tree so that his view of the Memorial Wall was more peripheral than direct through his dark sunglasses. The glasses helped to hide the earphone in Stryker's left ear. He opened a bottle of Diet Pepsi and a bag of chips. He ignored the chips as soon as he set them down, but he enjoyed the feel of the genuine glass of the old-fashioned bottle. He took a slow drink, then opened a book that he looked over the top of as he occasionally turned the pages. Stryker's cell phone sat on top of the crumpled clothes next to his left hip. The phone was turned on and ready to be connected to Jeffries' cell phone.

About 1:10 pm, Jeffries appeared in a dark blue police uniform at the Memorial Wall about a third of the way from the east end. He examined the names on the wall closely and made a careful rubbing of the name Carter Jeffries, although the name had no known significance to him. Jeffries alternated his position close to and back from the wall, and exchanged brief sympathy-sharing nods with other visitors.

At the far east end of the wall, a man in tan slacks and a white polo shirt squatted down on flexible knees and stood back up. His head swiveled frequently as his sunglass-covered eyes scanned the area. Immediately behind him, at the corner of the wall, a small pot displayed fresh pink begonias. The man, six feet three inches and narrow-shouldered, worked to appear relaxed as he continued to observe his surrounding. "Nothing yet," he spoke into the tiny microphone clipped to his shirt collar. Stryker had never seen the man before.

"Nothing yet," Stryker heard through his earpiece that received a signal from a microphone hidden in among the leaves of the begonias. He kept himself from looking directly at the speaker as he took a drink from his comforting glass bottle and returned his visible attention to his book. Nearly fifteen minutes later he heard: "You guys see anything?" in his left ear. The shifting sun rays had him more in the sun than shade now, but to stay in the shade would have had him completely facing away from his target.

A well-built jogger with little hair and brand new shoes slowed as he ran by Stryker, but then continued on his way. A single drop of sweat tickled Stryker as it rolled down his calf from the inside of his knee. He resisted the temptation to pick up the phone and check in with Jeffries. The sun beat down on the man at the end of the Memorial wall and he fidgeted in the heat without moving from his appointed spot. At nearly 2:30 the wait ended.

"We're done," Stryker heard in his earpiece. "In five minutes I'll walk slowly east on Constitution and then I'll cut back on Virginia. Team One, move two blocks ahead on Constitution so you're there when I pass. Teams Two and Three, stay in position and see if anyone follows. Grab anyone you see. If nothing turns up, you'll get the all clear to disband." While he listened to the instructions being given, Stryker was already up and moving, walking directly north to C Street where he would head to Virginia from the other direction. He waited till he cleared the area to talk to Jeffries and was about to remove his earpiece when he slowed as it spoke to him again. "It's Sedopoulus, Sir. No Sir, nothing. Yes Sir, we're checking. Yes Sir. Three o'clock, I would guess. Yes Sir."

Stryker walked one block north and then another block northeast to Virginia Avenue. He talked to Jeffries as he walked and told him where he was going and why. "I guess you get to watch the watchers," Stryker said. "He spoke to two teams, but whether they're teams of two or three, your guess is as good as mine. I don't expect we'll learn anything from seeing them, but you never know. I'll pick up my guy on Virginia and fill you in then."

"You be careful there, young man," Jeffries directed like a mother sending her son out with the car for the first time.

"Always," Stryker agreed. "Besides, I figure the police will come to my aid if there's any trouble. Protect and serve, right?"

"I never liked that 'serve' part very much. Later."

Stryker stopped briefly to slip his cargo pants over his shorts. He threw the tank top and sunglasses in a garbage can and put on the shirt and sweatshirt. Once he reached Virginia Avenue he walked two blocks southeast toward Constitution and stopped at a hot dog vendor where a woman placed her order and an overly large man sweated and waited anxiously for his turn. Stryker looked down to the corner of Virginia and Constitution, and as the woman moved away with her foot-long treasure, he saw the tan slacks, white polo shirt and sunglasses he'd been looking for move around the corner. The man paused in front of a rack of postcards and then again at a storefront window advertising historic tours of the city. Stryker bought his hot dog and added a thick line of traditional yellow mustard before he moved ahead on the street to follow from in front.

Stryker walked a full block before he crossed Virginia to walk on the side opposite his quarry. While waiting to cross he checked the man's progress and looked for a reasonable place to stop on the next block. His phone rang immediately after he cleared the intersection.

"Hey," Stryker greeted while balancing the hot dog in his left hand.

"Two teams of two," Jeffries informed him. "Gym bags. Got the look, but nothing specific."

"Alright." Stryker stopped at a newsstand and perused the papers and magazines. "I'm on Virginia and I just crossed 19th. Our guy's just a half block back. See if you can get a block or two ahead of us. North side of the street. Not sure how far we're going, but he said three o'clock and it's 2:50 now."

"On my way," agreed Jeffries before he disconnected the call.

Stryker moved a full block ahead to 20th street, which put him on the verge of entering Edward Kelly Park. Part of the park already lined the south side of Virginia Avenue and Stryker prepared to cross back to that side of the street. A tour bus roared by so closely that Stryker would have lost an arm had he extended it out to point ahead of him. Tired, elderly faces peered from the windows and Stryker wondered what the tour guide instructed the passengers to be looking for. After the bus cleared, Stryker saw the while polo shirt moving more quickly down the street. Apparently, he had given up on being followed.

The man pulled out his cell phone while he walked and Stryker did the same and changed his mind about crossing the street. "Where are you?" he asked as Jeffries answered the call.

"Just ahead of you, by the Frozen Yogurt stand."

"You see our guy?" Stryker asked as he spotted Jeffries.

"Got him," Jeffries acknowledged. "Looks like he's given up on trying to lure in a tail."

"My thoughts exactly," Stryker agreed as he moved toward Jeffries more slowly than the polo shirt moved. "Said he was going to meet someone at 3:00. We'll see who it is, then follow if we can."

"Roger Wilco, whatever the hell that means," Jeffries replied.

Stryker met Jeffries at the yogurt stand and their wait proved to be short-lived as polo shirt crossed the intersection on the opposite side of the street and met a yellow polo shirt with matching tan slacks. The two men spoke for a moment until white polo shirt pulled out his cell phone and made another call.

"As soon as we see which way they're going, I'll get ahead of them," Stryker said. "If they split up, I'll stay on the first guy. Let me know if they grab a cab, and then we'll both try to get one. We still can't rule out someone watching his backside, so keep your eyes open."

"You do know that you're working with a trained professional, right?" Jeffries did his best to sound offended.

"Can't be too careful about how much you've softened up over the years," Stryker teased. He nudged Jeffries as he saw white polo shirt pocket his cell phone.

At that moment, Stryker was bumped hard from behind so that he stumbled into a woman walking in front of him. The woman nearly fell into the street before Stryker grabbed her and offered a profuse apology. He quickly turned to find Jeffries face to face with a young Hispanic man who gestured at Stryker and spoke fast-paced Spanish. A handful of pedestrians, like school kids near a playground fight, stopped to watch as Stryker held up his hands and shook his head at the man whose embroidered work shirt read "Carlos" over the left breast. Stryker noticed the two polo shirts checking out the commotion before they began to move further on Virginia into Edward Kelly park.

Carlos continued his one-sided argument as Stryker moved quickly up the block. He stayed on the inside portion of the sidewalk, and ran ahead when cover was offered by the frequent buses. Jeffries pulled off his uniform shirt as soon as Carlos moved on, and bought himself a vanilla frozen yogurt. He felt better in a plain white t-shirt.

After two minutes, Jeffries called Stryker's cell phone. "Nothing," he shared as soon as Stryker answered.

"You still see our guys?" Stryker asked.

"Not anymore, but they can't be too far down," said Jeffries as he continued to scan both sides of the street.

"They're turning off the street. It looks like they're heading to the back side of the Federal Reserve building," Stryker explained softly into the phone as he watched his targets only a half block behind him. "If we're clear back there, why don't you head that way."

"Ten-four good buddy," replied Jeffries. "Over and out."

Stryker shook his head as he hung up the phone. He moved into the park, but not much in the direction of the Federal Reserve building. The two polo shirts headed directly for the building, but stayed on the back side. Rather than move toward an entrance, they closed in on a bench in the park, not far from the northeast corner of the Fed building. White shirt talked on his cell phone as they meandered slowly near the bench.

Jeffries joined Stryker and together they moved closer to the building, assuming that the polo shirts would direct any paranoid searching away from the building rather than toward it.

They sat on a bench with a partially obstructed view of the two men, Jeffries with his back to them, Stryker partially facing.

In just four minutes, a third man joined the two polo shirts. He looked to be of medium height and build and his short hair was graying at the sides and seriously thinning on top. He wore the dark green pants and light green short-sleeved shirt of an Army uniform. Stryker stared at his back as he talked to the two polo shirts with intermittent hand gestures. Jeffries fought the urge to turn and look for himself.

The three men talked for nearly three minutes before the two polo shirts turned and walked away from the building, back toward Virginia Avenue. The third man looked at his watch and paused for a moment before he turned back toward the side of the building from which he had come. As he turned, Stryker saw unmistakably the face of Major, now General, Teague Atkinson.

Stryker swallowed hard as he looked away from Atkinson and processed a hundred thoughts at once. General MacAfee. Atkinson replacing MacAfee in Omega. Axman. The continued postings after MacAfee's death. The killer in Independence. The "debt payment" from Larry and his friends using Sam. Teague Atkinson behind the search. "Let's go," he pointed with a nod of his head. He and Jeffries shunned the taxis and walked roundabout to Jeffries' car for the drive back to New York. Stryker had a plane to catch.

It wasn't until they were halfway to the car that Jeffries broke the ominous silence. "Well?" he questioned. "I take it we're done with the following. Anything worthwhile after all that?"

"Yeah, thanks buddy," Stryker clapped him lightly on the back as they walked. He still scanned the street carefully as they moved and knew that Jeffries did the same. At this point, however, he paid slightly more attention to the beautiful women on the street.

"Glad to hear it. Yes, I am glad to hear it indeed. Now, is it a secret from the unpaid help or are you going to fill me in?" Jeffries asked.

"I just can't believe I didn't see it earlier," Stryker shook his head in disgust. "It's all pretty obvious now."

"Glad to hear it," offered Jeffries again in minor annoyance. "Some of us are still in the dark, however. Ready to share?"

They stood at a light to cross an intersection that had them among a number of pedestrians, so Stryker waited until they moved once again and separated themselves from others. "Atkinson," he finally stated matter-of-factly. "Major Atkinson of Double O."

Jeffries quickly recovered from the slight hitch in his step. "Atkinson?" he asked although he knew that he had heard clearly.

"Yeah. That's who met our two guys just now. I should have seen it," Stryker chided himself once again.

"Wow," was the entirety of Jeffries response as he shared Stryker's litany of thoughts. They reached the lot with Jeffries' rental car and appreciated the shade that kept the year-old Taurus from stifling temperatures. Even so, Jeffries immediately turned on the air conditioning, then turned to Stryker before pulling out of the lot. "Now what?" he asked.

"What say we roll out of the city before we stop for a home-style burger somewhere. Then you've got to get back to work and I've got a plane to catch."

"No arguments from me," agreed Jeffries as he backed out of his parking space. "I assume there's something more, however." Without a response from Stryker, Jeffries continued as if the pause hadn't occurred. "Which I assume you'll tell me about when the time is right."

Stryker looked over at Jeffries and smiled as they moved toward the northbound interstate. "I'm starving."

Jeffries shook his head and reached to turn on the radio.

CHAPTER SIXTY

They stopped in northern Maryland for a late lunch, but otherwise proceeded non-stop to New York where Jeffries drove Stryker to La Guardia Airport. Miles Belo was booked for a flight to Chicago. Jeffries swung through the passenger drop off area rather than seeking out airport parking. Their discussion had focused primarily on small talk about baseball, movies, and Jeffries' job and family.

Jeffries pulled up to drop off Stryker who opened the door and grabbed his small bag from the back seat. "Thanks again, buddy," Stryker offered sincerely with a firm handshake. "You know I appreciate your help. Keep your ears open, and I'll be in touch soon."

"You do that," advised Jeffries. "And try to stay out of trouble, huh?"

"You know me," Stryker laughed lightly before closing the door and moving into the terminal.

Once Miles Belo reached Chicago, he rented a car with a GPS system that would guide him to the town of Peru, Illinois. Michael Carter's plane to Seattle didn't leave for ten hours. Stryker would use that time for a two-hour drive to Peru for a gift-bearing visit to Mary Arndt.

Before he left the airport, however, Stryker turned on his laptop and found wireless access. He quickly logged on to the HiJinxxx site and kept the computer screen down while he ordered a plain coffee with an apple fritter. Once he finished his snack, he re-opened the computer and jumped from the HiJinxxx site to the Axman page. A tingle of excitement surged through his chest as he saw the familiar page. The discussion blog carried a new entry that read: "Problems? We can try again."

Stryker logged in as Axman and hesitated with his fingers poised over the keyboard. After a calming reflection of nearly half a minute, he decided to skip the coded date and time. Instead he typed for less than ten seconds. "Teague Atkinson. Washington D.C."

Thorne Stryker logged off, shut down his computer, and walked to his rental car with a satisfied smile on his face.

CHAPTER SIXTY-ONE

The rifle lay gently along his comfortably extended left arm with the barrel caressed lightly in his left palm. Without breaking his visual concentration, the sniper found himself thinking about his hands and their lack of perspiration. He freed both hands from the rifle to rub his fingers lightly over the palms confirming their dryness. The palms probably should be damp, he thought, given that he was about to put an end to another man's life -- but then again, they'd never been damp before. A final slide of the fingers over the palms recorded no change, just as his eyes recorded no change at the front door of the house. His hands resumed their dry and relaxed, but lethal positions on the barrel and trigger guard of the rifle.

Made in the USA
San Bernardino, CA
05 May 2018